ANIMAL LIFE

*For Deb & Charlie,
Friends Forever!*

ANIMAL LIFE

by Jerry Mevissen

A publication of the
Jackpine Writers' Bloc, Inc.

© Copyright 2018 Jackpine Writers' Bloc, Inc.
Menahga, Minnesota
Printed in the United States of America
All rights reserved by the authors.
ISBN #978-1-928690-38-2

www.jackpinewriters.com
Send correspondence to sharrick1@wcta.net or
Jackpine Writers' Bloc, Inc., 13320 149th Avenue,
Menahga, Minnesota 56464.

Managing Editor: Sharon Harris, Tarah L. Wolff
Editor: Deb Nelson
Beta Readers: Paisley Kauffmann and Bonnie West

Abridged editions of stories have appeared in *The Talking Stick*.

This is a work of fiction. Names, characters, places, and incidents either are the product of the author's imagination or are used fictitiously.

CONTENTS

Prologue

Wolf 1
Bear 19
Rooster 35
Fish 51
Stag 71
Snake 85
Swan 105
Hamster 123
Spider 143
Pigeon 161
Moth 183
Butterfly 203
Lamb 227
Gopher 239
Chameleon 259

Epilogue

For my grandchildren
Sarah, Rachel, Peter, Mike, and Megan

ANIMAL LIFE

PROLOGUE

Drug busts. Meth labs in deserted farmsteads. Under-age drinking parties. Seems television news crews can't get enough. Kidnapping cases and aggravated arson where a barn is torched to avenge a stolen wife. All riveting stories with graphic footage. The barn blazing bright as the setting sun. Parents wringing their hands in worry. Scruffy teenagers being tried as adults while community elders pontificate, "I knew this would happen."

According to the news, rampant lawlessness is the challenge of out-state Minnesota law enforcement. That's not reality. I know, because I've been deputy sheriff of Browns County for decades.

My job is ninety-nine percent mundane and predictable — like patrolling lonely stretches of township roads, standing intersection guard at funeral processions, or rescuing a pup from a culvert. I haven't pulled my sidearm in years, except to end the suffering of a ten-point buck in a deer-meets-car incident. If you were to hear me address high school career days, you'd say my job sounds horribly boring. You'd say I make our townspeople out to be angels.

They're not. They've perfected the fence-walk between transgression and virtue. If you knew their secrets, you'd be shocked by their disregard for law, their morality, their stupidity. A drunk neighbor walking nowhere in the dark because he can't go home. Accompanying an abused woman through her house to get clothes and driving her to a shelter for the night, knowing she'd be back with the husband by week's end. Being there for a kid you know is in a bad situation, but you can't help.

This quiet stuff you don't write down. You don't tell anyone about it. Just stuff it in the back of your head and let it smolder until it burns out.

As I check my calendar for the number of days until

retirement, my people, the people of the county, stand out front and center—friends, neighbors, co-workers, merchants, everybody. These are people I went to school with, raised my family with, worked and played with. These are the people I took an oath to protect and serve. People who pretend to be one thing and who I know to be something else. Guess we all have our dark side. There's stuff about me I wouldn't want you to know.

Sometimes I feel I'm living in a world of animals. Other times, most times, they're just ordinary people.

WOLF

Lorna Martin suspected something unusual Friday afternoon. Turk had stumbled into the house not saying a word, grabbed a camera, and stumbled out. She watched him through the frosted window until he disappeared in the darkness of the pelt shed, then herded her daycare kids into the mud room to dress them for their rides home. Parents would arrive between five and five-thirty, their headlights piercing the November darkness of the long driveway.

Supper. She wondered what she would cook for supper. Turk would be hungry after a day of trapping. Hungry and ornery. Hash browns with onions, she decided. Fried baloney, creamed corn. He'd like that. But first she had kids to tend. *Let go of my leg, honey.* The older ones, first and second graders, dressed themselves. The toddlers scurried and tussled while she sorted through boots and jackets and mittens. Two infants sat in the playpen crying.

Today, Friday, she collected for her services. Some parents came to the door with a check, some sent the kids back in, some hustled out the driveway, forgetting or unable to pay. She would call them tomorrow. There would be time, with only toddlers and infants to tend.

Six o'clock and Turk hadn't returned to the house. Supper waited in the oven. She would be patient, not walk to the pelt shed door to ask the reason for his delay. He had discouraged her from entering. "You have your daycare. I have my trapping. Stay out of mine, and I'll stay out of yours."

She hadn't argued, but said, "I love the feel of the fur. I love to imagine the beautiful coat some woman will wear."

He turned his head. "Dream on."

Lorna stepped to the bathroom to freshen up. She looked in the mirror. New lines around her sunken cheeks. Loose skin below

WOLF

her chin. More gray hair than she remembered. *Maybe this is why Turk is cold.*

She walked to the kitchen window. A dull yellow light shone from the pelt shed. Lazy snowflakes tumbled in the glare of the yard light. She recalled Turk rushing in for the camera, grinning but saying nothing.

"I could start the laundry," Lorna said as if talking to the kids, a habit she had acquired that surprised her. "Get a head start on the weekend." But the rumble and roar of the washer and dryer irritated Turk. "Sounds like a war zone," he had said. She watched the snow fall. She could start cleaning, but not vacuuming. "Sounds like a helicopter."

The shed windows darkened and Turk limped to the house, powerful-looking in his winter jacket and insulated jeans. She had found his look sensuous years ago. Now she found it intimidating. She knew his strength, knew how to read him when he walked into the room, knew the importance of shutting her trap before he told her to.

Turk stomped his feet on the stoop and opened the door. "Smells good."

"Fried onions."

Lorna released a breath of air and reached for potholders to carry the heated platter and bowls. Fried baloney and onions. She had cooked that for Turk the first supper after they married. He had wrapped his arms around her and lifted her off the floor. "And she's a good cook too," he had joked.

Turk rolled up his sleeves and washed his hands in the kitchen sink. "Snow tonight, good trapping tomorrow." He dried his hands with a towel from the oven handle.

Lorna turned her head away, smiling as she poured milk in his glass.

"I'm hungry as a bear." Turk slid his chair forward. "Keep the jug on the table."

Lorna sat, waiting for him to fill his plate, waiting for him to talk. *Something happened today. Don't ask questions. Don't spoil it.* She took small bites of corn, watching Turk lean into his plate, lifting his head long enough to gulp a glass of milk. She poured a refill.

Turk scooped the remaining potatoes and baloney and corn on his plate and buttered a slice of bread.

"Good news." He chewed a bite of baloney and grinned at her.

◊ 3 ◊

Lorna relaxed, her fork halfway to her mouth, and waited. Waited for him to talk. Waited for him to share the good news. Not wanting to hear, *Don't get your underwear in a bundle*. She knew from his initial excitement he'd talk. If not to her, to one of his buddies at the Legion. She'd hear him on the telephone.

"I caught a wolf today." He drained his milk glass and slapped the table. "A young female. Caught her in a number three coyote trap."

"There's no wolf trapping season, is there?" she chanced. "Isn't it illegal?"

"Only if you get caught." He lifted his fork and pointed it at her. "And you're the only one who knows."

Lorna dropped her fork and shook her head. *No. No.*

Turk nodded. "Good girl. I built a cage for her in the pelt shed. Tomorrow I'll fence in a pen behind the shed and cut in a trap door."

"Caught in a trap? Is her leg broken?" Lorna felt a pang of sympathy. She pictured the wolf, limping in a cage, tracing a path along the short wall.

"You think I reached in there and inspected her leg? Use your head, woman. Where's the toothpicks?"

Lorna rose and walked to the cupboard, relieved to feel distance between them, however slight.

"I'm going to watch the fights tonight, then go to bed early." Turk pushed away from the table, held his stomach, and belched. "That's a compliment."

Lorna smiled, uncomfortable with his jocularity. "Thanks," she whispered. "Can I bring you a cup of coffee?"

"I said I'm going to bed early. Want me to lay awake all night?" He turned to face her. "And don't offer me decaf. I don't drink that pissy stuff."

Turk walked into the living room and turned on the television. Lorna sat at the table alone, picking at her food. She thought of the wolf, pacing the cage. *Was she hungry? What did she eat?*

Lorna busied herself in the kitchen, washing dishes, peeling carrots and cutting them in strips for the kids, fingering through recipes. Chocolate chip cookies. She'd bake a batch of cookies, the kind she mailed to Turk when he was in basic training.

She rose to check the supply of jelly for peanut butter and jelly sandwiches. From the top shelf, she pulled a small jar of

WOLF

strawberry jam, one she and Turk had made together last summer. She held the jar to her chest and closed her eyes. Warm summer morning, dew on the grass, wild strawberry patch by the vacated gravel pit. They picked into the same plastic pail, picked without eating, without talking, picked until their fingers were red, picked until the pail filled.

Lorna had brought a thermos of coffee. She spread a blanket next to a patch of unpicked berries. Breakfast. Turk sat beside her and kissed her, kissed her lips, her neck, her throat. Opened her blouse. Kissed her. Put his arm around her and lowered her to the blanket. Placed strawberries on her body. Closed his eyes and searched for them with his lips.

She shook her head to release the fantasy. Shook it again to rid herself of the fight announcer's banter on television, louder and louder. She counted the seconds of each round, waiting for the bell. The television snapped off.

"I'm going to town tomorrow morning after I check my trap line. Have your list ready. I hope you got money to pay for it." Turk stood in the bathroom door and turned. "Getting hog panels for my new critter's pen. Put 30-30 shells on the list. I'm going deer hunting this year, too."

"You'll need a license, right?"

Turk raised his arm and aimed it at her. "You don't pay attention at all, do you? Disabled vets don't need a license." He smirked as he walked into the bathroom.

Lorna gave him time for sleep after he closed the bedroom door. His first few hours were the soundest. Later, moans turned to wails, twitches to tremors. She would roll off the bed onto the floor to avoid his flailing arms.

The mantle clock ticked a restful cadence. No kids. No television. She brewed a cup of tea and sat at the kitchen table, closed her eyes, and deepened her breath. The quiet was welcome, but she needed to hear a friendly voice. Sal. She would call her sister Sal. Better than having Sal call her. Turk jumped when the phone rang. She dialed the number.

"Same old stuff." Lorna turned from the bedroom door to answer Sal's question. "Daycare kids Monday through Saturday. House cleaning, laundry, and baking on Sunday."

"Sounds exciting. Too bad they aren't your kids. Might

make it all worthwhile."

"I don't think that ever was an option," Lorna stammered, "what with Turk's condition."

"Oh yes, Turk. How is my favorite brother-in-law?"

"He had a busy day trapping." She thought of the wolf. "Went to bed before the news. Better than last night. George W. Bush was grinning like a spoiled prep school brat at the groundbreaking for the new Presidential Center. Turk yelled, 'War monger,' and threw his shoe at the television."

"I don't know how you manage. Stuck out there with somebody else's kids. When's the last time you went out for dinner? Went shopping with the girls? Does he let you drive his new truck yet?"

Lorna listened for noise from the bedroom.

"And no moral support from the old man," Sal continued. "When you come to your senses, Girl, call me."

"Sal, it's winter. His leg kills him in winter. He's miserable in winter. He'll be my loving Turk come spring. I can hold my breath that long." She rubbed her forehead. "And it's not that bad. I have a warm house. Plenty of food. I have . . ." *How often would she have to explain before Sal understood?*

"You have your high school wardrobe," Sal added. "Lorna, however you live your life is fine with me. I'm just saying, if you want to talk . . ."

Lorna placed the receiver on the hook and stared at the room, the wallpaper she and Turk had hung together when they married. Turk had held her legs as she stood on the ladder, tickled her on the way down, wrapped her in his arms when she stood. The fun of finding a home for wedding presents—dishes, pots and pans, Mixmaster, toaster, cookbooks, linens, towels. The joy of feathering their first nest, this nest, together.

And last fall, before Turk started limping, she had sprained her back from lifting a four-year-old. She fixed Turk's supper and told him she had to lie down. When she woke hours later, Turk stood in the kitchen, his arms extended for a hug. The kitchen shone brighter—higher wattage light bulbs in the overhead fixture. He pointed to the sink faucet, no longer dripping. The silverware drawer, now flush with the cabinet face with a repaired drawer slide. The table cleared, wiped clean, the dishes washed, the sink shining. Yes, she could hold her breath until spring.

The wolf. She thought of it pacing in unfamiliar darkness,

WOLF

dragging a broken leg, hungry, thirsty. What did she have for food? What could she use for water? She had a chunk of baloney. She would sneak to the pelt shed. Use a flashlight so she wouldn't need the shed lights. Turk mustn't know.

The pelt shed smelled musky. Lorna shone the flashlight around the walls, spotting the makeshift pen. The wolf coiled in a corner, head between paws, eyes alert and sparking defiance. Wounded, frightened, imprisoned. Light reflected from the wolf's eyes like two tiny mirrors. Lorna tossed the baloney chunk in the pen and rushed to the house.

When Turk returned from town Saturday morning, the daycare toddlers scrambled to Lorna and stood behind her sweatpants. Babies sat in the playpen rattling a string of bright plastic blocks. Turk set the groceries on the cupboard and the ammunition on the top shelf of the hall closet. "That racket drives me crazy. I'm going to build the pen. Keep the kids away. Today and forever. I'll be in for dinner at noon."

Hog panels overhung the Ford pickup as it backed to the pelt shed. Turk eased out of the truck, loosened tie-downs, and hoisted panels to the rear of the shed. Lorna stacked gallons of chocolate milk in the fridge, cereal boxes in the cupboard, bananas in a bowl to ripen. She refrigerated a block of Colby for macaroni and cheese, hamburger for goulash, more carrots. She checked the items against the cash register receipt.

Dinner. Turk would be hungry. He would eat in the kitchen, the toddlers in the living room in front of the television, the babies in twin highchairs fingering Cheerios while they waited.

At noon, Lorna set Turk's place at the table. Chicken noodle soup simmered on the stove; buttered cheese sandwiches waited on the grill. Turk limped in, shaking snow off his jacket and cap. "Got the pen pretty much where I want it. Had to cut through six inches of ground frost for the posts." He lifted the cover of the soup kettle and inhaled. "Eight feet long, four feet wide, a half-panel on the end, hinged like a gate in case she needs a quick getaway. Like a visitor from the DNR." He washed his hands and sat. "The gate is padlocked and the key is on the key rack."

"Are you expecting trouble? How would anyone know?'

"One of these days, she'll start to howl. Neighbors. And that damn daycare inspector that comes to check if the toilet's clean."

Lorna ladled soup. The toddlers watched from the living

room sucking their thumbs.

"I'll be hunting deer at sundown." Turk slurped his soup. "Snow will make for easy tracking. I'll need deer bones and guts for the wolf." He gulped his milk and rubbed his hand against his mouth. "I see you snuck her a hunk of baloney last night." He glared at her. "She didn't eat it." He pulled on his coat and returned to the pelt shed.

When he returned, Lorna watched a video with the kids. "I'll be out in the state forest. Back before dark. With a deer." He uncased the 30-30 and slipped shells in his pocket.

"Gun," said a toddler. "Bang, bang."

"Shouldn't you wear orange?" Lorna asked.

"Don't dress me, woman."

She stood and, through the picture window, watched him hobble to the orchard, to the stubbled corn field, toward the state forest. A car slowed at the driveway. A toddler watched from the living room window. "Mommy. Mommy."

No more kids today. Quiet. Lorna stacked dishes in the sink, returned plastic trucks and cars to the toy shelf, tossed plush rabbits and monkeys in the play pen. She hugged a plush wolf.

She straightened pillows and books and heated water for tea. The wolf. Still curled in the corner? Whimpering a muted snarl? Turk had cut a plastic jug in half for a water trough, still full when she checked last night. What had Turk fed her? Had she eaten? Lorna shut off the burner for hot water and grabbed her coat.

Darkness had fallen when Turk burst into the house. Lorna turned off the vacuum cleaner. "Got her." He stomped his feet. "Dragged her to the road. A big doe." He snatched truck keys from the key holder and hobbled out.

She stood, excited and worried. *What if the game warden caught him shooting after dark? Where would he hang the deer? Somewhere out of sight of the daycare parents. Could the freezer hold a hundred pounds of venison? But now the wolf would have something to eat. Something within her diet. Something better than baloney.*

"The woods are full of deer out there," Turk said the next morning. "I found an old deer stand. I'm going back out this

WOLF

afternoon. We won't buy meat all winter. All spring."

"Did the wolf eat the guts?" Lorna asked. She handed him a mug of coffee.

"No. Nothing yet. Don't eat, don't drink, don't walk around. Her leg will get stiff if she don't move. I prodded her, but she just curls up and snarls. She'll break in time. I'll have her trained."

"How long are you willing to wait?"

"As long as it takes."

Snow fell for days, for weeks. First inches, then feet. Turk stayed busy plowing the driveway and walking the trap line. "My leg's killing me again," he said one night. "I can feel cold metal in my thigh when I drive the tractor."

"You should buy an insulated work suit."

"I said, don't dress me." He plopped on the couch and turned on the television. "Tuesday night. NYPD Blue." He muted the volume during the commercials. "I wish you'd find some way to make money where I didn't have to plow snow," he yelled at her. "Or have to watch where I put my coffee cup, or could take a nap on the couch at noon."

Lorna sat in the kitchen out of his sight, scanning recipes. "You and me both," she agreed. "But you know, it'd be no different if we had kids of our own." She snapped her hand to her mouth and cupped it toward her, as if recalling her words.

Silence. Then the announcer's voice on television.

"I'm going to make venison jerky," Lorna said. "You could take it with you when you're trapping. And the kids will like it. Is the smoker still in the garage?"

"Quiet. I'm watching my program."

Lorna checked the cupboard for pickling salt, garlic powder, brown sugar. When she heard commercials, she walked to the living room archway. "I'm going to look for the smoker." Earlier today, she had tucked the kids' food scraps in her jacket pocket.

Turk likely knew she visited the wolf at night, but didn't comment, didn't seem to mind. Lorna had offered brief commentary. "Seems to be losing weight. Sleeping in a different corner, so she must be moving. Coat's losing its luster, mangy looking."

"I'm making progress," Turk maintained. "Old habits die slow."

Lorna trudged through fresh snow to the garage, elbowed

the door open, and stared at piles of broken furniture, discarded appliances, lumber scraps, plastic storage boxes marked CHRISTMAS and SPORTS GAMES, and BOOKS. Beside a black-domed barbecue grill, she saw the smoker. She wrestled it out of the garage and headed toward the house, stopping at the pelt shed. Inside she turned on the light. The wolf lay in a far corner of the cage, her head between her paws, her eyes alert. Lorna tossed food scraps in the pen. The wolf maneuvered toward the trap door, her eyes locked on Lorna.

November 29. Lorna would not forget the date. She rose early and padded out the bedroom into the darkened living room. Through the picture window, stars shone. The snow had stopped. A mysterious light reflected off heaps of snow on the picnic table, the birdbath, the sandbox, softening hard lines into gentle curves. She walked to the kitchen and turned the radio on low. An announcer read the weather forecast while she scooped coffee grounds in the Mr. Coffee basket. "Winter storm watch. Extreme cold with wind chills down to minus thirty. Beware of frostbite."

She poured coffee for herself when it stopped perking and arranged bowls of dry cereal mix and raisins for the kids. Turk walked into the kitchen wearing an undershirt and boxer shorts. He took the coffee mug she offered. He seemed to be sleepwalking, unaware of her, uncertain whether to stand or sit, kitchen or living room, say *good morning* or remain mute. She watched him while she prepared carrot sticks. His pronounced limp, his weight gain around the belly, his hair gray at the temples. *What happened to my hero?*

Through the kitchen window, a pale white sun peeked through black trees on the horizon. On either side, massive brackets of gold flared upward, bathed in white light.

"Look, Turk. Sundogs."

Turk grunted and limped to the bedroom with the mug.

"Sundogs," Lorna spoke to herself. "They're important in Native American culture. Signify a new age, a new beginning, a new something."

Turk crossed into the bathroom and closed the door.

Lorna stared at the phenomenon. *Oh, I wish the kids could see this.*

After breakfast, Turk announced he would carry his rifle

WOLF

when he ran the trap line. "Pack me a couple sandwiches. I'll have dinner in the deer stand." He slid into his coveralls, his parka, and grabbed his chopper mitts. "Good to get an early start. First day all week I haven't plowed."

"It occurred to me," Lorna hesitated when she handed him the lunch bag, "if you had an accident on your trap line, I wouldn't know where to look for you."

"Somebody would spot the truck along the road. A dog could sniff his way to me."

"You'd probably be dead by then."

"Don't get your hopes up." He walked out before the kids arrived.

The day grew bright, the sun a welcome stranger. Snow tumbled off boughs of cedars and branches of birch at the slightest breeze. Chickadees scrambled between trees and fluttered at the feeder. The image of sundogs, bright and lyrical, lent an aura of magic to the morning. It stayed with Lorna, its presence like an omen.

For afternoon story time, she concocted a legend of an Indian boy, blind since birth. When the boy's father saw the brilliant sun one cold winter morning, he wrapped his son in blankets and brought him outside facing the ball of white fire. The boy shivered in the cold. Father wrapped him tighter and targeted his face, his locked eyelids at the white-hot sun. The boy wriggled. Father held him fast. The fiery sun burned on his eyelids and, as if by magic, loosened their lock. Slowly, the boy's eyes opened. He squinted, squirmed. Father held him and prayed to the Great Spirit. The boy opened his eyes wide, took a deep breath of surprise, and screamed. Father looked at his son's eyes, black as night and brown as chestnuts. He lifted his head, and pools of tears flooded his eyes. "Sundog," Father cried. "I will name you Sundog." The sun reflected on his tears and bounced back to the sky forming lights on either side. They became known as sundogs.

"You shouldn't look at the sun," a second grader said. "You'll go blind."

"You're right. The father lost his sight momentarily, but his son gained a lifetime of precious sight."

"Is that a true story?" the kid asked. "Or did you make it up?"

"That's for you to decide." Lorna ruffled his hair. "Now it's time to go home."

When the last parent carried a daycare kid to the car, Lorna sat at the kitchen table twirling her wedding band, rapt in an odd feeling of well-being. Something strange, like closure of a door she hadn't known was open. *This is good.* She sprang up to brew a cup of tea. *I hope I'm not riding for a fall.* While she waited for the water to boil, she straightened the living room and thought about supper. Leftover venison stew. When she asked Turk how he liked it a couple days ago, he had said, "Not bad."

She turned on the radio. With Thanksgiving past, Christmas carols jingled without break. She thought about a tree. Decorations. Cookies the kids could bake for their families.

The teapot whistled, a low plaintive note, then higher. Eerie and wild. The wolf. She dropped the teabag and slipped a jacket over her shoulders, boots, a scarf.

The night crackled with cold. Stars shone in a cloudless sky. Red oak leaves hung lifeless, spared of breeze. A shadow of smoke from the chimney fell across her path. She shivered. Turk has been out all day in this weather. How could he handle it?

Inside the pelt shed, the air smelled of cedar shavings from new pelt stretchers. The wolf lay in the cage, then stood when Lorna approached. Tentative at first, the wolf stepped toward her. Deer bones lay on the floor, some gnawed clean, some bearing meat scraps. Her water dish was half-full. Turk must have thrown an old winter jacket in the cage which she had bunched into a nest in the far corner.

Lorna stared at the wolf's eyes. Yellow, moist, brilliant. Liquid topaz. *Sundogs.*

Back in the house, she busied herself preparing for tomorrow. Meals, snacks, activities. She checked the clock. Six-fifteen, and dark outside. She lowered the volume of the radio and listened for Turk, checked for lights in the pelt shed. Six-thirty. She swept the kitchen, vacuumed the living room, scrubbed the sink and toilet bowl.

Seven o'clock. The moon shone in a clear sky in the east where sundogs had lit the morning. *Was that Venus or Mars beneath the crescent moon? Such beauty. But shouldn't she be worrying?*

One way to get him home is to call Sal long distance. Lorna dialed the number.

WOLF

"Turk's not home from hunting yet. I thought I'd call."

"What can he hunt at this hour?" Sal asked.

"Who knows. Anything. Everything. Turk's happiest when he's killing something. Hunting or trapping." She paused. "That sounds terrible, doesn't it?"

Lorna heard pounding at the door. "My God, he's home." She dropped the receiver and rushed to open the door. Turk lay on the stoop, his jacket covered with snow, his face flushed, his beard frosted. "Help me in, for Christ's sake."

She grabbed his arm and tugged. He grunted and winced and collapsed.

"A little bit more." Lorna pulled. "A little more and I can close the door."

He lifted and pushed himself inside.

"Oh, my God. What happened?" She ran to the bathroom for a towel and scissors.

"Go get my rifle," he whimpered, measuring his breath.

"What happened?" she repeated, removing his cap, brushing snow off his jacket, his coveralls. Blood. Blood on the legs of his coveralls. "Oh, Lord," she screamed. "I'll call 911." She unzipped the leg of his coveralls to find the source of bleeding. Blood had coagulated around his thigh, his leg. It no longer bled. She wrapped the wounded area with the towel.

"No, you won't call 911." He spoke with quiet authority. "You'll walk back and get my rifle."

"How will I find it? Where will I find it?" She gasped at the bloodied pant leg. "It's your bad leg, isn't it? How did you get home?"

"On my belly. Now follow my trail across the corn field to the fence line at the state forest. My rifle is standing against a post. Now hurry, damn it."

She grabbed her jacket and slipped into a pair of Sorels.

"Water," he whispered.

She poured a glass for him and scurried over his body out the door.

When she returned, he had inched himself onto the carpet. Blood frozen on his pants had thawed on the kitchen linoleum, leaving a sordid trail. "I have it," she said. "I have your rifle."

"Dry it and get the truck ready."

"Should I call 911?"

◊ 13 ◊

"I don't want them messing around out here."

"How about the neighbors? They could help me lift you in the truck."

"That's worse. Get busy, woman. I'm in deep misery."

She wiped the rifle with a bath towel, hurrying, shaking, drying the stock, the barrel, the open chamber.

"Leave it on the table, chamber open." His head lay under his arm. "Now let's go."

"I'll bring the truck around." She ran for the door.

Back inside, she watched him take a deep breath, lift himself on his elbows, and inch his way to the door.

Later, she told Sal about the incident. "I have no idea where his strength came from. Or mine. We got him into the truck and to the emergency room. They treated him for a broken leg, his bad leg, and blood loss, and frostbite."

"How did it happen?" Sal asked.

"The ladder broke at the deer stand. He fell about twelve feet."

"What do the doctors say?"

"They may have to amputate. Turk doesn't know that yet. I don't want to be around when they tell him. One thing for sure. He'll never hunt or trap again."

"What are you going to do?"

"I've called my daycare customers and told them I'm unavailable for a while. Maybe never. Turk wouldn't survive in a house full of kids."

"Call me every day when you get home," Sal said. "Keep me posted."

"Hang on, Sal." Lorna turned toward the window. "There's a car coming up the driveway. Wonder who it could be this time of night. Stay on the line."

Lorna turned on the yard light. A car with SHERIFF in large gold lettering on the door parked at the garage.

Lorna grabbed the receiver. "It's Bear Braham, the county sheriff. You remember him from high school? I'll talk to you tomorrow."

Deputy Braham knocked on the door. He had called earlier today, left a message he'd stop by the next time he was in the neighborhood. Routine visit, he had said. Just wondering how she was doing.

WOLF

"Come in, Bear." Lorna combed her hair with her fingers and forced a smile. "Too late for coffee?"

"Never too late." Bear removed his cap and stomped his feet on the door mat. "I heard Turk's in the hospital. Everything okay?"

Did he know about the wolf? "Fine." Lorna's voice sounded more eager than she planned. "I'll be fine. And I have the truck if I need anything." She reached for a cup. "I brewed this when I got home from the hospital." Her hand shook when she poured.

Bear reached for the cup. "Don't be afraid to ask for help. That's what you pay taxes for. And I'll pop in when I see the lights on."

Lorna remembered Bear Braham from school, the big kid coaches eyed but couldn't convince to play football or basketball or baseball. "Don't have time." Bear had laughed when asked, according to school yard chatter. "Corn to shuck. Cattle to truck. Chickens to pluck. And girls . . ."

Grade school kid Lorna had sat in the school bus idolizing high school senior Bear—his butch haircut, the yoke of his western shirt, the stainless-steel expansion band glistening around the blond hair of his wrist, the red tab of his Levi's. She envied girls who stopped at his seat when the bus stopped to load, girls who giggled and made small talk. Girls who snugged books against their chests and under their breasts.

Bear had retained his commanding presence. Although his chest had gone south, he carried himself with authority. The blond butch haircut, now salt-and-peppered, blended with a trimmed beard. An easy smile brightened his face. The coffee cup disappeared in his outsized hands.

Lorna had seen Bear over the years since she married Turk but kept a distance. Turk was an outsider in this town and acted uncomfortable around law enforcement. "They wouldn't know what to do if a bomb dropped on them," he had said.

"I haven't seen Maggie for a while." Lorna hoped to steer the conversation from her and Turk. "Still at the beauty shop?"

"She's recuperating from knee surgery, but she'll be back. How else would she keep up with the town gossip?"

Gossip? In this town? Lorna flushed. *Surely not about me. Surely not about Turk. Hopefully not about Turk.* Her face reddened. Sweat broke out on her neck. *Was Bear hinting at something?* Lorna shook her head. "Oh, I don't traffic in town gossip. If I can't say something good about someone, I don't say anything at all."

15

Bear drained his cup. "A couple of your neighbors called the DNR. Said they heard a wolf howling in this direction. You heard anything?"

Lorna turned and stared out the window. Turk didn't need gossip and he didn't need legal trouble. Neither did she. "I've heard dogs barking a lot at night lately. Maybe coyotes. But not a wolf." Turk would be proud of her for quick thinking.

"Well, thanks for the coffee, Lorna." Bear reached in a pocket. "Here's my card. Don't hesitate to call."

She watched Bear's taillights trail down the drive, locked the door, and turned the yard light off.

Lorna called Sal daily, the news degrading from bad to worse. "They won't release him to come home, now or ever. At least he'll be in a Veterans' Home. Thank God for his GI benefits."

"What's his frame of mind?" Sal asked.

"At first, he was mildly sedated," Lorna said. "He wasn't conversational, but he recognized me, tolerated me. I fed him his meals, as much as he ate. Didn't like their eggs. Didn't like their chicken soup. He liked the peach yogurt. Imagine Turk eating yogurt." She smiled into the receiver, tapping a pencil on a note pad, her list of items to take to the hospital. "When an aide came for his tray, I asked if she had extra yogurt cups. She pulled a couple from her smock pocket. 'Don't tell anyone,' she said."

"Turk let you feed him? That's a surprise."

"Yes, he was very loving. In a passive way. I placed my hand in his, and I swear he squeezed it. I whispered 'I love you.' and he smiled." She tapped her pencil. "I wish he would always have acted like that." She stared out the window into the darkness. "Funny. He never liked me to touch him, especially if he didn't expect it. In the hospital, I shampooed his hair, trimmed his fingernails, massaged his shoulders." She laughed. "Gotta admit to goose bumps when I did that."

"That was then. What about now?"

"When he's not sedated, he's angry. At me. At the doctors, the nurses, the hospital. Everybody. He doesn't want me in the room. I sit in the Waiting Room. Good name for it. Waiting for what?"

Sal paused. "I have an idea. Come stay with me a few days. Tell the doctors. Tell Turk if he'll listen. I can be there in the morning."

WOLF

"I'll think about it." Lorna paused. "I'll call you later tonight."

Morning sun glistened on wind-packed snow as Sal followed tire tracks up Lorna's driveway and parked. At the house, Lorna opened the door, set a tan suitcase on the stoop, and closed the door to lock it. The quilted nylon fabric of her ice blue jacket swished when she reached for the suitcase.

Sal walked to the stoop and hugged her. "Sisters." She held her and felt Lorna's arms tremble, her chest heave. Sal released her. "My, you're all dressed for the occasion. Pearls, earrings."

"They were a gift from Turk before we married." Lorna wiped her face with her sleeve and led the way to the car. Sal opened the door, closed it when Lorna sat, and placed the suitcase on the rear seat.

"Oh," Lorna said. "I forgot. I'll be right back."

"What are you doing?" Sal called as Lorna walked into the pelt shed.

Lorna walked to the cage. The wolf paced the far side, cowered, and folded into a coil and snarled.

"You're free, girl. I'll unlock the gate." She took a key from her jacket pocket and walked outside.

"What are you doing?" Sal called.

Lorna trudged through snow to the rear of the shed. She opened the lock, cleared an arc of snow for the gate to swing, and walked around the shed.

Inside, she cried. Tears blinded her. She wiped her face with her sleeve. "You're free, girl. You can go."

The wolf eyed her, her head parked between her paws, unmoving. Lorna found a conduit pipe and braced the trapdoor open. From where the wolf lay, she could see the open gate.

"Get out, girl," Lorna cried. "Out, out." She grabbed a pelt stretcher and banged it against the cage. She reached for a bigger board. "Out. Out."

Her eyes flooded, her voice shrieked. "Get out, damn it. Get out."

The wolf coiled tighter.

"Get out, damn it. Out. Out, you stupid animal." Through her tears, she saw the wolf tremble.

Lorna stood shaking. She stumbled from the shed, her head bent, hands over her mouth. The snow, the trees, the house, the

◊ 17 ◊

car, all swam in dizzying circles. She stumbled toward the car and opened the back door, her face hidden from Sal. Tears froze on her cheeks. She lifted the suitcase.

"Lorna, what are you doing?"

"I can't," she said. "I just can't."

BEAR

Deputy Sheriff Bear Braham sits at his desk, oversized fingers hovering over undersized keyboard. "Missing Persons Report. Boy Scout," he pecks. With time added for corrections, one line takes a minute. Screw it. He pushes the keyboard aside and grabs the recorder.

"19 November 2010," he dictates. "At approximately 0-hundred hours, Browns County Sheriff's Posse located a missing youth from Minneapolis in Section 4 of Lyons Township. The unharmed youth did not require medical attention." He pauses and listens to the playback, cringing at his stilted phrasing, detesting his tired and whiny voice. He glances around his dark office, lit only by the computer monitor. Beside him on the credenza, a scanner blinks an agitated sequence of red lights that reflect on three photographs—a younger Bear with grinning son at his side holding a stringer of fish, a wedding anniversary portrait, a young marine in dress charlies.

The one o'clock siren wails.

Bear yawns and stretches his arms. He wants to be home, to curl up behind Maggie and sleep. But the sheriff will want a report in the morning, the paper will want a statement. Better dictate now while details are fresh.

The scout troop had arrived at Frame's Landing on the Crow Wing River on Friday evening after a three-hour auto caravan. Pent-up energy and away-from-home unruliness, combined with a near-full moon and a ritual game of snipe hunting ended with a lost scout—an eleven-year-old kid wearing a Guns N' Roses sweatshirt and carrying a burlap gunny sack.

Bear got the call from the scoutmaster early Saturday morning. Why the delay? "We didn't know he was missing until bed check at midnight. Then we thought he was pissed for being suckered in and decided to make us suffer. A couple parent

BEAR

chaperones and I combed the woods with flashlights near camp. I called the kid's parents. In desperation, I called the sheriff." Four o'clock.

Bear summoned the mounted posse to meet at the campsite. Mid-November flurries fell despite a temperature in the thirties. The kid wouldn't freeze. Not yet.

Late Saturday evening, a posse member found him a couple miles from camp in a wintered-down cabin up river. A broken pane in the back door aroused her suspicion. The posse woman called the scoutmaster and sheriff. The scout hid in a bedroom closet behind a rack of trashy sequined gowns, each with a matching wig.

"What you got to say for yourself, young man?" The scoutmaster stood with his hands on his hips.

The scout swung around to face him, anger burning in his eyes. "Assholes."

Bear wants to add a line or two about the relieved father, how he hugged his son. He didn't. How instead the father walked to his son, stern-faced, and raised his arm. How the scoutmaster grabbed it. "I'll handle it."

Fine. Emotional response didn't belong in the report. But he wished he had seen it.

Outside the sheriff's office and across the street, the manager of the local pub pulls out of the empty parking lot. Bear heads for the squad blanketed in fresh snow.

At home, the porch light glows a welcome yellow. A horse nickers. His beloved Morgan Misty stands in the moonlit paddock, new foal at her side. Bear detours and offers her treats from the tack room. Leaning on the gate, he admires the days-old foal, its size and agility. "You need a name, young fella."

In the house, he sits in the entry and removes his boots. He taps the coffee pot. Empty. He pours a cup of milk for cocoa, adding a shot of Baileys. Not something he wants to do, but, damn it, there's no way he can sleep tonight without a boost. He stokes the fireplace until the fire roars. The icy reunion of the dad and lost kid gnaws at him like an impacted tooth. He slips a CD of Schubert's *Great Symphony* in the player, and sits on the hearth, cradles the cup in his hands, and yearns for commiseration with the plaintive cello in the opening movement.

Moonlight casts an eerie light, creating unfamiliar shadows adding to his uneasiness. He rinses his empty cup and walks stocking-footed to the bedroom. Maggie sleeps in a half-sitting position, a magazine on her lap. He stubs his toe on her walker. She stirs. "What time is it?"

"One-thirty."

"Did you find the boy?"

"Yeah. Michelle found him."

"Did you pray he'd be found?" Maggie sounds groggy. "St. Anthony is the patron saint of lost things."

"I don't pray. I can't afford to distract my attention."

"I prayed for you, and it worked." She folds her hands in prayer position. *"Dear St. Anthony, please come around. Someone is lost and cannot be found."*

Maggie twists down to lie flat, groaning. On the bedside table, an empty wine glass stands beside a bottle of prescription narcotics. "Slide my leg over and hand me a couple of those pills. I can't tell you how tired I am of these aching knees. And to think I may have to go through this again."

A week earlier, Maggie had knee replacements, a procedure required to continue styling hair at Salon Chic. The orthopedist also predicted hip replacement. "That's where I draw the line," Maggie stutters. "Maybe I'll retire before you do."

Bear had considered early retirement; his years of service qualified him for a pension. Before the last election, he had planned to toss his hat in the ring for promotion from deputy to sheriff. When the current sheriff saw it differently and threw his support behind an outsider—*might be God's way of telling me to get out of the business*—Bear decided to hang in as deputy. He prays he will coast and finish his career without headline-grabbing crimes to wrestle with.

Maggie reaches for him, pulls his head to hers, and nuzzles his chin. "Did you forget to shave?"

"I'm growing it out for the Lions Club beard contest. Got to be one of the guys."

"Isn't there a department regulation about beards?"

"I doubt if they'll fire me after all these years."

Bear lies in bed, the young scout putting an adult face on his childish prank gnawing at him. When son Brian was that size but years younger, Bear had taught him to swim. Held him, one hand on his back, the other on his stomach in five feet of river water. Brian paddled like a dog, kicked like a frog. "Let me go, Dad. I can do it."

BEAR

Bear wanted to ask, *Are you sure?* but turned him toward shore and walked behind the new swimmer, hoping he would panic, tire, swallow the river, any reason for Brian to reach for him, to need him. Instead, "I've got it, Dad," as he turned to swim into the current.

With Dad as deputy sheriff, Brian led a fishbowl life. Bear piled on responsibilities, obligations—Black Angus heifers for a 4-H project, tractor driving as soon as he could reach the clutch, chores after school and before sports. Honor classes in high school, strict discipline on driving and curfews. Mandatory good deeds—driving a neighbor to her chiropractor appointment or hauling firewood for the old couple down the road. No one would say the deputy coddled his kid or gave him special privileges.

The summer after graduation, Brian enlisted in the Marine Corps.

"I feel cheated," Bear told Maggie on the muggy July day he left. "Just when he's old enough for me to enjoy him, he's gone."

"You're surprised? You had eighteen years to enjoy him. You held him to a higher standard than any kid in town. Remember when you taught gun safety? You praised every kid who did anything right. Brian did everything right, and not a peep from his instructor, his dad."

"Too late for that kind of talk." Bear slumped in his chair. "I just want someone to be proud of. I hope he doesn't have to win a Purple Heart for me to feel it."

Maggie raised a scolding finger. "You always told him good enough was not good enough." She walked out of the room. "I don't blame him for leaving."

After sixteen weeks of boot camp, Bear drove to the Fargo airport to meet Brian. Maggie had wanted to come, but Bear wanted time with his son for a few hours. "You'll have him while I'm on the night shift," Bear had said.

At Hector International, Bear waited at Luggage Claim, rehearsing his welcome home lines, eyeing passengers on the down escalator. Latinos, Asians, Somalis on Brian's flight from San Diego. He spotted Brian, running the staircase in dress charlies, cover, and black mirror dress shoes. Bear hurried toward him and extended his hand. "Damned if you haven't grown a couple sizes. What are they feeding you?"

Brian searched the waiting area. "Where's Mom?"

In the airport parking lot, Brian pointed to Bear's pickup. "Still have Ole Faithful, I see. I thought you might pick me up in the squad."

"Nothing but the best for you, Private." They exited the lot and headed for I-29. "So how was boot camp? Still as nasty as the basic training I recall?"

Brian scanned the billboards, the traffic, his head turned away from Bear. "I survived."

"Still have the chicken shit drill sergeants? The godawful c-rations? The *take ten, expect five, get two-minute* breaks?"

"Something like that."

"I remember the uniform of the day, posted the night before in our barracks," Bear said. "They didn't know it'd be raining the next morning, and the posting didn't mention rain gear. We fell out in formation and got soaked. The First Sergeant walked out and yelled, 'Dumb shits,' and told us to fall in and put on our rain gear. We trained and marched all day in wet fatigues. In December. In Indiana. Stupid."

"They have to break you down to rebuild you."

"Did they break you down?"

"They thought they did. It's a mind game." Then, quiet except for the swipe of windshield wipers, the hum of tires. Brian turned the radio on and dialed the local talk station. He frowned and turned the volume down. "Those guys still doing their insane stuff."

A Dakota headwind scattered wisps of snow. Lights from commercial buildings along the freeway blinked through fluttering snowflakes. Traffic zoomed by. Bear held the wheel with both hands. "You got plans while you're home?"

"Maybe some ice fishing. If there's ice."

"Great idea. I'll take a couple days off if you want to go for the big ones."

"Some of the old gang already invited me for a long weekend on Red Lake." Brian punched the radio station selector buttons.

Now, Bear is the seasoned deputy reporting to younger man Troy who leap-frogged Bear for the sheriff title. Troy is easy to work for, respectful of Bear's skills in diffusing explosive situations and for the trust he's earned from townspeople. Bear fantasizes about retirement, but feels a traitor doing it. Someday, he'll be a

BEAR

traitor to folks who rely on him. Best to get some practice.

Maggie has survived her knee surgeries and returned to work as stylist at Salon Chic. No thought of retiring unless Vernie allows her to sit in the salon and comment on what clients know about townspeople, and speculate on what they don't.

Brian has completed his enlistment in the Marine Corps and lives in Missoula, Montana, with his wife, daughter, and son. Maggie writes, "We know it's tough for you to visit us in Minnesota, what with the two young kids and all." So Bear and Maggie drive out each summer. Bear feels like a fifth wheel. Brian, forester for the Idaho DNR, doesn't take vacation from work, and Maggie has trouble understanding Brian's wife Kim, an Asian. And the grandkids have to be prompted to remember their grandparents. "Remember? We took you to the zoo to see the lions." The kids give a wide-eyed stare, like guppies in a bowl.

Bear pours a cup of coffee and checks his daily calendar.

Verify Stub Harrington's parole status
Deliver sentence-to-serve prisoners to construct hockey rink
Oil change on the squad
Address cub scouts at 4:30 den meeting
Check vacant homes of early snowbirds
Patrol New Germany township
Make an appearance at high school basketball game
Make hotel reservations in Minneapolis for prisoner transfer
Set up meeting with retirement administrator

Bear muses over the Stub Harrington visit. Young Stub was early-released from a fifteen-year sentence for vehicular homicide, and is now in home custody with his mother. Bear must affirm his presence, make a judgment about his alcohol and drug use, both prohibited, spend a couple minutes alone with Stub, another couple minutes with mother Rhoda. *Hope the stepdad isn't home so I don't have to listen to his litany of Stub's screw-ups.*

For the Minneapolis trip, Bear will drive a squad to the Hennepin County Detention Center, process out a local scum who jumped bail on a meth charge, and drive him back to Browns County jail the next morning.

The retirement administrator meeting unnerves him. Although word is out he's considering retiring, he's not

◊ 25 ◊

comfortable with it. "You're flattering yourself," Maggie had said when he mentioned his discomfort to her. "You think the county can't live without you."

"Exception, your honor," Bear had responded. "I don't think I can live without them."

Millie the dispatcher leans on his door and winks. "Your girlfriend is on line one. Second call today."

Bear rolls his eyes and picks up the phone. "Good morning. Deputy Braham here."

"Good morning, Bear. This is Anita Woods. How are you this morning?"

Bear pulls the phone away from his ear. "All's well, Mrs. Woods. Busy day."

"Oh, Bear. Please call me Anita. No need to be so formal." Bear pictures her sly smile, hears piano tinkling in the background. "I wonder if you could stop out today. I've noticed some strange footprints in the snow around my windows. Men's footprints. I think we have a peeping tom in the neighborhood."

"One of us will drop by today, Mrs. Woods. Nothing to worry about until we get there."

"I hope it's you that investigates. I trust you with all my heart."

Anita Woods has been calling Bear daily, creating absurd reasons for him to visit. Her husband Arlen died a few months back and, since he had been a member of the sheriff's posse, Bear attended the funeral. Anita hugged Bear at the graveside and collapsed in his arms. He must have spoken kind words, told her Arlen would have wanted her to be strong, to trust that her friends, his friends, would look out for her. She must have heard him, remembered his words and his comforting hug.

When Bear mentioned Anita's constant calls to Maggie, she laughed. "That explains why she asks about you whenever she comes in for a styling. Wants to know how you're doing, what you're doing. Says with your gray beard, you remind her of Sean Connery."

"Tell her I have a bad skin disease and she should keep her hands off."

"I'll tell her when I'm done with you, she can have you."

"When you're done with me? You have plans?"

"You better find something to do when you retire. You

BEAR

sitting around all day will drive us both crazy."

"I'm thinking about getting serious with my Morgans. Buy another mare and a stallion. Add to the barn. Maybe fence the woods for more pasture."

"Don't fence my woods," Maggie says. "I won't have horses clomping on my morels or eating my Lady Slippers." Maggie slides her glasses down her nose and stares at Bear. "I'm surprised you have enough love in your heart for another Morgan. Misty will die of jealousy." She returns to her magazine. "I can identify with her feelings."

Bear has heard this grousing before, but not so unfiltered. "Look," he says, "I allow myself one bad habit. For me, it's Morgans."

Maggie drops her magazine. "I want to be your bad habit."

"Sorry. You're my good habit." He reaches for her hand and kisses it. "Now I have to pack for my Minneapolis trip. Anything I can bring you?"

"A pound of Starbucks beans and a couple new hips."

Bear parks along Fourth Avenue in Minneapolis and heads for the Hennepin County Detention Center. An hour later, he retraces his steps to the squad and drives to a Motel-6 along I-94 on the west end of town. Not convenient, but priced right. Supper will be back downtown at a family-style Italian restaurant someone recommended. He changes out of uniform into Levi's and jean jacket.

Five forty-five, and traffic streams west out of town and trickles east back into the heart of the city. Bear slips in a CD of Schubert Lieder and lets the music relax him as he merges into a stream of red taillights. *Thank God, I don't have to do this every day.*

He finds the restaurant, a walk-down with small windows crammed with neon beer signs. Inside, the after-work crowd packs the noisy dining room. He raises one finger to the hostess. "Supper."

"*Buonasera.* You have a reservation?" She stares at his jean jacket.

Bear shakes his head.

"Well, cowboy, how 'bout you sitting at the bar?" She hands him a menu. "Abriana will be your waitress."

Bear sits at the U-shaped bar across from a man who pores over a notebook, writing while he struggles with a plate of spaghetti. A young woman watches him and nurses a glass of water.

She slides onto the stool next to the man. "How was your day?" She's pale, shaking. A struggling druggie. Her hair is bleached in streaks, her makeup overdone, her trench coat open to reveal a skinny chest.

"Rough one," he says not looking up. "And it's not over yet."

"Don't let it get to you." She nudges him. "You gotta stop and smell the roses."

He ignores her and checks his watch. He's middle-aged, wears a suit coat and open-neck shirt, tie loosened. A wedding ring. No ring on the girl.

Bear reads the menu, one eye on the girl.

"Just wondering what makes you so intense," she says.

The man points to the notebook. "Sales goals."

She smiles. "I know something about those."

"I'm sure you do." He punches numbers in a small calculator and jots notes. "Pardon me, but I have to make a phone call."

Bear studies the young woman. Is this what she has to do to make ends meet? He's happy he had no daughters. Worrying about this kind of behavior would drive him crazy. Bad enough to worry about son Brian. Not worry—wonder.

Newcomers fill the bar, and the man shouts into his phone to be heard. "Lorene, sorry to bother you so late. About those dining room sets . . ."

Abriana saunters over with a napkin and silverware for Bear. "Something from the bar?"

"Bud Lite."

"You sell furniture?" the girl asks the man. "Interesting. I'm an interior designer. What lines do you carry?"

"Look, lady." The man points his fork. "I've got one hour to do a day's work. Sorry to be rude."

"No problem." She elbows him. "I might be able to provide a few new accounts for you. How about we find a quiet spot and talk?"

He flicks his hand. "Not a chance."

"I know a couple tricks to relieve your tension."

"I'm sure you do."

She puts her hand on his arm. "You look like a kind and

BEAR

considerate guy. You're looking at a damsel in distress. I haven't made my sales goals tonight either."
"I'm sorry, ma'am, but I can't help you."
"Could you advance me fifty, sixty bucks so I can get home?"
"Long cab ride."
"Expensive cab ride. What d'ya say?"
Don't do it, Bear says to himself.
"Here's a twenty. Take a bus."
Abriana brings a Bud Lite. The man returns to his notebook. The woman leaves.
Two police officers approach the man. "Sir, come with us."
"What's going on?"
"Step outside. Don't make a scene and make us cuff you."
"Tell me what's going on first."
"You offered the young lady money. There's a law against that."
"For bus fare?"
"Don't be stupid. Come with us."
Bear listens and watches the man stuff papers in a briefcase and stand. A third police hands him his coat. They walk past the hostess. "Sorry 'bout this," one officer says.
Bear throws his napkin on the counter, hurries out behind them, and sees them force the man in a squad. "Hold it, guys. I'm a deputy sheriff from Browns County and I heard this man's conversation with the girl." He flashes his open wallet showing a badge. "She may have been a prostitute, but he's no john."
"Browns County," an officer says. "You're out of your jurisdiction, aren't you?"
"Don't take this any further," Bear says. "Trust me. I heard the entire conversation. She bugged him for cab fare. He offered her $20 to get her out of his hair."
A young officer, square-jawed, face made for TV, approaches him. "Listen, you frickin' hick. Leave this to us. You stick to cattle rustlers, hear?"
"You listen, asshole," Bear shouts. "This comes to trial, I'll testify in his defense."
"Hate to do this," the senior officer says, "but you're obstructing justice. Lay off, or I'll have to cuff you and haul you in."
"Guess that's what you'll have to do. Can't believe you guys

balance the city budget by creating crimes to solve." Bear places his hands behind his back.

Pretty boy, toned body stretching his uniform, stands nose to nose with Bear while the officer slaps on the cuffs. "You mean to say you'd testify against a fellow peace officer?"

"You fuckin'-A, I would." Bear hisses and blows a gob of spit across his face.

Pretty boy recoils and throws a punch at Bear, landing on his chest. Thud. He jerks his fist back, shakes it, rubs it, dances in a tight circle. "It's broken," he screams. "The son-of-a-bitch's wearing plated Kevlar."

December 1. Beautiful winter day. Brilliant snow glistening in brilliant sunshine. What will he be doing next year at this time, or the next year, Bear wonders. Sitting in front of the fire, second cup of coffee with Maggie, Schubert symphony in the background. Maybe take Misty for a ride through knee-deep snow. Today, he'll patrol Highway 10, from the north end of the county to the south. Check for abandoned cars that slid off the highway in last night's snowfall.

The dispatcher buzzes him. "Lakewood Hospital on line one for you, Bear."

"Sheriff Braham?" the hospital caller asks. "Our patient Anita Woods has requested we call you. Ask you to come."

"What's the problem?"

"I'm sorry. I can't discuss her condition with you. But I can tell you she's critical."

Bear grabs his jacket and heads out the door. Air is refreshing and sweet and tingles his chest. A winter-white sun dangles over a bank of lead gray clouds. *What's her problem? Why ask for me?*

In the hallway outside her door, the station nurse says Mrs. Woods suffered a stroke. "She speaks haltingly. You have to listen. She knows you're coming. She smiled when we told her." The nurse puts her hand on Bear's arm. "Be prepared. She's on a steady decline. Thanks for coming."

Inside, Bear slides the curtain open and steps beside the bed. Anita sleeps, hands parked on her chest. He lifts her hand. Rings dangle from twig-like fingers. She opens her eyes. "Bear," she mouths. "You came."

Bear holds her hand, brown and mottled, limp and quaking.

BEAR

"I knew you'd come," she whispers and tries to hold his hand, his finger. "Take me home." Her jaw is slack, her murky eyes floating in tears.

Bear leans and whispers in her ear. "I'll stay with you, Anita. Now relax and sleep."

"Will you be here when I wake?"

"I'll stay with you." He lowers his lips to her forehead.

She closes her eyes. A smile creeps across her thin lips. Her breathing is weak and irregular. Her hand reposes in his.

"Sleep, my beautiful Anita."

The nurse appears. "Best to let her rest."

Bear leaves the room and walks to the parking lot. He sits in the squad, fists clutching the steering wheel. For a long minute, he stares at his hands. *Should I pray for her? What's the prayer? Recovery? Painless death? Smooth sailing through heaven's gates?* He lowers his forehead to the wheel. *May she have courage to accept God's will for her whatever it is? Whoever her God is.*

He heads north on Highway 10 a few miles into town and pulls into the Burger King drive-thru for coffee. He calls Maggie while he waits. "Thought you should know Anita Woods is in the hospital. Dying."

"She's already dead."

"What? How do you know that?"

"Anita's living will requested we be notified when she died. The hospital administrator just called. She said you'd been up to see her."

Bear flushes.

"That's sweet of you," Maggie says. "You're a good man." Bear's hands sweat. He grabs his coffee and drives back onto the highway.

A man walks on the shoulder, his back to traffic, thumb extended, carrying a satchel. Bear welcomes the distraction, stops, and rolls down his window. "There's a law against hitchhiking, you know."

"Sorry." The man puts his hand in his pocket and keeps walking.

Bear inches the squad forward. It's a young man, late teens maybe. Mug doesn't ring a bell with any on the MOST WANTED roster. Clean-cut young man, honest face, doesn't act undone with a deputy sheriff tracking him. "I can't let you keep thumbing your way through the county, but I can give you a ride to the other end, if that's where you're going."

"Minneapolis," the young man says.

"Hop in the back seat."

"Beautiful day for a walk." Bear signals his way back in the traffic lane. "You been on the road long?"

"Started in Fargo a couple hours ago. Got a ride to about a mile from where you picked me up."

"Kind of risky riding with strangers, isn't it?"

"No more for me than it is for them."

Bear sneaks a glance at him through the rearview mirror. He likes the confidence the young man projects. It's a weekday and he asks why he isn't in school.

"I graduated."

"You don't look eighteen."

"I'm not."

They assume a spot in east-bound traffic, speeding drivers slowing when they see the profile of the warning light bar. Bear glances in the rearview mirror again. His passenger rests his head back and closes his eyes. "Warm enough for you back there?" Bear asks.

"Fine."

"I have to report passengers in the squad. Care to coach me on what to say?"

The young man sits up and slaps a flat palm against the grid separating them. "Jeremiah Dwyer, on his way to the Big City."

"Pleased to meet you, Mr. Dwyer." Bear reaches a flat palm to contact his. "Bear Braham, Deputy Sheriff, Browns County." He smiles when their eyes meet in the rearview mirror. "None of my business, but are you running from something or running for something?"

"Some of each." Jeremiah locks his hands behind his head and leans back. "Running from a bad family situation. Running for a chance to make it on my own." He closes his eyes. "I once heard no house is big enough for two men. Now I know it's true." He pauses and takes a deep breath. "My father's an ordained minister. Believes in predestination. Our lives are already determined for us. All we do is live them out in a Bible-prescribed manner."

"That's bad?"

"It's bad if you don't agree with it. Father doesn't believe in planning. He never talks about the future. Always about the past—how we must repent for our sins, and the present—say your

BEAR

prayers, live the virtuous life, put your trust in the Almighty. Never gave me advice for the future." He stops. "Except when I told him I was leaving. He said, 'Well, take it easy.'" He laughs. "That's invaluable."

"Did you feel he held you to a higher standard than other kids in his congregation?"

"He unloaded the weight of his calling on all of us kids. Told us we could make him or break him as a minister of the Lord. Exemplary behavior, daily works of charity, high scholastic performance, all of that was our constant challenge."

Bear listens, glances in the mirror at the young man spilling his guts. Feels a tinge of recognition, then guilt. The radio crackles. After a long silence. Bear asks, "You like music?"

"The only music we listen to is the Christian station. The only music I know is hymns, and much of that isn't music. It was written for a different generation. *Amazing Grace? Rock of Ages? Old Rugged Cross?* That stuff doesn't resonate with me."

"Let me treat you to some real music," Bear slips in a CD, Schubert's *Ninth, The Unfinished*. "You want to stop for coffee?"

"No thanks, I want to get to Minneapolis as soon as possible. My sister expects me this afternoon. I'll stay with her 'til I find a job and get my own place. Might be McDonald's where I work. There, in the morning. Subway in the afternoon. I'll do that until I'm eighteen and get a real job. Then get on with my education."

"You'll make it," Bear says. "I admire your confidence."

"Thanks. I'm not used to that. My father thinks praise is the devil's tool. Self-pride is the biggest sin of all."

"You seem to have your act together. Good for you. But don't be too hard on your old man. I'm sure he meant well. Did the best he could with what he had. Taught you lessons that will prove invaluable for life."

"That's true, and I already appreciate it."

"Did you tell him that?"

"He's the adult. It's up to him to take the initiative."

Bear stares at the highway. He slows when a group of snowmobilers chase in the highway ditch.

"You remind me of my father when you chew your bottom lip," Jeremiah says.

Bear pats his chest pocket, hears the crinkle of a letter from Brian he's read and reread and reread.

33

Dear Mom and Dad,

I'm writing from Lolo Pass in the Bittersweet Mountains, cooperating with Montana DNR on a wild game count. On my left is Montana, on my right is Idaho. Lewis and Clark country. How impressed they must have been.

No cell phones up here. No computer. No keyboard. Just old-fashioned pen and paper. Kim and the kids are doing well. Jeong is chatty, loves to set her mother's hair. Who does that remind you of? John is quiet, introspective, analyzes the entire situation before he acts, and when he acts, he acts with conviction. Who does that remind you of?

We're planning a trip home for Christmas since we visited Korea last year. Jeong wants to ride a horse. John wants to go ice fishing. Can you arrange that, Dad?

Love to both of you.

Brian.

Bear slows to a stop and signals at a crossroad. "County line. This is as far as I can drive you." He opens his door, and opens the rear door. "Good luck, Jeremiah." He offers his hand. "Tell me something. Did your father ever say *Good enough is not good enough?*"

"All the time. But sometimes *good enough* is all we have." Jeremiah smiles. "And that's good enough."

Rooster

This is a bad stretch of road here, halfway from town to the ranch. A mile back, a Norway pine plantation blocks the drifting snow. Now it's open fields—cornstalk stubble to the north with phantom beef cattle grazing way off and, to the south, random hay bales on a barren patch. That, and a gentrified old farmhouse city folks gussied up years ago and now occupy on an occasional weekend. All well and good, those city folks, but they attract a deer herd with the shelled corn they feed in the backyard. Locals know to watch for those traffic hazards.

Here, ice glazes the highway, and a scrim of snow scurries across the black surface. DeWayne scrunches over the steering wheel, the brim of his Stetson inches from the windshield. *Straighten up*, he says, and hits the rear window with his hat, tilting the brim over his eyes. *Damn. Next time, I'll buy a truck with an extended cab.*

DeWayne replays the conversation at the auction barn, pounding the steering wheel with his fist, then gripping it with both hands. *Damn that auctioneer.* DeWayne had been chatting with a buyer friend while a small lot of scrub steers, bony and manure-caked, mulled around the sale ring, awaiting an opening bid. No takers.

The Colonel chanted his singsong "Eighty, eighty, do I hear eighty?" He paused. "Seventy-five?" Buyers left their seats and headed for the coffee pot. "They need groceries," the Colonel twanged. "Buy these steers right today, and bring them back in the fall. You'll be a rich man." He pointed his pencil at DeWayne. "Hey, Rooster, you lookin' for a Christmas present for the wifey?"

The crowd turned to DeWayne, primed to laugh.

Ha ha ha ha.

A beefy stranger, hands buried behind his bibs, elbowed him. "That's a good one."

ROOSTER

DeWayne checks the time on his truck dash—four-thirty. A few chores to do tonight, check that the neighbor boys fed the cattle, check the water troughs for ice, check the sliding doors on the lean-to. Maybe time to stop at the Broken Hart, see if the new barmaid returns for her second week.

Eyes on the road, both hands on the wheel. The city folks' house is just ahead. He sees the picket fence, the spruce trees, the mailbox with three red reflectors.

There's deer walking out the driveway. Honk. Tap the brake. Easy. Tap again. Deer walk toward the road single file. *Must be ten or twelve. If the first runs, the last one's a goner.* Honk. The truck slides forward. The lead deer runs. *Damn. Tap the brake. Again. Stay on the road. You're gonna hit one. Damn.* The truck bumps, bumps again, slides, rises and clumps over an obstacle, slides, slides, noses into the ice-crusted ditch.

"Damn."

DeWayne stares into a snow-covered windshield, lifts a deadweight foot off the brake, releases his grip on the steering wheel. *Damn.* He pulls the ignition key and climbs out of the truck. A buck sprawls on the highway, bloodied and littered with scraps of chromed plastic and glass. It lifts a magnificent rack, wriggles its body, lays down, tongue out, bleeding. DeWayne picks his way back to the truck and grabs a pistol out of the glove, loads it, fires point blank. He jerks the buck onto the shoulder and kicks glass off the highway with his boot. The radiator hisses and steams and reeks of antifreeze. He wades through waist-high snow into the ditch and lifts the hood. Fan blades are buried in the radiator.

Damn. Damn.

He reaches for his cell phone. Dead battery, and no charger in the truck. *Damn.*

Nothing for DeWayne to do but walk it, wait for a neighbor to drive by and hitch a ride to town. A couple miles to the bridge, then a couple more to town. Not to worry. He'll have a ride before he reaches the bridge. There's blood on his new deerskin gloves. *Damn. And damn these Tony Lama boots and their slick leather soles, inch-and-a-half heels.* Slipping on ice, stiff-legged, he looks like a new filly trying out her legs for the first time.

Almost five o'clock. Someone's likely to be driving home from work. Thank God for this sheepskin-lined chore coat. Pricey, but the real deal. Gets lots of laughs at the coffee klatch, but it's warm. Let 'em laugh.

He presses the collar to his ears and picks his way down the highway.

DeWayne turns to look behind and sees headlights a mile or so back. Tiny blots of light in the snow. He tilts his hat back, a lock of salt-and-pepper hair dangling on his forehead. He unbuttons his coat, like he's out for a stroll. Headlights approach. Not a truck, a car. He steps backwards and waves his arms. Big smile. Car approaches, little red imported model, keeping its speed. He'll have trouble scrunching into the front seat of that one. DeWayne waves. Driver can't help but see him. Keeps coming. Small driver. He doesn't recognize the vehicle. He waves. Woman driver or girl. Keeps her speed. Looks ahead, not at him. He could reach out and touch the car as she passes.

"Hey," he yells. *Damn, damn, damn.*

The next morning, DeWayne walks into the darkness of the Broken Hart, blinded by the morning sun. Coffee drinkers go quiet, then snicker when they recognize him. He stomps his boots.

"Well, look what the cat dragged in."

DeWayne doffs his hat and slaps it against his leg. "G'morning, girls," he says, nodding as he passes the women's table. They dismiss him with a wave of their hands. He heads for his chair at the men's table.

A neighbor laughs. "Heard you were out for a stroll last night, Rooster."

"Yeah. Damn those city folks and their deer," DeWayne says, removing his coat and hanging it on the chair back.

"Heard the sheriff on the CB this morning. Twelve-point buck. Said he was shot, not run over."

"You telling me deer hunting season is over?" DeWayne jokes. He sits, leans into the crowd at the table, and splays his elbows.

"Said he banged up your truck, too. Now you gonna have to get up early and take the wife to work."

"I'm already looking at a new truck." DeWayne reaches for a cup. "Anybody heard from Mitch?"

"We're not talking about Mitch. We're talking about you. You musta stopped for a couple bumps at the Stockman's Café after the sale. Musta got silly."

DeWayne chuckles. "I've been known to do that."

"You don't impress me as the kind of guy who'd take a five-mile hike in a snowstorm. Musta looked like you were walking on stilts wearing those fancy boots. Probably the best dressed hitchhiker in the county."

The men laugh.

"A guy's gotta do what he's gotta do." DeWayne taps his empty coffee cup on the table.

"I expected you'd tell us you picked up the waitress at Stockman's."

"Well, she does have a problem keeping her hands off me. But I was alone when it happened, damn it. Any coffee in the pot?"

"Not 'til we get the scoop, Rooster. So you broadsided a buck, ran your truck in the ditch, and hoofed it all the way to town. Tell me you had some good luck yesterday, like you bought low and sold high at the auction."

"Saw nothing there of interest. A man only gets lucky like I did once in a lifetime." He grips his jaws tight, nods, and smiles.

"You still crowing about the overpriced Angus bull you bought for your wife last Christmas?"

"That would be the one." DeWayne points his spoon at his interrogators. "Two of his daughters took Grand Champion and Reserve Champion at the Angus Futurities in Wichita. Both heading for the National Western Stock Show next month."

"We've heard that song before, haven't we, men?"

Nods and chuckles all around.

"Believe what you want." DeWayne waves his spoon again. "I already got calls from a couple A-I suppliers. Offered me thirty bucks a straw for that boy's semen." He grips his jaws together again, smiles, loving the attention.

"This is starting to sound like another one of your get-rich-quick schemes. Weren't you gonna hit the jackpot raising angora goats?"

"Or your dude ranch wet dream," another chimes in. "Having those city folks haul your hay bales all summer. And they pay you for the privilege."

"Don't forget the catfish farm in the old barn foundation," another adds.

DeWayne shakes his head. "I'm just telling you. When my bull's daughters take first place at Denver, that thirty-dollar straw shoots up to three hundred."

"Might be a good idea for you to hire a chauffeur when your ship comes in. Keep you out of the ditch. I suppose you're buying a new truck for the wife's Christmas present this year."

"You're right for once, Buster. The dealer's delivering a demo model right here in a half hour. Ford F-350 XLT, extended cab, heated seats, loaded." He scans the table, locks eyes with all the men, and smooths his goatee. "Now, pass the coffee pot."

Back home, DeWayne parks in front of his garage enthroned in the cab of the new Ford F-350. He has driven to town, honked at neighbors who gave him a blank stare, faked a reason to stop at the drive-thru window at the bank hoping for a comment, a question, a compliment. Nothing. He lowers the seat height, tilts the molded steering wheel, and presets the radio push buttons to country western and talk show stations. The King Ranch interior is saddle-slick. The wife will like the heated seats.

He glances at the clock on the dash. Time to check cattle before dinner. Check Commander's King Cole, DeWayne's ticket to fame and fortune. Luckiest investment he ever made. That poor asshole rancher had to sell him. Now. Got a girl in trouble. Had to have cash. Today. DeWayne knew the pedigree, had A-I'ed his own cows with King Cole for a couple years. He knew the bull's worth. He also knew the rancher's desperation. Bought King Cole for a song.

The barn where The King rules is climate-controlled and opens to an exercise ring. Neighbors got a kick out of that. "You air-conditioned your barn before the house?" "Your bull has his own spa?"

"It's not air-conditioning." DeWayne had defended his investment. "It's a wall-hanging heater for winter and a couple fans for summer. And it's not a spa. It's an exercise ring with a hot walker." Let those assholes have their fun.

DeWayne walks into the house through the garage to slip into his work boots. Damn, his feet hurt from last night. Feels like they swelled a couple sizes. Outside, he pats the hood of the truck in the drive and crunches through snow to the barn. Cows, already fat with calves, snuggle at bale feeders due for reloading. Others waddle the worn path to the watering system. DeWayne had plugged in the block heater for the John Deere this morning. He'll feed hay after dinner.

"Old King Cole, you handsome brute." He leans on the corral rail. "You gonna make me one happy man."

The bull stands across the corral fence near the cows. His

broad masculine head is framed in a white leather halter. He raises his head toward DeWayne, as if he's posing. *Gentle giant,* DeWayne thinks. *Leads like a lamb.*

Damn, look at his conformation—wide shoulders, square body. Look at his deep rib. And look at that set of balls. Aristocratic is what you are. You are The King. DeWayne salutes him. *There's a million dollars standing there. Just hope your calf crop and semen sales cover the line of credit payment coming due.* He heads for the house. *Can't seem to get those desk jockeys at the bank to share my enthusiasm.*

In the kitchen, DeWayne lifts the Crock-Pot lid. Chili. He sniffs, closes his eyes, and grabs a bowl. The knotty pine cupboards are fitted with handles fashioned from pony shoes. A calendar picturing a Black Angus herd hangs by the door. Yesterday's dishes are piled in the sink. Cereal boxes stacked on the counter. A basket of recyclables waits by the door.

He walks through the living room where a collapsible aluminum Christmas tree with a few ornaments stands on the coffee table. Big enough tree, he figures, for the gift he'll place under it for the wife. Truck keys. He passes the telephone on the way to the bathroom. A red-light flashes—three messages on the answering machine, two with 303 area codes. Colorado. One number he recognizes as the truck dealer. No call from the wife. She must have found a ride home.

He scoops a bowl of chili and sits at the table by the window. His throne, his kingdom—the corral, the feed lot, the cows, the heifer calves, the steers. Soaking up brilliant December sun. Black gold. Cows fat and pregnant, due in late March, early April. Another crop of calves to sell. Prices projected to stay high. Not that he'll need the money, thanks to Old King Cole. "Thanks, buddy."

DeWayne leaves the house an hour before the wife is due to return from work in some co-worker's car, he guesses. Leaves to save himself from listening to them haggle as to whether the driver accepts a five spot for gas, the driver saying "'Tis the season," or "What are friends for?" or some malarkey. Get away now and spare him explaining the new truck. How he planned to pay for it, what with the line of credit payment due. Leave now and at least delay the explanation.

"This doesn't look like Happy Hour to me." DeWayne

removes his coat at the Broken Hart and pulls the corner stool out from under the counter. "Looks more like a morgue."

Two cowboys down the line crouch over their beers and glance at him. "Hey, Rooster, when'd you get outta jail?"

"Don't pay any attention to those young whippersnappers, Sweetie," DeWayne says to the barmaid, the girl he met a couple nights ago. "I'm DeWayne, new here and eager to make friends. Remember?" He extends a hand across the counter.

She lifts a tentative hand and presents it to him. She wears a different outfit tonight—black sequined jersey top, black stretch pants, black boots. "Name's Amber. What can I get you?"

"That's the best offer I've had all day. You'd look good in my new Tuxedo Black truck in that getup."

"Don't let his line worry you, Amber," Black Cowboy Hat says. "Rooster's all yack and no shack."

"I'll have a bottle of Bud. Got change for a hundred?" Dewayne asks.

"No."

"Maybe I got something smaller." He reaches for his billfold.

"Why do they call you *Rooster*? I thought your name was DeWayne." She hands him the bottle.

"You watch him and you'll know why," Tan Hat says. "And listen to him. Watch him strut and listen to him crow." He imitates a rooster crowing and damn near falls off the chair laughing.

"Kids," DeWayne says, pointing his bottle at the cowboys. "You stick with an older man, Sweetie. Old age and treachery trump youth and skill, you know."

She wipes the counter and stacks paper coasters.

"You from around here, Amber, or just passing through?"

She shrugs her shoulders. "Two dollars, please."

He offers her a five and squeezes it in her hand. "Keep it," he says.

"I hope I don't see the day when I have to pay for it," Black Hat says.

And from Tan Hat, "Heard you got a new truck."

"Yeah. The old one needed an oil change."

"That, and a new radiator. And a new grill. And new headlights."

"I wanted a rig with reclining seats." He winks at Amber.

"Don't promise more than you can deliver, Rooster," Black

ROOSTER

Hat says. "My old man went to school with you. Says you were cherry when you married your old lady."

Tan hat adds, "And you're smart enough not to screw up a free meal ticket by messing around now. Wifey caught you, she'd have you off your so-called ranch in less than an hour. It was her family's farm, right?"

"Where would you house your prize bull then?" Black Hat jumps back in. "I hear you expect him to put you in an upper income bracket."

"That could be the case." DeWayne picks the label off his bottle. "Got a couple more calls today. A-I suppliers wanting me to sign up with them for exclusive distribution rights. Nice offers, gonna get nicer." He empties his bottle and taps it on the bar. "Amber, dear, how about one more and a round for the boys?"

"Damn," Black Hat says. "I take back everything I said about you."

"The A-I sales are just the beginning." DeWayne watches Amber bend into the cooler. "Got a call from the *Western Farmer-Stockman* magazine. Want to interview me for the stock show special issue."

"What's that all about?"

"Two of my bull's daughters are contestants in Denver. And they're getting a lot of buzz. The owners took out a full-page ad in the magazine. Want me to pay thirty percent of the tab. I told them I wasn't in show business."

"Damn," says Tan Hat.

"There's more. They invited me to watch the judging from their box seats at the Coliseum. Free drinks, free food, free girls, for all I know."

Black Hat nods. "Damn, damn."

"It ain't over yet. Been invited to two, three hospitality suites during the show. This is Black Angus high society, I'm telling you. All free."

The cowboys are quiet, start to talk among themselves.

DeWayne takes a swig and licks his lips. He glances at the television. Two sports announcers haggle over a bad play, a bad call, a bad pass, anything bad. He glances around. Getting dark outside. Colored Christmas lights trace rectangles around the windows.

"Amber," he says. "Turn off that TV crap and play something on the jukebox." He hands her a dollar and watches her strut around the end of the bar. At the jukebox, she shifts her weight, one foot to the other, while she selects the songs.

"Looks like two puppies in a gunny sack," DeWayne says to the cowboys.

Black hat points to Amber. "Rooster, you'd have no idea what to do with that."

DeWayne grins. "Give me a couple hours to figure out just what I would do."

DeWayne lays on the horn outside the café where the community gathers for morning coffee and waits. Waits for someone inside to walk to the window. No one. Lays on the horn again. Watches and waits. No one. Oh, well . . .

"Keep your seats, gentlemen," he says at the long rectangular men's table. Four or five conversations mingle and merge. None involve DeWayne. A newcomer sits at DeWayne's customary seat and looks up at him standing beside the chair. No effort to move. DeWayne walks to the far end of the table, past the end chair conspicuously vacant, and slides a chair to the corner next to a quiet coffee drinker, one not known to talk or listen or shake dice.

"Sure like my new rig," DeWayne says, removing his coat.

The coffee drinker reaches for a napkin and blows his nose.

"Any of you guys need anything from town?" DeWayne calls down the table. "I'll be going to the courthouse to sign title papers."

A couple men stop talking, shake their heads *No*.

"Anybody hear the weather forecast?" DeWayne tries again. "Any more snow in the works? I'm thinking about adding a snow plow to my rig."

"We get the message, Rooster. We know about your new toy. Or your wife's new toy."

"Yeah, we know. I was behind you in the drive-thru lane at the bank."

"I saw that black and chrome piece of conspicuous consumption outside the Broken Hart," another says. "'Got to be Rooster's new wheels,' I said to the wife."

"And please, don't bore us with your Denver stories. My boy said he had to listen to your shit at the bar last night."

DeWayne grins at the attention. "You can't blame a man for wanting to share a little excitement. I'm debating whether to fly or drive."

"My nephew just flew home from school for Christmas vacation. Said the lines at security were blocks long. Makes Disney World look like a slam dunk."

"You're talking Denver, Colorado? One of the guys from work moved out there. Lasted less than a year. Smog drove him away."

The door opens admitting brilliant morning sun that silhouettes a man, a large man, square shoulders, chesty, boots.

"Holy shit," someone yells from the men's table. "It's the law. Hide the dice."

Deputy Bear walks in, nods to the ladies' table. "G'morning." Wipes his boots on the mat. He walks to the men's table and slides the end chair out. "Anyone sitting here?"

Silence until Ray at the far end says, "Have a seat, Bear. That's the Merlin Swanson memorial chair. The late Merlin of Merlin's Minnows. We're keeping it open a few months. Or for special guests like you."

DeWayne slides tighter into his neighbor. Bear sits.

"What's the buzz in the courthouse?" someone asks.

"Can't think of anything huge." Bear motions to Darla for coffee.

"What brings you to our fair city?"

"Routine patrol. And someone reporting cattle on the road."

"Better keep those cattle off the road. We got a driver here with a reputation of crashing into them." He points his cup at DeWayne.

DeWayne lowers his head and smiles.

"We was wondering if you're going to ticket him for hunting with an illegal weapon."

Darla hands Bear a cup of coffee and declines his offer of a dollar bill.

"You get your transportation issues resolved?" Bear asks DeWayne.

"Will have by the end of the day." DeWayne nods. The other coffee drinkers resume their conversations.

DeWayne turns to Bear. "We were talking about the National Western Stock Show. A couple of my bull's daughters will sell out there. Might make me a rich man."

Bear nods and sips his coffee.

DeWayne smiles and refills his cup. "Some of those

exhibitors are making offers that are tough to turn down. Free tickets to the show. Box seats. Hospitality suites. A pass to every Coliseum event."

"Don't listen to him, Bear," a man says picking up on DeWayne's words. "There ain't no such thing as a free lunch, Rooster. I heard the Coliseum parking lot is a hundred acres. Better switch boots if you park there."

"I don't understand what's the big deal," another says. "You don't have your cattle in the show."

"You don't understand the A-I industry," DeWayne says, rising to the resumed attention. "If King Cole's daughters win, place, or show, a couple distributors want me on hand to negotiate a price for semen and sign a deal. Start taking orders right there at the show."

"Can you hardly wait for someone to invent the telephone? Close a deal like this in three minutes of your time, not three days. Now, let's get those dice rolling. I've gotta win some Christmas shopping money."

"Oops," says another. "Not in front of the sheriff."

Bear smiles. "Other than present company," he nods at DeWayne, "are people behaving around town?"

Silence again until Ray says, "Yeah, except for the meth lab down the street. And a couple drunks with revoked driver's licenses still on the road. And a light-fingered kid who ransacks cars out front." He smiles. "But if we can't handle it, we'll sure call you."

A coffee drinker lifts his arms. "Frontier justice is alive and well."

Bear grins. "I'd better be going."

DeWayne stands. "I'm outta here, too." He reaches for his coat as Bear walks to the door.

"You must be expecting a cold snap," a coffee drinker says. "Sweatshirt for underwear, wool flannel shirt, vest, and that sheepskin leather coat."

DeWayne smiles, sucks in his gut, and raises his arms in a muscle man pose. "Big," he says.

Outside, he stomps snow before entering the truck cab.

"Hey, Rooster, hold on a second." A coffee drinker walks out. "If you're looking for a chance to spread some Christmas cheer and you got a few extra bucks, you might think about paying a visit to George Marin's family. He's in the hospital and his sick benefit check doesn't show until after the first of the year." He blows on his fingers. "His wife called me for a short-term loan and I couldn't spare anything. Just a loan is what she wants, you understand. That is, if you could spare it."

"Always better to give than to receive," DeWayne says. "Thanks for the tip."

"Watch your step with that woman. She's a ball buster."

"I never met my match yet. But thanks again."

No time like the present, DeWayne thinks as he steps in the truck after his business at the courthouse. He glides a gloved hand across the dash, the console, the steering wheel. Drive out to the Marin farm now? Or should he call her, make sure she's home, confirm she's looking for a financial lift? Or go home, shave, and shower? He doesn't remember meeting Mrs. Marin at the Broken Hart or shopping, although he remembers George from the coffee klatch. A good tractor mechanic. Not one to make a fuss.

You only get one chance to make a good first impression on the lady, he concludes, and heads for home. The wife has a few hundred dollars stashed away for property taxes he can borrow. After dinner, chores, and a shower, he'll call the Marin household.

"Mrs. Marin," he sweet talks into the phone. "This is DeWayne Dunne. I got a delivery for you from Santa Claus."

Silence.

"Mrs. Marin? I heard at coffee this morning you could use a small loan to tide you over the next couple weeks. Right?"

"Who is this?"

"DeWayne Dunne. I have the Angus ranch north of town."

"Oh, Rooster. I never knew you had another name."

DeWayne grunts. "You plan to be home the next hour or so?"

"I'm getting ready to go the hospital when the kids get home from school. But I'll be here 'til then."

"I'm on my way." He stuffs three hundred-dollar bills in his vest pocket.

It's a short drive to the Marin farm, through town, south on the tar to the second gravel, east to the third driveway. Long driveway, unplowed. Kids' boot tracks break the wide expanse of snow. He shifts into four-wheel drive and blows a cloud of powder.

He parks the truck in view of the front window and trudges to the porch.

Mrs. Marin opens the door. "Come in. Come in. Hey, thanks for making a trail down the driveway. I should be able to get out now." She smooths her white jersey blouse and backs into the house. "Let me take your coat. Coffee, or are you in a hurry?"

"I should keep going," he says, "but thanks." DeWayne stares. Her busty torso makes her top heavy, like she'd fall forward if she didn't bend back. She takes his coat and drapes it over a chair; he removes his boots. "I'd like to help you if I could," he says. "A loan, you understand."

"I wouldn't have it any other way."

"Anything you want to sell? Anything you want to get rid of?"

"Nothing to sell except maybe a couple dozen eggs. A dollar a dozen."

"I'll take those as a starter. Any machinery, tools, livestock? Stuff worth somewhere in the hundreds?"

"No, sir. Let me get the eggs."

DeWayne scans the room. An afternoon soap mutters from the television. A man's seducing a woman, she's seducing him; DeWayne can't tell. A scrawny jack pine with a string of lights stands in the corner, a few gifts piled below. The furniture and carpet are worn, the room sparse but tidy. He smells chocolate from the kitchen.

"Smells good," he says when she returns.

"A batch of brownies for the kids. Today is the last day of school before Christmas vacation. I was getting ready to visit George as soon as the kids get home." She looks at the clock, two cartons of eggs in one hand and a plastic bag in the other.

DeWayne hands her two dollar bills. She takes the bills with her bag hand and stuffs them in the neck of her blouse.

"Nice piggy bank," he says.

"Here you are, Rooster," she says ignoring him. "Grade A, extra-large."

"I was thinking the same thing."

She throws her arms back in a tease and wiggles her shoulders. "The girls," she says glancing down. "They're anxious to see Daddy."

"What kind of loan we talking about?" DeWayne asks. "How much?"

ROOSTER

"How much you got?"

"I've never heard any complaints."

"Come on, Rooster, we're talking business."

"I struck a run of good luck with my bull King Cole and I'm happy to share it. You've heard of a cash cow? Now you've heard of a cash bull." He grins telling the story. "But we're talking a loan, right?"

"I wouldn't want to be indebted to any man around here."

He winks. "Would a couple hundred dollars get me a roll in the hay?"

She places her hands on her hips and smiles. "Now, Mr. Rooster, you know what the ladies at the coffee table say about you? Say you're all talk."

"As if any of them would know."

"I'm not sure," she says, still smiling, "but I'm gonna call your bluff. Come here." She grabs his belt. "Nice buckle. *Ford Tough*. I've got a soft spot in my heart for a Ford man."

"Hey, take it easy, woman." DeWayne leans back.

"Well, about that roll in the hay. We're gonna have to get on with it. The school bus is due in a half hour." She tugs at his belt and reaches to unbutton his vest.

"Hey, hey, hey, slow down. Let's go in the bedroom."

"Can't. The baby's sleeping in there."

"You mean right here in the living room? In broad daylight? In full view?"

"That's what I mean." She lifts her hand off his vest and rests it on his shoulder twirling his earlobe. She leans forward, pressing against him.

He smells her fresh out-of-the-shower fragrance. Scented soap. Coconut.

"What's the matter, Rooster? You bashful?" She pinches his goatee.

He backs to the door, dragging her pressed against him. "What about your husband?" He lifts her hands away. She replaces them.

"No problem. I'm not gonna tell him. And I'm sure he'd do the same for me with the right woman."

"But won't he ask? Won't he know?"

"George and I share the same philosophy," she whispers in his ear. "Sex is like breathing, or eating. Just one more bodily function." She slips a hand under his vest and rubs his chest.

"Trouble is, people assign all kinds of moral and emotional baggage to it." She traces a finger down his neck, around his collar, under his shirt. "But in the end, it's just a roll in the hay." She snickers. "I'll bet your Old King Cole isn't bashful with his girls."

"We gotta slow down," he says. "I don't do this enough where I can predict my performance. I wouldn't want to disappoint you."

"You underestimate me," she says, unbuttoning his shirt.

"Mrs. Marin, this is not gonna work." He lifts her hands free and forces her away, holding her two hands in one of his. He reaches in his vest pocket and fans three hundred-dollar bills. "Take what you want."

She eyes the money, smiles, and takes three bills. "You're sweet. Your missus is lucky to have you."

DeWayne doesn't hear her. He's slipping into his boots, keeping one eye on her. He struggles with the sleeves of his coat. If he hurries, he'll clear the driveway before the school bus arrives. He grabs the bag of eggs and holds it against his chest, like armor plate.

He waves a hand, either in goodbye or to keep her away. He sneaks one last look at her, at her huge grin.

She leans against the open door, hand on her hip, and watches him take giant steps through the snow. "Hey, nice truck," she yells.

FISH

Joy shouldered her condo door open and struggled to the kitchen, a bag of groceries in each arm. *I hope this guy is worth it.* The phone rang. Maybe Bob confirming their dinner engagement as he said he would. Maybe wondering what he could bring.

"Hello," she sang. Her voice tightened down. "How is my boy today?"

She slipped out of her jacket and unpacked groceries as she talked. "No, I can't help you right now." She turned on the oven and unpacked frozen lobster cakes and scalloped potatoes. "Honey, believe me, I'm in no position to help you now. Maybe in a month or two, but not now." She balanced the phone on her shoulder and lifted the lobster cakes out of their aluminum pan and placed them on a baking sheet. Bob wouldn't know the difference.

"Honey, listen. I'm very busy. I have a friend coming for dinner." She checked the boxes for oven temperature. "No, you don't know him. His name is Bob. He'll be here in a half-hour." She set the oven temperature dial. "No, silly. I can't ask him that. It's only our second date. Men shy away from needy women, especially rich men." She sighed and rolled her eyes. "Have you talked to your brother?" She opened a package of bread sticks. "Don't talk about your brother that way. Now honest, honey. I have to get ready. Let's talk later, okay?"

After she finished dinner preparation, she brushed her hair, did her makeup, her nails. She set the dining room table. The sea foam blue linen, the good china, the sterling silver, the crystal goblets. She stood blue candles in crystal candleholders. *I should have bought the blue daisy bouquet at Walmart. But ten dollars?* After tuning the kitchen radio to the Golden Oldies station, she opened the oven, closed her eyes, and inhaled. Already the aroma of garlic

FISH

and seafood. Breadsticks lay on a baking sheet ready for warming. A bag of shredded greens chilled in the refrigerator. And for dessert, a Sara Lee cheesecake. How could she go wrong? She had hocked a marble tarpon sculpture owned by her late husband Chuck to fund this dinner. It had better be worth it.

What did she know about Bob? Not much. They had met on Craig's List where she scoured *Men looking for Women*, searching for an older man, retired, high income bracket, no plan to live to one-hundred. They had met for dinner once.

In his profile, Bob described himself as *affable, laughable, and ready to take the plunge*. He may have understated his two-hundred and fifteen pounds. But so had she. He parted his overly groomed brown hair on the side and flashed the practiced smile of a salesman.

This won't even be a challenge. I could have this babe-in-the-woods for breakfast.

Bob had invited her to dinner at the VFW where he held a membership. *What war? Maybe Vietnam, maybe even Korea.* He had mentioned he preferred pizza but felt an obligation to support his fellow veterans. Lobster cakes would be a huge step above the buffalo chicken wings they shared, her dining room chairs more comfortable than bar stools, her music better for conversation than the blare of country western. She had strained to catch every other word Bob spoke.

She remembered his discussion of an apple orchard, his retirement project, his dream. *Oh, yes, put the bowl of Red Delicious apples on the table. So perfect, they look plastic.* She had searched for his orchard on the Internet and driven there, curious about his house, his neighborhood. She copied names off upscale neighbors' mailboxes. "You must live near the Jacobsons," she would say later in conversation. "They were friends of ours."

And what about her outfit tonight? She flitted between the kitchen and dining room in her pink chenille robe. Would navy blue slacks, the white blouse, the red blazer be too much for patriotic Bob? Would he salute her like Chuck had done? Maybe her teal blue pantsuit to match the dining room table.

She had suggested dinner at six. At five forty-five, snow pelted the window and she pulled the living room drapes. Nosy neighbor across the condo hall would keep her drapes open and sit by the window, one eye on the evening news, the other on the sidewalk. Nosy neighbor would hear the main entry door open, hear his footsteps in the hall, hear him knock, hear her open the door. And if true to form, she'd call a few minutes later and ask Joy to play cards or something. Or *Are you busy? Do you have company? Someone new? Can you talk? Can you tell me about him?*

No. No.

Should she light the candles now? Or ask what's his name? Bob. Yes, Bob. Should she ask Bob to light them? And the wine. He drank beer at the VFW. She had asked the liquor store clerk to recommend a wine for dinner. *Good wine goes with everything,* he had said. *Bad wine goes with nothing.* Big help. She placed a bottle of Zinfandel on the counter along with an opener and two glasses. Bob could open the bottle. Men liked that sort of thing. Oh, napkins. She forgot the napkins. Good she remembered now, rather than have to get up from the table when Bob dribbled scalloped potatoes on his chin. What kind of country bumpkin would not have napkins?

Joy looked at the table, the Lennox china, Gorham silver, Waterford Crystal, all remnants of Chuck's dowry. All over-the-top for frozen Walmart lobster cakes. But so elegant. Bob would surely be impressed.

Damn that radio station. All commercials. She slipped in the new Holiday Sampler CD. Fresh snow tonight and Christmas carols. Hadn't Bob mentioned he loved Christmas?

The phone rang. Let it ring. Too late for Bob to call now. Probably a telemarketer wanting a donation. The answering machine played the recorded message. "This is Joy. Sorry I can't take your call." *Is that me talking? Damn that cracking old lady voice. How long have I sounded like that? Tomorrow. Switch to the generic message tomorrow.*

"Mom," came the voice on the recorder. Joy's eyes rose to the ceiling. She filled the water pitcher with ice to avoid the message. "Wondering if I can borrow your car tomorrow night. The warning lights are flashing on the friggin' Falcon. Blinks like a friggin' Christmas tree. I don't get my check 'til Wednesday. Love you, Mom."

Lord, when will he take responsibility for his own life?

Ten to six. Better change. What to wear? Nothing flashy about Bob. On their first date, a black leather jacket with an eagle holding an American flag embroidered on the back. A turtleneck and chino pants. Forget the blazer and pantsuit.

The doorbell buzzed. *My god, he's here.* She started for the

FISH

bedroom and turned back. She buzzed him in and started for the bedroom again, and turned back. *Make him wait in the hall? Have nosy neighbor crack her door and check him out?* She opened the door and leaned out. Bob carried a small poinsettia plant and a brown paper bag.

"Come in. You're early." She motioned him in with a robed arm. "I'm getting dressed. What a beautiful plant. You can put it on the coffee table. Take off your coat. Have a chair. I'll be right out." She hustled to the bedroom.

Bob elbowed the door shut. "Smells good."

Joy stood before the closet and grabbed a pair of slacks and sweater. "Open the wine if you want," she yelled from the bedroom, "and pour yourself a glass. And one for me."

She stood before the bedroom mirror. Were those new lip wrinkles? She tugged her sweater down, dispensing any definition of torso. She shook her head and fluffed the sweater up. And these fashionably short slacks revealing her thick ankles, oh my god, and these matronly half-heeled pumps. She shrugged her shoulders and walked from the bedroom, arms extended for a handshake or a hug, she wasn't sure.

Bob stood in the living room before a wall of portraits. With his black horn-rimmed glasses and a top-heavy body in bulky fisherman's knit sweater, he looked like Charlie Tuna. "Sorry I'm early. One of my bad habits."

He shook her hand and pointed to the portraits. "Who's the guy that looks like Colonel Sanders?"

"That's my father. Reverend Martin Luther Johnston. May his soul rest in peace."

"Oh, sorry. And these?" Bob pointed to portraits of two young men. "Your sons?"

Something about Bob looked different. In the VFW, he had brown hair. Tonight, he was bald. "They're both my sons. Ricky on the right, LeRoy on the left." She glanced at the wine bottle, still corked, and the brown paper bag beside his leather jacket draped on a kitchen chair.

Bob walked to the wall. "Neither one resembles his mother. Don't even resemble each other. None of my business," he chuckled, "but were they adopted?"

"No, no. They're both mine. Different fathers." She corrected herself. "Different husbands. Oh, this is more than you need to know."

"Not a big deal." Bob grinned. "So, you've been married twice? It's three strikes before you're out."

"Well, no," Joy stammered. "Well, yes." She looked at the pictures, the kitchen, the bowl of apples. "Oh, this is embarrassing."

"It's okay. May I open the wine for you?" Bob struggled with the bottle. "Many people our age have been married twice."

Our age? He's older than me. She lifted her glass and allowed him to pour. "Aren't you having one?"

"Nope. I'll have a beer. I brought a six-pack of my house brand. He opened the bag, pulled a key-chained church key from his pocket, and snapped a bottle of Corona Extra.

My god. Corona Extra. Ricardo's personal brand.

Bob lifted his bottle. "Cheers."

Joy considered guzzling the glass. She swallowed a lump and recovered. "Fact is, I've been married three times. But never divorced." She walked to the living room, shaking her head. "Not me divorced. Widowed three times." She lifted three fingers and took another sip. "Oh, that sounds terrible. Puts me in a terrible light. I'd better check our dinner." She hustled back to the kitchen.

"Beautiful furniture you have," Bob commented from the living room. "I haven't seen this quality for years."

"My late husband Chuck had excellent taste. And the wherewithal to afford it. I gave most of his stuff away when I moved from the house to the condo. The boys furnished their apartments in style. Most of it sold or ruined by now, I'm sure."

Bob returned to the wall of portraits. "I don't know which carries the worse stigma—you being married three times or me being not being married at all."

Joy carried the dinner rolls to the oven. She stopped. *Say something stupid. See if you can find his hot button.* "Never married? That's odd."

"Odd?" His voice raised a half-octave. "Taking care of your aged parents and sacrificing your personal life. That's odd? Loving the single life you're living. That's odd? Holding out for the right woman. That's odd?"

"Not odd. Unusual, commendable. I'm sorry. I'm not good with words." She rolled her eyes. *The guy's a pushover.*

"Your sons." Bob pointed to the wall. "Ricky is the older, right? Dark complexion, black hair, great smile. Latino?"

"That's good." Joy relaxed. "His father Ricardo was

FISH

Hispanic. Law enforcement guy. Twenty-four/seven policeman. Tough to live with. Hot tempered. Nasty tongue. Terrible drinking problem." She smiled. "My saving grace was his love of fishing. Summer and winter. Got him out of the house." She stared at a painting of a jumping sailfish, and shook her head. "I don't want to dwell on him. But I will tell you this."

Bob chuckled and swigged his beer.

"My mom hated him, said she'd shoot him if he ever set foot on her property. And what did Ricardo say? 'She'd have to outdraw me.'"

"Of course your dad loved him, right? They were great fishing buddies."

"What dad? He disappeared before I was potty-trained. Ma said, 'Good riddance. There's plenty of fish in the ocean.' And there were. Don't know what happened to them either." She motioned for Bob to sit on the sofa.

He set the beer bottle on the coffee table and stretched his arms. "Very comfortable."

Joy sat and rotated her glass of wine. What to say?

"Nice marlin in the photograph. Is that Ricardo?" Bob pointed while reaching for his beer. The bottle tipped and crashed to the table. Joy jolted, staring at the bottle dripping beer on the carpet. Ricardo's beer bottle.

"Bring my dinner out to the fish house at noon." Ricardo pounded a beer bottle on the table.

Joy stood at the window, patting the baby, watching the first flakes fall. "I don't trust my car on the ice. And I can't take the baby out."

"I'll take your damn car. You drive the truck. You remember how to drive a stick shift? Don't screw up reverse and first gear." Ricardo emptied the bottle and tossed it in the recycle basket.

Joy jumped.

"Grab me another one."

"I get nervous driving on ice. What if the ice can't hold the truck? I'll sink."

"The law of gravity takes over, woman. All you do is open the door and step out on the ice. Pedal your ass to the closest fish house. Somebody will help you." He snickered. "Might cost you something, but they'll help you. They're all my buddies." He looked outside. "Better get going. Looks like it's starting to snow. You be there at noon with dinner, got it?" He tickled baby Ricky. "Can't wait to take you along, kid."

Joy telephoned her grandmotherly neighbor. "Can I leave Baby Ricky with you for an hour or so at noon? I have to make a run to town." She grabbed a loaf of bread, mustard, sandwich bags, and placed a tube of sandwich meat on the breadboard. She held the cleaver high. *Treat me like scum and you'll get what's coming to you.* Her arm trembled. The knife wavered. She swung the knife down. Severed meat chunks rolled off the breadboard, off the countertop, onto the floor.

The truck stood backed against the garage door. She restrained her foot as she tested the gears. The truck inched backward and tapped the door. She found first gear and drove down the driveway.

Ricardo's spear house, an oversized Mexican flag, dominated the lake—red and green vertical stripes on the sides and white-painted door decorated with a golden eagle. Joy's white Chevy stood alongside, blending into a snow bank. She tested the brakes and ground into reverse, backed to the spear house, and stepped out of the truck. Snow continued to fall, heavier now, half-hiding beer bottles in the drifts. She pulled her collar up to keep the cold snow off her neck and tapped the horn to alert him she had arrived. She snugged her jacket and knocked on the door. "Hold it." Ricardo spoke softly. She waited. Ice fishing houses dotted the lake, the trucks beside them frosted with new snow. "Hold it," he spoke again. Her arms shivered; her knees rattled. *You're strong, woman. You can do it.* The truck purred with warm confidence beside her, its vibration strengthening her like a willing accomplice.

"Damn," Ricardo yelled. "Got away. Open the door."

Inside, thin light filtered through snow and ice into the water, creating an eerie green glow. Beer bottles crowded the narrow bench where Ricardo sat beside a minnow bucket. His feet dangled above a large rectangle of open water. He grabbed the lunch bag. "Move out. Close the door." He swung a gaff hook in one hand, a spear in the other. "I've got a trophy waiting for me."

Joy closed the door and climbed into the truck. *I've got one chance. Screw up and I'm dead meat. Which gear is first, and which is reverse?* She slipped into gear and released the clutch. *Oops.* She

FISH

shifted again and drove off the lake.

At home, she waited. She played with baby Ricky and poured a glass of beer for herself. Another. She started supper at five. Ricardo could arrive any time after dark. She heard herself humming Christmas carols and turned on the radio. She fed baby Ricky and put him in the jump-up seat. She hadn't picked up the mail. She threw a scarf around her neck and danced down the driveway, her arms spread, her chin tilted up catching snowflakes on her tongue. A star shone in the new darkness. *Twinkle, twinkle little star*, she sang in a giddy kid's voice.

Six o'clock, and no word from Ricardo. "Let's wait for daddy until six-thirty," she cooed to baby Ricky.

At seven, she called the sheriff's office and asked them to check on Ricardo. "I haven't seen him since he left this morning. He's always home soon after dark."

At eight, Deputy Sheriff Bear Braham knocked on her door. "Joy, please sit."

He explained Ricardo's spear house had moved, maybe been struck. Ricardo must have lost his balance and fell into the icy water.

Joy sat speechless.

A gaff hook lanyard had wrapped around his leg allowing the EMTs to recover the body. A lunch bag floated in the water. "We assume he was distracted while eating."

Joy stood, threw her arms to her face, and screamed. "What? How? When?" She fell forward. Bear caught her and held her against him.

"Heavy gusts of wind out there in the open." Bear rubbed her shoulders. "Could have moved the spear house. Lot of guys drinking too. Might have driven over and bumped him."

"Did you check for tire tracks?" Joy asked between sobs. "Those were Ricardo's fishing buddies."

"We checked for tracks, and there were lots of them. Unfortunately, they were all covered with snow. We couldn't tell new tracks from old." He stood her against the door frame. "I'll stay with you until someone else arrives. You have family? Neighbors? Church friends?"

Joy opened her mouth to speak, choked on her sobs, and fell back into Bear's arms.

"Sorry. Clumsy me." Bob blocked beer from dripping on the

carpet with one hand and held the poinsettia in the other. "Do you have paper towels?"

Joy stood, her knees unsteady, her eyes blinking. "I'll get towels." She walked to the kitchen. "Not to worry. That's why I have neutral Berber."

"Sorry," Bob repeated.

Joy stood beside him as he knelt to wipe the carpet, feeling superiority, control, advantage. He reached for her hand to stand. She smiled. "Let's eat." She pulled lobster cakes and scalloped potatoes and bread sticks from the oven and bowls of salad from the fridge. "Another beer?"

"Beautiful table." Bob reached in his pocket for a lighter. "Shall I?" He lit the candles.

She lowered the dining room lights.

"Beautiful." Bob opened his arms. "Looks like a serene moonlit lake."

The phone rang. "Let it ring." She motioned for Bob to sit. *Oh lord, I hope it's not some collection agency. They tend to call all hours of the day.*

He walked to her chair and slid it out. "Who said chivalry was dead?" He pointed to the phone. "You can take that if you want."

"No." She shook her head, dreading hearing her voice and the incoming message, hoping the Christmas carols would drown them out. "Let it ring."

"Hey, Mom, call me. I gotta know. By the way, what do you want for Christmas? I'll be waiting here by the phone."

"Ricky?" Bob lifted a lobster cake onto Joy's plate and one for himself.

"LeRoy." Joy filled Bob's salad bowl and her own. "He's having transportation issues. Again."

Bob tasted the lobster and waved his fork at her. "Great."

"My mother-in-law's recipe."

Bob grinned. "Which one?"

Joy poked her fork at him.

"LeRoy looks like he'll be portly in a few years. Light complexion. Scandinavian?"

"His dad Merlin was a Swede. Owned a sporting goods store and bait shop. We lived upstairs. People called or knocked on the door day and night, Sundays, holidays. No privacy ever." She lifted a potholder stamped *Merlin's Minnows*. "A relic of the old

FISH

days. One of the few."

"Merlin's Minnows on Central Avenue? I used to buy bait there."

"Well, then, you've been in my house before."

Bob pointed to the silver, the crystal, the china. "You've come a long way, my dear." He reached for her hand. She dabbed her mouth with a napkin and offered her hand to him.

Bob smiled his practiced smile. "The candlelight does wonderful things with your eyes."

Joy looked at *his* eyes. She hadn't viewed him head-on since they met. His left eye focused down and to the left, then wondered to the right. She stared, first at his right eye, then at his left. Which one focused on her?

Bob laughed. "You finally discovered my lazy eye. It's called amblyopia. I've had it all my life."

"Does it affect your vision? Isn't it treatable?"

"I see everything I want to see." He smiled and squeezed her hand. "Some of my female clients find it fetching."

"Clients? Are you an attorney?"

"Nope. Investment banker." He picked up a silver knife and spoon. "I make rich people richer."

Joy recovered her hand and sipped her wine. *So far, so good.* "I suppose you entertain your clients. Take them on expensive trips."

"I spent a few days on Lake of the Woods with clients last month. Three-bedroom houseboat, combination guide, skipper, and cook, imported Scotch." Bob killed his bottle of Corona and walked to the kitchen for another. He poured wine for Joy and droned on about the boat, the bait, the walleyes he caught and released.

Joy smelled minnows and fish-scented water in Merlin's bait tanks downstairs, saw the minnows scurry to avoid the net, felt their slimy bodies when they flopped on the floor.

"Well Merlin, this is the last supper." Joy scraped dishes and rinsed them in the sink. "I mean the last supper in this building. Did you like the salmon loaf? I saved it for a special occasion."

Merlin belched and held his belly. "What're you so peppy about?"

"Not peppy. A bit excited, I guess. And a bit worried." She warmed a bottle of baby formula in a sauce pan. "I blew a circuit breaker twice cooking supper. Shouldn't you have an electrician check the wiring?"

Merlin lit a cigarette. "That faulty wiring is going to be my ticket out of Dodge." He poured a glass of whiskey and headed for the couch. "Another year in this business, and, one night, poof. The whole thing goes up in smoke." Merlin mixed a whiskey soda.

"In the meantime, what about us? Me and the boys?" Joy leaned against the living room arch drying her hands. "What if the building catches fire some night when we're here?"

"I'll grab the big guy. You grab the little guy. Simple. Don't have a cow."

"But I can't plug in my hair curler if the television is on. I can't run the toaster if the microwave is on."

"You have any idea what it would cost to rewire this piece of crap? Drop it. Unless you got some coin tucked away from your Ricardo insurance settlement."

"Guess I have only a couple more days to worry about it. I was thinking about the kids, that's all."

"I'm thinking about the shit I put up with day in and day out. Those assholes who run up a big bill, then avoid me. Don't come in to pay, don't come in to buy. And that Fletcher dude who bought a depth finder two, three years ago, and wants his money back because it crapped out on him. And all those fancy duds and accessories they're pushing on us dealers. Looks more like a boutique than a sporting goods store." Merlin turned on the television. Click. The circuit breaker popped. "Shit." He gulped the whiskey.

"See what I mean?" Joy walked to the kitchen.

"I talked about our bad wiring at the men's coffee table. They all know this place is a tinderbox. No one will be surprised when it happens."

Joy looked at her child. "You're making me nervous."

He tapped his empty glass against the remote. "Put a head on this, woman."

Joy had tolerated much of Merlin's bad behavior, but she would not jeopardize the lives of her babies. And she tired, tired, tired of customers tramping upstairs looking for a dozen shiners or chubs while she cared for two-year old Ricky and baby LeRoy. Joy and Merlin occupied the one bedroom. The boys slept in the

FISH

living room. Slept, until someone knocked on the door and woke them.

She had found a small two-bedroom house on the highway leading into town. Bob had agreed to the purchase, thinking he might remodel the attached garage into a bait room. Sell minnows all weekend.

Why live with this low-life? Why tolerate all the intrusions? Why sleep in your clothes in case you need to run outside from a burning house? Joy didn't wait for Merlin to help her pack. Not that he had the energy or inclination,

Nights after work, after supper, Merlin predictably lit a cigarette, mixed a whiskey soda, and slumped to the sofa before the blaring television, reading today's mail and a newspaper. Two or three drinks and a cigar later, he'd plump down, newspaper covering his eyes, the cigar still burning.

Joy brought the whiskey bottle. "If you're going to the Sporting Goods Dealer Convention in January, you'd better get your reservation in."

"You do it. Tomorrow."

"How many days do you want to stay? Which hotel? Signing up for any workshops?"

"I said, do it tomorrow."

"Okay. After I feed the baby, I'm taking boxes of clothes over to the new house tonight."

Merlin had reset the circuit breaker and watched a hockey game.

When she finished feeding, Joy tucked the empty bottle into a diaper bag by the door. She slipped into her coat and snuggled baby LeRoy into a bunting and Ricky into a snowsuit.

"Hope you don't need help lugging stuff. Been a long day."

"I got it. I packed the car today. I packed my clothes. You can pack yours. We're down to the basics here. Just enough food and dishes to last until the Sunday move." She tucked the baby under one arm and grabbed Ricky's mittened hand. "Go through that pile of newspapers and magazines and junk mail on the floor," she called to Merlin. "Put what you want saved on the table."

Joy walked down the stairs to the car, started the ignition, and strapped in the kids. She turned the heater fan on and walked back upstairs. When she inched the door open, Merlin slept on the couch, newspaper over his head, cigar burning in his hand. She tiptoed to the bedroom and grabbed the bank deposit envelope and tiptoed back to the door. She stopped. Merlin snored with relaxed sonority. She flipped the light switch off and stared at the cherry red ash on the cigar. Grabbing the diaper bag, she tiptoed out the door, locked it, and padded down the stairs.

A light snow fell, nothing challenging. Christmas-card-pretty the way it formed a halo around the street lights. *Why do I feel this lightness?* Maybe memories of Christmas. Mom sitting on the couch in the trailer with little Joy. Her baby brother in the stroller. The unbearable excitement of watching Mom open the gift she had made in school—a woven potholder. A card with red poinsettia petals and tiny gold beads glued in the center. The tabletop tree made of pine cones. Rudolph cavorting on the television screen.

She tickled Ricky on the cheek as she drove. "Mommy will take care of you," she cooed.

At the house, she slipped baby LeRoy out of the bunting and laid him in the bunk bed she found at the Thrift Store. Ricky struggled out of his snowsuit, eager to sleep in the top bunk. "Mommy will be back and forth from the car." Joy tucked Ricky in. "You take care of your little brother. Everything will be all right."

She carried boxes, bags, laundry baskets from the car and hid the bank deposit envelope under the mattress. The radio in the living room played Christmas carols. Through the drape-less picture window, a neighbor's lighted tree blinked. Icicles shone from the porch roof.

The boxes felt lighter than when she packed them and lugged them down the stairs. Did the new space free her? Where is the bottle of wine? Why do I feel like celebrating? The Sporting Goods Dealers Conventions—what a laugh. She had thought they would be in San Diego or Miami. This year Dubuque, last year Superior, next year Fargo. She found a night light in the diaper bag and peeked in the boys' room. Both slept. She plugged in the night light and closed the door.

Joy walked around the rooms, furnished but not decorated. Decor could wait. She found the portrait of her father, Reverend Johnston, and stood it on the table. "Be with me, Father."

She needed fresh air and stepped outside with her glass of wine. So Christmas-y. So homelike. So quiet. No phone ringing, no door knocking, no highway traffic, nothing. Nothing but an easy falling snow softening the gaudy lights of the neighbor's tree.

FISH

Snow falling on her open hand in soft silence.

A siren wailed. Ambulance? Police car? Another siren. Fire truck?

She lifted her glass in a toast. "Good luck." She smiled.

"You must live near a fire hall." Bob held a beer in one hand, a bite of lobster in the other. "That's the second siren I've heard tonight."

Joy blinked her eyes, shifted her weight in the chair, reached for the wine. "Sheriff's squad cars. Coming from the courthouse."

"I was wondering . . ." Bob set his beer and fork down and rested his chin on his hands. Candlelight danced on his glasses.

She searched for the focusing eye. "Yes?"

"I was wondering what a nice girl like you is doing on Craig's List." He smiled his born-salesman smile.

"I know it's bad form to answer a question by asking one, but what's a nice guy like you doing on Craig's List?"

"Fair enough." He lowered his chin as if ashamed. Candlelight danced on his bald head. "I heard every guy on dating sites is looking for sex. I wanted to offer the ladies an alternative. I'm looking for their money."

"Really?"

"Not their money to spend." He laughed. "Their money to invest. For them."

Was this his idea of a joke? "I heard every woman, every woman my age on dating sites, is looking for money. I was looking for sex."

"Touché." He raised his hands, thumbs up.

She raised her glass to toast him, pleased to exhibit wit, pleased he appreciated it, pleased he communicated his appreciation. *He does something to me. Something new. Something wonderful.* His head shone in the candlelight. "Would you fill this for me, Chuck?" She handed him her glass.

"Who's Chuck? I'm Bob, remember?"

"Oh my god, I'm sorry. How stupid of me."

Bob laughed. "Not a big deal." He stabbed at his salad. "Who's Chuck?"

"My late husband. My third and final late husband. The man with the champagne taste. He wore his hair, or lack of it, like you. Shaved."

The phone rang.

"Saved by the bell. Let it ring. I'm not answering it." Joy clenched her jaw, hoping, hoping for another reprieve from an irate bill collector. She cringed when she heard her voice and relaxed when she heard the caller's voice.

"Joy, it's your neighbor," a woman's voice sang. "Have you looked out your window? It's snowing. I brewed a pot of decaf, if you're interested in coming over."

Joy shook her head. "I can't live in a condo. Can't stand the constant scrutiny."

"She sounded well-intentioned." Bob cleaned his plate with a spoon. "So Chuck had a house, not a condo?"

"A big house. On the banks of the St. Croix River. He was a boatman, a Chris-Craft boatman. Old classic boat beautifully restored on the outside, a few mechanical issues inside. Happiest when he cruised downriver at sunset, boat lights on, looking for a quiet bay to fish."

She looked through blue candles, through the watery blue table-setting at the man sitting across from her. Chuck, a bald, smiling Chuck. An affable, laughable Chuck, ready to take the plunge.

"I've never been so embarrassed in my life." Chuck whipped off his captain's hat and flung it at the door. "Those boys are trash. No manners. No social graces. No common sense. Nothing."

Joy stood on the porch, watching neighbors drive their cars down the drive, some honking, some waving. She managed a half-wave, a lame smile, and walked inside.

"Where have they been all their lives? Living in a rabbit hole?" Chuck opened the liquor cabinet. "Am I expecting too much to ask them to clean up before I introduce them to my friends? And where did they get those clothes? Didn't anyone tell them the grunge look is dead? That one kid, the skinny Mexican. I expected his pants to slide off his ass any minute."

"I'm sorry to have embarrassed you." She rotated her wedding band. "I thought some of the guests found their conversation entertaining."

"Trained seals are entertaining. And the other kid. The fat one. When's the last time he had his hair cut? And that wispy excuse for a beard. Christ. I didn't dare get close to him. Sure I'd smell booze. Or weed."

Joy shook her head. "No, no. Neither of my boys do drugs."

"They might want to look into it. It would give them an excuse for being weird."

"Please, Chuck. You're talking about my sons."

"I don't know whether to admire you for claiming those renegades or question your sanity."

"Please. The party's over. Your friends are gone. My sons are gone. We survived. No one walked out in disgust. Everyone seemed happy when it was over."

"Everyone seemed happy *that* it was over." Chuck poured a brandy and replaced the bottle in the cabinet. "By the way, how did they get home? You had to pick them up, as I recall."

"I loaned them my car."

"How can they not have a car? Tell me they have jobs."

Joy fidgeted with her bracelet. "Not at the moment. Ricardo is thinking about going back to school. LeRoy injured his back working on a road crew. No income. No car."

"Probably no driver's license either." Chuck drained his glass and reached for another. "So they smash your car on the way home. Your insurance . . . *my* insurance going to cover it?"

"Chuck, please drop it. They're my sons. I have to love them."

"I'm just saying I wouldn't tolerate behavior like that from my kids."

"Don't compare kids." Joy felt the blood in her neck pulse. "If my sons had the privileges yours had, things would be different."

"Being poor is not an excuse. In fact, it's an incentive. It's not all about money."

"It's not all about money if you have it." Joy held her arms across her chest and turned away. "If you don't, it *is* all about money."

"You think dumping money on the problem will solve it? No. If they were my kids, I'd drown them."

Joy gasped and grabbed for a chair. She walked to the porch. A breeze off the river rippled the flag on the pole. Her stomach roiled like the threatening clouds tumbling in from the west.

Chuck walked out the door, a glass of brandy in hand. "I'm going to take a boat ride. Got to settle my nerves."

Joy grabbed a rain slick and trailed behind.

The angry river rocked the boat. Rare whitecaps splashed against the sides and sprayed the air. Chuck slammed the gears into reverse and sped from the dock into the current. The motor roared. He pulled his captain's hat down tight, gulped his brandy, and headed upstream full throttle. Joy stood behind him, steadying herself with the back of his boat seat. Chuck took a sharp right and headed for the west shore. He throttled back into the river's protected side. The planed bow lowered. The motor hummed. Chuck relaxed his grip on the steering wheel and flexed his fingers. He lifted his cap and placed it on the dash.

He slowed at a bay, circled it twice, and shifted into neutral. "I'm going to cast for a few bass. You take the wheel. Just give the engine enough gas to keep up with the current. Keep me in this spot." He grabbed his rod and reel and stood in the stern, casting to a shore shadowed by weeping willows. Joy sat with a nervous hand on the throttle, edging it up and down to remember which was fast, which was slow. Wind whistled over her head.

"Damn. Snagged a deadhead." Chuck handed his rod to Joy and took the wheel. He maneuvered the boat to a sunken log exposed like a black crocodile head. "Keep it right here." He climbed onto the bow and leaned over the edge, jiggling his line.

Rain trickled through the umbrella of foliage and splattered on the mahogany planks. Huge random drops at first followed by a steady pour, the rain skidding off the waxed surface in tiny droplets. "Edge up a little closer." Chuck yelled. "A little closer."

Joy heard a buzzer, noted a warning light. "What's that noise?" she yelled.

"Probably the bilge pump. It'll kick in later. Run me in a little closer."

Joy wiped rain from her eyes, reached for the gear shift, reached for the throttle. The boat veered backward. "The other way," Chuck yelled. "Forward."

Joy pushed hair that matted her forehead. She wiped her eyes. *Throttle. Gear shift.* She pressed down. The boat careened forward, smacked the deadhead, and headed to shore. She turned the wheel in a sharp right, listing the boat to the river's level. A warning light flashed. A buzzer growled. She drove to the center of the river and slowed the engine. Wind rocked the boat. She wiped rain from her eyes and looked at the bow.

"Chuck," she screamed. "Chuck."

FISH

Rain smacked the deck. The light flashed. The buzzer growled. A cloud of fog tumbled up river, wrapping her in a sudden blanket of contentment.

She tossed the captain's hat overboard.

Joy lifted her head to a smiling Bob. She turned toward the kitchen. "What's that buzzing?"

"Sounds like a timer."

She rose from her chair. When she walked past Bob, he opened his arms. She let him hold her, his arms around her hips, his head nestled against her stomach. She rubbed his scalp. Smooth.

Bob. Gentle, affectionate, funny Bob. Maybe not as rich as she'd prefer, but . . . courteous, respectful, presentable. And his hobby farm in the country. Apple trees, maybe a dog. A garden. Dump this godforsaken condo living. *Maybe time to find the right man for me rather than a rich man for my kids.* And who was she to compete with the tanned slender widows who drove a Lexus and whose kids matriculated at Ivy League colleges or cavorted in Spain? She pulled away and turned off the timer.

Back at the table, she motioned to sit on his knee. "I haven't rehearsed this, and I don't know how it will sound and I'm surprised I'm saying it, but please, hear me out."

He patted his knee and nodded, his eyes smiling, his face at full attention.

She sat and reached for his hand. "In all my years, and I won't tell you how many that is, I've never gone to bed with a man on a second date. I was always disciplined in that department. I admit to making bad choices, ugly choices in men. My first marriage was a young girl's mistake. The second two were not for me. They were for my sons. Follow me?"

Bob nodded, eyes still smiling.

"And I'm not drunk, not even alcohol-impaired. Watch this." She lifted one hand high above her head, index finger pointing down. She lowered the other hand, index finger pointing up. She brought the two fingers together in perfect alignment.

Bob patted her on the thigh. "Bravo."

"So tonight, I'm going to initiate a first, a first for me. I'm going to invite you to stay the night."

Bob pushed his glasses higher on his nose. He nodded and

smiled.

She searched for his working eye. "I presume that means yes."

Bob squeezed her waist. "I'll pile these dishes in the sink."

"Great. Let me have the bathroom for a few minutes."

In the bedroom, she fingered through her lingerie drawer, grabbed a flimsy peignoir with a mermaid design, a gift from Chuck. She held it up. Mermaid. Fairy tale. Happy ending. She slipped into the bathroom and turned on the shower.

She emerged minutes later, refreshed, excited, smiling. At an empty bed.

"Bob?" She walked to the living room. "Bob, where are you?" Into the dining room, the kitchen. "Bob?"

The kitchen chair was bare. His coat and the paper bag . . .

Gone.

STAG

"Gentlemen, we have gathered here tonight to celebrate a game-changing event, a rite of passage for our friend Mike. Our buddy, our co-worker, our go-to guy when we need an extra hundred. Mike has opted to marry Diana." Todd raised a glass in one hand, a bottle of Jack Daniels in the other. "After twenty years of relative celibacy, Mike will bite the silver bullet he has so heroically championed. It is incumbent upon us, his scarred, married friends, to welcome him into our ranks. And to advise him of the pitfalls that lie ahead."

Red raised his glass. "I'll drink to pitfalls."

Mike sat on one of the double beds in a motel room, elbows resting on his knees. Tan nubby drapes were pulled shut. Tan oversized bedspreads sprawled to the tan blotched carpet. A huge television set appropriated half of a water-stained credenza.

"Tonight," Todd continued, "we celebrate the old and embrace the new. Al, pour the guest of honor a drink."

"Easy, guys." Mike flapped his fingers down. "You know I'm on call."

"Not to worry." Al, the fourth member of the party, continued to pour. "I talked to the union steward, and Line 2 will not go down tonight. If it does, they'll call some other electrician."

"*Some other electrician* got fired last week. I'm sum and substance of electrical maintenance. If they have problems, I'm there in fifteen minutes, or I'm on the street."

"Such dedication. I'm impressed." Al handed Mike a glass with a dark tint.

"Whoa," Mike said. "I'll nurse this all night."

Two wall sconces on either side of the television provided scant light for the makeshift bar on one end of the credenza—Jack Daniels, a couple quarts of soda water, tan ice bucket, plastic glasses. A small table lamp on the nightstand between the beds shone on an ash tray and Gideon Bible.

"You'll notice we rented connecting rooms at this no-tell motel out in the middle of the boonies." Todd scooped ice cubes into his glass. "Herman's Hideaway, with strategic rear-of-the-building parking. Our logic will become apparent later in the evening. But we'll open with our Words and Whiskey segment. Mike, does the prospective groom have an opening statement?"

"No, but I'll say it anyway." Mike stood and walked to Todd, towering over him. His square jaw, muscled arms, bristle-top haircut suggested, rightfully, an ex-marine. (Not ex, Mike would add. Once a marine, always a marine.) An OD T-shirt hung outside his camo pants. "I want to thank you guys for shoring me up at this critical moment. You know, the idea of a big wedding with three groomsmen wasn't mine. I had no idea who to ask. 'How about the guys at work?' Diana said. And the rest is history." He raised his glass. "So, thanks. But remember, I'm on call."

"Relax." Todd resumed command. "Gentlemen, our guest being on the cusp of a new life, it is appropriate that we be properly dressed for the occasion." He reached for a shopping bag beside the credenza. "And here's our uniform." He lifted a neon-colored T-shirt that read TEAM MIKE, OFFICIAL DRINKING SQUAD. "Grab a shirt and slip it on."

Todd struggled into a neon pink tee over a gray sweatshirt. Red helped Al and Al helped Red. Mike slipped into his. Todd swigged his whiskey. "Now, in a couple days, we'll all have something sweet to say at the wedding reception about our friend and his lovely bride. But the really good stories, the ones that defy mixed company telling will go untold unless we tell them tonight. Somebody care to start?"

The rattle of a heater fan shattered the brief moment of silence.

"Anybody mind if I put the basketball game on?" Al grabbed the remote. "I got ten bucks on the Gophers tonight." Television reception was blurry, the sound full of static. He searched for the channel. Two announcers in headsets hypothesized in dead-serious tones about the impact of an overinflated ball.

"Turn it down." Red waved his glass at the screen.

"Turn it off." Todd grabbed the bottle of Jack Daniels and cocked his arm.

Al muted the television and sat on the edge of the bed.

"Good. I can lip read."

Red stood and leaned on an orange vinyl side chair he had pulled between the beds.

"Would you stand away from that chair?" Todd nudged the air with his hand. "The orange clashes with the pink."

"Up yours. You asked for a story. As you know, I'm not the jokester, but I have a true story about Mike." Red swigged a drink and twisted a finger in his red beard. "Over the years, we've all tried to line our friend up with a good woman. A couple years ago, I lined Mike up with a retread named Melissa. Melissa had her flaws." He wavered his hand back and forth. "But she had one extraordinary talent." He looked at Mike and winked. "I told her he was bashful, but if she played her cards right, she might score."

Mike dropped his head and covered his eyes.

"Somehow, they ended up at Mike's apartment. The next morning, I asked him what was the highlight of the evening. Without a moment's hesitation, he responded, 'The minute she walked out the door.'" Red walked to Mike and slapped his back. "That's my man. That's my story."

"I remember her." Mike laughed. "If she had one extraordinary talent, it was alcohol consumption. Half a fifth of vodka before midnight."

"And counting," Red added.

"I have one." Al pulled away from the television and stood. "My engineer friend Mike was out walking one day when he saw a frog. 'Kiss me,' the frog said, 'and I'll turn into a princess.' Mike picked up the frog and put it in his pocket. 'Hey,' the frog cried. 'Kiss me and I'll turn into a princess and I'll spend a month with you.' Mike kept on walking. 'Listen,' the frog said. 'I'll turn into a princess, I'll spend a month with you, and I'll do anything you ask. What could be better than that?'" Al stopped and grinned at Mike. "Mike, the consummate engineer, looked at the frog and said, 'A princess, that's no great shakes. But a talking frog, that's cool.'"

"Lying asshole." Mike laughed. "It was a talking toad."

"I know how you guys hate one-upmanship." Todd stood as if he addressed the United Nations. "But did I tell you about the time Mike asked my advice on how to talk to the woman he was dating for the first time? I told him to stick to the three basics: family, sports, and philosophy." Todd hesitated and rubbed his pink T-shirted belly. "So, Mike and his date are sitting at this restaurant, and Mike asks, 'Do you have any brothers?' She looks around and shakes her head *No*. 'Do you like to bowl?' She raises her eyebrows and shakes her head again. *No*. Mike is distraught. He reaches for her hands, looks her in the eye, and says, 'If you had any brothers, do you think they'd like to bowl?'"

"Lies," Mike said.

"That's not the way I heard it." Al stood again. "The three basic conversation starters are shopping, recipes, and what's that gal in the next apartment doing with a different guy every night?"

Mike pulled a pillow over his head. "Holy shit. I expect the Goddess of Thunder to strike us all dead."

"Enough of this levity. Let's play some poker." Al pulled the legs down on the card table borrowed from the motel office and set it between the beds. "Holy shit. What's on this table?"

"You don't want to know." Todd walked to the bathroom and brought a soaking towel to wash the table, another to dry it. "Sorry, you guys, if anybody wanted to take a shower. No towels."

"Some in the next room." Al pointed to the adjoining room door.

"Not likely." Todd shook his head. "Save those for Mike."

Al pulled a deck of cards from his pocket. "The Gophers look like a Junior Achievement project tonight."

"I ordered pizzas from Chuck Purdy's Purdy Good Pizza Parlor." Todd lifted a folding chair over the table in front of the nightstand. "The one with the knockout delivery girls. How's your drink, Mike?"

Mike rattled his glass. "I'll take some ice."

"So, how did a Lutheran like you end up with a good Catholic girl?" Red asked. He looked older than the rest, the once-red hair on his head transplanted to his chin. A band of skin on his ring finger showed a telling pinkish white. "Church wedding, high mass, communion. And wasn't she married before? You said she had a kid. How did she swing getting married in the church this time?"

"Time and money." Mike twirled the glass in his hands. "Her mother wanted her to get an annulment, and since Diana was a minor when she got married, without parental approval and without benefit of clergy, it was a matter of only a minor investment."

Al sneered at Mike. "How does that make you feel? She has a kid. On the receiving dock, we'd consider her returned goods."

"Spoken like a true shipping clerk." Red stood in Mike's

defense. "I think we all married divorced women, or we're divorced ourselves." He pointed to himself. "Exhibit A." He put his hand on Mike's shoulder. "If Al wants to hold out for a virgin next time, good luck in this town."

"Diana has a great kid," Mike said. "Miles. Twelve years old. Been raised by his grandparents, Diana's mom and dad. Grandpa was a career army guy and still plays the part. Miles may as well be in basic training. His hair is cut shorter than mine. You can bounce a quarter off his bedspread. And he calls me *Sir*. On top of all that, he's an A student and starting quarterback on junior varsity."

"Does he like you? Do you like him?" Red asked.

"I love him."

"You know my story, don't you?" Todd asked. "My first wife asked me for a divorce after about six months of marriage. Said she decided she was a lesbian, wanted to try someone else, someone different, someone . . . better. Talk about a lesson in humility." He rapped on the table. "Deal those cards, Al. The pizza should be here any minute."

"So, tomorrow night at this time, we'll be enduring or enjoying the groom's dinner and telling lies about how happy we are for the bride and groom. Why can't they learn from our mistakes, men?" Todd asked. "And Saturday night at this time, the happy couple will be on their way to where, the Cozumel Copacabana?"

"More likely the Brainerd Best Western." Mike laughed. "Diana has to work Monday. So do I."

"I can't believe women left you alone this long." Al mixed another drink. "Ex-marine, handsome hunk, straight, good job, silver bullet. I ought to thank you for laying low. You made it easier for clods like me to score. Which reminds me. How are the Gophers doing?" He glanced at the television. Half-time. Gophers trailing, 51-49.

"But Diana," Al continued. "Who'd have guessed? I went out with her in high school. Not a pleasant memory." He walked to the window and peered through the drapes.

"She mentioned that." Mike shook his head. "Said it wasn't one of the highlights of her life."

"Diana." Todd jumped in. "I remember her as Lincoln town car. If anything, Mike, you're Chevy pickup."

"Whatever happened to her ex?" Al asked. "Bill. We played

basketball together. Bad ass, as I recall."

Mike shook his head. "Not good."

"Does he see his kid?"

"Rarely. Miles is moving in with us. Already decorated his new room."

"Don't you worry about Diana comparing your performance to Bill's?" Todd asked. "He was quite the stud."

"Do you compare the performance of your wife with your ex?" Mike asked.

"Men are different from women," Todd huffed.

"Men are different from men, too."

"What's your game, Mike?" Al returned from the window and sat. "Let's get this poker party underway."

"Five card draw." Mike looked at his watch. "Deal 'em out."

Al dealt, picked up his hand, and turned to the television. Play had resumed. "Hold it a second," Al yelled. "The Gophers have a chance to tie the game."

"You're watching television while history is being made?" Red held a pillow in front of the screen. "Turn the damn thing off."

"You live your life, I'll live mine. Now get out of the way."

A car screeched off the highway into the parking lot and squealed to a stop. Al folded his cards and listened.

"Al, you worried your wife will drive up and find you with some hooker in a motel room?" Red rose off his bed seat and refilled three glasses.

"This place gives me the creeps." Al sniffed the air. "And why do all motel rooms smell alike? Like they all use the same disinfectant."

"Or don't use," Todd added. "Smells like air out of an inflated tire."

Al looked through the open bathroom door at the pink plastic shower curtain. "Reminds me of the motel where 'Psycho' was filmed."

"I was thinking of doing a little filming later myself." Todd tapped his folded hand of cards on the table. "Might be like money in the bank if I decide to blackmail somebody."

"Damn, the Gophers screwed up again." Al snapped the remote and threw it on the bed. He fanned his cards. "Whose play?"

"Will Diana keep working at the hospital?" Red asked. When he talked, his beard wiggled. "Or are you going to concentrate on having a family?" He laughed. "I presume she's pregnant."

"She's not pregnant, and we've talked about kids. But not yet."

"Interesting how a woman is willing to give up her working life with the promise of having your babies." Al folded his cards and snapped them on the table. "Why wouldn't she? You have a good job, own your house, probably have a huge IRA. As of Saturday, she'll qualify for early retirement on your nickel."

"Hey, Al," Red growled. "Take it easy."

Mike dropped his cards and grabbed the edge of the table. "I don't know anything about your personal plans, your finances, or your wife's career," he barked at Al, "but you're quizzing me a lot about mine. Trust me. I know what I'm doing. And lay off the questions."

"Whoa." Todd took command again. "Settle down, guys. It's going to be a long night. And the best is yet to come. Come on, Al. Chill out. What are you so nervous about?"

Al took a deep breath. "Sorry, fellows. I can't concentrate." He put his face in his hands.

Todd rose from his chair and hopped over the bed. He grabbed an imaginary clipboard, sat on the end of the bed, and crossed his legs. "Lie down, Mr. Albert. Would you like to talk to your friendly shrink about your issues?"

"The white Impala, the one with a sunroof. It belongs to my girlfriend. It was here when we arrived. It's still here. What's she doing?"

"Altogether now, boys." Todd raised his arms as if directing a choir. "She's cheating on you."

"That little wench. I wondered about her."

"She's cheating on you. You're cheating on your wife. What am I missing?"

A horn honked outside the door. "That must be our pizza." Todd walked to the door. "Okay, you guys, move the card table to the corner. Be on your best behavior. Keep your hands in your pockets." He opened the door.

"You the host of this party?" a woman asked.

"That would be me." Todd pointed to his chest. "Come in."

"And who is the guest of honor?"

Todd pointed. "That would be Mike."

"Well, I have this for you." She handed Todd a large flat

box. "One jumbo pizza with almost everything on." She walked to Mike. "And for you, one delivery maiden with almost *nothing* on." She flung open her trench coat. Mike jerked back, spilling his drink on himself, on the bed. "Oh, my god."

"I love to get that kind of reaction." She twirled in front of him. "What's your name, Big Guy?"

"Mike O'Neill."

"We're going to get to know each other really well, Mike." She traced her finger along his cheek, his chin, his chest. "You can call me Daisy. Daisy DelRio." She reached for the pizza and leaned it in front of him. "Would you like a piece?"

"Take off your things, Daisy, and get comfortable." Todd lifted her coat. "Wow. That's a lot of torque to put on those bikini straps."

"What's the worst thing that could happen?" Daisy shook her shoulders and danced around the room, bumping her hips into the men.

She looked to be young thirties. Toned athletic body that challenged her bikini, comfortable in heels. Farrah Fawcett hair, mascaraed brown eyes, glossy pink lips. On her hip strap, she wore a small posy of daisies.

"I don't know if this is such a good idea." Red spoke like a spiritual counselor. "Is this fair to Mike? Is this fair to Diana? The guy's been Old Faithful up to tonight. Do we want to be part of his undoing?"

"Yes," Al said. "Infidelity seems to be the name of the game."

"A little late for Monday morning quarterbacking, Red." Todd put an arm around Daisy and Mike. "Would you two mind cavorting in the next room? We have a serious poker game in progress here. I'll fix you a drink, Daisy. And I'll refresh yours, Mike." He kept an eye on Daisy as he poured. "Her contract expires in an hour, Mike my friend. Make the most of it."

"Come on, Big Guy." Daisy led Mike to the door. "I'll need my coat too. My phone and keys are in it."

"Done. Daisy, I give you the boy." Todd handed her the coat and pointed to Mike. "Give me back the man."

"Lock the doors," Mike said when they entered the adjoining room. "Draw the drapes. I don't trust those guys." He scanned the room for cameras—the light fixtures, the drapery rods, the air conditioner above the door. He sat on a bed and turned on the table lamp. "Daisy DelRio. Not too original a name."

"All Purdy Good Pizza delivery girls are named for flowers. Daisy DelRio, Rose LaRose, Lili LaCrosse. House rules."

Mike lowered his head and ran a hand through his hair. "Let me be straight with you, Daisy. This extracurricular activity is going nowhere. I'm not about to cheat on my soon-to-be wife a couple nights before the wedding."

Daisy sat on the opposite bed facing him. "I'm not surprised." She tossed him a teasing grin. "You're not the type."

Mike snapped his head up. "I'm not? I'm not."

She detached the posy on her hip and tossed it on the bed. Mind if I put on my coat?" She draped her coat over her shoulders and leaned against the headboard. She twirled ice cubes with her finger. "So, how do you propose we spend our sixty minutes? You got a deck of cards?" She laughed and kicked off her heels and crossed her legs.

"We could chat for a while." Mike scratched for a topic of conversation. *Family? Sports? Philosophy? No.* "I'm curious how you got into this line of work."

"This is funny as hell."

"It's funny for you. Guess what? I'm feeling clumsy, nervous, guilty, stupid. And I feel let down. Todd knows I don't mess around."

She recrossed her legs and stirred her drink. "How did I get in this business? I suppose I should feel defensive. I don't. I could tell you some trite clichés about needing to pay the rent, to support my son because his deadbeat dad doesn't pay child support. Not true. I could say I hated my father and I'm taking revenge on every man I meet. Wrong. I could say my uncle abused me as a kid and I never grew out of it. Wrong again." She sipped her drink and stared at the blank television screen. She turned to Mike. "My name is Robin."

Mike smiled and offered his hand. "Robin. That's much better than Daisy DelRio. Glad to meet you, Robin."

"You're curious about how I got into this line of work. Would you believe I meet some fabulous guys?" She pointed to him. "Present company included. I love men. I do. I love you, too."

Mike retreated, hid his expression behind his drink glass.

"I love men and, in the best of all possible worlds, I'd *maybe* find the right one." She grinned at Mike and turned. "I have a degree in mathematics with a minor in statistics. Let me offer a simplistic probability analysis. What's the probability of my finding a man I'm physically compatible with? Pick a number. Fifty percent? The probability of a man I'm emotionally compatible with? Another fifty percent of fifty? We're now at twenty-five. Probability of intellectual compatibility? Down to twelve. Sexual compatibility? Six. Cultural? Psychological?" She smiled at Mike as if she believed what she said. "The probability of my finding a compatible partner is down in single digits. Way down. One in a hundred? That's not my idea of acceptable odds."

Mike let out a woof of air. "But in small town Minnesota at the dawning of the twenty-first century, doesn't a woman need a man?"

"Another cliché, Mike. For many women, yes. But I'm past needs. *Way* past needs. I'm into *wants*." She sipped her drink and sighed. "And for all the men who have tried to *save* me, I say, save yourself."

They sat without speaking. The fan started and rattled in the heater. An occasional hoot came from the room next door.

Robin broke the silence. "So, tell me about your big day ahead. And the lucky lady. And your plans for the next hundred years."

"We marry Saturday. Big church wedding. My first, her second. She presents an exciting dowry, a twelve-year old son. No waiting for kids at our house. Like buying a new car and they throw in airfare to Paris."

"Congratulations. I don't talk about my personal life on the job, but I have a twelve-year old son, too."

"What should I expect?" Mike asked.

"Depends on the kid. Mine has already assumed the alpha male role. More than ready to rule the roost. He's home now, doing homework, I'd guess. I should call him."

"Speaking of," Mike interrupted, "if my phone rings, I have to answer it. I'm on call at the plant."

"Saved by the bell, kind of?" Robin leaned on the pillows, smiled, and sipped her drink. "So you'll have a new son. You have a demanding job. What else?"

"I have this great bride. Wonderful lady. Has already lived through all the shit in her life. It's clear sailing now, at least until Saturday." Mike leaned on his pillow. "I should probably be having second thoughts soon. I'm not."

"What does this fairytale bride do when she's not planning her wedding?"

"She's a nurse. Ask me about her tender loving care routine. Gives great backrubs."

Robin smiled. "Interesting. I'm a licensed masseuse. That's how I got into this business." She sat against the headboard, crossed her legs, and pulled the coat around her. "How long have you been at the plant?"

"Ever since I got discharged from the Corps. Eight years."

"You're a marine? So was my dad. You know your way around the hard stuff—flak jackets, assault rifles, personnel vehicle carriers. And you're about to learn your way around the soft stuff—female mood swings, the demands of in-laws, the challenge of raising a stepson."

"You make it sound enticing."

"I'm sorry. Let me rephrase. You're about to learn your way around the soft stuff—temptation, passion, surrender. Looking at you, I'd say she's one lucky lady."

"Thanks, but sometimes I feel sorry for her. Taking on a confirmed bachelor, green as grass when it comes to sharing a house or raising a kid."

Robin sprang forward, her coat falling off her shoulders. "Sorry for her? You're kidding. That's what every woman wants—a man she can train from Step One."

Mike's phone rang. "I have to take this." He looked at the screen. "Damn, it's Diana."

Robin jumped from the bed. "Take it. I'll be quiet in the bathroom."

"Hi, Hon." He paused. "Sure, sure, that's fine." Pause. "No problem, I'd rather talk to you than them. Good night, Honey. I'll call you in the morning." He closed the phone. "Coast is clear, Robin. Thanks for understanding."

"Doesn't she trust you?"

"Her sister called. The one who was supposed to do a reading at the mass. Can't make the flight from Denver. Would it be all right with me if she asked her coworker?"

"Sounds trumped up to me." Robin walked to the bed. "Does she always check on you?"

"She wasn't checking. After hearing what I heard from those guys," he pointed to the door, "checking her turf might be good advice." He leaned on the pillows and stretched his arms, his legs.

"Didn't mean to snap at you. I'm feeling tension. Wonder if I'm getting opening night jitters."

"I have a cure for that. And it would clear my conscience if I did something to earn my hundred bucks." She stood and tossed her coat over a chair. "Take off that crazy T-shirt. Pink is not your color. Lay down."

He set his drink on the nightstand and flopped down on the bed. She leaned over him and pressed two strong hands on his shoulders. "Does that hurt?"

"Yes, in a good way."

"Roll over on your stomach." She kneaded her way down his spine, watched him cringe and relax. "I have to sit on you to put on pressure. Do you mind?" She straddled him, sliding her palms down his back, kneading, tapping. "I can't believe anybody would feel sorry for your Princess Diana." Robin huffed. "You, with a body right off the cover of *Iron Man*. Nice guy. Respectful. Good listener. And, best of all, wouldn't think of yielding to temptation." She leaned and blew on his shoulder.

"You're overstating your case to make a point," he said. "And you're making me shiver."

"Am I?" she asked. "Good to know I haven't lost my touch."

She massaged his scalp, worked around to his neck, his jaw, his cheeks. "Why are you grinning?" she asked.

"I smell pizza."

Robin stopped. "May I step out of character for a moment?"

Mike turned his head and rested on an elbow.

"Oh, the things I could have done, the person I could have been if I had a man like you." Robin sighed. "A man of principle. If chivalry is dead, principle is extinct. Please. Allow me a moment of fantasy."

She turned, and Mike watched as she faced her image in the door mirror—her near naked body sitting on his. She covered her face with her hands. "What the hell." She threw her arms in the air. "It is what it is." She straddled his legs and worked his lower back.

"I'll give you one hour to stop."

"Sorry. We're down to thirty minutes." She leaned on him, pressed hard, slid her hands across his shoulders, along his sides, around his waist. She leaned lower, her body touching his, startling him.

"Am I getting a response?" she purred.

Her hair tickled his shoulders. He inhaled. "What is the

alluring perfume you're wearing?"

"Chocolate chip cookies."

He reached for her hand. She lay still. He reached with his other hand and turned off the table lamp. They lay in the dark, Robin breathing in his ear, Mike feeling sweat trickle under his arms. The red neon MOTEL sign flashed and reflected through a crack in the drapes. He moved her hand across his body, reached back and moved his hand on her thigh, her leg. The fan on the wall heater clicked and rattled.

Mike tensed up. She lifted herself slightly.

"Robin. Stop."

A door slammed and a man shouted. Mike lifted himself. "Sounds like it's coming from outside the other room."

The shouting continued from the parking lot, the cursing, the yelling. "You little tramp. What the hell you think you're doing? And who is this asshole?"

Robin rolled off Mike's back. "One of your friends?" she asked.

"Sounds like Al." Mike sat up. "I better get out there before this thing escalates."

The screaming continued outside their window. "I'm done with you, understand? Get out of my life, you little tramp."

A loud male voice hollered, "Who you calling an asshole?"

"You," Al shouted. "I'm calling you an asshole. But you can have her. And you can thank me for doing a good job of breaking her in."

"Yep. You did a great job, as far as you went."

A husky voice bellowed from outside the office. "You guys knock it off. I called the sheriff. And I'll press charges. You're ruining my business."

"I'd better be going." Robin stood and felt for her heels in the dark. "Sometimes I don't understand this job." She opened the drapes, slid into her coat, and stood silhouetted in front of the window. "How shall we consummate this transaction?"

Mike sat on the bed and buttoned his shirt.

"I'd give you my card," she smiled, "but that sounds tacky." She walked to the bed, leaned, and handed him the daisies.

He reached to touch her.

She pulled keys from her pocket, jingled them, and walked to the door.

SNAKE

The rock pile at the edge of the cornfield seemed smaller than she remembered, the rocks themselves smaller, less intimidating. Their once-stark surface now softened with lichen to a gentle gray. The swamp beside the rock pile felt the same—cattails in full bloom waving in a breeze, the chirp of crickets, the trill of red-winged blackbirds. And the air, so pungent. The sky so bright, so wide.

Shirley Reichert eyed the rock pile, warmed by September sun. She stood her tripod and mounted a camcorder, then made notes on a tablet—time, date, location—and tucked the tablet in the pocket of her lab coat, the pencil behind her ear. She watched for movement. After minutes passed, she threw a small rock. The pile came alive with garter snakes, coiling, writhing, slithering in and out of sight. A brood of young wriggled on a flat surface; adults, large and lethargic, stretched their necks and waddled into crevices.

"They're still here." She scanned the area again and smiled at the dichotomy—how much the place had changed, how much it had stayed the same. She walked through the swamp, poking a path through reed grass with tripod legs. How much she, Shirley, had changed—a professional woman with salon-styled gray hair in Calvin Klein jeans—and how much she had stayed the same.

"They're still here. Fifty years, and they're still here." The country school house at this intersection of two gravel roads was gone. The swing set, gone. The ball diamond beside the box elder grove now overgrown with golden rod and purple aster. A couple remnants of the school remained—a concrete cap over the well and two depressions where outhouses stood.

She parted foxtail and canary grass, looking for frogs. And snakes. Grasshoppers jumped in random arcs before her.

The acrid September air, the murky swamp, the buzz of

SNAKE

insects—none of that had changed. Miss Bennett, her teacher here at Four Corners School, had changed. Shirley, her sister Prudence, and brother Gordon had changed. The intermittent insanity at her family farm down the road had changed. But on this spot, fifty-plus years ago, she realized her life's calling. That hadn't changed.

Back in the late forties on a warm September afternoon, kids, all from farm families, were less ready to learn than to socialize and play after a summer of isolation and work. For them, vacation started the day school started. No more long hours herding cows or picking cucumbers. No more riding a monotonous cultivator through an endless cornfield or pitching alfalfa off the hay fork in a sweaty haymow. Sitting in school was a piece of cake. Playing kitten ball at recess was fun.

Four Corners—a one-room schoolhouse with thirty or forty students in eight grades who learned from Miss Bennett, a late teenager fresh out of normal school. She had been a town girl, always considered herself up for the challenge of teaching, until now. Now she faced frightened first graders and stoic or defiant eighth graders. *Demure but determined*, her yearbook had described her.

She stood at the blackboard, pink-plastic-rimmed glasses perched atop her soft brown hair. She wore a powder blue sweater set, *not too fancy*, she had been counseled, *nothing to draw attention to yourself*, and black wedge pumps for elevation.

During lunch hour, Shirley Reichert had found a garter snake swallowing a frog by the swamp. As a science project, Miss Bennett lent her watch to Shirley and assigned her the task of noting the snake's progress. At afternoon recess, her notes read: *One-thirty, feet in snake's throat, frog struggling; one-forty, half legs in snake's throat, frog still struggling.*

On the playground, brother Gordon Reichert mesmerized the younger kids with his antics on the swing. Gordon, an eighth grader, stood a head taller than Miss Bennett and half a body taller than the first graders. He'd mess their hair as he strode to his desk in the back row in his high-water overalls. There he'd throw one leg over the back of the seat, flop, and stretch his lanky legs past his sister Prudence's desk in front of him. Students pretended not to notice his mousy hair chopped from a kitchen haircut, not to cringe from his teenage body odor and pimpled cheeks, not to jump when he crossed his hands behind his head and cracked his knuckles.

"Dad warned us to stay away from Gordon," a girl whispered to Shirley and Prudence, "and not to cross him." Another student touched their hands. "We prayed for you last night." Prudence smirked. "Save your breath." Everyone knew Mr. Reichert had spent time in the Browns County jail, and Mrs. Reichert had her share of nervous breakdowns.

The other eighth-grade boy Alistair Braham, short and stocky, quiet and respectful, sported a respectable crop of facial hair which earned him the moniker *Bear*. The boys avoided each other, not competing, not cooperating, not engaging. School yard chatter had it that Bear had warned Gordon to keep his distance or he'd kick the shit out of him.

Today Gordon swung on the chain swing, pumping, pumping higher, yelling he'd loop the loop, pumping higher and higher, yelling louder and louder. Kids circled the swing holding their heads in disbelief, in fear, in anticipation. Higher, higher, until Miss Bennett rang the bell. Gordon jumped at the high point of the arc, landing like a string-less puppet. He stood and brushed sand from his overalls. Kids ran for the school door. Shirley stayed with the snake and frog.

For the last class of the day, seventh and eighth grade literature, Miss Bennett called students to the front of the classroom with their faded red *Prose and Poetry* books. Miss Bennett taught literature by having students read aloud. The current story was "The Pit and the Pendulum."

Shirley heard Miss Bennett ask Gordon to read and walked to the screened back door. Gordon strode up the aisle to read, small kids ducking, squirming. Grades one through six turned from their books, unable to concentrate on addition and long division.

Gordon stood to read, holding the book with one hand and tossing a pencil in the air with the other, always catching it. He began where the prisoner finds himself bound to a wooden bier with a surcingle. He stumbled over the word.

"Think of it as a belt," Miss Bennett said.

When he read of red-eyed rats swarming over the prisoner's body, he gloated. And when he read, "their cold lips caught my own," first grader Sandra screamed.

Outside, a car approached. Not Mr. Snyder's muffler-less

SNAKE

truck across the road where Miss Bennett stayed, but a car. Through the open windows came the yowl of chewing gravel, braking to a quick stop at the school, a car door slamming. Gordon stopped reading.

Shirley burst through the screen door. "Gordon, what's Pa doing here?" She shuddered, waving her arms at the younger kids as if to tell them to take cover. "Gordon, Pa's here. Pa's here."

Gordon dropped his book and ducked to the floor behind Miss Bennett's desk. The front door crashed open, and Henry Reichert marched in. "Where is she? She's coming with me." He wore a visor-less black cap, sleeveless shirt under bib overalls, and black rubber barn boots up to his knees. A husky man with dark whiskers and bushy eyebrows that filtered steel-blue eyes. "You." He pointed to Miss Bennett with his big farmer hand. "You're coming with me."

Miss Bennett must have known about Mr. Reichert, must have been warned about him, must have been instructed what to do if he confronted her. "Of course, Mr. Reichert." She spoke with everyday calm. "But I'll have to make a few preparations. Why don't you wait for me in the car?" She flicked her hand as if brushing away a fly. "Yes, wait for me in the car. I'll be there shortly."

Henry Reichert marched out the door.

"Alistair." Miss Bennett pointed. "Run over to the Snyders and ask Mrs. Snyder to call the sheriff."

Alister bounded out the back door.

Gordon cowered. "He'll kill me." He folded into a tight ball under the desk. "He'll kill me."

"Children," Miss Bennett spoke in a calm voice, "you are excused now. Leave by the back door. Stay out of sight of the car parked in front. Walk in the ditches until you're away from school. If you hear a car approach, run into the fields."

Gordon remained under the desk while students sneaked out the back door.

Miss Bennett touched Gordon when the room emptied. "You may leave now."

Gordon shook his head.

"I'll stay with you then. Don't worry. I'll stay with you." She reached down and placed her hand on his head. He unfolded and stood, holding Miss Bennett, leaning down on her, shivering, shaking, crying.

"It's all right, Gordon. I'll stay with you."

Shirley and Prudence entered the back door. "Looks like Pa's sleeping," Shirley said. Prudence hustled to the coat closet where baseballs, bats, and gloves were stored. She grabbed a bat and pointed to Gordon. "Get him out of here, Miss Bennett. We checked on Pa. He must be drunk." She swung the bat in a strong arc, then pointed it toward the car. "If he comes in here, he'll find his head in centerfield."

Miss Bennett and Gordon snuck out the back door. Minutes later, a siren wailed from far, far away on the road to the county seat. Louder now, louder and closer. Miss Bennett and Gordon heard it. Shirley and Prudence heard it. Henry Reichert slept.

"Ma, when's Pa coming home?" Shirley sliced cheese for school lunches the next morning while Emma fried potatoes and scrambled eggs. She poured a cup of coffee, then started toward the window and stared, a tall, slim woman in faded yellow dress, bib apron, bare legs, lace-up oxfords. "They probably gave him a cot to sleep it off. We'll see him for breakfast. That's how they did it in the past."

"Don't you worry about him, Ma?"

From the living room radio, Clellan Card cracked jokes in exaggerated Scandinavian accents, drowning their conversation.

"Turn that darn radio off." Emma shook the spatula at Shirley. "This is no time for funny stuff."

Shirley walked to the living room and glanced out the window. Through the elms and maples and oaks in the yard, she saw Gordon drive milk cows along the lane to pasture. Prudence would be feeding calves in the barn. Shirley looked down the windbreak of poplars along the drive for the sheriff's car.

The dog barked.

"That must be them," Emma said. "Quick, set the table, then make toast. I'll talk to the sheriff on the porch."

A black Ford slowed at the mailbox, then turned up the drive and stopped at the house. No one moved inside the car. Emma stood on the porch, drying her hands on an apron. Sheriff Berquist opened his door. "Good morning, ma'am."

Emma nodded.

He walked to the rear door of the Ford and unlocked it. Henry stepped out and walked ahead of the sheriff to the porch. He stood at the step and stared at the thermometer.

SNAKE

The sheriff removed his hat. "Mrs. Reichert, your husband has been booked for disorderly conduct and property destruction. Judge Hewitt has scheduled a hearing for a week from Wednesday. Mr. Reichert has the option of hiring legal counsel, or the court will provide a public defender. In the meantime, he's being released on his own recognizance."

He returned his hat to his head and stared at Henry. "We know you have a farm to keep, winter to prepare for. But," he placed a hand on Henry's shoulder, "this is your third offense in two months. Judge Hewitt is not likely to be lenient." He looked at Emma. "Do you have any questions, ma'am?"

Emma shook her head.

"All right, then. You'll get a notice of the hearing time and date in the mail. Call Court Administration if you have any questions." He tipped his hat. "Thank you, ma'am. Goodbye, Henry."

Henry walked in the kitchen, glanced at Shirley, then turned into the wood room. He dumped kindling from a cardboard box onto the floor and walked to the bedroom. He closed the door.

Gordon and Prudence opened the screen door and waited.

"Get a move on," Emma whispered, pulling them inside. "Wash up and change your clothes. I'll make you an egg sandwich to eat on the way to school. Now hurry."

Shirley stood in the kitchen. The room smelled of breakfast—fried potatoes with onions, eggs, toast, coffee. Food steamed on the table, but no one ate. She glanced out the window. The sheriff's car made the corner at the mailbox.

Emma grabbed Shirley's arm. "Take your plate upstairs and stay home for a while. I'll want someone around."

Henry walked out of the bedroom with a box stuffed with clothes.

"What's that?" Emma asked.

"Clothes. I gotta leave town."

"You can't." Emma swung a spatula. "You got a court date."

"They don't have the money to find me or the manpower to bring me back."

"Where are you going?"

"I heard on the radio about the Harvest Brigade. A company hires hands to work the grain and corn and hayfields up and down the Dakotas. It's good money, and they house you and feed you."

"The Dakotas? North Dakota? Do you think you'll be near

Rugby? You could visit my folks." Emma perked up. "I could quick fix a package for them."

"Hold your horses, woman. This is work, not vacation. Who knows if I'll be near Rugby? And if I am, I won't have time. Now get me some breakfast. I gotta scoot."

Emma grabbed a plate and dished up eggs and potatoes. "And what are *we* supposed to do?"

"Listen." Henry shook a fork at her. "I've thought this out. Either I'll be in jail earning nothing, or I'll be in the Dakotas making money. Either way, I won't be here. You do what you have to do."

"But the milking, the harvest, the wood cutting. We can't do that."

"What would you do if I fell off the silo?"

"We'd probably have to sell the cattle."

"Well, that's probably what you'll have to do." Henry wiped his plate with a crust of toast. "How much money do we have?"

Emma held the spatula, turning it, turning it.

Henry stared at her. "You got some put away for taxes, right? When does the milk check come?"

"Yesterday."

"Give me both of those. And pack me some food. I'll need to eat until I find the harvesters and get a job. I'll send you money soon as I get a check." He finished his coffee and grabbed the box of clothes. "I'm going to gas up the Chevy."

"You're taking the car too?"

"You think I'm gonna hitchhike? Have the food and money ready for me when I come back."

When the screen door slammed, Emma walked to the wood room, took the shotgun off the rack, and stashed it under the strewn kindling. She packed loaves of bread, jars of canned meat and vegetables and fruit, jam, a brick of cheese, plus a plate, cup, fork, and knife. She filled the thermos with coffee and placed it on the table with the property tax money and milk check.

Henry walked in, stuffed the money and check in his billfold, and walked to the wood room. "Where's the shotgun?"

"Isn't it on the rack? Gordon was shooting pigeons last night."

"Damn that boy of yours. He's the devil's child, I swear. I don't have time to look for it now." He grabbed the box of food and thermos and tramped out the door.

SNAKE

When the Chevy started and rolled out the drive, Shirley walked down the stairs. "What are we going to do, Ma?"

Emma watched the Chevy fade in a cloud of dust. She held her arms out, then up. The walls pushed in on her. The ceiling pressed on her neck and back. The floor trembled. She twisted the spatula, twisted and turned it, choking back a sob.

"Ma?"

"Oh, no. Not now," Emma whimpered. "I can't break. Not now."

Shirley poked her tripod through flowering heads of reed grass to the pond. Ahead, perched on a log at the shoreline, frogs lazed in the sun. She extended the tripod and aimed the camcorder at the frogs, the same leopard frogs that inhabited the pond years ago. They eyed her, intent on her, not vigilant to ground motion. Shirley identified trails where snakes had tunneled through grass from the rock pile to the pond. It was a matter of time. A dragonfly lit on her hand and flexed its wings. She waited.

"I'm glad you could join us for supper, Miss Bennett." Emma Reichert ladled mashed potatoes into a bowl. Around the table sat Gordon, Prudence, and Shirley. Emma's chair sat next to Betty's. Mr. Reichert's chair sat empty. When Emma sat, she nodded. "Prudence, please lead us in prayer."

They folded hands and bowed their heads.

"Make yourself at home, Miss Bennett," Emma said when Prudence finished. "Or may I call you Betty?"

"Please do."

Emma handed Betty a platter of fried chicken. "We've talked it over as a family and decided we have no recourse but for Gordon to quit school and tend the farm. He'll be sixteen soon, so we won't be breaking the law."

Betty looked at Gordon, watched him load his plate and slather a slice of homemade bread with butter. "That would be unfortunate, but I understand."

"We were wondering," Emma handed Betty the plate of bread, "if you'd be interested in moving from the Snyders to here. That way, you could tutor Gordon in exchange for your room and board. And Gordon could graduate."

Betty looked at Gordon and Prudence and Shirley, wondered how other families would react to her living here, given the Reichert reputation. Would she have her own room? Would walking to school in the winter be a problem?

Prudence met her stare. "We'd like to have you. Shirley and I will share a room. You could have my room."

"I could use tutoring too," Shirley added. "I'm planning to go on to high school, maybe college."

"I know the Snyders are wonderful people." Emma placed a hand on Betty's arm. "But Betty, you should be around people your age. What are you, eighteen? Gordon is only a couple years behind you."

Gordon dished up another helping of potatoes.

Betty scanned their faces. "I'll give it serious consideration. I don't know how I'd break the news to the Snyders."

A week later, Betty sat at the same chair in the Reichert kitchen and spoke to Emma. "The Snyders understood. Mr. Snyder offered to drive us to and from school on stormy days. You have wonderful neighbors."

"Yes, we do." Emma handed her a platter of meatloaf. "The neighborhood men offered to have a wood-cutting party when they finish picking corn. I could use help feeding that crew."

"Gordon, I brought your books." Betty passed the platter. "We'll set aside a couple hours each night and a few more on weekends to keep you current. We'll call it an excused absence so you can take your eighth-grade finals at the end of the school year."

Gordon nodded. "I already know that stuff."

"Well, then we'll skip to something you don't know, smarty pants."

The sisters giggled.

After supper, Gordon and Prudence shuffled to the barn for milking. Emma set up the ironing board and sprinkled dresses for the girls. Shirley wiped the red oil cloth and washed dishes. Betty dried.

"I'm happy to have you here." Emma spit on the heating iron. "If something happens to me, it's comforting to know the kids have someone to turn to."

"Have you heard from your husband?"

"No, and I don't expect I will. He said he'd send a check

every payday." She shrugged her shoulders. "I'll believe it when I see it."

"How long will you be able to keep on? Gordon's too young to take the responsibility of farming this place. I've seen him with the horses, and he's not good."

"Neither was Pa."

"And the old Farmall. Does it even run?"

Emma slid a school dress onto the ironing board. "Beats me. I have enough to worry about."

After chores, after the kids were in bed, Betty sat with Emma in the living room and listened to Cedric Adams and the ten o'clock news, Emma listening for word on the Harvest Brigade, Betty for Current Events topics. Emma reached for a sewing basket and a pile of socks. She turned to the lamp and threaded the needle, her eyes narrowed, her wire-rimmed glasses riding down her nose. "Don't expect too much from Gordon." She kept her eyes on the needle. "He's not right, you know."

"I know he's very intelligent."

"Intelligence don't make him right. He's been a thorn in his father's side since the day he was born. Even before that." She slid a light bulb into the sock, concentrating on her work. "Henry didn't believe Gordon was his child."

Betty turned the radio off, threw a questioning glance at Emma, and grabbed a pile of homework and pencil.

"Henry overheard some braggarts in the tavern shortly after we were married. One of them said, 'Too bad for Henry. He got stuck with two-bit Emma. She's got to be knocked up. Hope the kid don't look like me.'" She wove the needle through the threads of the heel. "I swore to Henry that wasn't true, but bull-headed Henry, he'd rather believe some drunken sot than his own wife." She pushed her glasses up. "And to think I saved myself for him. How stupid."

Betty set the homework down. "But you know whose child he is, right?"

"Small consolation." Emma poked the needle into the sock. "It gets worse. My dad hated Henry. Said he could tell Henry would be a troublemaker. That he couldn't handle his whiskey. When Henry and I told him we were getting married, he said to me, 'I suppose you're pregnant too. And if you are, that's the devil's child you're carrying.'"

Emma finished the sock, folded it with its mate, and placed

the sewing basket under the table. "Pa treats Gordon terrible, just like his pa treated him. Thank God he doesn't treat the girls that way." Emma clung to the chair. "Don't expect too much from Gordon." She stared at Betty. "And don't be hard on him. Promise?"

Betty stared in disbelief. "Of course I promise."

Emma stood, her long fingers flexing like knitting needles. "You know I'm not well. But I'm comfortable with you here. More comfortable than I've been in a long time."

Betty leaned forward to stand, to hug her.

Emma turned. "Let's call it a day. I'll turn off the lights when you get upstairs."

While Betty gathered homework papers, Shirley crept to her shared room from her listening post at the top of the stairs.

Shirley leaned against a massive white oak where she could see the frogs, and wondered if this tree stood back then, back when she collected leaves and pressed them in a huge geography book for a science project. She found herself in a time warp, a young country girl interested in snakes then, a professional city woman now, still interested in snakes. Miss Bennett would be proud.

A breeze rattled the cattails, discharging tufts of cotton and a patter of acorns. Strings of cobwebs caught the sun and floated past. She trained her binoculars on the frogs. Motion, lower left. Yellow stripes on black, gliding low and slow. Crows squawked. Blackbirds trilled in alarm. A snake slithered to the nearest frog, recoiled, and struck, catching a leg.

"Everything okay back here?" Shirley jumped and reeled to see a uniformed man, familiar but unidentified face, and a white car with door emblazoned BROWNS COUNTY SHERIFF. "Just patrolling the country roads, ma'am, and I saw your car. Everything okay?"

"Yes, Officer. Thanks for checking." Shirley peered at him. "You wouldn't be Bear Braham perchance? You and I attended school together here. You were in the same grade as my brother Gordon."

"Shirley or Prudence Reichert, which one are you?"

"Shirley. I'm on the staff of the Minnesota Science Museum filming a documentary on ophiology, or snakes to the rest of the world." She handed the camcorder to Bear. "Would you mind filming me while I narrate this drama that's unfolding? Then I want to hear what you've done with your life. You know you're the first boy I ever kissed."

Bear blushed. "That kiss doesn't really count. It was in our class play."

"Might not have counted for you, but it did for me."

"Eat hearty," Emma said on Saturday morning. "We have a busy weekend ahead." Betty and the Reinhart kids loaded their plates and sat around the table. Emma filled a blue canner. "Don't wait for me. I want to sterilize a few more jars for canning this afternoon." She spoke with nervous excitement, flitted from cupboard to stove, pantry to kitchen.

"Gordon, there's no dew on the ground this morning. You can rake hay right after milking. One of us will drive the team when you're ready to pitch it on the wagon."

Curtains fluttered in the kitchen window across a calendar with 4 marked on today's date, then 3, 2, 1. Emma lowered blue Mason jars in the boiling water, humming.

After breakfast, Gordon slipped into Pa's barn boots and carried a milk pail to the barn. When a neighbor had offered to buy two Jersey cows, Gordon had twelve Holsteins to milk. The haymow was stacked to the rafters; the silo would be filled when the crew made rounds. Gordon would drive his team and wagon to the neighbors, as he and Pa had done, to become part of silo filling rotation.

Emma led Betty, Prudence, and Shirley to the garden with bushel baskets, gunny sacks, and garden forks. Betty dug potatoes, and the girls picked through dirt, tossing potatoes in the sacks. On to carrots, beets, rutabagas. Emma stooped over a row of green beans, stretching her apron to form a basket.

By noon, the garden was decimated. Only winter squash and pumpkins remained, yellow and orange globes tethered to gray vines and black leaves pressed to earth. Beyond the garden, Gordon cursed the horses as he sat on the hay rake, trailing a ribbon of alfalfa.

"Girls, pick a couple pails of crabapples for apple butter," Emma called. "I'll fix dinner."

The porch was a cornucopia of fruits and vegetables in

bushel baskets, cardboard boxes, gunny sacks, pails. Tomatoes lined the handrail, bottom side up, sunning to blood red. Cabbage heads were stacked near the sauerkraut crock like cannon balls. Baskets of cucumbers and bunches of dill waited near the pickle barrel.

At noon, Gordon unhitched the team from the rake, removed their bridles, and walked the horses to the water tank, harnesses jingling, Gordon yelling, "C'mon Dolly, move it." When they finished drinking, he tied them to a tree in the shade of the barn.

In the kitchen, the huge Presto pressure canner commanded the stove, a smaller pot of boiling water and aluminum teakettle dwarfed beside it. Sterilized jars waited in rows on the kitchen counter, next to boxes of metal lids and rings. Emma hummed as she sliced baloney and smeared mustard on bread for sandwiches. After lunch, production would begin—peel, cut, blanch, fill jars, pressure cook, cool. Admire.

Emma shouted orders: *more beans, slice the carrots thinner, keep an eye on the timer*. She filled jars with carrots, blanched them for five minutes, added salt. She checked the kitchen clock, then placed filled jars in the cooker, released the pressure, and lowered the temperature.

Prudence and Shirley dumped potatoes in wire baskets, shook off sand, and hauled them down the outside stairway to the cellar. "This place gives me the creeps." Shirley's voice echoed in empty space. The rock walls, once whitewashed, were draped in spider webs, the dirt floor pocked, the air chilled and earthy.

Emma hustled the girls, barked orders, slapping her thigh with a wooden spoon.

"Take it easy, Ma." Prudence hugged her waist. "It's only the middle of October."

Emma hummed as she checked the pressure gauge on the Presto, hummed while she aligned the sealed jars of vegetables, hummed as she slapped her thigh.

At nine, after a catch-as-catch-can supper, after Gordon finished milking, after the beans and carrots and tomatoes and beets were canned, Emma stood in the kitchen, eyeing jars of blue-tinted fruits and vegetables. "You kids get some sleep. I'll pack a couple more batches before I call it a day." Emma reached for a jar of pickled beets and cradled it like a baby. "We're on schedule." She attempted a smile. "Tomorrow is another day. Wild plums for

SNAKE

jam, apples and rhubarb for sauce, and, if we have time, hazelnuts."

"I'll stay up with you for a while," Betty said.

Emma pulled the bead chain on the overhead pantry light bulb and washed shelves before storing the canned goods. She arranged the jars like jewels, carrots beside beans, corn beside beets.

Gordon walked from the barn lugging a half-pail of milk. "I'm too tired for school tonight. I'm going to bed."

"Not until we review our spelling and capitals of the states." Betty grabbed his sleeve. "We'll sit on the porch. We won't need light." The pressure canner whistled. Emma hummed. Prudence climbed the stairs to bed. Shirley read a history book at the dining room table.

"Would you have a cup of tea with me?" Emma asked when Betty returned. She stood in the pantry doorway, her back to Betty, her hands on her hips, humming. They sat in the living room when the ten o'clock news began. Emma didn't listen. She walked to the calendar in the kitchen and drew a line through the day's date, 2. "There'll be food for all winter." She placed her apron on a chair. "We're on schedule."

Back in the living room, she picked up her sewing basket. "Is Gordon learning?" she asked, her hand to her mouth deflecting the conversation from Shirley.

"He has a great memory, and a knack for mathematics. We're past multiplying and dividing fractions, past decimals, well into square root. Ready for geometry, if I remember it."

"And the other classes?"

"We're locating the hot spots in the news on the world map. We sidetracked a bit on literature." Betty smiled. "We're reading 'The Scarlet Letter.' I had to tell him what the A stood for. He asked what adultery is, so I told him."

Emma whispered to Betty. "Shhh." She pointed to Shirley in the dining room. And in a quiet voice, "How would he have known? Did he understand?"

"He wanted to talk about it. I shut him off."

"Pa should have talked to him. But I expect Pa figured he knew all he had to know from watching the cows." Emma leaned back, exhaled, and dropped her arms. "Long day," she sighed. Then, in an aside, "Did your parents talk to you about that? Guess I should talk to Prudence and Shirley."

"My parents never thought it necessary to talk to me about the birds and the bees. Look at me. Stringy hair, thick glasses, overweight. I heard Dad tell Mom when I left to teach he wouldn't have to worry about me being chased by any boys." She faked a laugh.

Emma lifted a thimbled finger. "When the right one comes around, you'll know."

"No. I'll end up an old maid school teacher, or I'll take what I can get."

"I noticed Gordon stares at you when you're not looking."

Betty blushed. "You're teasing."

Sunday, Emma finished canning and stood in the pantry door with crossed arms. In front of her, in perfect alignment and brilliant coloration, Mason jars stood as if in a homemaker's magazine. Shirley walked behind her and hugged her waist.

The girls pushed wheelbarrows of squash to the cellar, braided onions to dry on the porch, picked pails of crabapples. The wind shifted from the south to the west, then to the north. Tan leaves fluttered off oaks and scattered the yard. Crisp air tasted of winter.

"After dinner, we'll pick hazelnuts," Emma said. "The bushes are loaded."

They carried gunny sacks to the pasture and filled them with nuts—large, brown, and loose in rough husks. Shirley watched a wooly bear caterpillar climb on a leaf, then onto her sleeve. "What's its real name?" she asked Betty.

"Wooly Bear is good enough," Betty said. "It will become an Isabella tiger moth someday. That much I remember."

At home, they hung two gunny sacks of nuts from rafters in the granary, safe from mice and birds. The sacks dangled and twirled in the breeze from the open door as if they were dancing.

"I should dress them up and scare Henry." Emma faked a laugh. "If he comes home."

Monday, Gordon harnessed the horses to haul deadfalls from the pasture for sawing. Betty and the girls bagged text books and notebooks for school. Betty reached to hug Emma. "You're due for a day off."

Emma looked at the calendar.

SNAKE

Shirley returned from school Monday afternoon as Gordon unhooked a log chain. "Where's Ma?"

"The house, I suppose."

"When's the last time you saw her?"

"Dinner time. Change your clothes and help me."

"Was she okay? Did she say anything about walking to the neighbors?"

Gordon ignored her.

Shirley ran back to the house, called, opened the outside door to the cellar. "Ma. Ma." She ran to the barn, the woodshed, the granary.

A third form dangled from the rafters beside the bags of nuts, rotating in a breeze. Shirley stood in the door, threw her hands to her face, and screamed.

Shirley crept to the camcorder, checked the focus, and zoomed in on the snake's head. She felt gratified to reconnect with Bear, but she had a mission—snakes. The snake's disconnected jaws maneuvered around the frog. Two top teeth curved backwards, securing its prey. The frog stood helpless, wide eyed, and stoic—Gordon's look when their dad burst into the schoolhouse years ago. The snake rotated its head with a snap, upending the frog. The frog twisted, righted itself, and clung to a twig on the log. Shirley returned to the tree where a squirrel chattered and dropped acorn shells.

Betty stayed on while the Reinhart kids wondered about their future. She called the sheriff and asked for help finding Henry and heard a disinterested response. "We already have a warrant out for his arrest. Contempt of court."

Betty found herself in charge of cleaning, cooking, laundry, arranging for rides to town with the Snyders. "I can't play with you," she told the girls. "I have work to do." She moved her clothes to the downstairs bedroom, to be closer to the kitchen.

"Gordon, you're getting behind in your school work, and it's more important than chores." Betty washed dishes. Shirley wiped. "We'll study each night until ten."

They sat at the kitchen table, Gordon with math worksheets, Betty with the day's lessons and homework to grade. Shirley sat at her perch at the top of the stairs. After a few minutes of math, Gordon reached for *Prose and Poetry* and opened it to "The Scarlet Letter." "What does the A stand for again?"

Gordon's knee must have touched hers under the table. She jerked, then eased back. Paper trembled in her hands. She flushed. Gordon glared and grinned. Betty pretended to read and reread the spelling words. Sweat broke on her neck, her arms.

Gordon closed the book and stood. "I'm going to bed." He walked to the downstairs bedroom, loosening a suspender and tossing it over his shoulder.

Indian summer stumbled into winter late that year. On the walk to school, the sun lit the naked treetops, and wispy clouds floated soft against a pale sky. By afternoon, the sky glared a bold blue. Leaves of cornstalks raced across the road. A formation of Canada geese circled the cornfield, swooped down, then ascended, flying south.

After supper, Betty prepared a shopping list for the woodcutters' dinner. Prudence and Shirley argued in the kitchen while doing dishes. Gordon milked the cows.

Rain pelted against the windows. The kitchen light flickered. Betty placed the list in her pocket and drew designs for the school Halloween party—cats with arched backs, pumpkins, witches and ghosts for the early grades.

The dog barked. Betty glanced out the window. Two faint headlights cut through rain and searched the driveway.

Betty stood. "We have company. Maybe Mr. Snyder wondering if we lost power." She opened the screen door and stood on the porch with Shirley and Prudence. Headlights dimmed and the car door opened. A bolt of lightning struck, revealing a figure, a man, stockier than Mr. Snyder. Not as tall. Thunder rattled the windows, shook the porch. The man reached into the rear seat and retrieved a duffel bag. He walked with slow, deliberate steps through the pelting rain to the porch.

"Mr. Reichert," Betty yelled. "You startled me."

"Who are you?"

"I'm Miss Bennett, the school teacher at Four Corners."

Henry stepped on the porch and stomped his feet. "What are you doing here?" He didn't wait for an answer, but walked into the kitchen. Prudence and Shirley stood in the doorway.

"Fix me some supper," he barked. "I'm hungry as a bear."

SNAKE

He walked to the bedroom and threw the duffel bag inside, then to the washroom, dried his face and combed his hair. Back in the kitchen, he glared at the girls. "Where's your ma?"

Betty stood with the girls.

Henry reached for an envelope in his pocket and fanned a handful of bills. "I saved enough for us to get off this godforsaken farm and get a decent place." He counted the bills. "How's my supper coming?"

Betty grabbed leftovers from the refrigerator and dumped them in a fry pan. Henry flicked through mail on the table.

"Gordon milking the cows?" Henry asked when Betty handed him a plate.

The girls nodded.

"Where's your ma?"

"Girls, go to your room." Betty nudged them toward the stairs. They squeezed past Henry's chair and stood at the landing.

Betty met his stare. "Emma is dead."

Henry stopped chewing and stared. "What do you mean *dead*?"

"Dead," Prudence shouted. "D-E-A-D. Dead." She ran upstairs crying.

Henry looked at his plate, looked at the pile of bills, looked at Betty. "God damn that kid of hers."

Betty walked into the living room and waited, then walked up the stairs to the girls' bedroom.

"Where're my boots?" Henry yelled.

"Gordon's probably wearing them." The door slammed. When lightning flashed, they saw Henry walk to the barn. Betty ran downstairs and grabbed her clothes from the bedroom and ran back upstairs.

"Will Gordon be all right?" Shirley asked.

"He's young and he's fast." Betty hugged her. "He'll outrun him."

Lightning struck again, and the house was black. Betty groped in a drawer for candles and matches, then walked downstairs with the girls to light a lamp. Thunder cracked, shaking the house. Wind blew and snapped a tree in the yard.

Henry staggered into the house trancelike, walked to the wood room, and hung the shotgun on the rack.

He sat at the table and stared at his supper. "Call the sheriff."

Shirley eyed the frog-snake struggle through binoculars. The snake rotated its head and lunged forward. The frog clung to the twig. A swoop of wings startled her. In a dead elm, within view of the snake, a marsh hawk flapped graceful brown wings. The snake reacted, twisting, turning to drag the frog to cover. The frog clung to the log. The snake tugged, tried to release the frog. In an instant, the hawk dove, clutched the snake in its talons and lifted. The snake curled and coiled, its mouth open, empty. Shirley retrieved the camcorder. "Excellent footage."

She packed her equipment, walked to where the school stood, walked to the spot where her desk would have been, and remembered Miss Betty Bennett. Remembered the letter Betty wrote when she left the Reichert house. Remembered it word for word.

Dear Prudence and Shirley,

As much as I hate to, I must leave for my own survival. Too many memories, some good, some bad. I shall miss you and always love you.

Continue with your studies. When the New York Yankees recruit women, Prudence, I expect to see you in the World Series. Shirley, savor your interest in science. I see a Nobel Prize in your future. You're both resourceful, brave, and intelligent, and you have good neighbors. You'll do well.

As for me, I must break away. I look forward to some day meeting your mother and brother in heaven.

Love,
Betty

Shirley remembered the letter and the brief obituary in the Minneapolis Star Tribune that prompted her trip today.

Betty Bennett, age 75, lifelong elementary teacher in Minnesota rural schools, died on September 16, 2011, in the loving arms of her friends. Preceded in death by her parents George and Stella Bennett and brother Clarence. Survived by her loving son Gordon.

SWAN

"I must have done something right." Lowell Ward stands on the shore, his right foot on a boulder, a hand on his knee. He corrects himself. "Many things right. Our beautiful home, a comfortable retirement, excellent health, all the result of informed choices along the way." He turns to Barb. "Don't you agree?" He turns back to gaze at a flock of mallards barnstorming the bay.

Barb sits at a park bench reading. She lifts her glasses and eyes him. Erect posture, Stetson expedition hat, fresh-pressed khaki pants, spit-shined jodhpurs, all side-lit by a yellow morning sun. *Give him a red cape and you'd have "George Washington Crossing the Delaware."* "Yes, Captain," she says. "Many things."

Lowell and Barb prefer this end of the park, its privacy secured by a long wood-chipped path emblazoned with flowering crabs, its peace from squealing toddlers at the swing set ensured by a copse of blue spruce. Now and then, a high-pitched child's scream floats through spring air and mingles with the cacophony of frogs gargling in the reeds.

Lowell snaps a willow twig and taps his knee. "What are you reading?"

Barb raises her book and displays the jacket. "The same book I've been reading for days."

"Of course."

Wind rustles the waxy green willow leaves, their catkins falling and carpeting the riverbank. The air smells of winter's dead foliage rotting in the shallows where anemones poke through last year's residue. Under the willow, patches of marsh marigolds gild the shore.

Lowell steps off the boulder and swings an imaginary tennis racket. "Tennis was good this morning. I finally had decent competition. I despise a doubles game with an uncoordinated woman."

"Or man," Barb adds.

"True. I've had my time with incompetents. The army was a haven for them. Top brass. Non-commissioned officers. Recruits. All incompetents when I met them."

"Modesty does not become you, Captain." Barb knows the drill; he's asking for praise, his daily ego reinforcement. "Look at the lives you influenced. All the young soldiers you trained. All the young officers you encouraged." Her litany is solicitous and she knows it. He must know it, too. "We've been through this before, Captain. Look at the worlds you changed. Isn't that gratifying?"

Lowell lifts his foot back on the boulder and resumes his pose. "You're right, Barb. I needed a challenge. All my life I needed a challenge. The Army provided that." He glances at Barb. "What about you? In retrospect, was the life of an officer's wife fulfilling?"

Lord. Barb closes the book and slides the small gold cross on her neck chain. She snaps her head and stands. "Look." Barb points. "The swans. The swans are back. How many years has it been?"

Lowell stares ahead.

"So beautiful." Barb smiles. "This must be their tenth year. I'm certain it's the same pair. Always swimming out from the point. She in the lead. He, watching, guarding. I wonder about their life span."

Lowell clenches his fist and taps his knee.

"Do you know their life span, Captain?"

Lowell lowers his head.

"Captain?" Barb whispers.

"I'm thinking."

The sun slides behind a wisp of clouds, encouraging a cool breeze. Barb folds her arms.

"Thinking of what?"

"The name. That type of swan."

"It's a trumpeter swan, Captain."

"Of course it is. I knew that."

Barb watches the swans, their pretentious poses, their affected togetherness. "Do they truly mate for life or is that silly folklore?"

"What difference does it make?"

"None, really, but it's interesting. Do you know?"

"Did you bring snacks? I'm hungry."

"I wonder if they nest beyond the point." Barb stands and points. "And when does she set on the eggs? Remember last year? Two cygnets."

Lowell taps his fingers on his knee, his eyes locked, his jaw clenched. He lowers his head, then snaps it up. "*Cygnus buccinator.* That's what I was looking for."

Barb shoots a questioning glance. "What?"

"The Latin genus for swans. *Cygnus buccinator.*"

Barb shakes her head and sits. "You are such a lovable old naturalist."

"And such a lovable old Latin scholar," he adds.

The breeze is steady now, sweeping last year's leaves into the river. The link chain on the park's huge American flag clangs against the pole.

"I've been thinking about your brother," Lowell says. "What do you hear from him?"

"My brother? Dale?" She sets her book on her knee. "Dale died last year. May 12. Remember?"

Lowell glances at her, then shifts to the river. "Oh, yes." He forces a smile. "Let's walk. The first warm day of May. A walk will be invigorating."

"Captain, it's ten-thirty. You have a haircut appointment at eleven. We should go back to the house."

The wind picks up and ripples the willow leaves. Frothy water laps at the shore. Lowell lifts his foot off the boulder, faces her, and looks at the walking path, right and left. The swans swim behind the point. Thunder rolls across the river. Discrete raindrops pelt sideways, blurring vision. Barb tucks the book in a bag and places it on her head.

Lowell looks left and right again, rain dripping off his hat mottling his pressed shirt. He takes an uncertain step.

"Captain, this way." She approaches him and reaches her arm to touch him.

He squints his eyes to tiny circles of black. Rain streams down his scrubbed cheeks, his squared jaw. He pushes her away, teeters, and stops. He reaches for her, grabs her arm, and clings with both hands.

"How long has this been going on?" Kim hands Barb a container of kimchi with a mock bow. "When did you first notice his memory lapses?"

Barb straightens the towels on the oven handle and glances at the bedroom door. She stalls. "I hope I did the right thing getting you involved." She motions for her to sit at the kitchen table.

Kim glances around—the aligned books in the bookcase, the fanned magazines on the coffee table, the *place for everything and everything in its place* demeanor. "Pardon me," she says, "but your home looks like a military barracks. Me being a social worker with Veterans Affairs, I see that eight hours a day. Don't you sometimes want to jumble stuff up, make a mess, and revel in the disorder?"

Barb smiles. "I could tell you stories. On rainy days, he alphabetizes my spice rack."

"Other people have daily routines," Kim says. "We have SOPs." She digs through her bag, finds a notebook and pen. "Sorry for my distracting observation. You did the right thing. I'm your friendly neighbor; he's a veteran. You're entitled."

"Maybe it's my imagination," Barb says. "The Captain is in excellent health. Has been all his life."

Kim smiles. "Why do you call him *Captain*? He has a name."

"Everyone calls him *Captain*. He calls himself *Captain*. I think he enjoys the stature it implies."

"Sounds impersonal to me," Kim says, "but if it works . . ." She points her pen at Barb. "When and what did you notice?"

Barb leans on the cupboard, watching the bedroom door. "A few months ago, maybe. At first, I wrote it off as casual forgetfulness. A name, a date, a place. Then he became disoriented. Forgot where he was going. Forgot the way home."

"Of course he's defensive about it," Kim adds.

"I wouldn't dare confront him."

"Does he know I'm coming? Does he know I'm here?"

"I told him I needed new activities, new friends. He thinks you're a lifelong learning consultant." She shakes her head. "Certainly not a VA social worker. I told him we were discussing adult education classes."

"He's home?"

Barb points to the bedroom. "Napping. His daily regimen. Twenty minutes. No more, no less." She checks her watch. "He'll be out in five minutes, pour himself a glass of water, and walk to the mailbox. Normally, he would sit in that chair, but today he might not join us."

"Any medical history I should know of? Any family history of dementia?"

Barb snaps her head toward Kim. "Please."

"I'm sorry," Kim says. "For this visit, I'm not a social worker. I'm your lifelong learning consultant. We can talk adult education. I have the Summer Class Registration bulletin. Interested?"

"Are there music classes? A chamber music ensemble? I'm a cellist, always looking for like-minded musicians."

"I see your instrument," Kim says, pointing to the cello in the living room. "Beautiful. Play it for me sometime."

"I'd love to. Sometime when the Captain isn't around. He's not a musician, thinks music is superfluous." Barb glances at the bedroom door. "I keep trying to dissuade him."

"Too bad. Music is excellent therapy."

Barb checks her watch again. "He'll be out within the minute. Call me later today, in case things get out of hand."

The bedroom door opens. "Ah, we have company." Lowell walks to Barb and places his hand on her shoulder and drums her neck with his fingers.

"This is Kim, the consultant I mentioned. We're talking adult education classes."

"Splendid," Lowell says, walking to the kitchen sink. "Never too old to learn. But you," he turns to Kim, "you're young for that group."

Kim grins. "I learn from my elders."

"You're Korean. Your English is good. How long in the United States?"

"I was adopted when I was twelve, twenty-eight years ago."

"Have you returned to your homeland?"

"Once, when I was sixteen. I wanted to meet my birth mother. We located her, and she agreed to meet."

Barb twists the cross on her neck chain, awaiting Lowell's discounts of her story, his litany of questions, his demeaning banter.

"And?" Lowell asks.

"Within ten minutes, she asked for money."

"Were you surprised?"

"No, disappointed. I left."

"And your father. You have Caucasian features. Any attempt to locate him?"

"No. He was a military man, a U.S. Army officer. My mother

doesn't know more."

"Not an unusual event, I'm sorry to say. Are you curious about him?"

"Not really, and don't ask why. I should be but I'm not. His contact with my mother maybe took all of five minutes."

"By nature, you're half him."

"By nurture, I'm zero him."

Lowell stares at her, stares at Barb. "I'll get the mail," he says. "You girls talk education."

"One of his *on* days," Barb says when the door slams.

"Typical," Kim says. "And more *on* if he thought I was a professional. Is he likely to return soon?"

"No, he'll read the paper on the porch."

"I need background," Kim says. "If you don't mind a social worker prying in your past. How long you've been married. Any children. Any service history I should know."

"He was an army officer. In Korea." Barb grins. "But you haven't found your birth father."

"I wasn't looking. Any children?"

"None. Military life is the wrong environment for a family. Moving every three years. Father in a foreign land not knowing his children. The gypsy camp mentality of living on base. Not for me."

"It's been done. There must be a million army brats on the planet."

"I gave you my stock answer." She gazes at Kim as if to calibrate her trust level. "The real story is the agony my mother endured when my brother was born. Three days of intense labor. In the end, it killed her."

"And your brother?"

"He was vegetative all his life. Died a year ago, a ward of the state. No chance ever to contribute to the betterment of society. A sinkhole for taxpayers' money."

"That's harsh, Barb." Kim takes a deep breath and continues. "You decided not to chance a complicated delivery?"

"*We* decided not to chance it."

"There's always the adoption option." Kim points to herself.

"We discussed adoption. Briefly. We both knew of adoptions that had gone sour. It was such a crap shoot. What if we adopted *The Bad Seed*? The Captain had his reputation to protect."

Barb stands and walks to the front door where the Captain sits reading the newspaper. Kim scans the room. A wall is decorated with framed photographs of a young officer, a diploma from American Military University, framed merit commendations with gold-embossed seals, service medals and multi-colored ribbons mounted on black velvet. Barb turns and gives the all-clear sign.

"Your mother died when you were a young girl. How about your father?" Kim asks.

"I remember every detail. I was eight. We were at the hospital together when Mother died. The doctor walked into the waiting room, pushing his mask on top of his head and sliding out of his rubber gloves. He put his hand on Dad's shoulder. 'We couldn't save her.'

"I waited for permission to scream. Dad stared at the doctor, shrugged his shoulders, and lifted his hands in surrender. He cackled a nervous laugh and walked out the door. The next day my aunt picked me up. That's where I lived for years." She reaches for her neck chain. "This cross is the only keepsake I have of Mother. That and a photograph." She walks to the bookcase and pulls an album. "Here," she says, showing a black and white snapshot to Kim. A dour woman in cotton dress stands in front of an open porch. Beside her, a gangly girl in pigtails and jeans holds a rabbit.

"What happened to your dad?'

"Who knows? Who cares? We heard from him occasionally. Interesting he gave away his daughter but kept the dog."

"And the Captain. What do you know of his childhood?"

"He never discusses it. And if I ask, he says, 'What's over is over.'"

"Where did you meet him?"

"We met at a USO dance. He was a young lieutenant. At ten years his junior, I think he was attracted to my immaturity. Or my dependency."

"Were you working at the time? A student?"

"I was an aide at a children's day care. I loved caring for babies. Thought I might become a nurse."

"It's not too late."

"The Captain wouldn't approve. It would look like I had to work."

"It's still not too late."

"Yes, it is. I'm yesterday."

A gust of south wind billows the curtains. "More rain." Barb closes the windows. "The Captain will be in soon."

"How about your brother?"

"I visited him once a year when the Captain and I were stationed here. Delivered my Care Package and left. I couldn't forgive him for what he had done to Mother."

"He was a baby."

"I fight to not think of him as causing her death."

Kim stares at Barb and makes notes. "Anything I should say to the Captain? Not say?"

"Let's play it by ear."

Lowell walks in, his eyes on the paper in front of him.

"Care for an iced tea with us?" Barb asks.

Lowell lifts his head, looks at Barb, looks at Kim. "Who are you?"

"This is Kim, my consultant friend. We were discussing classes." Barb glances at Kim. "We settled on music, right Kim?"

Lowell stares. "Why are you here?"

"She's our guest, Captain. I invited her."

He points to Kim. "What do you want?"

Kim stands, extends her arms, and smiles. "World peace."

"What is your village?"

"Yongsan. The home of the USAG Army base. I cook for you. Clean your office."

"I don't need you," Lowell yells, "or any of your people. Get out."

Kim nods at Barb and holds an imaginary phone to her ear. She sidles past Lowell and inches through the door.

"Consorting with the enemy," Lowell shouts to Barb.

"She's not the enemy, Captain. She's our neighbor."

"You don't know. They all look alike. You can't trust them. What do you know of her motives?" He stares at her, his eyes shrinking to tiny circles of black.

"I can trust her, Captain. I know her background."

"Have you had her vetted?"

"Of course not."

"How can you be certain?"

"Captain, please. Listen to me." She extends her arms and approaches him.

He grabs her shoulders and shakes her. "You can't trust them."

Barb twists to loosen herself from his grip, her arms

twinging, her teeth shaking. She stands in front of him, sees the set of his jaw, the terror in his eyes. With a burst of adrenaline, she elbows him in the stomach.

Lowell buckles and wraps his arms around his waist.

"Captain. Captain. I'm sorry. I'm sorry."

He curls forward, then straightens. His tiny eyes stare at the ceiling. He leans toward a chair, reaches for her, and eases himself toward her. He holds her arm. One hand. The other.

The Captain capitulates to Barb daily, surrenders to her in minute increments. What to eat, when to sit, where to walk. To *her*. God, what a transformation. What an unexpected transformation. But what a commendation, coming from the commandant. She finds herself gratified to care for him, gloried to be his nurse, realizing an imagined destiny. A nurse. To her surprise, her love remains constant: a selfless doting love, now rewarded with half-smiles and nods of approval.

With the emotional flattery comes the physical challenge. Dressing him, undressing him, lifting a leg into the bathtub, steadying him, easing him down. Washing him, helping him stand, drying him. Then what? Feeding him, monitoring his intake. Solids, liquids. Prescribing his exercise. Planning and announcing the daily agenda.

"Let's go to the park today," Barb says over coffee. She wipes a splotch of jam on the Captain's chin with a napkin.

He's in a chatty mood this morning. He eats toast, talking about the weather, the lawn that may need mowing, the lawn mower. Will it start? Do we have gas? When did we sharpen the blade? "I'd love a walk in the park," he says, another splotch of jam on his cheek. He places an arm on Barb's shoulder and drums her neck with his fingers. "Thank God I can still drive."

Barb stops her coffee cup halfway. "We'll see," she says, like the mother of an impetuous five-year-old. Barb has learned to select her battles. "We'll see."

Barb drives to the park, agreeing the Captain can drive home. On the wood-chipped walk, she reaches for his arm, nesting her head into his shoulder. A robin scolds from a branch. "We must look like a couple of teenagers," she says. He wraps an arm around her shoulder and drums her neck.

Past full bloom, the faded petals of flowering crabs grace

early shoots of grass. Capricious clouds shade the sun rousing a chilly breeze off the river. Barb snugs her sweater and holds the Captain's arm tighter. "I wonder where the swans are."

Around the hill of blue spruce, another couple stands, pointing at the river. Barb sees the swans. No, the swan. "Look, Captain. The swan. He must be on guard while she sets on the nest."

"Did you hear of the tragedy?" a man in tweed sport coat and binoculars asks.

"What tragedy?"

"The cob was killed by predators. The Park Ranger found a mess of feathers upstream."

"But isn't that the cob?" Barb points to the lone bird.

"No, that's the hen. Seems dogs or coyotes attacked her and the nest. The cob died defending her."

Barb gags, feels an urge to vomit. She holds her throat and turns. "Oh, no."

"She'll find a new mate," the man says. Barb feels his words patting her on the head. *Not likely. Not at her age.*

"Captain, I want to leave." Barb twists a kerchief around her finger and turns to the couple. "So nice to meet you folks."

At the car, he walks to the driver's door and holds out his hand. "Keys, please."

"Are you sure you feel up to it, Captain?"

"Keys, please."

She hands the keys and walks to the passenger side. Lowell hums while he inserts the key in the ignition and buckles his seat belt. He adjusts the mirror and lowers the window. He tosses a smile at her and shifts into reverse. Barb looks right and left, front and rear. They leave the parking lot and head down the drive to the County Road where he stops for the sign. He looks right, left, right. He waits, looking ahead, looking right, left. Barb twists her kerchief. He waits.

From behind, a horn honks. Again. Again. A car pulls beside them, and a female passenger gives Lowell the finger and shouts, "Get off the road, you old fart." The car screams around them and peels rubber down the highway.

Lowell leans forward and grips the wheel. "You son-of-a-bitch," he says, and pounds the accelerator.

"Captain, Captain. Don't follow them."

He's at forty, fifty, sixty miles an hour. The car ahead stays a comfortable distance but within view. The passenger lifts her arm through the skylight and flashes the finger.

"Captain, Captain. Stop. You'll kill us." She reaches for the ignition key. He slaps her hand. The car ahead speeds through an intersection while the stoplight is yellow. Lowell continues toward the intersection at full speed. "Captain, stop. Do you hear me? Stop."

A car to the right moves into the intersection and screeches the brakes. Lowell speeds through, his eyes glued to the car ahead. Barb reaches for the gear shift lever on the console. She jerks it into neutral and clamps it with both hands. A siren wails, screams behind them. Lowell continues his pressure on the gas pedal. The engine revs and whines until the car rolls to a stop.

They sit in the middle of the lane. A squad car pulls up behind them, its siren dying. Barb reaches and turns off the ignition. She pulls the keys.

Deputy Bear Braham approaches the driver's side, sun glasses tilted on his forehead, name badge over his left pocket. "You came close to causing an accident, sir. May I see your driver's license?"

Lowell reaches for his billfold and hands Bear a card.

"This is your military ID, sir. May I see your driver's license?"

Lowell stammers. "Military ID not good enough for you?"

"No, sir."

"Were you a military man?" Lowell asks.

"No, sir. My son was a marine."

"What rank?"

"Second Lieutenant."

"Huh." Lowell sorts through his billfold for a driver's license and hands it to Bear.

Barb gets out of the car, walks to the driver's side, and stands by Bear. Lowell sits, stoic, his fists clenched, color draining from his clamped jaw.

"When you finish, I want to talk to you," Barb says to Bear. She waits while he returns to the squad car and writes the ticket. When he returns, he hands the ticket to Lowell. "I'm giving you a citation for speeding and reckless driving."

"Why don't you arrest the car ahead of me that sped past me and harassed me?"

"The judge may recommend an Anger Management

sentence. Think about it."

Barb follows him to the squad. "Thanks for doing what you did. And doing it before he killed someone."

"I recognize your husband Captain Ward. Is he likely to start the car and drive away?" Bear stands by the squad door.

Barb pats her jeans pocket. "Not likely." She points to his name badge. "You're Maggie's husband. She's my hair stylist."

"That's how I'm known around here." Bear smiles. "Maggie Braham's husband."

"I'm Barb Ward." She offers Bear her hand. "I feel today is the first day of the rest of my life. I've been waiting to act on my husband's . . . his condition. He's been ready. I haven't. Now I am."

"Happy to be of service, ma'am. Keep me posted. I'll tell Maggie we met."

Barb waves goodbye and walks to her car. She opens the driver's door. "Get out." The Captain walks to the passenger side, and Barb drives home. He says nothing, nothing for hours.

After evening dinner, Barb walks him to the living room to his recliner and turns on the television. "There," she says. "We must keep up on the news." She hands him the remote, like a mother handing a rattle to a toddler. He stares his trademark vacuous stare. "You're very nice," he says. She smiles. Later, in the kitchen, she cries.

In bed at night, he cuddles into her shoulder. She rubs his neck, his back, rustles the military cut of his hair. He's silent, breathing relaxed. He whimpers into her hair. She pats his back and tells him a story.

In the quiet of night, she considers options. Now? Wait? What for him? What for me?

"Thanks for coming." Barb motions Kim through the front door.

"I heard you playing. That was beautiful. What was it?"

"Saint-Saens. A piece for cello. I love its mood—melancholy with a hopeful resolution. Care for an iced tea?" She pours two glasses and sits at the kitchen table, an arm supporting her chin, her gaze fixed on the window. The spring morning sun promises unseasonable heat. Last night's rain promises intolerable humidity. But this morning, the air is clement and fresh and smells of orchard blossoms.

Kim sips her tea. "So, you bit the bullet, so to speak."

"I promised myself if the Captain was irrational or violent, I'd act. He was. I did." Barb scans the room, landing on the cello. "Funny, I've played more in the last few days since he's been gone than I played for years. What a friend."

"Music has charms . . ."

"And I'm sleeping again. Six, seven, eight solid hours. It's been a while. I didn't realize how tired I was. Have you lifted a six-foot man out of a bathtub? Chased him down the street when he went for the paper? Tried to put socks on a grown man, or tie his shoes? And that's just the physical stuff. Living with the uncertainty was even harder."

"He's where he belongs," Kim says. "What was his reaction to the Memory Care Center?"

"Better than I could have hoped. The regimentation of the place appealed to him. He asked about the chain of command, the daily schedule, the uniform of the day, all military stuff." She smiles and fingers the cross on her neck chain. "They mentioned the locked doors and stressed the penalty for unauthorized departures." She laughs. "He asked if it was a court martial offense, like AWOL. 'Something like that,' they said."

"I surmise he was ready to go," Kim says. "It's been a while since we first talked."

"He was ready, but I wasn't ready to release him. Until now. Same old story."

"What tipped the balance?"

"A lot of small things, leading to the big thing. Asking the same questions minutes apart. Delusion. Thinking his wallet or keys were stolen. Suspicion when a neighbor drove by. Threatening phone calls from sworn enemies." Barb pauses, concentrates on a flock of finches at the feeder, their plumage already an indulgent gold. "One day he wanted to drive home from the park. Damn near caused an accident." She puts her face in her hands and shakes her head. "I called the Veterans Memory Care Center."

Barb glances at the bedroom door and pauses. She fingers her cross. "The drive in was completely uneventful. The place has a military feel about it which resonated with the Captain. The gate at the entrance is marked Fort Sibley. He didn't ask questions. I didn't offer information."

Kim reaches for her hand. "They were ready for him?"

"I'll say. The director, the nurse, the social worker, and a volunteer, a pink lady. All waiting for us. We finished the paperwork and the pink lady offered to show us around. The dining room, marked *mess hall*. The gathering room, marked *day room*. The Captain's room."

Barb sneered. "The pink lady grated me somehow. All touchy-feely stuff. Holding my hand with both of hers when we met. Holding the Captain's hand the same way. Her every word accompanied by a gesture of welcome. She looked the part. Pink cardigan over pink pullover tossed over her shoulder. The pearl clasp, of course. Lovely complexion. Short blond curls, fresh from the salon."

"Am I sensing a tinge of jealousy?"

"More than a tinge. She has this chirpy canary voice. Of course she's slim and walks in heels more comfortably than I do in slippers." Barb lifts her arms in surrender. "As if that should be a problem for me. Back at the office, the director must have sensed my reaction. 'Don't worry about her,' she said. 'We call her Miss Velcro. She attaches to everyone she sees.'"

Barb stirs her iced tea and dangles her chain. "I'm still conflicted about my decision. I loved caring for him these past months. I felt empowered, making decisions I've never made. Never had to make. I loved the turnabout in roles—his dependence on *me*." She taps her chest with a spoon. "Little old groveling, agreeable, whatever-you-say me. I loved it. I loved him. Now, forty years later, I understand how fulfilling married life can be."

Kim smiles. "You're a saint."

"Now that he's comfortably cared for, I've spread my wings. Mondays, volunteering at the Senior Center. Wednesdays, a rosemaling class at the gallery. Sunday afternoons, playing cello at Good Shepherd Assisted Living."

"*Chuk-ha-hae*."

"Which means?"

"Congratulations."

"New distractions but old habits. I continue to love him." Barb fondles her cross again, slides it up and down the chain. "The highlight of my day is my visit to the Center. My life revolves around those visits. I feel giddy when I drive to meet him."

"Can you tell him how you feel?"

Barb shakes her head. "I baked his favorite chocolate chip

cookies." She points to a plate wrapped in Saran Wrap with a small blue bow. "I'll bring these today. And," she points to a gift bag, "I ironed his pajamas."

"You spoil him rotten. And the Captain. Is he acclimating?"

"He is. His residence wing is his command. He's assigned rank to all the staff and thinks the residents are a Battalion of which he is Commander-in-chief."

The clock chimes eleven o'clock. "Eleven hundred hours." Barb smiles. "I'll see the Captain at noon for lunch."

"Any power struggles with the residents?"

"Staff advised me of an aggressive female. A Colonel. She has a habit of claiming male residents as her husband. 'We humor her,' they said. 'Nothing untoward, you understand,' all said with a smirk."

"Interesting. Does that worry you?"

"Romance is not the Captain's strong suit. I saw the Colonel in the mess hall. Big, imposing woman. Loud voice. Gray bobbed hair with just a hint of mustache gracing her upper lip. She's in an advanced state of dementia. Her swings are wider than the Captain's."

"You're comfortable with his placement? Comfortable everything's under control?"

"Yes, everything's under control. Going so well I feel I'm riding for a fall."

"Guilt is a virtue." Kim rises. "I'll leave so you can get ready."

At the Memory Care Center, Barb strides with plate and bag toward the entry door expecting to see the Captain. Nothing. Inside, she walks to his apartment and knocks, pacing and smiling while she waits. No answer. She places the plate and bag on the floor and walks to the mess hall. No one. She walks to the office and asks for him.

"Check the day room," the aide says. "I saw him playing cards earlier."

When Barb enters the day room, the Captain is seated at a table, his back to her. He is seated with a woman in a pink sweater. The Captain rests his arm on her shoulder and drums her neck with his fingers. Beside them a large woman stands in khaki blouse and slacks. Barb walks to the Captain's side. He continues to play, unaware. The pink lady deals the cards and coaches him, points to cards to play. "The ten on the jack," she chirps.

"Captain." Barb taps his shoulder.

He turns his head and stares at her, his eyes adrift.

"Captain, are you ready for lunch?"

"Oh, my, my." The pink lady smiles. "Lowell, look who's here."

He sits immobile and glares at Barb with steel-blue eyes.

Barb reaches for him. "Captain, it's noon and I came to join you for lunch."

"Who are you?" His voice is muted, his tone serene but alert. "What do you want?"

"Captain, it's me, Barb. Your wife."

He attempts to stand. The chair tips. "Who?" he asks with a cynical smile.

The Colonel reaches and grabs Barb's shoulder. "You. Not his wife." She pulls at her sweater. Barb feels the gold chain tug her neck.

She struggles free and circles the table toward the Captain, now seated. He cowers when she grabs his arm. He shrugs his shoulders, lifts his hands, palms up in surrender, and utters a nervous chuckle.

"Captain, please. Please."

He gazes at the pink lady, at the Colonel, at Barb. He reaches for the pink lady's arm, first one hand, then two.

Barb stumbles out of the room, grabs the handrail, and staggers down the hall, past the Captain's apartment. She stops, kicks the plate of cookies, and continues down the long aisle toward the glass entry door where sunlight streams. She pushes the buzzer allowing the door to open. An office voice from the speaker says, "Have a nice day."

She stands on the porch and deep-breathes warm spring air. Again, again.

From behind, a lone bird honks and flies low, casting its shadow on the walk in front of her. She reaches to finger her cross and chain.

Nothing.

She negotiates the steps, facing the unrelenting sun, the brazen optimism of spring.

HAMSTER

"This is Tim Kelly, signing off for Wednesday's edition of 'Happy Hours,' KBOB's musical marathon from four to six weekdays. Time for me to go home and feed the kids. Until tomorrow, be good to each other. Love ya." He triggers his theme song, removes the headset, and kisses his reflected image in the glass of Studio B.

Listeners know who the kids are—two hamsters, Ham and Cheese. Listeners also know Tim is recently divorced, and when ex-wife Paige scuttled the marriage, she retained the assets. Listeners know all about Tim. He's chatty and can't keep his personal life private.

"Is nothing sacred?" Paige asked when he detailed their anniversary weekend on the air. What she wore, what she looked like, what she smelled like. He walked his listeners though dinner, through the spa bath, to the hotel's bedroom door, then segued into "Afternoon Delights."

"This isn't junior high," Paige said. "I'm outta here."

Paige bankrolled the Kelly household; Tim's salary at KBOB was pocket change. She hired the attorney, retained the house and furniture, her Infiniti, IRA, and stock portfolio. Tim, representing himself, settled for the hamsters and his rusty Dodge Horizon.

Tim pressured Manny Sanchez into tuning his radio to KBOB. They've been friends since college when Tim hosted a radio call-in show on campus. Tim, a known quantity, turned heads when they walked into Illiterati, the student hangout. Manny bought the beer and handpicked from Tim's rebounds. "You can meet a new groupie every night," Tim had said.

Tim called Manny during the divorce and asked for lodging *until I get my act together*, which Manny knew would be never. "One caveat," Tim said. "I'm light on personal property like furniture, lawnmowers, and big-ticket appliances. But I do have what means the most to me—Ham and Cheese."

HAMSTER

"What?" Manny asked.

"My hamsters. But not to worry. They can live in the garage with Beyond."

"Beyond?"

Tim chuckled. "Thanks for asking. My rusty blue Horizon. Beyond, the Blue Horizon."

Nothing had changed. Tim moved in and, as instructed, parked in the garage to keep Beyond out of sight.

Manny's house is classic two-story colonial—white narrow-lap siding, black shutters, red geranium window boxes below small-paned windows. Inside, authentic colonial furnishings—maple floors, braided rugs, six Windsor chairs around a cherry dining table. Rock fireplace with a brass eagle and pewter candlesticks. A million books, some first edition. Tim lives in the expansion space apartment above the garage.

Monday noon, and while Tim prepares his throat for broadcasting, he stands before the sink, on tiptoes to see into the Moroccan-tiled mirror frame. He has counted the bathrooms in the house and settled on five if he includes the half-bath in the kitchen. Bedrooms? Maybe six.

Weeks later, Tim walks down the stairs and retrieves the hamsters. Manny sits in the library at his laptop surfing the Internet for real estate. In Spain. He's of Spanish descent, Cordoban, and curious of his lineage. He inherited a patch of property in Cordoba he knows nothing about. Nothing, except he pays a modest amount to the local province in taxes each year and receives an equally modest income. From his father's recollection, it's an olive grove. Or it was a hundred years ago.

Manny baffles Tim by spending the day writing his memoirs. The estate and his genealogy intrigue him. He fantasizes finding renowned statesmen and artists on the family tree, but expects rogues or indulgent landed gentry. He knows he's a distant cousin and namesake of Manuel Rodriguez Sanchez, the matador. It'll take months to visit the courthouses, the churches and graveyards, meet the remnants of his family. And why rent a small room at an inn when the real estate market is so attractive? Chalets, villas, *fincas*, all at depressed prices. Maybe he'll stay. Maybe he'll find a castle and princess, maybe find his soul. Maybe not.

"How goes the search?" Tim walks in the library carrying

the kids.

"You can buy a dozen *cortijos* on the Andalusia countryside," Manny says. "There's a glut of high-end properties. At unbelievable prices."

"Are you going?"

Manny shrugs his shoulders.

"What does that mean for me and the kids?"

"Grab a couple beers and we'll talk."

Manny tells Tim about the plan. Tim will have to leave the house. Maintaining this property is not a responsibility to which Tim is accustomed. But . . . but Manny has talked to the widow next door, Maria Alexander. Manny is her unofficial guardian and chauffeur. Before Manny could tell Maria of his travel plan to Spain, he had to have a replacement Guy Friday. Maria lives alone in a house bigger than Manny's. No one uses the second floor. Maria agreed to meet Tim and consider a lodging arrangement, although she stressed one point. "I will not ride in that rattletrap car of his."

"No problem," Manny says. "I'll leave the Lexus in the garage."

"Try not to gawk, Tim, when you see Maria's decorating scheme. She has a hodgepodge of a dozen eras, but no furnishings younger than a hundred years." They ring the doorbell and listen for her tapping her way in the foyer.

"What do you want?" they hear from inside.

"Alms for the poor," Manny says.

"Come on in, whippersnapper."

Inside, off the foyer, a green leather fainting couch occupies half a pink-walled parlor. Crystal beads drip from a Tiffany lampshade. The walls are crammed with Turkish tapestries, oval framed portraits of a jolly bearded man and braided-hair woman, oil paintings in gilded frames. In the living room, crossed Civil War swords reign over the white marble fireplace. A suit of armor stands in the corner holding a tray of aperitif glasses.

"Have a seat," Maria says as she taps her way to a red velvet boudoir chair in the sunroom. "It's a beautiful view of the garden; at least they say it is." She lifts her glasses on her nose and peers out the window.

Manny walks to a gold frieze loveseat. Tim gawks at the rooms. French provincial tables, Moroccan rugs, silver candelabras, maroon drapes and valances the density of carpeting.

"I'd offer you coffee, but I'd likely spill it." Maria laughs. "Getting old is the shits."

"Better than the alternative," Manny offers.

"Cripes. How would you know?"

"Just trying to humor you, Dearie." Manny points to Tim. "I brought my live-in friend to meet you. Maria, this is Tim."

Maria scans the room, lands on Tim, and studies him over the rim of her glasses. "Huh. You the radio guy? I pictured tall, dark, and handsome. What are you, five-foot six?"

"Five-foot eight, ma'am."

"Bullshit. Unless you're on your tippy toes." She stands tall, chin up, chest out. "This is five-foot eight." She leans forward, steadies herself on the chair, and wrinkles her glasses up her nose. "You do have a great radio voice. Do the world a favor and don't switch to television."

"No, ma'am. You listen to the show?"

"I like your show. Too much schmaltzy music though. You need more rock and roll." She wiggles her hips, then steadies herself on the chair.

Tim glances for a place to sit, a chair that won't collapse. He spots a raised wooden bench with carved angels on the head rest, likely from a European cathedral. He sits and pounds an imaginary gavel. "The meeting will come to order."

"You're crazy," she cackles.

"Therein lies his charm." Manny laughs.

"You're looking for temporary lodging." Maria attempts to focus. "I never fancied myself in the hospitality business, although," she swings her arm, "this place is bigger than a hotel."

"And more interesting." Tim swings his arm in a mock gesture. "I'm sure every piece has a story."

"Wrong. Every piece has a price. My late husband was a compulsive buyer. We'd walk into an antique store and he'd say, 'There's something we don't have—a stuffed peacock.' Check out the attic." She dabs an imaginary tear. "Lovable old fart, but he had a few loose screws."

"In case we can put an arrangement together," Manny interjects, "do you have questions, Maria? Care to state the house rules of conduct?"

"The rules are simple. Mind your own beeswax, no friends over unless I meet them first, put your dirty dishes in the dishwasher, do your own laundry." Maria points her cane at Tim. "I can be a mean son-of-a-bitch if you cross me." She smiles. "But I can be a honey bun if you treat me right."

"Of course, I'd be willing to help around the house, around the yard," Tim says.

"You won't touch a thing around here. If you do, you'll answer to the housekeeper and the lawn guy. They're both meaner than me. Your job will be to squire me to the clinic, the grocery store, and the beauty shop once a week. And not in that rusty piece of crap you drive."

Manny pulls keys from his pocket. "I'll give him these."

Tim squirms on the bench. "I'm sure Manny mentioned my two precious kids, the hamsters."

"Criminy sakes. I know all about Ham and Eggs."

"Ham and Cheese," Tim corrects.

"Whatever. They can live in the garage. And, you." She points to Tim with her cane. "Pick a room upstairs. I'd suggest the one in the back of the house. It has a nice view of the garden and an even nicer view of the toilet across the hall. Check it out."

Tim walks to the grand staircase, climbs a few steps, and turns. He places a hand on his hip and raises the other arm. "I'm ready for my close-up, Mr. DeMille."

"Do you think you can tolerate the guy?" Manny asks.

Tim listens from the upstairs bedroom door.

"On one condition." Maria sounds concerned. "You come back. Don't find some storybook castle and hot *senorita* and settle down to raise olives."

"If I buy a castle, I'll buy the one down the road for you."

Tim checks the bedroom, the bath, the garden view and closes the bedroom door.

"Spooky," Tim says from the staircase. "The back bedroom with all the mounted animal heads. It looks like something from Dr. Seuss."

"I'll have the housekeeper change the linen." Maria waves her arms. "And throw extra sheets over the critters. When are you leaving, Manny?"

"Monday morning. Tim will drive me to the airport." Manny touches Maria's hand. "Do you think it will work?"

Maria twirls her cane. "What the hell . . ."

"With your permission, I'll be over after work Monday," Tim says. "I should be able to make the move in one armload.

HAMSTER

Two, counting the kids."

"You and Manny, you're an unlikely combination." Maria sits across the kitchen table from Tim and watches him devour a bowl of soup.

Tim grins. "He had the cash. I had the cache."

"Cripes all Friday," Maria says. "You slurp just like my late husband." She folds her hands in prayer and looks skyward. "May his soul rest in peace."

"Today is beauty shop day, right?" Tim crushes crackers in his bowl.

Maria has scheduled her appointments to accommodate Tim's shift at KBOB. He'll drop her at Salon Chic on the way to work and pick her up two hours later. In Manny's Lexus.

"I must say, you have beautiful silver hair. And a full head of it."

"My crowning glory," Maria says, fluffing it. "But I don't go to the shop to get my hair done. I go to keep up on who's doing what to whom. And find out what lies this town is telling about me."

Tim places his bowl in the dishwasher. "You play cards?" he asks.

"I'll whip your ass in cribbage. There's a board on the sunroom table."

"Mind if I bring in the kids?"

Maria dismisses him with a wave of her hand and taps her way to the sunroom. Tulips bloom in blots of color in the backyard garden. The apple tree hovers like a white cloud. She opens the window to the smell of lilacs.

"The kids get lonesome out there," Tim says. He waits for a response.

"Deal the cards. You'll have to peg for me. But don't get a bug up your ass and cheat. I can count."

"Want to hold one of the kids?" Tim asks. He hands her a hamster. "This is Cheese, I think. Tough to tell them apart."

"Male or female?"

"Who knows? They know. Aren't they about the cutest things?"

Maria holds the animal and strokes its fur. "Soft."

"And beautiful. And smart. I give them a hundred affirmations a day. They have the best self-image of any animals on the planet."

She holds the hamster at arm's length and stares at it, at Tim. "Huh. There's something to the old adage about pets resembling their owners. Cute. Round furry face. Beady eyes." She laughs. "I feel sorry for them though."

"Why? They lead a charmed life. Three meals a day. Someone who cares for them. A space where they can run and go nowhere."

"Like I said, pets resemble their owners. Now deal."

They play a few hands, Maria humming and snapping her cards when she scores big. Tim, corralling the hamsters on the floor with his slippers, recognizing the right play seconds after he played the wrong card, counting Maria's points aloud while he moves the pegs.

Spring sun floods the room, and a slight breeze billows the Irish lace curtains. With it, the aroma of blossoms and the trill of finches at the feeder.

"Saved by the bell," Tim says as the grandfather clock in the foyer chimes one o'clock. "Time for me to shower up and gargle fifteen minutes to get the perfect coloratura vibrato."

Maria fingers the board, figures she's about two hands from winning. She hasn't played cribbage since her husband died. She shuffles the oversize cards with large numerals and exaggerated figures. "That was fun."

"Who is this vision?" Tim opens the car door for Maria at Salon Chic. Her silver hair is rinsed to a dashing blond and falls low across her forehead to a rolled flip.

"My spring do," Maria says. "Like it?"

"Makes you ten years younger. Maybe twenty." He slides into the leather driver's seat. "*Quo vadis*, ma'am?"

"Home, James." She drops the visor and peers into the mirror. She extends her hands and splays her fingers, tipped in hot pink polish. "Good radio show today," she says, "but it could be better."

"I played 'Maria' for you."

"I got that. We talked about your show. Maggie doesn't often listen to it. Too chatty, she says, and I agree."

Tim snaps a look at her, not accustomed to negative criticism.

"We don't need to know Jo Stafford married Paul Weston

and the names of the Rat Pack and the seamy side of Doris Day."

Tim stares ahead and hears himself breathe through his nose.

"And who allows Lenny of Lenny's Lawn Service to voice his own commercials? His nasal twang drives listeners crazy."

"He pays in cash."

"In an earlier life, I was a media consultant. You couldn't afford me, but I'll give you a few tips. For starters, cut the gab. Everybody likes the *feed the kids* bit at signoff. Add another trademark. At the end of the Friday show, play 'It's a Wonderful World.' Louie Armstrong."

Tim taps his fingers on the wheel. "I like that."

"There's more, but I'll give it to you in small doses."

"Can't wait," Tim says. "And I have news for you. I was asked to emcee the Hospital Auxiliary Ball. Care to be my date?"

She raises her arms, "I don't have a thing to wear." She relaxes. "Take that back. I have two closets full of party dresses."

"I'll wear a tux, so the sky's the limit."

"Count me in. When is it?"

"Same day as your salon appointment."

On the evening of the ball, Tim stands in the foyer struggling with a cuff link. In the gilded mirror, he sees a stubby, white-jacketed smiley figure, like the plastic groom doll on a wedding cake. He rises on his tiptoes. *Elevator shoes. Buy them.*

Maria opens her bedroom door wearing a silky black dress slit to the knee. She places one hand on her hip, the other on the door frame. "Fasten your seat belts. It's going to be a bumpy night." Her neck, wrists, and fingers dazzle with diamonds.

"Wow."

"I eschewed the heels," she says, grabbing her cane. "No sense falling on my keister."

"Look at you." Tim walks to her. "You're beautiful." He stares at her face. "One problem though. Your lipstick is crooked. If you have a tissue and the tube, I'll fix it. Sit here."

Maria sits, removes her glasses, and tilts her head back into Tim's palm. He brushes her lips with the tissue. Her eyes are closed. Tim sees her at close range. Sees her creamy porcelain skin, her classic cheek bones, her squared chin. This precious object in the palm of his hand, dear and fragile, makes him giddy, like holding a newborn baby. This is Helen of Troy with shimmery summer-blond hair, piled high by Maggie this afternoon.

"What's the hold up?" Maria opens one eye and sees Tim inches away.

"You are one beautiful woman. So beautiful I could kiss you."

"Don't."

Tim applies the lipstick and hands her a cosmetic case mirror.

Maria moves the mirror forward and backward. "Looks pretty good for an old bag."

"We'd better be going." Tim checks his watch. "We're late already."

The Lexus waits for them outside the garage. Tim waves. "Bye, bye, kids."

"Don't wait up for us," Maria adds.

"How do you want me to introduce you?" Tim asks.

"Not as your mother. And not as Maria Alexander. I've always wanted to be Brandy. Introduce me as Brandy Alexander, your live-in girlfriend."

"You'll probably know more guests than I will."

"Well, I'll know the hostess Louella. And Maggie and Bear Braham. Maggie said they'll be there if Bear can fit into his sport coat. How do you want me to introduce you?"

"I'll think about it."

"Tim, you're late." Guests smile, turn, and whisper, "Who's he with?" The chair of the auxiliary plows through the crowd. "Tim. Finally. We had about given up on you."

Tim shakes her hand. "I had to feed the kids. Louella, I'd like you to meet my friend Brandy Alexander."

Louella stares at Brandy. "Maria, you charlatan." She hugs her. "So good to see you again. Nice hair." She puts her hand over her mouth. "This party could use some class." She points to the diamonds. "And some donations." She takes Tim's hand. "Is this woman always late?"

"How can you make a grand entrance if you're the first one at the party?" Maria laughs. "Where's the bar?"

A stout man in a KBOB T-shirt under a sport coat grabs Tim's hand. "Finally. Welcome."

"Brandy, this is Syd, station manager. I mentioned to him

you were a media consultant in an earlier life. Stick with him while I check out the PA system."

Maria links her arm in Syd's. "Interesting programming you have. I shared a few ideas with Tim."

"I'd like to hear them," Syd says. "Do you mix business with pleasure?"

"Best offer I've had all day," Maria says, as they walk to the bar, leaving Tim standing.

Tim wrangles through the crowd after his sound check. Maria is easy to spot, her blond hair the highest point in the room. Guests crowd around her, smiling, laughing. She holds a glass in one hand, pats her hair with the other. "Why, thank you," he hears her say. "It's my spring do, courtesy of Salon Chic. I love that place because . . ." She pauses. "Because it's so much more than a beauty shop. I learn more there than I do from the ten o'clock news. And Maggie," she waves her hands in a time-out motion, "limits the customers' organ recitals to five minutes."

"Organ recitals?" someone asks.

"Whose organs are functioning, whose aren't."

Tim reaches for her arm. "I'm on stage in a few minutes. Don't steal all my fans."

After Tim praises the hostess, hypes the hospital auxiliary, and entertains the crowd with familiar banter, he returns to Maria. She stands holding court with admirers half her age. Maggie and Bear stand behind her, Maggie aglow, sipping wine. Bear fidgets, one foot to the other, tugging his collar, buttoning and unbuttoning his coat.

Tim slips an arm around Maggie's waist. "Recognize any of the hairdos?"

"About fifty percent. The rest are men." She points her glass to Maria. "What do you think of Marie Antoinette?"

"Never been lovelier. Let's crash through these groupies."

"Maggie. So glad to see you," Maria trills. "It's been what? Hours? And Tim. Such comfort and ease on stage, and such mellifluous tones."

Tim hides his face in his hands. "Aw, shucks."

"And Bear," Maria continues, "I didn't recognize you in civvies. Wow." She scans him head to toe and fondles his muscled arm. "Better keep your eye on this hottie, Maggie. Lots of old-money widows in the crowd tonight."

Bear lifts her hand and kisses it.

"That's quite a strain you're putting on those coat buttons, Bear. Somehow, when I see you in my fantasies, you're not wearing a coat. Not wearing much of anything." She roars and slaps him on the back. "I hear you're counting the days to retirement, Bear. What's next?"

"Please, Maria. Don't get him started. He'll talk about his Morgans."

"Continuing my fantasy," Maria says, "I see you as my private bodyguard, sleeping outside my bedroom on a stormy night, telling me a story if I'm frightened."

"Don't make him promise more than he can deliver," Maggie says.

Bear rolls his eyes.

"You're stunning, Maria," Maggie continues. "Clearly the belle of the ball."

"Thanks, Maggie." She primps her hair. "But back to you, Bear. I wonder if I might call you about a peeping tom in the neighborhood, or has that trick been overplayed?"

A man walks up to Bear and taps him on the arm. "Well, if it isn't Smokey. Without his funky hat and shiny badge." He extends a hand to Maria. "Wayne's the name. New here and eager to make friends."

Maria extends her hand but says nothing.

Wayne turns to Tim. "And who might you be? And for god's sake, man, get off your knees and stand up." He slaps Tim on the back and giggles.

"I'm Tim Kelly, your emcee tonight."

"Is this your lady?" He turns to Maggie. "I don't know what she sees in you. Maybe the top of your head." He giggles.

"Is your wife here, Wayne?" Maria scans the room.

"Which one?" Wayne cackles and pats Maria on the butt.

Maria jumps. "Well, it's been a while since that happened."

Wayne turns back to Bear. "Is that all you stuffed in that coat, or are you packing a couple 45s?"

Bear pats his armpit. "Don't leave home without it."

"What brings you to Browns Prairie, Wayne?" Tim asks.

Wayne studies Tim's face. "Are you the dude on the radio with the guinea pigs?"

"Hamsters," Tim corrects him.

"Hamsters. That is one weird fetish. You maybe oughta try a

plastic doll. Less maintenance." He giggles and slaps Tim on the back again.

"Tim," Bear says. "Let's bring the ladies a drink. Care to join us, Wayne?"

Wayne bows to the ladies. "It was your pleasure to meet me," he says and walks with Bear and Tim.

They elbow through the crowd, out of Maria and Maggie's sight, and head for the porch.

"Hey," Wayne says. "The bar's over there."

"I know a shortcut," Bear says. "Follow me."

Bear closes the porch door behind Wayne and plants his hands on his hips. "I know who you are, Wayne Casperson. Recently from Milwaukee. Conviction for drug trafficking. A couple outstanding warrants. We have enough goods on you to book you tonight."

Tim scans the porch for an easy exit. Wayne forces a grin and shrugs his shoulders.

"But you know what, Wayne? We're not gonna do that. We're more interested in the conduit. We're going after the Big Guy. For us, you're nothing but bait. We'll wait. Your day will come later. Unless Big Guy does our job for us."

Tim wants to hide behind Bear. *Conduit for what? Big guy? Are they talking murder?*

Wayne smiles and the porch light reflects off a row of gleaming teeth. His body is dwarfed in Bear's shadow. "Guess the party's over," he says and turns to leave. "Have a nice day."

Tim feels it's safe to project a tough guy image. "Before you go," he says, "why in god's name would you introduce yourself to a sheriff?"

Wayne giggles. "He has a reputation of being a softie. Doesn't want trouble in his county. Won't pursue it. And he's a short-timer. Wants to ride out the rest of his days without issues." Wayne pauses. "On the street, they call him Teddy Bear Braham."

"Get outta here," Bear snaps.

Tim follows Bear through the crowd to rejoin Maria and Maggie. "Where are the drinks?" Maggie asks.

Bear shakes his head. "They were out of Dad's Root Beer."

At eleven-thirty, Tim finds Maria regaling another group. He listens to her describe a flight with her late husband, *bless his soul,* from Tokyo. "He sat across the aisle from a young student who was reading a textbook and said, 'I've heard flights go faster if you strike up a conversation.' The student put his finger in the book. 'What would you like to talk about?' My late husband leaned across the aisle. 'How about nuclear physics?'

"The student gave him a puzzled look. 'Let me pose a question first,' he said. 'Sheep, horses, and cows all eat the same hay, yet sheep excrete pellets, cows excrete pies, and horses excrete biscuits. Why?' My husband shrugged his shoulders. 'Well,' the student said, 'if you don't know shit, why should I talk to you about nuclear physics?'"

Tim reaches for Maria. "Time for me to bring this party to a close. Join me up front for a curtain call." Maria follows Tim to the stage, hugging ladies, tickling men on the chin as she passes.

Tim takes the mic. "Ladies and gents, what a great evening. And what a great cause. Time to sign off. But no one passes *go* without a signed pledge card. Louella is at the door." He waves to her.

"I want to thank my chaperone for accompanying me tonight. Marie, Brandy, come on up." The crowd applauds, whistles, chants "Brandy. Brandy. Brandy." Tim reaches for her as she walks onstage.

"I have to get this little lady home before midnight or she'll turn into a . . . into a . . ."

Maria reaches for the mic. "Into a crabby old bag. Sorry to call this party to a halt, folks. This is the most fun I've ever had with clothes on." She waits for the laugh. "But Timmy has to get home—to feed the kids."

The audience hoots.

"Thanks," she says. "It's been a slice of heaven. Until next time, as he says, be good to each other. Love ya." She grabs Tim's arm and leads him off stage.

"You beat me at my own game," Tim says the next morning. "You got more laughs than I did." He serves Maria coffee at a windowed kitchen alcove, the table between them covered with a Gauguin print tablecloth. A warm breeze waves lace café curtains.

Maria lifts her cup and inhales the aroma, her ringed porcelain hand mimicking the rose design of English china. She sips her coffee and grins.

"Syd said he plans to put you on a retainer as media consultant." Tim eyes her over his coffee cup. "As your agent, I get

HAMSTER

five percent."

"Five percent of nothing is nothing."

"And you're having lunch with him?"

Maria points her spoon. "Is somebody jealous? Watch your ratings rise. And I get five percent of your pay raise."

Tim pours another cup of coffee. "Let's sit in the sunroom."

The gardener mowed the lawn the day before, and a heady aroma of chlorophyll trails a breeze. Squirrels chatter under the birdbath. Hummingbirds dart like fighter pilots around the feeder.

Tim slumps in a rattan settee and stares at the lawn and garden. "Makes life worth living. Now, what can we do for a follow-up? Or have we peaked?"

"Lordy, no. You know anything about motorcycles?"

Tim jolts forward. "Hell, yes. I know bikes. Harley is my middle name. I rode before I walked."

"There's a 1946 Indian Chief in the garage. Another of my late husband's extravagances. He never rode it, but he had it serviced every year."

"I want to see it," Tim says. "A vintage Indian? What's the story?"

"It belonged to the New Jersey State Patrol. Has a sidecar. Gleaming black. Shiny as a baby's butt. I'd like to go for a ride."

"I'm your man. I led the first Ronald McDonald Benefit Ride in 2001."

"My son wants it when I kick the bucket."

"You have a son?"

"He lives in California. Hear from him once a month. See him once a year."

"Does he know about me?"

"What he doesn't know won't hurt him. Let's look at the bike."

Tim gulps his coffee and follows Maria as she taps her way to the garage, past the hamster cage, past two empty stalls to a third stall, walled and secured by a locked service door. Maria unlocks the door and turns on the lights. A shrouded vehicle sets in the center of the stall, and on the far side, several smaller shrouded objects. "My late husband had a weakness for antiques." She laughs. "It worked for me."

Tim lifts the canvas wrap over the center vehicle. "Holy Toledo, a Corvette. 1956. I'm trembling."

"We should take it for a spin sometime," Maria says. "Come

look at the Indian."

Tim follows her around the Corvette to a white-blanketed object. She lifts the cover. "Presto."

"Don't do this to me," Tim says, grabbing his chest. "You hear that thump? That's my heart." He reaches to touch a fender and stops an inch short. "Exquisite."

"When do you want to go?" she asks. "How about a trip to Duluth on your weekend off?"

"You got yourself a date, sweetheart."

"I'll ask the cleaning lady to feed the kids while we're gone."

Saturday morning, Tim presses the garage door opener. "Open Sesame." He lifts the white blanket covering the Indian Chief like a magician ready to expose a table full of rabbits. He places his hands on the handlebars. "Magic," he whispers. He slides a leg over the rear fender and sits on the fringed leather seat. The throne. He lowers his head into imaginary wind. "Vrrroooom." He slides off and lifts the kickstand upright. It's heavy. Heavier than he remembers.

He rolls it out of the garage, throws a leg over, and sits. His heart beats. He breathes in short huffs. He closes the choke, retards the spark, primes the bowl, the sequence as natural as breathing. He turns the ignition on, engages the clutch, throttle wide open. He takes a deep breath and stands on the kickstart. He pushes once, twice, three times. The engine fires and roars. He throttles back, feels the vibration, the sensuality, the majesty. He glances up and down the street, hoping to wave to neighbors. He slides the vintage aviator goggles over his head and glides down the drive.

Tim returns from the gas station and roars up the drive, makes a U-turn, and glides to a stop. "This baby is ready to roll. Are you?"

Maria stands in her white leather jacket and fringed gloves, holding a helmet and goggles. "This is insanity," she yells. "I love it."

"Get in," Tim says. "Slip on your helmet."

"It'll screw up my hair."

"Which is more important? Your hair or your brain?"

She bites her lip. "I'll have to think about that."

She steps into the sidecar, stashes the helmet between her

HAMSTER

legs, and slides on the goggles. "Let's go. I'm so excited I could pee my pants."

Tim eases out the drive, down the street, to the highway. He stops at the sign and removes his helmet. "How's it going?"

"Sweet, but it smells smoky. And it's bumpy."

"These old bikes don't have much for shocks. That's all part of the package."

On the highway, Tim glances at Maria. Her head tilts back, her hair billows, her eyes close. She mouths a song. *Born to be wiiiillllllldddd.*

At the halfway mark, Tim stops. "Want to keep going?"

Maria tames her hair. "For the rest of my life."

"Just in time for lunch," Tim says as they park at a restaurant on the North Shore. I'll order sandwiches, and we'll eat on a rock by the water."

They drive to an empty scenic overlook parking lot and walk to the shore. Maria sits on a boulder and stares at the horizon. "Heaven on earth," she says. "What power. What magnificence."

Tim opens the sandwich boxes. Gulls circle overhead. A cool breeze off the lake sways wild roses above the shoreline.

"Well," Maria says, "I've accomplished two of my bucket list tasks since I met you. I always wanted to be a blond, and I've always wanted to be a motorcycle mama. One more task to go. A huge party."

"You make it sound like you have a deadline."

"At my age I'm on borrowed time," Maria says. "Carpe Diem." Maria places her sandwich in the box and sits with her knees tucked under her chin. "And I've got this day seized by the balls."

Tom laughs at her. "What would your son say if he saw you now? Does he know about our excursion?"

"Of course not. It's his weekend to call. I'll tell him about it."

"Do you want to head home today? Or maybe relax at a hotel tonight?"

"Hotel sounds good. Take me to dinner at an appropriate restaurant in Duluth. How about Grandma's? We'll drive back tomorrow morning."

"I'll find a high-end hotel on Park Point. Close to Grandma's. The Presidential suite. Peach down comforter folded back with Lady Godiva chocolates on the pillow. Ankle-deep plush carpet. Terrycloth robes in the bath. The windows ajar welcoming pristine Lake Superior air."

She smiles. "You ought to be a writer."

Noon Sunday, they pull into the home drive. "Great fun," says Maria. "Help me out of this cage. I'm stiff as a board." Tim lifts her arm and walks her to the front entry. "The phone's ringing," she says and unlocks the door. Tim walks to the mailbox, then follows her in.

"Just walked in," he hears her say. *Pause.* "Duluth, on the old Indian Chief." *Pause.* "No, stupid. I didn't drive. Tim did." *Pause.* "He's my in-house chauffeur. You sold my car, remember?" *Pause.* "No that's not why God created taxis. And if He did, He didn't create any in Browns Prairie. This isn't Los Angeles, you know." *Pause.* "Relax. The Indian Chief is not yours. Not until I croak. I have to go to the bathroom. Goodbye."

Tim sorts the mail, one letter with a foreign stamp. "A letter from Manny," Tim yells.

"Open it. I can't read."

"He says he's coming home next week. No, he didn't buy a castle. No, he didn't marry a *senorita*. No, he's not wired to grow olives. He'll call from New York City before he boards the plane."

"Great," Maria yells from the bathroom. "We'll celebrate."

"There's another letter from the Animal Rescue League. Looks like an invitation."

"Open it."

"*The SPCA requests the honour of your presence at the Annual Tuxes and Tails Ball. Saturday, May 30, 7 PM at Cranberry Falls Country Club. Tuxedos for the gentlemen. Gowns for the ladies. RSVP.*"

"Let's go," Maria says. "Manny will be home. RSVP for three. I wanted one final big party. This is it."

Tim drives the Lexus to the airport to meet Manny. Maria rides along and waits in the car. They see her wave when they walk out the Arriving Passengers turnstile.

"*Saludos, amigos,*" she yells.

"Sounds like she's in great form," Manny says.

"She made plans for you Saturday night. I hope you're free."

Manny opens the passenger car door and gives Maria a hug.

"Look at you," she says. "Tanned and handsome. Good trip?

HAMSTER

Find any interesting ornaments on your family tree?"

"More than I care to talk about." Manny slides into the driver's seat. "And you? Are we still speaking after I introduced you to Tim?"

"We had a ton of fun. And more to come."

"I hear you have plans for me Saturday night."

"I received an invitation for the Tuxedos and Tails Annual Benefit. I thought the three of us would raise the bar for elegance in this town. It's formal formal."

"Sounds great, unless Tim has plans to squire another lady."

"Not a good idea," Maria says. "The Benefit chair is a good friend of mine. Young, well-heeled widow. Red-headed spitfire. Dedicated to stray animals. Convinced every animal . . . *every* animal deserves a home. It's her challenge to find it. I hear she has dozens of orphan pets at her estate."

"Hamsters?" Tim asks.

"No hamsters I know of." She turns to Manny. "Do you see where I'm going with this?"

Tim leans forward. "Tell me more. I think I'm falling in love."

SPIDER

"You know, Bear, it started with an apparition. A mirage. The first time I saw him, he was standing in the driveway. In front of the garage. He wore brown. Stood beside a brown sedan. Just stood there with a pleasant smile. Then he turned and disappeared." Rolf combed fingers through his graying hair, down smooth-shaven cheeks. He scanned the front yard from the porch glider. "Was I seeing things? I checked for tire tracks, foot prints. Nothing." He tilted forward, talking into his hands. "And my grandson..."

Bear visited Rolf on his annual trip to St. Cloud with Maggie where she attended the Hair and Beauty Expo. Rolf had told the grandson frustration story before. Bear was patient. He'd listen.

"Maybe you're working too hard." Bear nursed a cup of coffee. "Maybe you expected too much."

Early Saturday morning sun melted the treetops across the bay of Deer Lake, reflecting yellow-green on the water. A family of Canada geese stood silhouetted on the shore, the gander tall and alert, the goose pecking at clover, the huddled goslings stretching and preening tiny wings.

"Maybe I just screwed up my last chance." Rolf scraped his chair backwards and stood. "I think better when I'm walking." He snapped his fingers at the sleeping yellow Lab. "C'mon, Buck." Buck rose from under the glider and ran to the steps.

Bear gulped his coffee. "You're the boss."

Dandelion stems stood naked, their seed carpeting the ground like late snow. Waxy leaves on the cottonwoods fluttered with the breeze in a dainty dance, floating fuzz puffs in the air.

"You ought to do something about those dandelions." Bear strove to lighten the moment.

"They're green." Rolf kicked at a stem and kept walking. "I

thought if I could spend time with the kid, lure him away from his mother for a few days, I might help him, might get something started between us."

Bear slapped him on the back. "You act more scared than frustrated."

"Maybe I am scared. Maybe I'm losing my mind."

Rolf's house stood on high land with back-to-nature landscaping—a view of Deer Lake, the horse pasture framed in split-rail fencing, the spruce-lined driveway. From his porch, Rolf could watch his Morgan horses graze or sip a glass of wine as the sun set over the lake.

Both Bear and Rolf farmed, Rolf for a tax dodge, Bear to unwind after a harrowing day as deputy sheriff. Both attended Browns Prairie high school, separated during their working years, now reconnected thanks to the North Central Morgan Association. Rolf looked at home in suit and tie; Bear owned neither. Rolf graduated from the Carlson School of Management, founded an accounting firm in St. Cloud and retired, married and divorced twice. Bear attended Community College, earned a Criminal Justice certificate, and married his high school sweetheart. When quizzed about their seemingly incompatible friendship, Rolf said, "We don't compete in anything. I'm good for occasional financial advice. He's good for an occasional welding job."

They walked past the barn, past the silo, past the pole building to an empty square of concrete. "What happened to the windmill?" Bear asked.

"It jammed in a storm, and I wasn't about to climb the ladder. I pulled it down. I miss it though. The staccato beat. The wind singing through the blades."

The morning was calm, as if a storm had passed. Bear tolerated silence for a few minutes while they walked to the pasture. "Tell me about your grandson's visit."

Rolf unlatched the gate and followed the fence, side-kicking bull thistles under the electric wire, silent.

"One thing about kids," Bear said, "they're pliable. One mood, one mindset today, another tomorrow."

Rolf tramped ahead, batting weeds.

Bear followed, watching for imbalance, limping, erratic motion. "Take my Brian, for example. A more peace-loving kid you'd never meet. Then he joins the Marine Corps."

Rolf stopped. The powdery blue summer sky shone like a calendar picture. Oaks sported shining foliage; the pines, tender candles. Spider webs in the grass flashed intricate patterns of diamonds. Buck trailed into the woods and scattered a flock of cawing crows. "I wanted this to be his someday. It won't happen."

"Fill me in." Bear leaned on a fence post. "You were looking forward to the visit. Something went wrong."

Rolf grabbed a downed branch and tossed it over the fence. "Where do I start?" He lifted his cap. "I contacted my ex-daughter-in-law and asked if grandson Derek could spend a weekend with me. She sounded eager to make it happen, said he was out of high school for the summer, hadn't found a real job, had time on his hands. Sounded like he was a pain in the ass for her. She asked when could I pick him up. I said I'd like to talk to Derek first. There was a long pause, and then she said she was sure he'd want to come to the farm. Sure, like if he didn't come, he'd have to clean the garage. I drove down last Saturday morning. When I arrived, they were both sleeping."

Rolf took a deep breath and shook his head. He stared at his world of summer green, his legacy.

"I rang the doorbell two or three times, then knocked. She came to the door looking like she was rode hard and put away wet. She roused Derek, and, I swear, he sleepwalked to the car and nodded off the entire trip. No breakfast, no coffee, nothing. When we got home, we walked around the farm. I wanted to show him what someday might he his. No discussion of inheritance, you understand." He stopped, rubbed his eyes, cleared his throat.

"We walked this same path . . . There's that feeling again, like I can see the future but can't remember the past. God, it's unnerving." Rolf scanned the pasture, the trees, looking for clues. A warm breeze hummed through the Norway pines and ruffled his hair. Sunlight filtered through the branches. Green grass, green trees, green brush, everything green. And crows. The ozone smell after rain.

"We'll see a snake soon, I swear," Rolf whispered. "You'll hear deer flies."

"Rolf, take it easy. What's your mother's maiden name?"
"Saunders."
"What's the capital of South Dakota?"
"Pierre."
"What's your zip code?"

SPIDER

"Look, I'm not crazy. Yet. Have you ever had the feeling you've lived this moment before? Like you know what'll happen next but can't remember the chain of thoughts that got you there?"

"Let's head back. I'll brew a pot of coffee."

"We were on this same path, Derek and I. A snake was sleeping in that sand patch. A blow snake. A big, harmless blow snake. Derek freaked." Rolf glanced back at the house. He jerked. A car in the driveway. A brown sedan and a man standing beside it. In a moment, he disappeared. He and the car disappeared. "Did you see that, Bear? Did you see that man?"

"C'mon, Rolf. We're going home."

Days earlier, Rolf and Derek had walked the fence line, Rolf ahead, Derek steps behind. The sun had yet to thaw mid-morning chill. Derek scanned the path, watching where he stepped in his red high-top Nikes, laces flapping.

Rolf pointed to a burr oak. "Do you know what that is?"

"A tree."

"Do you know what kind?"

Derek looked at his cell phone, his face hidden by a mop of unruly blond hair. "Hey, I don't get a signal here?" He tucked the phone in his baggy jeans, a studded belt riding on his hips.

"You'll survive." Rolf pointed to a honeysuckle. "Do you know what that is?"

"A flower."

"How about those big, black birds circling up there, squawking at us. They're crows."

"Can we shoot them?"

"Not unless you eat them. Your dad could identify hundreds of birds, knew every tree in the county. Won a blue ribbon for his leaf collection at the State Fair."

"I'm not my dad." He stopped and wrapped his arms around his thin chest lost in a baggy rock concert T-shirt. "I'm cold."

"Walk faster."

They neared a patch of sand where a snake slept, blending with scraps of branches and leaves. It coiled when it felt their footsteps, raised its flattened head, and hissed.

Derek jumped and screamed. "Kill it. Kill it."

"It's a blow snake. It's harmless. It's afraid of *you*."

Derek stood paralyzed, arms in the air. "Kill it." He eyed the snake. "Kill it." He stepped backwards.

"Take it easy. It won't hurt you."

"I'm going to the house. And I'm not coming back. I can't believe you don't kill snakes."

"Snakes predate us. We're the intruders, not the snakes."

Derek crossed through the barbed wire fence and walked toward the house, beating the ground ahead of him with a stick.

"Wait up," Rolf called. "I'm right behind you. It's lunch time. Hungry?"

"No."

Rolf glared at him. "Well, you can sit with me while I eat."

A killdeer swooped out of pasture grass, squealing and screeching, and circled Buck. It landed, spread one wing, and faked a limp, then swooped around the Lab again.

"What's that?"

"A bird protecting its nest of babies," Rolf said. "Preservation of the species."

In the house, Rolf headed into the kitchen. "There's the bathroom if you want to wash up. And this will be your chair for the next couple days."

Derek stood in the doorway, hands in pockets. "I'll sit in the car."

"You'll sit in the house." Rolf took a deep breath. "Now, wash your hands."

Derek nibbled at a sandwich, looked out the window, checked his cell phone.

"There's a spot on the driveway where you can get a signal," Rolf said between bites. "You're not abandoned."

Derek sat against a wall where his dad's portrait hung. Phil, a young man in Army uniform. Healthy, handsome. Alive. Rolf glanced at Derek's face and his son's portrait. No resemblance. His son resembled his mother's side—tall, angular, dark-skinned. His grandson skipped a generation and resembled Rolf, his grandfather—slight build, light hair and complexion, large hands with long fingers. A pianist's hands, Rolf's mother had said. A carpenter's hands, according to his dad.

"After lunch, we can go horseback riding or fishing. Your choice."

Derek sipped his milk and put it down. "What is this, skim?"

"Have you ever ridden a horse?"

SPIDER

"No."

"I have just the horse for you. Easy going. No bad habits. Comfortable gait."

"I'm not riding a horse. My friend got bucked off and broke his arm. Not me."

"Guaranteed safe ride." Rolf circled an imaginary lasso. "We'll make you a cowboy."

"Not happening. I have these fingers to protect." He held up his hands. "I play guitar. Not taking chances."

"We can go fishing. The pan fish are biting. We can catch our supper."

"I don't have a license."

"You're a veteran's dependent. You don't need one," Rolf lied. "When was the last time you went fishing?"

"Never. And I hate fish."

"I'll eat yours. I cleaned the boat yesterday. We'll have to slide it into the lake and walk it to the dock."

"Are there snakes in the water?"

"No water snakes. Nothing to worry about. Just a short walk, a few yards in shallow water. Piece of cake. Speaking of, do you want dessert?"

"No."

"Stack your dishes in the sink. And grab a towel. I'll take bug spray. The deer flies are biting."

Derek grabbed his stick by the door and followed Rolf, beating the grass ahead of him. "What are those strings in the air? They're getting in my face."

"Spider webs." Rolf continued his path to the boat.

"Spiders. I'm getting out of here." He turned and ran toward the house.

"Get back here. Trust me. They're less bother than a housefly. Walk right behind me. I'll clear the path."

Derek stopped. "I hate spiders."

No snakes or spiders. Remember that.

At the dock, Derek slid out of his tenners and rolled up his jeans. He stood on the shore scanning the water, trembling while Rolf wrestled the boat in the lake. Buck jumped in the water rousing a family of mallards.

"What are those things swimming?" Derek asked.

"Minnows. There's a million of them. That's why we can't fish here. Too much food for the big fish. Wade in. I'll pull, you push."

Derek dangled a toe in the water. "You're sure there aren't snakes?"

Rolf rolled his eyes upward. "Positive."

Derek waded in, arms above his head, feeling his way forward on the lake bed, staring in the water. "What are those?"

"Those little critters spinning like tiny boats? They're water beetles."

"Do they sting?"

Rolf ignored him.

Derek stopped. "Those little fish are getting closer. Do they bite?"

"They're curious, not hungry."

"Are they piranhas?"

"Wrong hemisphere."

Derek reached the bow of the boat and walked behind, watching the shore. Rolf towed the boat and tied it to a pillar on the dock. "I'll mount the motor. You check those fishing rods and grab the bait can. We'll catch some crappies."

Derek stared at minnows swimming around his legs and swatted the water. He screamed, jumped from one foot to the other, waved his arms, screamed again. "It bit me. It bit me." He stumbled to the shore, trembling, screaming. "It bit me. I'm not going back in." He brushed his hand down his leg and screamed again. "Something's stuck on my leg. Get it off. Get it off."

"It's a leech, for god's sake. Just pull it off."

"I'm not touching it. Get it off."

Rolf jumped off the dock, checked an urge to kick Derek's ass. "It's really a blood sucker and you are one doomed dude."

Rolf remembered a paralyzing incident from his youth. Uncle Merle pitched hay from a wagon to form a haystack. Teenager Rolf stood atop the forming stack, taking hay from Merle's fork onto his own, lifting it to the middle, and tromping it. The stack grew to twelve feet, fourteen, sixteen. Rolf topped off the stack with a dome and craned his neck to see the ground. "How am I going to get down?"

"You got the law of gravity working for you." Merle jumped on the tractor. "Man up, kid."

Rolf stood, frozen.

Derek scrambled for shore and grabbed his shoes. "I'm going home. Take me home."

SPIDER

Bear poured coffee and carried it to the porch. "It might help to talk about it."

Rolf stared at his hands, rubbing them, pinching his fingers to prove they existed, to prove he could feel pain, to confirm he was alive. "I feel like I'm transparent, like I can see through me."

"Drink your coffee." Bear sat in a rocker. "Just wondering. Do you get into town much? Interface with your old friends at the office?"

"Not any more than I have to. Traffic congestion makes me nervous. How I did it all those years, I don't know. My office was on the sixth floor. I couldn't look down at the street from my window." He grinned an embarrassed grin. "Never rode in the tiny elevator either. Developed strong legs from all the stair climbing." He paused. "I'll hand it to Derek. He's front and center with his fears. I kept mine under wraps."

"Might be good for you to get out once in a while." Bear tried for a neutral tone. "I know how you feel about this place. Maybe have the guys out here for a poker party once a month."

Rolf stared at a bland summer sky. Stared as if he hadn't heard.

"You have me to talk to for the afternoon." Bear rocked, his hand on Buck's head. "Feel like talking?"

Rolf lifted his head, searching for courage, searching for words.

"Go ahead," Bear said. "Start at the beginning."

Rolf sat facing the lake, his homestead, his home. The apple orchard he and son Phil had planted, the cove they fished for bass, the tin shed they sided, the hip-roofed barn, the silo. And beyond, the pasture they fenced, the hay field they baled, the treed horizon where they hunted squirrels.

"Phil stayed with me when his mother left." Rolf fixed on a giant cottonwood in the yard. "Said he wanted to graduate with his friends. We got along, had good talks, stayed out of each other's personal life. He talked about making the break after graduation, wanted to prove to himself he could make it on his own. He got a job with a road construction outfit up near the Canadian border. Long hours, good money, no social life. After a summer of that, he came home with a pile of cash and a conviction—he'd use his head to make a living, not his back. He checked out colleges, found how expensive they were, and opted to join the

Army. Let Uncle Sam pay the tuition bill."

Rolf relaxed, surprised at how easy his story unfolded, how easy he delivered it. As if the times he had replayed the events in his head were rehearsals for this moment.

"Before he left for the induction center, we had a good talk." Rolf leaned back in his chair. "Turns out he had made some bad choices over the summer, got into trouble, bought his way out. Wanted to distance himself now from the events, the people, the place. But trading three years of his life and risking a combat assignment to escape a bad experience and collect a few tuition dollars, that seemed radical to me. He wasn't a hawk, and he wasn't out to save democracy. Military service would be the acid test for a guy like Phil. Independent. Logical. Not a team player." He stopped. "Unfortunately, he failed the test."

Bear held a flat hand in the air. "He didn't fail."

"It was the summer of '90, the start of the Persian Gulf war. Rumsfeld wanted troops on the ground in Kuwait. Now. They cut Phil's basic training short and shipped his unit over, half-trained. He got himself shot during Operation Desert Storm and ended up in a hospital. That's where he met his wife, another patient now his widow. Derek is the product of a lot of downtime at the hospital and rehab center."

Rolf sipped his coffee and closed his eyes. His jaws clenched. He shook his head. The ease of delivery slipped away. "Rehashing this shit isn't easy."

"I see you in Phil—focused, confident. But I don't see you in Derek," Bear said. "Are you sure he's *your* grandson?"

"Sometimes I wonder. I was also a skinny high school kid. Bullied, scared, didn't beef up until college. Once I understood the world rewards brains over brawn, I blossomed. That, plus the help of a mentor, a professor who cared. I could be that man for Derek."

"*You* were scared?"

"I had a closet full of irrational fears, maybe phobias. Heights. A trip up the windmill paralyzed me. Small closed spaces. I couldn't shit with the outhouse door closed. Crowds. I stood near the door, the aisle, the gate in stores and theaters. Elevators killed me. With help, I worked my way out of those fears. With help, Derek could do the same."

"Why hasn't he spent more time with you?"

"He's a fish out of water here on the farm. That, and his mother doesn't trust me, doesn't call or write, doesn't invite me down for holidays. She's comfortable with her pensions. She doesn't need me." He sighed a sigh of defeat. "She doesn't want me to know too much. She's cautious around me, cuts me off when I mention my son."

"Like there's something she doesn't want you to know?"

"I have questions." Rolf spun the cup in his hands, staring at the tiny funnel he created. Spinning. Staring.

Bear waited. A deer fly buzzed the porch and lit on Rolf's head. Rolf sat still.

"Rolf." Bear shook Rolf's shoulder.

"Where was I?"

"You had questions about your son."

Rolf took a deep breath. "He was listed as missing in action. MIA. Later he was reported recovering in a Kuwait hospital. There were conflicting stories about his condition. Meanwhile, his wife, I think they were married, was pregnant and reassigned to Germany. The Department of Defense notified me weeks later Phil had died. His wife returned to the States and delivered Derek. She didn't contact me. I had to locate her through the Department of the Army."

"What are your questions?"

"Phil was not one for casual relationships with women. It's hard to believe he'd father a child with this woman. Maybe he was on pain killers. Maybe he was losing it. Maybe an anxiety disorder. Maybe."

A breeze picked up from the east and flooded the air with cotton fuzz. Rolf sniffed the air. "Rain coming."

Bear stood. "I'll close my truck windows."

Rolf looked at his hands, wiggled his fingers. He lifted one leg, then the other. His boots. The same Wellingtons his dad wore. The same Phil wore when he was home. Not the red high-tops Derek wore. His jeans. Levi's. Cowboy fit. Same as Phil's. Not half way down his butt. His hands. Hefty, rough like Phil's. Not lanky, pink.

Bear walked up the steps. "You were saying . . ."

Rolf glanced at the sky, at Buck, at his hands. "Where was I?"

"You were talking about Phil, wondering about his whereabouts, his condition."

"There's that feeling again. Like someone watching me. And when I turn, nothing. Has that ever happened to you?"

Bear stood and placed a hand on Rolf's shoulder. "You were saying about Derek..."

"No, we were talking about what Phil and I had in common. And what I don't have in common with Derek." Rolf stopped. His hands trembled and sweated. He thought of the characteristics he did share with Derek, Derek's phobias, and his own irrational fears at his age. Derek's brash reactions and his own confrontational responses as a teenager. "No, we were talking about how Derek and I are different. And how we're alike."

"All right, you win." The boat rocked at the end of the dock. Rolf stood on the shore, hands planted on hips, and stared at Derek. "We can't be in the woods. We can't be in the water. We can't be outside."

Derek stood high on the bank, stomping his feet, scanning the ground for critters.

"And I can't take you home now." Rolf climbed the bank. "Too much driving for one day. I'll fix an early supper, and we'll spend the rest of the day inside."

Derek wrapped himself in a towel and marched behind Rolf and Buck.

"I'll light the grill." Rolf strode ahead. "I saved a couple venison steaks for this occasion. Unless you're vegetarian."

Derek yelped when an insect buzzed his shoulder. "What was that?"

"A dragonfly. Harmless."

"What's venison?"

"Deer meat. I shot a buck last fall."

"You shoot deer and you don't shoot snakes?"

"It's them or me. They keep the auto body shops busy up here. Now, you take it easy." Rolf held the screen door. "Take a shower. Check out the guest room. Might get a signal for your cell phone upstairs. I'll bet your mom would like to hear from you."

Rolf stood in the open door watching sunlight play on the leaves, hearing the chatter of wrens, inhaling the aroma of summer. Not a day to be inside. But every mosquito, every screeching hawk, every scampering squirrel threatened Derek's visit.

Inside, Derek lingered on the stair steps. Rolf reached for a photo album on the coffee table. "I have a few family pictures to show you. Have you ever seen pictures of your dad when he was your age? Or when he was in the Army?"

Derek stood, his back to Rolf, and fondled the cell phone in his pocket.

"Here's one of him on the track team. Must have been a senior in high school. About your age." He carried the album to Derek. "See any resemblance?"

"No."

"Neither do I." Rolf flipped through pages. "Here's one of him halfway through Army basic training. Weighed more than any time of his life. He was taller than you and me. Darker hair and skin." Rolf hid a proud smile.

Derek lifted his cell phone from his pocket.

"Here's the last picture I have of him. He's in a Kuwait hospital. That's where he met your mother. I saved the letter that came with this picture. He talks about her. Want to read it?" Rolf traced his finger on the picture. His throat constricted. He stared at it, saw desperation in his son's eyes, anxiety, impatience.

Rolf glanced at Derek's eyes and saw a mirror of his son—desperation, anxiety, impatience.

Rolf returned the album to the coffee table. "I'll light the grill and cook supper."

Later, Rolf carried the grilled steaks to the kitchen. "Supper time," he yelled.

Derek shuffled down the stairs.

"How's that for aroma?" Rolf waved steam from the sizzling steaks toward Derek.

"I'm not hungry."

"What's your favorite meal?"

Derek leaned against the window frame, tapping a finger on the sill. "Bacon cheeseburgers."

"Do you like to cook? Your dad could cook circles around me."

"I told you. I'm not my dad."

Rolf turned the kitchen radio on, tried different stations, tried to find something to appeal to Derek. Nothing. Nothing but country western. "Sit. Try the steak. Catsup? Steak sauce?"

"No."

You and your mother travel much?"

"No."

"If you could travel anywhere, where would you go?"

"Nashville. And not come back." He clamped his jaw. Rolf detected a smile.

"Good choice, Nashville. What would you do?"

"Play backup in a rock band."

"You play guitar?'

"Electric and acoustic." He held Rolf's stare. "And I'm good."

"I'm sure you are. Who's your idol?"

"Steely Dan. When I do 'Reelin' in the Years,' I stop the show." Derek lowered his head and pegged the air. "We played a dozen graduation parties this year. A couple teen dances. We auditioned for the State Fair, but didn't make it."

"Next year." Rolf wanted to touch him, to hug him, to encourage the conversation.

"You guys have a band?"

"We've had a garage band for two years. I play lead guitar."

"Name?"

"Code Red."

"Love it. Maybe I take you to Nashville sometime. See if we can wrangle an audition or two."

"You have a guitar?" Derek asked.

"No."

Derek shrugged his shoulders. A slight smile brightened his face, then the familiar scowl.

Rolf took a deep breath, like preparing for a dive from the high board. "I played jazz piano when I was your age. Oscar Peterson was my man. Ever heard of him?"

Derek cocked his head. "Thelonious Monk. Dave Brubeck. Count Basie. No Peterson."

Rolf cleared the table in front of him with a sweep of his arm and plunked single notes. Impressive full octave chording. He broke into a run up and down the scales, crossover hands for effect.

Derek strummed accompaniment. "Yeah, yeah."

Rolf played a two-finger melody. He smiled. "When I was in the groove, you couldn't stop me."

"What happened to it?"

"The piano? We sold it."

"No, man. The groove, the zone?"

Rolf clamped his jaw and shrugged his shoulders. "Guess I felt I needed to make a living." He looked at the table and plunked

SPIDER

a few more notes. "I was always a math whiz and wondered what I could do with numbers. I settled on accounting."

"The world needs accounting more than it needs music?"

Rolf pulled his plate back and cut a piece of steak. Cut it in smaller pieces. Smaller and smaller.

Rolf struggled through dinner, a *déjà vu* feeling hovering over him. He rehearsed conversations in his mind and scuttled them. Tried silence and found it clumsy. Having penetrated Derek's veneer of bluster, he wouldn't risk destroying their tentative bond with too many questions.

He scratched his memory for Steely Dan recordings, classic rock artists, their hit songs. Nothing.

"I'm calling it a day." He carried his plate to the sink. "Let's hit the sack and get an early start tomorrow morning. Miss the rush down there. You can give the rest of your steak to Buck." Rolf walked to his bedroom carrying a book of crossword puzzles. Something to relax him, something to cancel the day's fumbles tossing in his head.

At eight o'clock, Derek rapped on Rolf's bedroom door.

"What's up?"

"A spider bit me. On the foot."

"A spider or a wood tick?"

Derek opened the door. "A spider. I walked to the end of the driveway and googled toxic spiders. It's a black widow bite."

"We don't have black widow spiders this far north. Besides, they aren't aggressive and rarely toxic."

"You have four hours to be treated after you're bit. Where's the closest hospital?"

"We passed it on the way up here. Remember? I pointed it out to you. But we're not going to the hospital. I've lived here for years and never had a black widow spider bite."

"Look," Derek said lifting his foot onto the bed. "See this swollen spot between my toes? It's turning red. I need to see a doctor."

"I guarantee you it's not a black widow spider, and it's not toxic. I'll give you a dab of bite and itch cream. Give that a chance. You'll be all right. And get some sleep. We want to get an early start tomorrow." He handed Derek the tube off the nightstand.

Derek looked at the tube of cream and walked out of the bedroom, closing the door. Rolf heard him pace the living room, heard the bathroom door open and close, heard Derek climb the stairs and return. Thought he heard a soft knock.

At 10:15, the telephone roused Rolf.

"I was driving your car to the emergency room and hit a deer. Your car is totaled. Come and get me. I only have a couple hours left."

"Derek? Where are you? My car? Are you hurt?"

"My foot is bleeding. Some glass broke. I called my mom. She said to call you and get me to a doctor."

Rolf sprang up and stumbled for the light. "I'll be right there. While you're waiting, call 911. Tell them you don't need help. I'll bring my truck and tow strap."

"I already called 911 and told them to have the police meet me at the hospital."

"Where are you?"

"I'm on the county road and I can see the highway streetlight ahead. How long before you get here?"

"Twenty minutes. I'm on my way."

"So," Bear said, "you drove to the city to get your grandson. He spent a day with you. How did it end?"

"Catastrophe. He thought he had a spider bite, found my car keys, and drove himself to the ER. But he hit a deer en route. He was convinced he would die, so I drove him the rest of the way in the truck. Turns out the doctor didn't diagnose a spider bite and treated the cuts on his toes with Band-Aids. We were home by one o'clock."

"I see your car in the garage. It doesn't look totaled."

"Cracked windshield. Derek talked about the moment of impact, how the deer's eyes reflected. How the deer stood paralyzed. How he swerved to miss it and ended with the deer on the hood. He wondered how the deer could have survived, but it was gone when he opened the door."

Rolf rocked in the glider, clinging to the arm rests, and shook his head. "I drove him home in the morning. He slept, and around St. Cloud, he popped in ear plugs and strummed and picked his imaginary guitar for an hour. I swear he stripped the piety of that instrument with all his shaking. I dropped him off at his house. Didn't want to talk to his mother. I suspect she didn't want to talk to me what with her thinking Derek totaled my car."

"How did you leave it with Derek? Did you give up the

grandfather role?"

"I thought about that. If I do something, *when* I do something, I'll do it on his turf. Maybe a trip to a Dragons and Dungeons theme park, if there is such a thing." Rolf snapped the wristband on his watch. "I don't know what I was thinking. Transplanting him up to foreign territory and expecting him to buy into my dream."

"Preservation of the species," Bear said. "A natural male response. So, what's going on with you now?"

"Confusion. Sometimes I doubt my sanity. Not Alzheimer's, *Some*-timers." He stared at the porch ceiling. "More often lately, I see apparitions. I'm concentrating on something—mowing the grass, walking the fence line, splitting wood, and I sense I'm being watched. I expect to see a car in the drive, a man standing beside it. I look and there's the man with a trace of a smile on his face. He turns away and dissolves. Or I'm doing morning chores, and he's standing in the driveway, leaning against the car, smiling. Then he disappears." Rolf looked at Bear. "Has that ever happened to you?"

"Reminds me of my Uncle Harold," Bear said. "Remember him? He was old enough to be my grandfather. I spent my summers working for him on the farm. I must have been about Derek's age. The last summer I worked for him, he talked about visits from The Spirits. I didn't know what he was talking about. His visitor was a friendly-faced man, too. Always showed up in the barn after milking. Stood by the separator or leaned on a stanchion. Spooky stuff. Uncle Harold said he didn't want to trouble Aunt Ruth with the visits, but he had to tell somebody, so he told me."

Rolf interrupted. "When I got back to the farm after driving Derek home, I had to get busy to keep my mind occupied. There were a dozen windfalls in the pasture, so I hauled them home. I cranked up the chainsaw and cut them at the woodpile. Whenever I straightened up, I expected to see him. And then, there he was, standing by his car in the drive wearing a brown shirt and pants. No cap. Pleasant smile. No hurry. Just turned and disappeared."

"Do you know who it was?"

"I didn't recognize him."

"Was his outfit brown or khaki tan?"

"It's not Phil. It's not a real person. It's an apparition. What about Uncle?" Rolf held Bear's gaze and rocked the glider. Buck jumped and meandered to the far end of the porch. "Did he figure out who his visitor was?"

"Yeah," Bear stammered. "You're not going to like this. His visitor was the Grim Reaper. Mr. Death himself. Uncle Harold figured these visits were warnings of an early demise. His, of course." He put his hand on Rolf's arm. "That was Harold's reading of the situation, not yours."

"How did he respond?"

"He did all the right things. Talked to his lawyer about the will. Made peace with a couple neighbors he hated. Told Aunt Ruth he was tired of farming and scheduled an auction. For a month, we repaired machinery and painted the tractor. We built a sale ring with sixteen-foot gate panels to parade the cattle. We sorted tools, drove a dozen loads of iron to the scrap yard. We did fifty years of deferred maintenance in a month."

Bear stopped and dropped his head.

"And?"

"He died the day after the sale. Electrocuted himself disabling a circuit breaker in the barn. Right next to the separator."

A gray cloud strayed over. The wind picked up. Rain pattered on the porch roof. Rolf sat in a trance.

"Of course, that was Uncle Harold." Bear reached a hand. "Not you."

Rolf sat stoic. Buck crawled back under the glider. Rain fell faster, drowning the silence.

Rolf stood, put his hands in his pockets, and stared at the rain. He turned. "Do me a favor, Bear. Take Buck home with you. I'll hire a neighbor to keep an eye on the horses. I'm going to Nashville. With Derek."

Rolf glanced at the driveway and through a veil of rain, he saw the man in brown.

The man smiled, then disappeared.

PIGEON

I'm not sure why I married Sandy. I've had women, but never one I couldn't live without. I was fifty-one and never married. Like my two brothers, never married. Not that I needed a woman. But neighbors cracked jokes about three bachelors living at the big farm house, wondering what was going on back there.

We operate a dairy farm, Brust Brothers Jerseys. A hundred registered Jerseys and an open-ended contract to sell high butterfat milk to a cheese plant in La Crosse. Leo worries about nutrition and raises feed. I'm a veterinarian and worry about health. Claude is bookkeeper. It's a full-time job for all of us. We dedicated our young lives to building the farm, scrimping back then to have what we have now. No time for socializing and meeting future wives. Guess you could say we were married to the farm.

For distraction, I raise homing pigeons. I mended a broken wing on a client's bird and was struck by its docility, its devotion, its sense of purpose. It recuperated at the farm for a month, long enough to lose its home orientation. Its owner tired of retrieving the bird and made him a gift. Homer soon ruled over a flock of birds.

A year ago last July, neighbors Ben and Betty introduced me to Sandy. Sandy. Small town girl and will never outgrow it. Narrow vision. Can't see beyond the county line. Pretty, not beautiful. Smart, not savvy. Dependent. Three kids, also dependent. On our first date, I asked her to dinner at my country club.

She grinned. "Why not?"

"You live with your two brothers?" she asked, scanning the walls, fingering the linens, the silver, the crystal. "That's interesting."

I nodded.

"My three kids live with me. Off and on. Seems they're always on the verge of the next big thing. What's a mother to do?" She raised her arms in surrender and dangled her bracelets. "I can't kick them out."

Yes, you can, I thought.

"Do you have a housekeeper? A cook? A gardener?" she asked. "I've driven by your farm, Brust Brothers Jerseys. The lawn is immaculate. And that beautiful flower garden. You must have a lot of help."

No, no, no, no.

"Something from the bar?" the waiter asked.

Sandy looked at me for permission. I shrugged my shoulders.

She shrugged back. "Why not? Maybe a red wine? Something not too dry."

"The usual for you, Doc, I presume."

"He calls you Doc. Your name is George. May I call you Doc?"

Why not?

The waiter brought drinks, a glass of red wine for Sandy. She looked at me. "Did I order a half glass?" She sipped, pursed her lips, and frowned at the waiter. "It's warm. Do you have a couple ice cubes?"

She talked about her part-time job, her kids, two in their twenties and one graduated from high school this year. Their problems, challenges, and disappointments. After a second glass of wine, she shared stories of her failed marriages and relationships. How she had to leave each man *to keep her sanity*. How she returned because she couldn't make it on her own.

She ordered steak. *Well done, please. Not bleeding.* While foraging through her salad and carving her steak in bite-sized pieces, she mentioned her sister who lived in New Jersey. Lynn had recently survived a nasty divorce from a mobster, *certainly a mobster*, and Sandy worried about her being strangled. The husband had not declared hidden assets in the divorce proceedings which Lynn discovered. The judge awarded triple damages making Lynn a rich woman.

I yawned and said I had an early appointment tomorrow morning. "One final glass of wine for the road?" I asked.

She emptied her glass. "Why not?"

She rambled on about her kids, her job, her crummy,

crowded apartment. I studied her and felt an animal attraction. She had physical assets. I could tolerate her. My brothers and I weren't bachelors by design. It just happened that way. Our accountant didn't encourage marriage. "Today you have it. If you marry you'll halve it."

What made me change my mind? Her compliance was flattering, bordering on patronizing. My friends were married, some two or three times. The pool of eligible women was shrinking. I was aging. It was now or never. My feelings for Sandy were different, new. I found myself washing the pickup on date night.

She had needs—financial. I had needs too—physical. I could help her, maybe help her kids. I knew farms and businesses that were hiring. My references would be respected.

We'd need a house in town, but close to the farm. Maybe a fixer-upper. Something the average family couldn't afford to maintain or heat. I'm a rough carpenter, can finish, can wire and plumb. The old Mansfield mansion, an Italianate Victorian classic, had sat vacant for years in neglected condition. I could buy its brick walls and tiled roof, its built-in walnut cabinetry, its leaded glass windows and Corinthian-columned front porch for a song.

I did.

I brought Sandy to see the house. She was smart enough not to ask my plans, but our relationship assumed a different tone. I didn't ask her opinion on updating, but she tossed out hints. "The kitchen would be so cheery if it were light yellow," she chimed.

She threw her arms around me when she saw the living space above the garage, the maid's quarters. "What a perfect mother-in-law apartment," she screamed, although her mother and mine were dead. "So wonderful for company."

I knew *her* company.

I cut my vet practice to a couple days a week and called in IOUs of local tradesmen and leaned on friendships of others. Together we reinforced plastered walls and coved ceilings. Tore up worn carpet to expose honey birch floors. Replaced windows and refinished doors, stripped wiring, scrapped cast iron plumbing. The foundation was firm, the walls plumb, the rafters level.

Homer kept me company in a cage on the porch, shared my lunch, and raced me back to the farm at day's end.

Sandy visited once or twice a week, always in a dress and heels. She couldn't see beyond the mess, couldn't project the finished product. She'd trip over a two by four, run a chastising finger along a dusty window sill, or gape at an empty white-walled room in confused amazement. All the while smiling.

I hired a crew to sandblast and tuck the brick exterior. The tiled roof had another hundred years. As a finishing touch, I painted the wrought iron gates and paved the drive.

I knew the ultimate goal was Sandy. While remodeling, I'd find myself allocating closet space for her, designing a kitchen nook overlooking the garden for morning coffee, ensuring ample light over a bathroom mirror. Whatever it took to impress her.

I mentioned my intentions to brothers Leo and Claude, and asked Leo if he'd be best man at the wedding.

"If I'm not baling hay."

Sandy and I watched Fourth of July fireworks from the mansion's front yard. Near the end of the spectacle, I knelt in mock chivalry. Streamers exploded and arced to earth. Mortars shattered the night and lit the sky.

"Marry me."

The grand finale. Blinding colors, deafening noise, the smell of sulfur.

She proffered a surprised smile and lifted fingers to her mouth. Her eyes reflected streams of red, white, and blue. "Why not?"

Tough day, beginning with a pre-dawn call from Juanita whose Arabian gelding, twenty-three-year old Pepper, was down. I had treated him monthly, then weekly. Pepper was terminal, I knew, and Juanita knew. We had run the gamut of options to keep him alive. I'm good, but I'm not God. Pepper was ready for horse heaven. Now it was time to open the gates. When I mentioned euthanasia, she fell against me and held on, sobbing and trembling. I expected her to ask me to give the needle to both of them.

She knelt beside Pepper and lifted his head in her arms, crying and stroking his neck while I administered the first shot. In seconds, he was unconscious. I administered the second shot and suggested she call her daughter and bring a blanket. When she left, I administered the final shot and waited until she returned. I blanketed the calm carcass and sat on the animal while she recalled the day he arrived, how well he responded to training, how he loved apples, Granny Smith apples, etcetera, etcetera, until her daughter arrived.

I made a second stop that morning to castrate a half-dozen calves before heading home to finish chores and cultivate field corn. Monotonous hours in the air-conditioned International listening to Chet Atkins provided time to plan my days. Before we could marry, I had hay to cut and bale, cows to milk, my vet practice, and a house to restore.

Sandy wanted a small wedding at the mansion in July, the one month, she chuckled, she didn't have an anniversary. She talked of a catered reception; I asked for a delayed honeymoon, sometime after harvest. Sister Lynn volunteered to fly in as bridesmaid.

I had scoured used furniture stores and estate sales to accumulate the lion's share of furniture—dining room set, kitchen set, bedroom sets, upholstered chairs and sofas, rugs. The mattresses and appliances were new. Sandy had no preference for décor. She liked Victorian, but couldn't articulate her vision. Her furniture, she decided, would stay in the apartment where the kids lived off and on. When she moved, they would pay the rent, which would be a short-term arrangement.

"I have to buy my daughter's birthday present," she said on the way to dinner. "Will you stop at Walmart?"

She agonized over T-shirts or blouses, cotton or synthetic, pastel or primary, medium or large, button-down or pullover. We'd never move into the house by the end of July unless I selected furnishings myself.

I asked about kitchen appliances. "Any preference?"

"People say I'm a good cook, but I don't cook much. It would be best to leave my cooking stuff in the apartment."

"Any must-have appliances? Upright vacuum cleaner? Food processor?"

She grinned her signature smile. "A can opener. And a television."

At three in the morning, I'd lie awake, rehashing yesterday's progress and planning today's. And dealing with a specter of doubt. Why was I remodeling a house and marrying Sandy? Bringing an old classic house back to life gratified me. But Sandy? What could I do for her? What could I do for myself? Would she be happier? Would I? She was capable of more than serving lunch at the elementary school cafeteria. Did she want more? I didn't know. If she did, I could help, help her be all she could be. A rebuilt Sandy, like a rebuilt house. I played Henry Higgins to her Eliza Doolittle.

I invited Sandy to Sunday dinner at the farm to meet my brothers and tour my world—the house, the barns, the clinic, the land. I roasted home-grown beef and served green beans and potatoes from the garden.

Sandy arrived at eleven in a dress and heels. Leo and Claude were cleaning the milking parlor and feeding calves. "Give them a wide berth when they walk in." I held my nose. "They'll head straight for the shower."

Sandy surveyed the table set for four, the serving dishes, the pitcher of iced tea, pots steaming on the stove. "What can I do to help?" she asked, knowing there was nothing.

"Pour yourself a glass of tea."

Leo and Claude made a swift entrance, nodded at Sandy who extended her hand, and headed for the shower.

Sandy sipped her tea and grinned. "I could hardly get a word in edgewise."

After dinner, we toured the house downstairs and my bedroom upstairs. I held the door open. Sandy made a cutesy stall before entering. "Naughty, naughty," she whispered.

I walked ahead and pointed to the view from my window—the garden, the orchard, the rows of field corn stretching to the horizon. She sat at my desk and scanned the computer and sound system. On her left was my library wall.

"Have you read all these?"

"Yes. Some of them many times."

"Why do you keep them?"

While Leo and Claude snoozed in their rooms, Sandy replaced her heels with tennis shoes and we toured the farm. She had heard about my vet clinic and feigned eagerness to see it. I mentioned my plan to construct a lab for embryo transplant and artificial insemination which caused a shrug of her shoulders. At the pigeon coop, I introduced Sandy to Homer. He paraded along the perch rail, head nodding, body erect, confident and graceful.

Sandy stared. "I wish I had his poise."

The lane to the pasture was a pleasant walk. A hefty breeze kept flies at bay. A pair of hawks circled. A robin scolded from a tilted fencepost. Round hay bales dotted the field and perfumed the breeze.

"What's that?" Sandy asked, pointing to a weed.
"Curly Dock. *Rumex Crispus*. Indian tobacco to us as kids. We rolled our own."
"What's that?"
"Creeping Charlie. *Glechoma Hederacia*. Invasive species."
"What are those?"
"Gooseberries. The black ones are ripe." I picked one and offered it to her.
She gave me a quizzed look. "Why do you remember all this stuff?"

Back at the house, I poured iced tea. "You met my family. When do I meet yours?"
She held her glass to her lips. "In time."
"Before the wedding?"
"Probably not. I'm not sure where my son is." She whirled her glass, her eyes down.
"*At* the wedding?"
"For sure." She perked up. "They wouldn't miss a party."
I asked about the invitation list.
"Just my kids and sister Lynn. I don't want people snickering, 'Oh, there she goes again.'"
"What about Betty and Ben? They introduced us."
"God, no," Sandy snapped. "Her brother was my first husband." She sipped her tea and grinned. "Just my family. My sister and my kids."
I had planned to invite dozens of neighbors, friends, cousins, my clients and suppliers and told her so. The house would hold a hundred.

Sandy monitored my progress on the mother-in-law apartment and notified sister Lynn when it would be habitable. At dinner, after two glasses of wine, she asked about a wedding dress. She'd need a new dress. She didn't want to embarrass me in front of my friends. Everything she owned was *so out of style*.
"Not a problem," I said.
"I hope my kids have something decent to wear," as if to piggy-back on my generosity.
"They'll be fine."
We selected July 29, the last Saturday of the month, three weeks away, and printed and mailed invitations.

"One awkward chore." I gritted my teeth. "Prenuptial agreement. I'll make an appointment with my attorney. Think about any property you want to declare."

She grinned. "No property and no problem."

Remodeling proceeded without a hitch. The finished rooms sparkled, screaming for furniture and furnishings. Windows waited for drapes and curtains. Appliances accumulated, waiting to be plumbed. We concentrated on the master bedroom and bath. I had shopped a used furniture store in Browns Prairie and found a cannon ball four-poster bed. Massive, cherry wood, perfect.

"It's been sitting here for years." The shopkeeper dusted it with his sleeve. "Too big for today's houses. It's from the old Mansfield mansion."

"It's coming home."

We spent an afternoon assembling the bed and washing linens, drying them on the clothesline. Sandy selected a couple framed Monet prints and Ansel Adams photographs for the bedroom walls. She held the antique satin matching drapes and bedspread to her cheek and smiled.

After our first dinner in the house, seated at packing crates and drinking wine from paper cups, I asked her to spend the night. She gave me her coy *why not*, and drove home to gather her trousseau.

In the bedroom, a low July sun beamed gold on the burgundy rug, like a Rembrandt painting. Sandy tittered a nervous giggle and opened her valise. She removed something flimsy, then returned it. She unbuttoned her blouse, looked at the open window, then re-buttoned it. She wagged a finger at me, closed her valise, and carried it into the bathroom. I lay on the bed, alternately hopeful and confident. The shower sputtered. I waited. The grandfather clock downstairs struck nine. The shower stopped.

"Close the drapes, hon," she called. Nine-fifteen.

I closed the drapes, stripped, and walked to the other bathroom. A hair dryer whirred. I waited.

I was asleep when she emerged.

Thursday before the wedding, Sandy met sister Lynn at the airport and drove her to the mansion. Lynn offered her hand to me, held my gaze, and gave me a body hug. "I'm so happy for you and Sandy." Worldly Lynn knew the way to please a man was to praise his woman. As we toured the rooms, she credited Sandy on her exquisite taste in color, in décor, in furniture, commenting on the complimentary and contrasting textures, the eclectic mix of old and new. "It's all so perfect." She hugged Sandy. "And so *in.*"

Sandy was attentive to Lynn's running commentary on the woodwork, the cabinetry, the staircase. She memorized the periods and styles and varieties of wood and repeated them verbatim, which developed into a new interest in the mansion, an ownership. In the master bedroom, Lynn commented, "Stiffel lamps. I have the same lamps in my condo." I learned if it was good enough for Lynn, it was good enough for Sandy.

Lynn unpacked her bags in the mother-in-law apartment and changed into bling jeans and a T-shirt. She resembled a Sandy in tailored clothes, her hair styled, not cut. Her gold necklace must have cost thousands. I knew high-maintenance women like her.

Lynn asked about the reception plans in her take-charge voice and led us through the living room, the den, the wraparound porch, her arms to her chest, holding an elbow in one hand, her chin in the other. "What a beautiful space for a reception." She walked by Homer's cage. "What have we here?"

Homer sidestepped on his perch, blinked, tilted his head, puffed his chest.

"My honey's best friend." Sandy winked. "Until now. They race to the farm every night."

Lynn smiled. "Amusing."

Sandy described the menu, the caterers, the tables and linens and china. The crystal and silver. The bar.

"I'd set up the bar on the porch." Lynn, fortuitous home entertainment consultant, spoke with authority. "Convenient to guests inside and out. And flowers?"

Sandy's eyes met mine. We had forgotten flowers.

Lynn rushed to save us and raised her arms to hug us both. "My responsibility. I'd love to help."

Sandy stayed at the mansion Thursday night to talk to Lynn, or listen to Lynn. Friday morning, they announced their shopping trip. Seems Sandy's dress made her look matronly, and her feet and legs would ache after walking in *those* shoes all day.

Mid-afternoon, they returned with bags under both arms. Sandy sashayed toward me with a seductive smile. Her tinted and styled hair slimmed her face. Never before had she worn eye makeup. She extended her hands to display ten brilliant pink nails.

PIGEON

"Nice nails." I was impressed. "Nice eyes. Nice hair."

Sandy executed a clumsy pirouette. "Maggie at Salon Chic is a magician. I invited her and her husband to the reception. You know him, don't you?"

"For years. Bear's beloved mare Misty is my patient."

"My son knows him, too." Sandy turned toward the window. "Lord knows, they've had plenty of contact." She turned toward me suppressing a frown. "You can't see my new outfit," she teased. "Not until the wedding."

Lynn leaned against the door wearing a smug smile. She winked.

I liked what I saw in the new Sandy. A woman with class clinging on my arm when I entered the country club. Not someone I snuck in the back door of the farm house after Leo and Claude went to bed.

Saturday morning. T minus six hours and counting. I made a quick trip to the farm to confirm Ben and Betty's son milked my share of the cows. I reminded Leo of the ceremony at one, and Claude, the reception at one-thirty. My suit and shirt, fresh from the cleaners, waited in the closet.

Lynn had offered to prepare an easy brunch at ten and invited Sandy's kids, all present when I returned. Caterers commandeered the kitchen, so we retreated to the porch. Sandy's older daughter, a clone of her mother, acted bored, unimpressed. Sandy's jaundiced son sported a stringy goatee and seemed unaccustomed to functioning at this early hour. The Lord didn't create losers, but these two came close. The younger daughter must have resembled her father. She greeted me with a handshake, saying how much she had heard about the house, and how it exceeded her expectations.

I congratulated her on her graduation and asked what the future held.

"I have plans."

The next hours blurred. Sandy left with Lynn to dress in the apartment. At one, she followed Lynn down the stairs in her new outfit—a slimming soft gray pantsuit with a plain white silky blouse and Lynn's gold necklace. The ceremony followed in front of a ton of company. A friend of Sandy's officiated. In the photographs, Sandy and I look happy, Lynn looks satisfied, and Leo looks uncomfortable.

The caterers placed trays of food inside and out, the

bartender hummed on the porch as he polished glasses. The florist had distributed a truck full of flowers, a bouquet for each table. According to the guest book, over a hundred attended.

Sandy clung to my arm for the first hour, then shadowed Lynn, giving mini-tours of the house with amazing detail, as if she had discovered this hidden treasure, polished it to perfection, and furnished it for the Parade of Homes. Her ownership in the project surprised me, and pleased me.

Maggie and Bear stood on the porch, surrounded by a gaggle of freshly preened Salon Chic clients, some wearing brimmed hats, some in long dresses, one in white gloves.

"I didn't recognize you out of uniform." I reached for Bear's hand. "Or without your chore coat. Welcome."

Bear pinched a stemmed champagne flute between his thumb and finger. "What is this thing called?" he asked, jerking my tie. "Misty wouldn't recognize you."

I blushed. "Great to see you both."

"Quite a party." Maggie glanced around the porch and lawn. "Like a scene from *The Great Gatsby*. White columns, groomed grounds, ladies in chiffon. Good to see the Mansfield mansion back in its glory. Great job on the furniture and decorating. Exotic."

"Speaking of," Bear interrupted, "count the silverware when the party's over. One of your guests lifts shiny objects like a magpie."

"I heard you might know him."

"We have a cellblock with his name on it. I could arrest him right now for parole violation."

Maggie poked him.

"But I won't."

After that, more blur. I do recall my classmate in vet school and his wife buttonholing me and inviting us to honeymoon at their condo on Maui. "We would have put it in writing," he said, "but Elaine wanted to check out Sandy first."

Elaine placed a hand on my shoulder. "Nice girl."

"Great offer." I shook my head. "Sorry, but we've already booked the Androy Hotel in Hibbing."

He looked surprised and laughed.

I also recall sharing my piece of wedding cake with Homer. He perched on my finger to the crowd's delight and pecked at the frosted roses.

"Look." Sandy pointed to her suit. "Our colors match. Dove gray."

With that, I swept my arms up, and Homer flew to the farm to warm applause.

Sandy's older daughter snapped me out of my reverie when she motioned me into the den. "Don't trust Mother." She tilted her wine glass at a perilous angle. Her eyes floated in and out of focus. "This," she swept her arm around the book-lined walls, "is not her world. She's a conniver. And for God's sake, don't trust Lynn."

Seven-thirty Sunday morning, the phone rang. A good client, young farmer, apologized for the bad timing, said he had a first-calf heifer in delivery trouble. I slid out of bed. "I'll be there in fifteen minutes." I kissed a sleeping Sandy and left a note on the kitchen table.

The young cow lay sprawled on the grass, her breath labored and heaving. The calf's nose protruded, its tongue extended. The cow's water had broken.

"I tried to pull it out, but couldn't find its feet." The farmer looked helpless, worried. A boy paced between his dad and the laboring animal. "It's my boy's cow, his 4-H project. We sure want to save that calf."

"The calf is dead. We'll work to save the cow." The boy's hands shot up to his face. I slipped on plastic gloves and reached in to tie a nylon rope to the calf's hooves. When the cow pushed, I pulled. Push-pull. Push-pull. The cow took a long break and heaved hard. I pulled. The calf slid out. A big bull calf, perfectly formed.

"When did she go into labor?" I asked.

"Sometime last night. She was in the barnyard when we went to bed. She's a couple weeks early."

I slid the calf in front of the prostrate cow. She licked its lifeless body, slick and warm. I stood with them, dealing with my own grief. The boy rubbed his eyes.

"Go ahead and cry, son." I placed an arm on his shoulder. "If you don't, I will."

The drive home was filled with contradictions. Yesterday's joyful celebration with this morning's tragedy. I needed caffeine, needed to talk to Sandy, needed sleep. I entered the welcoming mansion gate, the mansion door. Inside, the aroma of coffee blended with the strains of Tommy Dorsey. Rich wood and warm textures of Oriental rugs and pillows and paintings created a comforting opulence. I stood in the foyer, reveling in my new environment, my new home. Sandy stepped out of the kitchen, fresh in a white T-shirt and bling jeans. She rushed to kiss me and asked how the call went.

"Fine," I lied. "New?" I asked, pointing to the jeans.

She placed her hands on her hips and pirouetted. "Like them?"

Lynn would be joining us for breakfast, Sandy announced. They had a million things to talk about and we had gifts to open, cards to read, and a refrigerator full of leftovers. Sandy handed me a cup of coffee. "My kids will be handy for something." She poured her coffee and, hand in hand, we walked to the porch. The house and lawn were immaculate, thanks to the catering crew. We sat in wicker rockers, cooled by a breeze that carried the aroma of fresh-cut grass. I listened to her monologue. *This is good*, I thought, over her banter. *I could make this work.*

Lynn joined us, wearing an outfit identical to Sandy's. She hugged her sister. "Twins."

They rehashed the reception, who attended, what they said, what they wore. "I was asked to join everybody's club." Sandy threw her hands in the air. "A bridge club, but I don't play bridge. A garden club, but I hate to garden. A golf group, but I've only played once in my life. And a book club. I haven't read a book since high school."

"Do you plan to join any of them?" Lynn asked.

Sandy squeezed my hand. "I have everything right here."

Lynn announced her eagerness to return home, that she felt like a fifth wheel interrupting our honeymoon. After breakfast, she called the airline and changed her reservation for the next flight to Newark. Sandy and I drove her to the airport.

She thanked us; we thanked her. "I'd love to return the favor." She hugged us. "You two fly to the Jersey shore. I know it's crowded, the air is foul, and the traffic nightmarish. It might be a challenge."

Right.

Monday, I returned to my schedule, back to the farm in the morning for milking, two vet appointments, hay to cut in the afternoon. The construction bug had bit and created an urgency for completing the lab.

My brothers and I had invested in high value Jersey livestock, a blue-ribbon bull and a dozen record milk-producing cows. Our herd topped the state for production and butterfat. The creamery announced plans to expand and asked us to increase our output. We were at optimal capacity, but we could increase cattle production and sell the progeny. I attended a seminar on embryo transfer technology, and thus the lab project evolved.

I shared details with Sandy nightly, in retrospect maybe over-shared. The numbers intrigued her. An average of seven viable embryos per monthly flush, ten or fifteen choice donor cows, hundreds of dollars per fertilized embryo.

She scribbled numbers on a pad. "Wow."

Maybe the potential profit lured her. Maybe genuine interest. Whatever the reason, Sandy bought into it. She asked if she could be my assistant, travel with me for vet calls, take appointments, stock the truck with meds. Of course she could. She bought tailored coveralls, designed a logo "Brust Veterinary," inquired about typical vet cases. She googled them for diagnosis, prognosis, and terminology. For a couple months, it was heaven.

Summer turned to fall, and my work schedule accelerated. Sandy tired of the long hours and resumed playing *grande dame*, inviting new friends for lunch, shopping with old friends.

We didn't hear from her kids. They lost the apartment or were evicted, the older daughter moving in with a boyfriend, the son disappearing again. Younger daughter left for college.

Homer had assumed a patriarchal personality with the new pigeons. He selected a matriarch and circled her on the coop floor, fanning his tail and cooing, reluctant to enter the travel cage alone. The hen followed him, and we had two pigeons for company.

"I don't know if I can handle two pigeons on the porch," Sandy commented one morning. "They're dirty and they carry infectious diseases."

"The pigeons are healthy," I said, "and they're staying."

We planned an October honeymoon in Maui, after chopping corn and baling last crop alfalfa. We sold the first batch of fertilized embryos and had a waiting list for the next batches. Life unfolded in generous leaps, maybe too good to be true.

It was.

Leo tangled with a hay baler and lost his right arm. Goodbye predictable schedule. Goodbye Maui.

Sandy understood. She shared the news with Lynn. "I know you were looking forward to a vacation," Sandy told me Lynn said. "Join me on my trip to Florida after the holidays."

The offer assuaged my guilt at canceling our honeymoon. "Go."

Late fall, Sandy discovered mail order. Catalogs occupied the foyer table, the coffee and end tables, the kitchen table, the bedroom nightstands. Lynn must have precipitated this. They talked for hours about swim suits on page 44, beach robes, the cute jeweled sandals on page 71. In December, packages of resort wear arrived weekly.

Leo continued physical therapy and aftercare, including a prosthesis fitting which he rejected. "It feels weird," he said. Claude and I, with hired help, completed the harvest and fall plowing. The embryo transfer business burgeoned, with orders backlogged into next year.

On the coldest day of the new year, we drove to the airport. Giddy Sandy held her airline ticket to Tampa in her hand, her first flight since a high school class trip and her first visit to Florida. I envied her, even considered hiring extra help to join her.

I wish I would have.

The house felt empty without her. Quiet and cold. I missed the music when I opened the door, her perfume in the foyer, the aroma of supper cooking, her warmth at night. She called twice a day—in the morning before I left for work and at night when I returned. She loved Tampa, loved spending time with *wild, wild* Lynn, loved the sunshine and warm temperature. She couldn't imagine anyone spending winter in Minnesota. I imagined her smile when she said, "We should talk about retiring here."

The day before her ticketed return, she asked if she might extend her visit. Lynn liked the idea of retiring in Florida and planned to purchase a condo. Would I mind if she, Sandy, helped her sister? The way her sister helped her at our wedding?

She had already decided to stay, I knew. She didn't ask about the house, about Leo, about the farm. She raved about eighty-degree temperatures, the plush five-star resort hotel, the miles of ocean beach. It sounded too perfect. Or was I jealous? I missed her.

At the end of the month, a new Sandy returned, tanned and trim. She offered an eager hug, followed by an eager retreat. No excitement in her voice, no play-by-play excerpts of her fun-filled days. I excused her dejection, having to abandon temperatures in the eighties for readings below zero. Substituting swimsuits and sandals for parkas and Sorels. Her phone calls to Lynn, however, were animated and cheery. I was curious.

The Visa bill was not in the stack on my desk. Nor was her Verizon bill. Since I was applicant for both cards, I could access the statements on the Internet.

In five minutes, I read my Visa January statement showing charges at the Paradisio Resort Hotel. I read Sandy's Verizon statement showing multiple late-night calls to a local number. On the White Pages Internet site, I reverse-checked the phone number—Ramon Hernandez, Tampa, Florida.

I swallowed guilt to check the statements and a Facebook page. Smiley Ramon, a cute, curly haired Latino. Occupation: Resort pool bartender. His photo album featured pictures of him with a bevy of women, including Sandy hugging Lynn, Sandy hugging Ramon, Ramon hugging Sandy. I studied the Visa statement. Two women could not consume that much food and liquor.

I called the resort manager, identified myself and asked him to call up Sandy's statement. Then call up the Facebook page of his employee Ramon Hernandez. "The woman in pictures seven through fourteen being mauled by your on-duty employee is your guest, my wife. What kind of house of male prostitution are you running? Does your parent company in New Jersey know about this? Does the Tampa Visitors' Bureau? The Tampa police?"

"Sir, I'm sure we can explain."

"Great. Call me within an hour."

I checked the Verizon statement again, highlighting Ramon's number, and noted a pattern of recent noontime calls. When I returned from the farm at 12:30 today, Sandy hung up the phone. I dialed Ramon's number.

"*Sandeee*. You call again? You must *meese* me."

I hesitated. In my richest baritone: "We both *meese* you."

I sat in the den reviewing the statements. Sandy walked from the kitchen to the dining room carrying a tray of sandwiches and milk. She wiggled her little finger as she passed.

The phone rang. The resort manager assured me my complaint would be investigated. Paradisio valued my business. *Muy agradecida* for the opportunity to rectify the situation. Mr. Hernandez would be given an opportunity to explain the photos.

The charges did seem excessive, and Paradisio would agree to a *significant reduction*.

I walked to the dining room and sat on a chair facing Sandy. "Who called?" she asked.

"The Paradisio."

"Did I forget something?"

"Yes. Your good judgment."

I handed her the credit card and cell phone statements and left for the farm.

No aroma of dinner cooking when I arrived home that evening, no Glenn Miller. A penitent Sandy sat alone in the huge living room, holding her head in her hands. "I can explain everything."

Sandy learned a lot from Lynn, but not how to lie. She explained the credit card purchases. The telephone number highlighted, she said, was assigned to a temporary telephone Sandy bought for the trip.

I held flat opened hands in front of her. "Stop."

Her shoulders slumped, her eyes burned watery pink. If she retained anything from her Roman Catholic upbringing, it was guilt.

I packed a few things and said I'd be staying at the farm. "Get your story straight and decide what you'll do."

She called the next morning and asked me to come in.

I came, carrying the cage with Homer and Helen.

"Seems you know everything, Mr. Sam Spade detective." She stood with her hands on her hips. I smelled gin. "What *I* don't know is why I married you. Lynn agrees. You can't imagine my embarrassment. We visited a friend of Lynn's on Treasure Island. Her husband owns a company that buys distressed businesses. He turns them around and sells them for big bucks. 'It's a dirty business,' she quoted him as saying, 'but someone has to do it.'"

She motioned to me. "'And what does your husband do?' 'My husband preg checks cows,' I said. 'You want to talk about dirty business?'"

I shrugged my shoulders and brought the pigeon cage to the porch.

Sandy followed, steadying herself on the doorframe. She trembled, crying. She clasped her hands to steady them. "Lynn's friend has this modern house on the beach. All white, with a full glass wall facing the water. White upholstered furniture, white carpets, and two white cockatoos on the veranda. And what do I have?" She pointed to the birds. "Two god-damned pigeons."

She took a deep breath and wiped her nose with a Kleenex. "You think you know everything, but what you don't know is that I've talked to a lawyer in Tampa. Lynn knows her and she's tough. She's preparing to serve you with divorce papers. I'll see you in Florida."

"Not likely. We're both residents of Minnesota."

She hesitated. "No matter. She said if you cooperate, it'll be painless for you. She knows your net worth, knows your income stream."

Sounded like Lynn talking.

"Does she know Minnesota divorce law? Does she know about the prenuptial agreement?"

"I signed it under duress."

More Lynn. My attorney would testify Sandy filed her nails during the entire discussion.

"Anyway," she dismissed me with a wave of her arm, "she advised me not to discuss it with you."

I expected this conversation and had stopped at the bank. "You'll be out of here by six tonight." I handed her a clip of bills. "This will tide you over, pay your rent, cover expenses, until you find a job. Don't use your Visa card. It's canceled. The joint checking account is closed. You still have your cell phone."

I grabbed my computer from the den and the pigeon cage. At the door, I stopped. "A locksmith will be here this afternoon, so be thorough. By the way, nice photos on Ramon's Facebook page."

I stayed at the farm for days, maybe weeks, and came back to empty the refrigerator and clear the mailbox of catalogs. Early spring, and lilacs budded, blue scilla poked through a mat of leaves beside the foundation. Early sunrise animated the rooms of the mansion with dancing shafts of light. Despite the season's rebirth, I felt dead. Sandy had sent her new address, and I mailed her a check monthly. Other than that, no word.

Neighbor Betty said she met Sandy cashiering at Walmart, that her daughter had returned and moved in. She shook her head. "The more things change..."

I felt remorse bordering on depression. I, the alpha male who uncorked Sandy's first champagne, who bought her first new car, who introduced her to country club living and dinner parties. And Florida vacations. I felt responsible for creating a new world for her, then denying it.

Someone some time back diagnosed me as passive aggressive, and maybe I am. I felt responsible, yes. But I felt wronged. Someone had to teach her she couldn't flee the coop and return at her whim. I was conflicted. I wasn't her life coach; I was her husband. But why had I married her? Because I loved her? Someone also diagnosed me as a caretaker. Because I wanted to save her?

My attorney suggested I proceed with the divorce. I doubled his suggested settlement at the hearing, which was uncontested. The judge signed the decree in May.

I returned to the mansion one day a week, then two, then three, always with trusty Homer and Helen. I slept well after the divorce, ate regular meals, concentrated on my vet practice. And I saw other women, including Juanita whose Arabian I had euthanized. I invited her to dinner at the mansion and invited Maggie and Bear Braham, too.

On July 29, Sandy's and my first anniversary, she called. She wanted to talk. Lynn thought that was a good idea. She had made a huge mistake, had learned an important lesson. Might I reconsider? Might she move back? Say, for a week or so? Say, for a trial run?

I thought about the good times and the grief, my new freedom and the old uncertainty. "I'll think about it. Call me tomorrow." I hesitated. "There would be conditions, of course."

"Any conditions," she agreed. "I'll accept them."

In the morning, she drove to the mansion in a noisy Ford Falcon. She approached me outside carrying a suitcase and valise and reached to kiss me. I held the pigeon cage between us and turned aside.

"Hmmm." She raised an eyebrow and walked to the house.

For most of my life, I've had my way, although I've busted my ass to get it. I'm also wired to avoid conflict. I'd walk across the street, drive across the state to avoid confrontation. I screwed up all my resolve to say what I had to say. "Where are you going?"

"In the house, hon. To unpack my bags."

"No. Up there." I pointed to the mother-in-law apartment. "You'll clean the house tomorrow when I leave. I'm having company this weekend."

"Oh, great." She recovered. "I loved our parties. Who's coming?"

I turned, embarrassed. Sandy had pride. I knew that. Knew when she heard what I had to say, she'd hightail it back to her noisy car and leave.

"You don't know her."

MOTH

Terry Clark stands erect in the dim light of the hall, creases in his cheeks bracketing a huge grin. One arm is locked around wife Connie's waist, the other around Sue Ellis. He sucks in his gut and puffs his chest. Music murmurs from a wall speaker. "Yesterday." Couples shuffle in shadows behind them into a line along the wall.

"Ladies and gentlemen, may I have your attention?" Overhead lights in the Community Hall dim. A spotlight glares and reflects off a mirrored disco ball, bouncing shards of light off walls, off the ceiling, off white-clothed tables.

Terry snugs Connie closer to him and buries his face in her auburn hair, the soft texture, the familiar aroma of green apple shampoo. He turns to Sue, her hair coiffed and shining even in dim light. And the fragrance—mega-hundred dollars an ounce, for sure. Sue glances at him and flashes a smile. Connie looks straight ahead.

"Ladies and gentlemen. I'm Tim Kelly, your fellow classmate and emcee for the night. It's now my pleasure to introduce," he pauses and raises his voice, "the Browns Prairie class of 1975 at its twenty-fifth class reunion." He waits for applause that doesn't come. "We begin with the grand march to our class song."

"Yesterday" blares from the PA system.

Terry squeezes his hand around Connie's waist. It yields to his fingers, soft and resilient. He squeezes Sue. Taut, toned.

"Alphabetically, may I introduce our class beginning with Alice Amundson Morse and Cliff Morse." In the center of the hall, shimmering streamers part under a white trellis festooned with Ben Franklin blossoms and greenery. A second spotlight glares at the couple struggling through the streamers, arm in arm, she squinting and waving to an imaginary crowd, he untangling a streamer snagged on his belt buckle.

Terry eyes Sue's profile, remembering her white off-the-shoulder gown at the homecoming dance. Her long blond curls, crystal blue eyes, tanning-booth tan. He remembers her generous smile, her infectious laugh. He remembers dancing, holding her close.

"Next, class clown Jeremy Benson and Felicity Benson."

The spotlight hits the Bensons as Jeremy snaps a startled look and pretends to zip his fly. Felicity shakes her head and smiles.

Terry remembers the beach at Spider Lake, the midnight skinny dip, the conversation when they rolled up in a blanket. Remembers his offhand comment, something he hoped to be a compliment, an invitation. "You and me, we could have beautiful babies."

Sue raised herself on one elbow, her face rigid. "I'm not having babies."

"Alice Bradford Finch and Marvin Finch."

A small contingent in the darkened room whoops and hollers. A young voice yells, "Way to go, Grandma." Alice wears pink sweatpants and sweatshirt with the inscription *My greatest blessings call me Nana*. Marv shades his eyes from the glare and pulls a baseball cap from his back pocket.

"Nothing changes." Sue shakes her head. "Those two have been an item since seventh-grade." Sue, in heels, shifts her weight and smooths her dress, anticipating the emcee's announcement. She's wearing shimmering gold that plays with the rotating spotlight.

"Probably the most contented woman in the room." Connie sounds defensive. "All she wanted was Marv and a bunch of kids. She has that and grandkids to boot." Connie wears a white blouse with three or four top buttons open, snug Levi's, and western boots.

Terry pulls the women closer. "Ready?"

"What have we next?" the emcee asks. "*Menage a trois* in sleepy little Browns Prairie? Who'd a thought?" Connie digs her fingers into Terry's arm.

"Ladies and gentlemen, Connie Carlson Clark and homecoming king Terry Clark. And on Terry's other arm, homecoming queen and country western recording star Sue Ellis."

Loud applause and catcalls. Terry steers them through the

trellis, down the aisle to a table and sits between them.

"So, tell me about the country western recording star thing." Connie points to Sue's dress. "That outfit isn't how I pictured a cowgirl."

Sue leans toward Connie, a breath away from Terry. "I front a country western band called Ten Gallon Hat. Jingle a tambourine, hum the chorus. Mostly I close my eyes and wiggle."

"Really?" Connie raises her eyebrows. "Guess it beats working for a living."

"Am I the only one who left Dodge?" Sue tilts her head back and tucks hair behind her ear. "Looks like everyone married her high school sweetheart and gave up."

"Not really." Connie talks about her career as a nurse at the county hospital. And the kids, her daughters in college, one in a four-year nursing program, one in TBD. How she, Connie, looks forward to devoting twenty-four hours a day to training Quarter Horses.

"Sounds like work." Sue turns to Terry. "How about you? Still with the county Highway Department?"

"Can't beat the job security." Terry smiles and talks about the pains and pleasures of being crew chief, how he's toying with the idea of opening a small engine repair shop when he retires — outboards, four-wheelers, snowmobiles, maybe lawn mowers, to pay the rent.

Connie smirks. "More likely to justify owning and maintaining all his toys."

"My investment in toys is nothing compared to your investment in horses." Terry turns to Sue. "Where do you play in Denver? I might be out there next month to pick up a boom truck for the county."

Sue digs in her gold purse and hands Terry a card. "We're at The Prospector every Saturday. All over town the rest of the week."

Emcee Tim continues the roll call as couples walk down the spot-lit aisle and sit at tables. Terry winks at his guy classmates as they pass and shake their heads. A woman approaches the table with a napkin. "Sue, would you autograph this for my daughter? She has your Ten Gallon Hat CD and plays it constantly." She points to the emcee. "Tim played it once or twice a day on KBOB the first month it was out."

Sue smiles and looks for a pen. She sees one in Terry's shirt pocket and reaches for it. "And what's your daughter's name?" she asks.

"Our final couple." Emcee Tim taps a drum roll. "Yearbook and school paper editor and now county sanitation engineer Wynn Walters and Nona Walters. Let's give the class a huge round of applause."

Someone whistles, someone claps. Women lean in and chat at tables. Men crowd the bar.

Terry glances around the room, people standing, sitting, talking, some staring at Sue. He sneaks a glance at her, the best-looking woman in the crowd. He remembers their breakup after the beach party. Remembers rationalizing if he couldn't date the queen, he'd date the first princess, Connie.

"If you're looking for a rebound romance, keep on looking," Connie had said.

"*Au contraire,*" Terry said, in his best French I diction. He had expected this from her and rehearsed his response. "She was the warm-up. You're the main event."

Connie had laughed. "Bullshit."

"Before we open the dance floor to the crowd," emcee Tim says, "how about we ask our homecoming king and queen to lead off with a dance to the class song?"

Polite applause again. Terry looks at Sue and offers his hand. They walk to the center of the floor. He lifts her hand above her head. She twirls and tips back in his arms.

"Yesterday."

Terry grins his trademark grin. "Just like old times, huh?" He pulls her close.

"Not quite." Sue nods in Connie's direction.

Terry feels Sue's shameless pink nails tap his back. He glances at Connie, tapping her stub nails on the tablecloth.

"How's your dad?" Sue asks. "How's my old buddy Roger?"

"You know, of all the women in my life, you are his all-time favorite."

"Someone said he was in the nursing home wing of the hospital."

"Still is." Terry looks around for Connie. He spots her walking to the bar. "Connie knows more about his medical condition than me. He was her patient."

"If he can have visitors, I'd love to see him. Good old Roger. Tell me he hasn't changed."

"Let's give them a hand," emcee Tim says. Silence. "Okay, everybody. Dance."

"I didn't tell him you were coming home." Terry keeps one eye on Connie. "He'd have been on my case to bring you over." Connie stands at the bar with her back to Terry, her finger linked in the belt loop of a cowboy-looking dude. "I'm going to visit Dad Sunday afternoon. Connie has to work. If you're free, join me."

"I'll do it." Sue slides out of Terry's arms. "Right now, I'm thirsty. Let's get a drink."

They wend their way through dancing couples, Sue leading and wiggling her fingers in petite hellos.

August, and Terry prepares for his trip to Colorado to pick up the county's new boom truck. He packs a satchel, checks his billfold for driver's license and credit cards. Sue's gold business card gleams at him. He fingers it, checks the website address for the band. Connie feeds the horses at noon today, her day off. He'll check the website then.

He leans against the wall, eyes closed, and sees Sue in a gold dress, sees her rolled up with him in a blanket, feels a quiver in his groin.

This is insane, the right half of his brain says. *But insanity is what it's all about*, his left half responds.

Connie should applaud his middle-age machismo, Terry reasons. He's still ready and willing. And *able*. But how would he feel if a man hit on her? Like the classmate at the reunion who said to Connie, "Can we talk?" The classmate sat close to her, his face touching her ear, the music and chatter making it difficult for Terry to hear. The classmate placed a hand on Connie's and explained a horse ailment. Connie responded with confident authority. The classmate gushed to Terry about her talents—nurse and equine trainer and healer, and still a looker. They stood, and he hugged Connie. With one arm around her waist, he smiled at her. "You're a lucky man, Terry, to bed down with this woman every night." Terry considered it a compliment other men found his wife attractive. Wouldn't Connie feel the same?

He's mulled the pros and cons of a side trip to The Prospector, screwed up courage, and talked himself into it. Now, he's turning off the freeway west of Denver, out where the plains meet the foothills.

MOTH

The Prospector is a dive. Four or five miles off the interstate, it's an orphaned pole building in desolate cattle grazing country. A neon goldminer swings a pick ax at a rock on the highway sign. *What the hell.*

He pulls into a parking lot full of trucks—semis, cattle trailers, pickups—and circles the main entrance. A poster on a sidewalk sign reads APPEARING TONIGHT: TEN GALLON HAT. He parks in the rear and shades his eyes from the glare of a security light flooding the back lot. From a kitchen fan, the aroma of fried onions wafts in the sagebrush-scented night. Gravel crunches beneath his boots as he walks past refrigerated trucks humming in monotone. He runs a comb through his hair, tugs up his pants, and tucks in his shirt. From inside, the bass line of a guitar beats like a lusty heart.

Terry stands at the door and studies the poster. Sue with her sly mischievous smile, blouse tied beneath her boobs, fringed short shorts, two guitar guys and a drummer behind her. He opens the door to a dark room. Guitars scream. He bumps a figure. "Excuse me," he says.

"Watch it, buddy." A blob of a guy, the bouncer, holds a small flashlight. "Five dollar cover tonight."

Terry flips him a five and looks for a stool along the bar.

"What'll it be?" the barkeep asks.

"Coors Light." Terry thinks this a safe choice in Colorado. "Cute canary there on stage making time with the music."

"Sweet Sue." The barkeep wipes the bar. "Magnetic Mama. Attracts men like bees to honey."

Sue steps offstage tapping a tambourine and sidles up to a table of truckers, bumping them with her hips. A man holds a bill up and shakes it. Sue leans forward, and he stuffs it in her blouse.

"Nice cash register," says Terry. "She's from my hometown. Any chance I could talk to her?"

"Every stranger who comes in here is from her hometown." The barkeep smiles and leans forward. "I'll see what I can do."

Terry high-fives him. "Thanks, buddy." Sue moves to another table, another.

The barkeep looks at the clock. "They're due for a break after this song. I'll give her the good news."

Terry has adjusted to the low light, glances across the silhouettes of men sitting at small tables. Neon signs glare for Millers, Bud Lite, Heinekens. Sue moves among the tables, tapping the tambourine, bumping, dipping. Icicle lights dangle from the stage. Disco lights render the drummer red, blue, green.

"All I got's a twenty," a man grumps. "Can I dig for change?"

Sue wiggles to the beat, reaches for a few bills, and hands them to him. He tucks the twenty in her blouse to applause from his table and takes a bow. Sue heads for the stage. "Last chance, boys," she teases. On stage, she grabs the mic. "Break time, America. Order up. See you in a few." The drummer punctuates with a riff.

Terry turns to the bar when the barkeep leaves. He sees himself in the mirror, an anxious dude, maybe confused, maybe guilty, maybe guiltier if things work out. Behind him a blond woman approaches.

"Terry. It's you. I couldn't imagine who. How did you find me?"

"You mentioned The Prospector at the reunion. Good to see you, friend." He reaches to hug her.

Sue turns her head and braces her arms against his shoulders. "What brings you to Colorado?"

"I'm picking up a truck for the county, remember?" He reaches for her hand. "Want a drink? Is there someplace we can talk?"

"Not really. I'm back on stage in fifteen minutes."

"Can we go to your dressing room?"

"That would be the ladies biff. And you wouldn't be the first man in there." Sue steers his hand to the bar. "I could use a breath of fresh air though. Are you parked close?"

"What will the management think if you go to the parking lot with a customer?"

"Terry, you're not in Minnesota."

He follows her to the door. A man at the bar yells, "Hey, Lucky."

The guy next to him wonders aloud, "What do you suppose that'll cost him?"

Outside, Terry steers Sue toward the truck and opens the passenger door.

"This is a surprise seeing you, Terry."

"Talk about surprises, what I saw in there was not what I expected."

"Welcome to my world. How's your dad? How's my old

buddy Roger?"
"He has the picture you gave him on his bed stand. Where Mom's used to be. He knows I'm here." Terry studies Sue in the dim light of the cab. The eye shadow, the lacquered hair, the scanty outfit. "I don't know what I'll tell him." He studies her again, suddenly feeling paternalistic. "And you? Are you doing what you want?"

"It's a living. Not something I'm proud of, but it's a living." She pokes around the console. "Got a cigarette?"

"Nope. Sorry." His mind wanders around the possibilities of *It's a living*. He feels the forbidden fruit attraction, yet feels protective, like a big brother. He's eager to change the subject. "I don't know where you picked up the twang in there. But it works."

"All part of the act. If I'm from Minnesota, I'm country but not western." Sue glances out the side window, then at her watch. "How long are you in town?"

"Leaving tomorrow. Unless I get a better offer." No longer paternalistic, he slides his hand to her shoulder. "Any chance you could put a homeless man up for the night?"

Sue turns. "You're kidding."

"Couch? Floor? Anything?"

"I might have trouble explaining that to my boyfriend."

"He lives there?"

Sue reaches for the door handle. "I'd better get back to work. That's a generous crowd tonight."

Terry follows her through the gravel lot, through the aroma of frying onions, past a white floodlight where a huge Luna Moth circles and dives at the light.

"Crazy bug," Sue says. "He'll kill himself."

Days later, Terry walks to the hospital cafeteria, spots Connie, and walks over to peck her cheek with a kiss.

"How was the trip?" Connie asks, chewing a sandwich.

"Perfect. Sweet truck, open highway, good weather." He sits and twiddles the ignition key.

"I didn't expect you till tomorrow."

Terry inspects the keys. "Guess I was eager to get home." He slides the keys on the bead chain. "How's Dad?"

"He's great. Saw him this morning. Cute picture he has on his table."

"Picture of what?"

Connie watches him as she chews. Terry looks at her, looks away, twiddles the keys.

"Aren't you going to ask how things went back home?" she asks.

"Just about to do that. What's new?" Terry sits across the table.

"Absolutely nothing." She glares at him. "Same old shit."

"Meaning?"

"Meaning I checked the Recent Searches on your computer. *Ten Gallon Hat. The Prospector. Sue Ellis.* You saw her, didn't you?"

Terry meets her gaze and drops his head. "Saw her. That's all."

"Makes me wonder what you had in mind. It's pretty obvious to me how she makes a living. And it's not jingling tambourines."

"Connie, this is not my idea of a welcome home party. Am I giving you shit about your cowboy friends?"

"You don't have to, and you know it. Look." Connie points and shakes a plastic knife. "If you want to screw around, go ahead. But if you do, you're out. And if you're out, you ain't never coming back."

"Listen to me. I'm innocent." Terry pounds the table. An aide in blue scrubs lifts his tray and walks away.

"Maybe you are." Connie returns to her sandwich. "May I add this bit of womanly advice? Sue is high-maintenance. You couldn't afford her on your salary. But it's your life. Live it. I just want to make sure you know the rules if you stick around."

She finishes her half-pint of milk and looks at her watch. "I've got to get back to work. And your dad's expecting you. We'll continue this discussion tonight."

Terry sits in the empty cafeteria. The PA system pages Dr. Someone to report somewhere. He taps the keys on the table. "Shit." He pushes his chair back and it falls to the floor.

"Hey, you're back." Roger grins as Terry enters his room. "How was the trip?"

Terry walks to the bedside and hugs his dad. "Horseshit."

"Did you see my girl?"

Terry hesitates. "Yes, I saw her. No, I didn't do anything else."

MOTH

Roger drops his head. "Pity."

Terry sits on a chair beside the bed. Sue smiles at him from her photograph. "Connie gave me the third degree a few minutes ago. Accused me of fun I didn't have. I'm still smarting from that."

"Trouble in paradise?" Roger asks. "How long you been married?"

"Forever."

"And you're surprised? What are you going to do?"

"No idea."

Roger places his hand on Terry's shoulder. "Want my advice? Follow your instincts."

"That might cost me a bundle."

"You can pay in cash, or you can pay in flesh. Cash is easier." Roger lifts a shoulder, faces Terry, and reaches for his hand. "Allow me to further ruin your ruined day. Your mother ceased being a wife when you kids were born. Meaning her maternal instincts outshined her conjugal ones. There's more. You want to hear it?"

"No. Why are you telling me this?"

"There's a silver lining to your cloud, son. A man is destined to suffer time in hell, a hell he creates for himself. He can suffer when he's alive, like I did, or he can wait until he dies. I've suffered. So for me now, it's clear sailing."

"Dad, what kind of pills are you on?"

"It hurts me to see you hurting, son." Roger stares at a silent Terry, shoulders down, face distraught, fingers fiddling with keys. "Let me tell you something. I heard a lot of talk when I was in Connie's ward. Those nurses love to gossip. They must have known she was my daughter-in-law, but didn't care or just wanted to be catty. They had her hooked up with a new intern one day, the hospital administrator the next. I can give you chapter and verse if you want."

"No thanks." Terry wants to stuff a pillow in his dad's face. "I don't believe you."

"Remember what I told you years ago. Never trust a horsewoman. A good man for her is someone who'll feed the critters in the morning and muck the stable at night."

"You wonder why I never ask you for advice?" Terry rises from his chair and looks at the door. He wants to hear more. But he doesn't want to hear more.

"Look." Roger raises himself to sit. "Can't you see you've

done her a favor? Now she can rationalize her bad behavior by accusing you of yours. It could be a tied score, but I suspect she has points on you."

Terry jingles his keys. "So now what, coach?"

"How long till you leave the county Highway Department and open your shop? Five years? You can't hold your breath that long. Go for it now. Don't waste precious time in hell while you're alive. Do that when you're dead."

"That won't work. The kids . . ."

"Look. You screwed up, and you know she knows it. She screwed up and she doesn't know you know it. Who has the upper hand?"

Terry looks at Sue's photograph, the Mona Lisa tease of her smile.

"I've watched enough episodes of Dr. Phil in here to qualify as a family counselor." Roger tugs a pillow behind him and sits erect. "Dr. Phil would say *Turn the page, begin a new chapter.* If that doesn't work, I've watched enough of Judge Judy to qualify for family law practice. Judge Judy would look you straight in the eye and say *Get on with it.*"

Terry covers his eyes and inhales sterile hospital air. He needs fresh air. Or the scent of mega-dollar perfume. Or green apple shampoo. "Guess I'll be on my way." He waves goodbye. "You're crazy."

Terry taps his fingers on the steering wheel as he drives the county's new truck to his hobby farm. It's Friday. He isn't due back until tomorrow. Why report early?

He hikes the air conditioner up, then down. He opens a window and closes it. Turns on the radio. Frank Sinatra sings "The Second Time Around." He shuts if off. *A Coors would taste good tonight.*

At home, Connie's horses whinny from the corral. The dog barks. Crows yack in a neighbor's corn field. *Everyone's yelling at me.* He grunts and grabs his satchel.

The house is cool, quiet. He glances through mail stacked on the kitchen table and grabs a beer from the fridge. He checks the hall calendar where Connie records her work schedule. Double shift today. She won't be home until midnight. He recalls his dad's comments. Midnight, unless she makes a stop.

August 14 is circled in red. *Holy shit. That's our anniversary.*

MOTH

He walks to the living room and turns the television on. A game show. He switches channels. A Twins game. The six o'clock news. He turns the television off and stares at the black screen. *I need my support group at the Broken Hart.*

Outside, the county truck dominates the front yard, dwarfing his pickup. *Might as well burn county gas.* The dog barks again. "Later," he barks back and hops in the truck cab.

"Hey, the world traveler's back," a regular yells from his stool at the Broken Hart. "We saved your seat." He pats a stool.

"How did you know I was gone?"

"There's not much in this town everybody doesn't know." He laughs. "Some good. Mostly bad."

The barmaid hands him his regular Coors. "Welcome home, handsome. How was the trip?"

Terry swigs the beer. "Good to leave. Better to get home."

"Weren't you in Denver?" a second regular asks. "Any chance you might have called on Sweet Sue?"

Terry closes his eyes and rotates the bottle in his hands. *I don't need this.*

"One of your classmates said you two looked like lovebirds on the dance floor at the reunion."

"You score with that girl and it goes on your resume," number two guffaws. "Also on Connie's complaint when she files for divorce."

"C'mon, guy," first regular retorts. "Connie's broadminded. She'd tolerate a little hanky-panky between friends."

"Knock it off, you guys." Terry stares at the television. "Hey, the Twins have a man on second. What's the score?"

"That's what we're asking you, Terry. What's the score? Suzie four, Terry four, Connie zip?"

"You guys got nothing better to do than speculate on my sex life?" Terry walks to the jukebox and slips in a dollar.

"Nothing personal, you understand," first regular chuckles. "But none of us would fault you if you scored with Suzie."

Terry walks back to the bar and guzzles his beer. "I'm outta here."

In the lot, he hops in the truck, guns the engine, and spits gravel until he hits tar. He glances at the speedometer—thirty, forty, fifty when he reaches the RESUME SPEED sign. The engine purrs. Steering is tight. The truck hugs the pavement as he rounds the corner toward home. He looks in the mirror and sees his trademark grin. He also sees an advancing flashing light, *Damn,* and slows to a stop.

Deputy Sheriff Bear pulls behind him, and walks to the cab. "What're you doing, Terry? Acceleration test on the new county truck?"

Terry leans out the window and shakes his head.

Bear lifts a foot on the running board. "I didn't think you were due back until tomorrow."

Terry clutches the steering wheel. "Damned if everyone doesn't know everything about me."

"Long day?" Bear asks. "Tough day? How much you had to drink?"

"Two beers."

"I'm going to believe you, Terry. Now, you drive this baby to the county garage. Forty miles an hour. Hazard lights on. I'll drive you home from there in the squad."

Terry shrugs his shoulders, stares through the windshield, and moans under his breath. "Damn, everybody runs my life."

"Sorry," Bear says. "I missed that."

Terry sits in the front seat, his first ride in a squad in forty-three years. He noses around the dials, the gauges, the switches, the radio, the lights panel. He glances at the log book and sees his name.

Bear notices his glance. "Nothing official. I have to log in each of my incidents, each of my passengers."

Terry glances at the clock. Half-past seven. Light rain falls. The *clack clack* of wiper blades breaks the silence. That, and an occasional unintelligible transmission on the scanner.

The rain eases up, and Terry looks for a handle, a button to lower the window.

"Want some fresh air?" Bear asks and presses a button on his door panel.

Moist August air is laden with ozone and the pungent aroma of fresh-cut ditch hay. Approaching headlights appear, advancing rapidly, then braking, slowing, slowing to a legal speed when they meet the squad. "Peder Davidson," Bear says. "Got two speeding citations and working on his third."

Tires hum on the slick pavement. The squad throbs like a nervous heart, beating from asphalt dividers in the pavement.

MOTH

"Easy drive home from Denver?" Bear asks.

"The drive was a piece of cake. All hell broke loose when I got home. First Connie confronted me with the results of her amateur detective work. Then Dad repeated the gossip he heard about Connie from the nurses. Then the guys at the bar were giving me the third degree for something I didn't do. I've got until midnight tonight to concoct a plan. Connie gave me an ultimatum. Said we'd talk about it tonight." He pauses. "Assuming she comes home tonight."

Bear shoots a glance at him. "What do you want to do?"

"Truth be told, I don't know. Got to admit I placed myself in harm's way looking up an old high school sweetheart."

"Maggie mentioned your class reunion dance with Sue was the talk of the town."

"That's what pisses me off. Nobody knows but everybody talks. And when they don't know, they guess."

Bear grins. "If you want anonymity, move to the Big City."

The rain subsides, and Bear turns off the clacking wipers. The scanner sputters a garbled message. "What do you want to do?" Bear repeats.

"I have a few hours to cogitate." Terry looks out the window. "This much I know. I don't want to trash everything I've worked for in twenty-three years to satisfy a long-delayed seven-year itch."

"You're the architect of your own fate, son," Bear says. "You'll do the right thing." He offers Terry his card and lands a hand on his shoulder. "My cell number is on there. Call if you want to dry-run your speech to Connie."

Eleven-thirty Friday night, and Terry stands in the hall peeling the label off a bottle of water. The kitchen table is cleared of dishes. Cupboard doors and drawers are closed. Cabinet countertops are bare and wiped. The sink is empty of dishes and pans. Towels hang neatly from the oven door handle. Terry practices his opening lines as he cleans, dusts, and straightens.

The living room is lit by three table lamps. Magazines fan across the coffee table. The television is hidden behind the doors of the entertainment center. Terry argues an imaginary point to a lamp, speaks it aloud, modifies the wording, changes the emphasis.

Bedside lamps glow on either side of a taut bedspread and

three casually tossed silky pillows. The dresser is bared of bunched clothes as is the bed footboard. He stares at a bedpost and denies an imagined accusation, admits to slight misconduct, understands how that could be misconstrued.

Terry considers confrontation and speaks to a mirror. "Maybe I'm not the only one messing around."

He sees Connie's response, hands on hips, head tilted. *Are you insinuating . . . ?*

Terry fans his hands in a baseball *safe* signal. "Just sayin'. Word gets around."

He listens to the playback in his mind shakes his head. *No. Don't do that.*

He leans against the doorway, his face in his hands. The only sound in the house is the washing machine in death throes of the spin cycle.

Terry watches the driveway through the kitchen window and glances at the clock. Eleven forty-five. Connie's shift is over at 11. She stays for shift report for ten to twenty minutes and drives home. He empties his water bottle, crushes it, and opens the fridge for another. Connie's car pulls into the drive. The washing machine beeps and stops. Horses whinny from the corral. Terry meets Connie when she opens the door. Her head droops, her shoulders slump forward. She hands Terry her canvas lunch cooler.

"What happened?" Terry asks.

"Patient fell. I should have asked for help."

Terry pulls a chair away from the kitchen table. "Water?" he asks. "Iced tea?"

"Ibuprofen," she mumbles. "And a hot shower." She heads for the bathroom and stops in the hall. "The answering machine is blinking. Who called?"

"I didn't notice. I must have been preoccupied."

"I can't imagine with what. Nice job on cleaning the house, by the way." She walks to the telephone and presses *play*.

"Hi, Mom and Dad. This is Rachel."

"And this is Sarah. We're calling from Minneapolis to be the first to wish you a happy anniversary. I talked to one of your nurse-y friends, Mom, and she said you were working a double shift today and had the weekend off. Dad, I know you don't work weekends, except for winter snowstorms."

"So," adds Rachel, "we're coming up to celebrate. We're

both done with our summer internships and we'll spend a week or so with you before fall semester."

"We googled anniversary symbols," Sarah chimes in. "We learned the twentieth is china and the twenty-fifth is silver. Guess what? The twenty-third is steak. So, make no plans for Saturday eve. We're coming home to cook an anniversary dinner for you."

Connie leans on the bathroom door. A tired smile escapes her lips. "Those girls." She walks into the bathroom.

Terry stands in the living room alone, like a boxer in the ring. Over-trained. Floodlights glow and burn. Hearts pound. Adrenalin courses. The crowd waits in awed silence.

And no opponent.

Saturday morning, and Terry sneaks out of bed. Connie lies comatose. He brews coffee. He's tired, didn't sleep well. He contemplates the night before as he walks to the porch with a glass of cranberry juice.

It's a classic Minnesota August morning. Heavy dew on the grass, a Kodachrome sky, air sweet and tinged with clover. Mourning doves coo on the power line. The dog crawls from under the porch and rubs against Terry's leg. Horses graze at the far end of the pasture.

After coffee, he'll mow the lawn, make a run into town for beer and charcoal, maybe gather sticks and scrap lumber for a bonfire. The girls love a bonfire. He returns to the kitchen for coffee and hears Connie pad to the bathroom, shake a bottle of pills, and return to bed. She'll be out until ten. Best to shop now and start the lawn mower later.

Connie sits at the kitchen table drinking coffee when Terry returns from town. He glances toward her to take a reading. She fingers through a recipe box.

"Good morning. I thought I'd make the layered salad the girls love."

Terry heaves an audible sigh.

"What was that?" Connie asks.

"Allergies." Terry wipes his nose. "Might be corn tassels." He stacks a twelve-pack in the fridge. "I'll mow the lawn now, spiff up the yard." He pauses and turns toward her. "Unless there's something you want me to do."

Connie shoots him her *Are you kidding me?* look and waves

her hand, as if shooing a fly. "Be a nice guy and feed the grass clippings to my ponies."

The girls arrive mid-afternoon. Connie had coaxed an appointment at Salon Chic for a hair styling at noon. She's fresh and rested and attractive in a white starched blouse and bling-pocketed jeans. Terry walks from the porch to the car, sucks in his stomach and puffs his chest, stretching his Menards T-shirt.

The lawn is manicured. Phlox satiate the perennial garden in pinks and roses and purples. Zinnias and marigolds and cosmos collide in colorful competition in the annual garden, vibrating with the buzz of bees and the whirr of hummingbirds.

"So great to be home." Rachel hugs her mom. "You look great."

Sarah hugs her dad. "And you look great, too. Studly. Got a beer for your legal-drinking-age daughter?"

After the steaks, after the report on the internships, after the predictions for the school year ahead, after a few too many beers and a celebratory round of Baileys, the family retires to the porch. Connie and Terry sit on the glider. The girls perch on the broad porch railing and lean against opposing posts. Terry walks his fingers to Connie's hand and squeezes.

The sun drops behind the horizon and peeks through the trees. The girls have played an old Bruce Springsteen CD on the stereo inside. Porch lights glow a soft yellow. It's country quiet.

"This is how I want to remember it." Sarah closes her eyes in the twilight. "Don't change anything."

"For sure," Rachel adds. "And happy early anniversary. May you have many more."

"That's sweet of you, girls." Connie rises. "How about I brew a pot of coffee?"

"How about we stoke up the grill again and make s'mores for old time's sake?" Rachel bounces off the railing. "We brought the ingredients."

Soon charcoal blazes, casting shadows on a table spread with marshmallow crème and graham crackers and Hershey bars. Insects buzz toward the fire and glide through the column of smoke. As the fire grows, the insects grow larger. Moths, acrobatic and persistent, circle the flames.

"Where did all the bugs come from?" Connie asks.

MOTH

"They're sphinx moths," says Rachel. "Probably Great Ash, one of dozens in Minnesota. I wrote a term paper on moths for Biology I. They're attracted to light. I postulated in my paper they also might be attracted to heat, even to aromas like perfume."

"How did you do on the paper?" asks Terry.

"C plus." Rachel laughs. "My prof said I should have skipped the heat and aroma stimulants and concentrated on light types, like infrared and ultraviolet and X-ray. Where's the fun in that?"

The fire burns bright and cherry red, lifting tiny flecks of ash in the column of smoke. Moths circle the flame, some diving into the coals.

"Why do they do that?" Sarah asks.

"They navigate by light." Rachel eyes the circling moths. "They confuse the light of the fire with the light of the moon."

"Ever see a Luna Moth?" Sarah asks. "Beautiful. I'd shoo them away before I'd let them self-destruct."

Terry recalls the Luna Moth in The Prospector parking lot. He recalls the aroma of fried food from the residue of tonight's steak on the grill. He glances at his daughters peeling Hershey bars, laughing, dribbling marshmallow crème on graham crackers.

He glances at Connie. She sits in a lawn chair within reflection range of the flames. She twists a curl and wears a tearful melancholy look that says she's savoring this transitory moment.

Terry reaches for his wallet, pretends it's Kleenex, and turns to sneeze. He pulls Sue's card from the wallet and slips it through the grill onto the coals.

He walks to Connie, stands behind her, and places his hands on her shoulders. She lifts her hand to his. He stoops to kiss her hair.

BUTTERFLY

Helen stepped down the path from the parking lot to foot-sized landings of red clay, over gnarled roots and jutting rocks, down toward the lake below. Beside her, shivering birch trees in white uniform stood like soldiers. Behind her, Harold picked his way, balancing a picnic basket landing by landing. "Careful, careful," he repeated. "Be careful."

Along the path, daisies bloomed. Sweet clover. Queen Anne's lace. Butterflies drifted flower to flower. Honeybees buzzed and disappeared among the blooms.

Over the lake, wisps of fog floated and softened the horizon like a curtain of gauze. Far out on the water, a muted fog horn hummed a two-note arpeggio.

The late afternoon sun broke through hazy clouds and warmed the south hillside. Helen stopped to roll her sleeves, to feel the sun warm her arms.

"Careful," Harold called from behind. "And watch the sun exposure."

Helen planted hands on her hips and inhaled cool lake air, then stretched her arms upward. Wind tousled her bobbed hair. She stood on her toes, silhouetted against water and sky that melded into gray-blue panorama divided by a pencil-line horizon.

At the shore, she sat on a driftwood log, bleached and smooth, sharp on one end, a tangle of roots on the other. Quiet water lapped at the rocks. Perpetual, relaxed, rhythmic.

Harold sat on a boulder at the waterline removing his shoes, his eyes fixed on a group of monarchs at the rock's watery recess. "Puddle club. Adult males."

Helen untied a scarf. "In all our years at the North Shore, I don't recall seeing the lake so quiet."

BUTTERFLY

Harold waded ankle-deep in water, pants rolled up and holding polished loafers. "Maybe it's getting old. Like us."

A car hummed on the road above.

Helen closed her eyes and lifted her chin. "Next month, I'll be in Evanston."

Harold turned to face the water, hiding his reaction.

"I still question my decision." She looked at him. "I'll miss you."

Harold turned. "We've been through this a hundred times. Don't tell me you're feeling remorse."

"Not remorse. Regret. Allow me a moment of regret. I don't want this to be an ego trip. It's highly flattering. Hugely gratifying." She clapped her hands. "But I don't need it on my resume or my obituary."

Harold lifted one finger. "Peer recognition is number one." He sounded like he read from a script. "You're tops in your field. No one knows contemporary American fiction like you. It would be different if you lectured at an Ivy League school. The students at Northwestern should be a walk in the park."

"The teaching component isn't my concern," Helen said. "Being away is. Being away from you and home, being away from the kids and grandkids, being away from Kat. I will definitely miss Kat."

"You encouraged us to be independent. Give us a chance to show our stuff." He reached for a flat rock and skipped it. "If you get lonesome, I'll schedule emergency surgery."

"Why don't you come with me?"

"We've been through this a million times. Someone has to stay home and feed Kat."

He stepped to shore and sat with her while the sun dried his feet.

"It's beautiful." Helen raised her arms and lifted her head. "The lake, stormy or serene. I feel small and insignificant in the face of such vast beauty. Yet I'm proud to be part of the universe. I love the ambivalence."

"Sorry, *ambivalence* is taken. It's my excessive trait." Harold replaced his shoes and sat, muffling his labored breathing. "I'll walk down the shore."

He felt her eyes on his back and strode with intentional erectness, his arms in an exaggerated swing. Pebbles crunched beneath him, rust and gray, matte finish on shore, glossy in water. On a flat boulder in the lake, a large cairn stood, human figures leaning toward each other, defying gravity and wind, in perfect balance.

He leaned to inspect a potential agate and staggered, caught himself with his right hand, and stabilized himself against the rocks. His left arm dangled numb and leaden. He waited, mindful not to project his difficulty. A muscle spasm maybe, from lugging the picnic basket down the path.

When the numbness subsided, he straightened, feigned a long inspection of the agate, and hobbled to an outcrop of driftwood, out of sight. He extended his arms, closed his eyes, and waited. When he opened his eyes, his left arm had dropped.

"Harold," Helen called. "I'm hungry. Let's eat."

He returned to a makeshift dining room—driftwood chairs and boulder table. A red-checkered tablecloth fluttered in the early evening breeze. Dishes were set, wine glasses stood at attention, a bouquet of daisies graced a castaway bottle.

"Sorry I forgot candles." Helen poured wine and handed him a glass. "To fifty years, and fifty more."

A smile relaxed his face. "It's been a ride. An interesting, challenging, fun ride."

Seagulls screamed and circled. Harold pinched his left arm under the tablecloth, checking for numbness.

Helen licked her spoon. "Now is the time when someone says, *Food always tastes better outside.*"

"Food always tastes better with a glass of wine." Harold raised his glass.

Helen swirled her glass and looked at Harold. "In all our fifty years, fifty years of my cooking for you, have you always been faithful?" She dropped her head. "Don't answer that."

"I think you know."

"I know as much as I'm willing to know."

He grinned. "Have you always been faithful to me?"

"Since you know I often lie to you, the answer is no."

"Tell me about him. Better than me?"

"Who said anything about a *him*?"

Harold raised his eyebrows and turned. "Look." Far out on the lake, an ore boat floated, or hovered in the air. All quiet, except the gentle lap of water at their feet.

Helen broke the silence. "We should talk about the party."

"What's to talk about? The invitations are mailed. The Club is reserved. The menu is set."

"The details, Harold. Don't you want to be involved?"

"You're better at details. Bankrolling the affair is involvement enough for me."

Helen speared a raspberry. "I'll buy a dress for the occasion. I'll ask Anita to take photos. I'll review the seating arrangement with the dining room manager."

"Why not leave that to the kids?"

"This is my one and only fiftieth. I want it done right." She sipped her wine and glanced at the water, a shimmering mirror, serene, languid. "Did you believe it would last?" she asked. "Fifty years. Did you ever expect it?"

Harold swirled the wine in his glass. "A couple times I wondered."

"Like when?"

"Not worth mentioning today. I don't want to destroy the moment." He touched her arm.

"Unfair." Helen shook a finger at him. "You don't suggest disappointment in marriage and then drop it."

"All right." Harold set his glass on the rock and rested his chin on his hand. His stomach tightened. "A month after you delivered Anne, you announced you were returning to teaching. We hadn't talked about that. Back then, fathers earned the living and mothers stayed home with children. You shattered my pride."

"Why is this news to me forty years later?"

"If I had told you, would you have acted differently?"

"Probably not."

"So, I didn't discuss it with you."

"But you remembered it, stuffed it in your resentment file for forty years."

Harold turned and held Helen's hand. "Let's stop. I said I don't want to ruin the moment."

"Stopping is not an option. You either deal with it or forget it. You don't stuff it."

"All right, I forget it. In retrospect, you made the right choice. I bonded with the kids as a result. It's history, it's done. And I forgot." He held her gaze. "And you? Did you expect it to last?"

Helen smiled. "I don't know. Suddenly all I remember are the good times."

He glanced at her, silhouetted against the lake. Breeze tousled her short wavy hair. Her gaze fixed on the ore boat. He knew her classic profile, her signature pose—chin high, shoulders square. A glint of sun sparkled in her wine glass. "I'd do it again," she said.

The sun dropped below the tree line behind them, and whiffs of breeze stiffened. The ore boat hovered, unmoving, marked by faint intermittent red lights. Distant trees became silhouettes. Far to the right, city lights flickered like candles.

Harold stood. "Let's walk up the path while there's still light."

Helen placed dishes in the basket and folded the tablecloth. "I'll carry it this time. Lead the way."

"May I have your attention?" Son Hal tapped his glass with a knife. He stood at the head table in the Country Club dining room, Harold and Helen in center; Hal and wife, right; daughter Anne and husband, left. Grandchildren sat facing them at another rectangular table. Around the grandchildren, tables seated friends, neighbors, coworkers, clients, and extended family. At each table, candles flickered beside an autumn bouquet, and tissue butterflies floated from the ceiling. Strains of Kenny Rogers drifted from the bar area.

"Ladies and gentlemen, we have a short program—the requisite speeches about how fifty years seems like yesterday, the *For better or for worse* thing, the regrets and the rewards." Hal looked at his mother, wearing a simple black dress, spaghetti straps, pearls. "Hard to believe this tennis-bodied woman could have been married fifty years."

Applause.

BUTTERFLY

"Don't miss the slideshow Anne assembled." Hal pointed to the lobby. "Pictures beginning with Mom and Dad's wedding, all set to 'Through the Years,' sung by Mom's *other guy*. Thanks, Anne."

More applause.

Hal waved an arm at the grandchildren's table, six youngsters in party dresses or shirts and ties. "I'd introduce them, but if you follow Mom's Facebook page, you already know more than you need."

Helen reached for Harold's hand and looked at Hal.

"Who am I to comment on your achievements?" Hal said. "Fifty years. Two strong, independent personalities, each going his or her own way, yet always staying close. Parallel paths, and still moving forward."

He looked at his mother. "Back when, it was fair game for kids to complain about their working mothers. I didn't feel that. You may have had extended faculty meetings after hours, but Dad was there. And he learned to bake a five-star mac and cheese. I learned to appreciate Mom's presence as a gift. I took her Contemporary Lit course and she was unrelenting. Held her students to high standards, high expectations. I sense she did the same to you, Dad."

Harold dropped his chin and nodded.

"I hope you'll share the good news tonight about your Northwestern contract, Mom."

Helen squeezed Harold's hand and nodded yes.

"May I propose a toast?" Hal raised his glass. "To the lucky couple."

"Here, here," guests chanted.

Knives clinked against glasses at the grandchildren's table. Harold feigned annoyance. Clink, *clink, clink, clink*. Harold pecked Helen on the cheek.

Grandchildren shuffled pages of tablets and lifted numbers above their heads, like Olympic judges.

1, 1, 2, 1, 0, 1.

Laughter.

Harold leaned toward Helen, placed a finger under her chin and, eyes closed, kissed her.

8, 9, 8, 9, 10, 10.

Applause.

When Hal sat, Anne stood. "Whose kids are those?" She smiled her mother's smile. "Looking through fifty years of photos was a revelation. Dad wears a freshly ironed shirt in every picture. And polished loafers. And hair cut the first Saturday of every month." She placed her hand on her dad's shoulder. "This man lived life to the fullest. When he wasn't financing start-up companies and turning them into profitable ventures, he was an amateur lepidopterist. Did you know he double-majored in college? Financial Management and Entomology. In his day job, he provided employment for thousands of people. In his spare time, he restored butterfly habitat and studied migratory shifts of monarchs. He built canoes for Hal and me. He plays oboe in the community orchestra. He ran Grandma's Marathon three times. And finished."

"And lost," Harold added.

"A real renaissance man." Anne raised her glass high. "So, here's to the happy couple. May your first fifty years be the hardest."

The crowd raised their glasses in a toast.

Anne smiled and reached for Helen. "Mom, would you say a few words?"

"A very few words. Thank you, Hal and Anne, for all your work. And thank you," she waved her arm at the tables, "for sharing our joy. Yes, with my family's consent and blessing, I have accepted a one-semester contract with Northwestern University to guest lecture on American Literature. Harold has opted to stay home and feed the cat. You're right, Hal. Harold does bake a knockout mac and cheese. But just in case, there's a sign-up sheet in the foyer to invite Harold to dinner for the next three months. Ease my guilt and sign it." She sat.

Applause.

"Dad?" Anne said.

Harold stood. "You've heard enough speeches. All I can add is this: If I ever did anything right in my life," he placed a hand on Helen's shoulder, "it was marrying this woman."

Applause.

BUTTERFLY

"Anyone in the audience want to offer an anecdote?" Hal asked.

Grandson Ryan raised his hand. "Grandma, what's the story behind the tattoo?"

Helen tossed an embarrassed hand over her shoulder. "It's a butterfly. A spontaneous, irrational gift to your grandfather on our tenth anniversary. He did appreciate it."

"Still do," Harold said.

Missy, the youngest granddaughter, raised her hand. "Grandpa, how did you meet Grandma?"

Harold looked at Helen and grinned.

"You wouldn't," she said.

Harold stood, took a long sip of wine, and clasped his hands.

She buried her face in her hands. "He would."

"I was visiting a friend at . . . at an *institution*." He made quotation marks with his fingers. "Poor gent was in a bad place, thought he was Dionne Warwick."

Helen turned away and buried her face in her hands. A few in the crowd snickered.

Harold continued. "I talked to my frenetic friend in the sunroom of this institution when a woman walked in. 'Who is that woman, that *vision*,' I asked. Dionne stood, lifted an imaginary mic to his lips, and sang, 'The moment I . . .'"

The grandkids chimed in. "I say a little prayer . . ."

"It's his favorite movie," Anne said. "'My Best Friend's Wedding.' We knew how he'd respond."

Applause.

Hal stood. "If you're ready to dance, DJ and local radio personality Tim Kelly is ready to play. We're leading off with a song for the happy couple, 'Through the Years.'"

Harold took Helen's hand and followed her to the dance floor.

Anne and husband followed. Then Hal and wife.

Hal tapped his dad's shoulder. Anne held her arms to Harold. Daughter-in-law danced with son-in-law. Hal and Anne motioned for guests to join the dance.

Everyone danced the next hour—neighbors, friends,

grandkids, the waitresses, the bartender, DJ Tim, everyone.

"I'm tired." Hal took Helen's arm. "Do you think we can slip out?'

"We can't slip out, but we can make a gracious, hasty departure. I'll tell Hal and Anne."

In the car, Helen inserted a compact disc in the player. "A gift from the kids. A Kenny Rogers CD."

"Confession," Harold said. "I wasn't tired. I wanted to save my energy for later."

Weeks later, Harold welcomed Anne into his kitchen. "Where are Ben and the kids?"

Anne held a serving bowl and stood before a cluttered kitchen table. "The kids wanted to go to the State Fair, and I didn't. Ben *volunteered*."

"Nice guy."

"Nice kitchen." Anne scanned the cupboards. "No dirty dishes. No empty cereal boxes. No banana peels. And you in a freshly ironed shirt. And shined loafers."

"One of my better habits."

Anne reached to brush away envelopes, account books, legal documents on the table. "Looks like you're using the kitchen for your office. Let's eat on the porch." She brought glasses, plates, silver for two and served the salad. "Do you miss her?"

"Of course, I miss her. At the same time, I'm proud of her for going."

"It doesn't feel like Mom's porch without her."

"Nor does the living room." He chuckled. "Nor does the bedroom." He glanced at the back yard, the flower gardens bordering the fence, the circular bench around the apple tree. Glanced, as if looking for Helen.

"Did you make the right choice, staying behind?"

Harold picked at his salad. "Maybe. Maybe not."

"If you decide to join her, I'll care for the damned cat."

"You think she'd want me? She has dinner with a different faculty member every night." He set his fork down. "Tonight, she's guest of the Department Chair."

"Sounds like you're jealous, Dad."

"As if jealousy is a bad thing." He pushed his plate away. "Great salad."

Anne looked at him. "Let's call her."

"Not a chance. I've talked to her once today. She'd think I was checking on her."

Kat walked through the porch and brushed against Anne's legs. "She thinks I'm Mom."

"I haven't told you about my appointment with Doc Kramer." Harold tried for a casual tone.

Anne set her fork down and rested her chin in her hands. "No, you haven't."

Harold gazed through the window. Noon sun poured down on the butterfly garden—delphinium, phlox, Oriental lilies in brazen bloom. "I had a couple self-diagnosed mini-strokes. Doc ran the tests—MRI and CT scans. He prescribed statins for my cholesterol. That and a half-hour walk daily. His prognosis? Come back in a month."

"Does Mom know this?"

"No. But I'll tell her when I see her. At the end of the semester."

"Probably not a good idea."

"If I tell her, she'll worry. If she sees me, she won't." He looked at her. "Do I look like I'm on my last legs?"

"Dad, you look great." Anne placed her hand on his arm. "I glanced at the pile of paperwork on the kitchen table. Your Last Will and Testament, your IRA accounts, your Health Care Directive. Are you telling me everything?"

"What I'm telling you is I'm not immortal. I have plans to make, not the least of which involve your mother. She's younger than me, in excellent health, probably will outlive me by a decade. I want her to be happy. I don't want her spending ten years alone."

Anne held his hand.

"That's part of the reason I consented to her guest lecturing. Check out the territory. See who's out there. Who might be available. Someday."

"That's thoughtful, Dad, but you have good years ahead of

you, too."

"Maybe." Harold rolled his napkin.

"Have you seen your old friends from the office?" Anne asked. "Enjoying your brief bachelorhood?"

"Not many old friends around."

"Godfrey?"

"Dead."

"Mackenzie?"

"Nursing home."

"Jordan?"

"Tucson"

"Walter?"

"Dead." He finished his iced tea. "Depressing, isn't it? But it comes with the territory." He slid his chair back. "I want to show you my specimens in the atrium."

In a south-facing room off the kitchen, French doors opened to a room of glass walls and ceiling filled with humid greenery and the aroma of moist earth. Potted orchids bloomed. Milkweed stems stood in ceramic vases. Butterflies fluttered toward the glass. Harold scanned the kitchen for the cat. "Close the door behind you," Harold said. "The monarchs and swallowtails like to explore the house, much to your mother's dismay." He stopped. "But she's not here, is she?"

Chrysalises dangled from milkweed stems, some compact, some emerging, some empty. "These little critters are skippers. There must be fifty varieties in the state. I'm writing an article for *Nature* on them."

He held a twig with an emerging monarch chrysalis. "Interesting how far they migrate and return to the same place. There's no place like home, right? I hope that's right."

"Dad, are you worried about Mom?"

"Not worried, concerned. She's talented, attractive, energetic. She's the one who's in demand. I'm dead weight." He replaced the twig and stood before the window, hands in pockets, his back to Anne.

"Are you not feeling needed?'

"Your mother is not a needy person. I worry about not feeling wanted. How far could she go without me?"

BUTTERFLY

"Look how far she's gone *with* you."

"I've read about how our youth informs our adulthood," he said. "How it affects it, impacts it, determines it. To a point. One day we wrest control of our life from our genetics, from our youthful environment, and become our own person." He turned to face Anne. "What decisions have you made in the last week, month, year that were informed by your childhood?"

Anne shrugged. "None, directly."

"Say you reach your goal of self-determination at age twenty-one," Harold continued. "You didn't need me, or us, for the next twenty years. Your mother and I have been married for fifty years. Do you think she needs me? Or am I just a convenient habit?"

Anne placed her hands on his shoulders. "Let me rephrase the question. Do you need her? I think you do." She turned him toward her, fingered his ironed collar, and smiled. "And what's the matter with habits? They're not all bad."

Harold lifted a pencil from his shirt pocket and placed it beside a new butterfly, its wings wet and crinkled, the undersides dull and contorted. He touched the wings together. "I have here a common, nondescript creature." He tickled the wings open to reveal brilliant orange and black monarch markings, an intricate architecture, an elegant design. "But if I loosen my hold and allow it to fly, it becomes a thing of beauty."

Anne wrapped her arms around his neck. "You love her, don't you? Her birthday is coming soon. Let's drive to Evanston and celebrate."

The phone rang.

"Hello," Harold said.

"This is Bella Meyer. How are you?"

Harold cupped the phone with his hand. "Bella Meyer," he whispered. "Probably collecting for the Red Cross."

"I'll leave," Anne said. "Think about Evanston."

"Bella, I have company. My daughter. What can I do for you?"

"Well, Harold, I volunteered on the imaginary sign-up sheet at your party to bring you dinner while Helen was out of town." Her voice smiled. "Might you be hungry tomorrow night?"

Harold looked at the calendar hoping to see an engagement. None. Might as well accept. Bella would continue offering until he agreed. "Thank you, Bella." He tried for solicitude. "I'm a six o'clock diner. Would that work for you?"

"You got a date," Bella said. "See you then."

When she arrived the following evening, Harold met her in the drive. "Here," she said. "You carry the salad. I'll take the basket. I'll come back for the hot dish."

Harold didn't remember the hair, bottle-red. Didn't remember she stood a head shorter than Helen. Didn't expect her in perky low-cut blouse and snuggy jeans. He recoiled from her musky perfume.

"Such a beautiful evening." She returned from the car and followed Harold. He had set the table on the porch, the wide paddle blades of a ceiling fan slowly blending cool outside air with the warm September air of the house.

"Glass of wine?" Bella asked. She uncovered a sweating bottle of white wine and two glasses. "Sit while I pour. Hope you like chicken and rice."

Harold folded a napkin across his lap, straightened his silverware, sipped his wine.

"Did you know I was a home health care specialist? Did this all the time."

"I'm not ready for home health care."

"Of course, you're not. What kind of salad dressing would you like?"

Harold sampled the chicken. "Wow. What kind of spice is that?"

"Oh, is it too hot? I'm sorry. I don't have dependable taste buds anymore."

Harold took another bite. "It's fine. Just threw me for a loop."

After dinner and a second glass of wine, Bella stood. "I'll put these leftovers in the refrigerator. You won't have to cook for days."

Harold stood, felt a sudden rush of blood, tipped forward, and leaned against the table. His left arm felt lifeless, leaden, like

BUTTERFLY

the sensation at the North Shore.

"Harold, are you all right? Here, let me help you." She supported him to the bedroom and lowered him to the bed. "Do you want me to call 911?"

"I'll be all right. Just let me rest a while."

When he awoke, the room was dark. A light from the hall shone on the floor. He lay under a sheet and stirred. Beside him on the bed sat Bella. "Good morning." She turned on a table lamp and tousled his hair. "Although it's not morning. How do you feel?"

Harold lifted the sheet, saw his underwear. He turned and saw his clothes hanging from the closet door. He stared at Bella. "You're wearing Helen's bathrobe."

For days, Harold didn't answer the phone unless he recognized the number on the caller ID. A sheriff's patrol car pulled in one evening and tapped the horn in the driveway. Harold recognized Bear and walked to the door. "Come on in, Bear. Am I under arrest?"

"Purely a social visit, Harold. Maggie's been calling you and not getting an answer. She asked me to check."

"It's a long story, Bear. And if you like happy endings, you don't want to hear it."

"Spare me. We wondered whether you would join us for dinner some night."

Harold enjoyed the stories Helen brought home from Maggie and the Salon Chic. He also tired of frozen dinners and chicken pot pies. "Pick a date."

Maggie met him at the door when he arrived the next night. She held out her arms to hug him. He hesitated, then moved forward. Maggie held him. "I worried about you."

"Pardon the delayed reaction," Harold said. "I've developed an aversion to being close to another woman."

"So I hear." Maggie laughed.

Harold pulled away. "What did you hear?"

"Well, of course, Bella is my client. She told everyone in hearing range about the chicken curry hotdish she made for you.

How you enjoyed it, but how you got dizzy afterwards and she had to put you to bed."

"She said that in front of your customers?"

"Don't worry," Maggie said. "Everyone knows Bella is a talker."

They walked into the living room. Paneled walls, plaid upholstered furniture, braided rag rugs, a coffee table made of wagon wheels. "Have a chair, Harold. Can I get you a beer? A glass of wine?"

"Red wine, if you have it. Where's Bear?"

"On his way home. He got stuck with a report that was due."

Maggie returned with two glasses and sat across from Harold. "What do you hear from Helen?"

"Sounds like she's having the time of her life. Right back in her element."

"Do I detect resentment?"

"You might detect apprehension. I don't want the widows in this town making up stories."

"If Helen has concerns, ask her to talk to me."

A car pulled into the drive, and the garage door opened. Maggie rose and hustled to the service door. She opened her arms. "Welcome home."

"Hello, gorgeous." Bear gave her a long hug. "What smells so good?" He glanced in the living room. "Hello, Harold. Feeling better?"

"You heard, too? Truth is, I think Bella dumped a ton of cumin in the hotdish. I had heartburn for days."

Bear sprawled in a recliner. "Tough day."

Maggie brought a glass of wine and stood behind him. "Supper's ready in ten minutes, gentlemen."

"Well, Harold, is batching all it's cracked up to be?"

"'For none of us lives for himself alone.' Romans 16."

"I'm impressed. How many more weeks before she returns?"

"Too many. We're heading down for her birthday next week."

BUTTERFLY

"Mother." Hal rushed to the cottage, outpacing Harold and the grandkids. Helen stood in the doorway, her arms open. Anne opened the hatchback and unloaded Harold's suitcase. Grandkids scurried between the two cars, then up the sidewalk to hug Grandma. Anne carried Harold's suitcase. "Mother, it's so good to see you. And what a charming cottage. And what a spectacular view. Lake Michigan."

Harold busied himself at the car, retrieving sun glasses, a water bottle, slipping into a sweater, wondering whether to appear excited or reserved. Helen had greeted everyone. He turned toward her. She was halfway to the car.

"Hello, stranger." She kissed him and held him.

Harold closed his eyes and buried his face in her hair. "Don't ever do this to me again."

The family toured the cottage with Helen, walked around the yard, admired the park separating the house from the lake. "Mom, what's the plan?" Hal asked.

"You and Anne and families check in at the motel. Then come back here for lunch. Quiet afternoon while you catch your breath and I catch up on the news. The kids can play in the park or swim at the beach. Tomorrow, the English Department is hosting a brunch at the Faculty Club for all of us."

Hal put his arm around her. "In honor of your birthday, I'm sure."

"I'm missing a grandson." Helen counted the kids. "Where's Michael?"

"Football team retreat weekend. Command performance. He sends his love," Anne said. "Dad occupied his seat in the car."

"Surrounded by grandkids." Harold attempted irritation. "Ask me my best Super Mario score."

"I let him take a nap with Marshmallow." Granddaughter Missy held a stuffed toy lamb.

"I noticed Marshmallow goes everywhere you go. Don't let him get away." She hugged Missy. "Harold and I will start lunch while you check in. Be back in an hour."

"So, how goes the guest lecturer gig?" Harold reached for a supportive tone.

"Different." Helen took silverware from the drawer. "I love

the faculty. I love the students. I love the curriculum. I hate being alone." She wrapped an arm around him. "Don't ever let me do this again."

"That's my line."

"So, how goes the bachelor bit? And how is Kat?"

"Kat asked me to give you this." He kissed her cheek.

"Other than that?" Helen asked. "Eating well? Sleeping well? Walking your thirty minutes a day?"

Harold stopped with a handful of plates. "How did you know about that?"

"I talked to Anne. I also talked to Doc Kramer. He said he couldn't discuss a patient's condition with another, not even a spouse. He would have told me if it was important to come home."

"I didn't want to trouble you." Harold felt betrayal by Anne, but relief.

"You look great. You'll follow doctor's orders. I'm not troubled. Let's get lunch on the table."

Sunday morning, the phone rang. "Mom," Hal said. "We'll be over shortly. Brunch is at noon, right?"

"Yes, here on campus at the Faculty Club."

"How's Dad?"

"He's reading the Sunday paper. Want to talk to him?"

Silence, then, "Missy wants to leave Marshmallow at your cottage, so we'll stop in for a while."

"I can't wait."

Sunday noon, Helen sat at a table in the Faculty Club, Harold to her left, Department Chair Dr. Marcotte, right. Anne, Hal and families sat interspersed with English Department faculty and administration.

Helen turned to Harold. "Dr. Marcotte spent the summer on a sabbatical in the Galapagos."

"Interesting." Harold poked at a salad. "What are the penguins reading?"

Helen poked him with an elbow and sipped her wine.

Harold reached ahead of Helen. "Did Mrs. Marcotte enjoy the lizards?"

Helen poked him again. "Dr. Marcotte is in early widowhood," she whispered and pointed to her chest. "Breast cancer." She sipped her wine.

"Helen is a formidable addition to our staff." Dr. Marcotte leaned forward. "Thank you for sharing her with us, if only for one semester." He raised his wine glass. "Students are asking if she'll return. She's a breath of fresh air for this stilted, stale, stoic institution." He smiled a deprecating smile.

Harold tilted his head and looked around the room, waving a finger at the grandkids.

"I've never known Steinbeck and Faulkner and Hemingway to generate so much excitement among students," Dr. Marcotte continued. "What a joy to have someone so literate gracing our campus."

Helen waved a dismissive hand and sipped her wine.

"With all her scholarship, you have an opportunity to discuss a myriad of contemporary and classic American authors," Dr. Marcotte continued. "What are you reading now, Harold?"

"He hasn't read anything more current than *The Iliad*." Helen nodded at Harold. "Right?"

Harold twisted his napkin.

"We're excited about Helen's proposal for the department to host the first annual Midwest American Literature Festival. I'm sure she's shared her ideas with you."

"No, she hasn't."

Helen dropped her head. "So little time."

"I swear she knows every living author in the Midwest. And they've agreed to attend, for only a modest stipend, I must add."

"Feed them and they will come." Helen waved her wine glass at guests enjoying brunch. "Exhibit A."

"We hope Helen will return to moderate subsequent Festivals. We're considering naming the Festival for her."

"Oh, please, Dr. Marcotte. That isn't necessary."

Harold groaned and pushed his chair back. "Excuse me. I want to meet the faculty. And ensure my grandkids eat their vegetables."

Helen held her wine glass and wriggled her free fingers. "Toodle-oo."

Harold walked to a guest table and placed a hand on the shoulders of adjacent faculty members, prepared to introduce himself. They continued the conversation—nodding, talking, ignoring him. He listened, nodding his head in fake concurrence. The same at the second. More shop talk, department gossip. At the third, a red-haired woman turned and stood. She was short, wearing a form-fitting jersey top, and reeking of warm spicy perfume. She reached for his hand. "So you're the husband of our new Shakespearean Beatrice. We've wondered about you."

Harold choked a response. He retrieved his hand and walked to Anne's table. "Get me out of here before I lose it."

Later when Harold returned from his walk, he braced himself in the shower at the cottage, hoping warm water would calm him. He played back the Marcotte flattery, Helen's attempt at naivete, the faculty's aloofness. *Stupid, stupid, stupid.*

"I can't believe what I saw today, what I heard today." Harold stood in the bedroom doorway, toweling himself. "You pedagogues have your own language. *Transdisciplinary. Metacognitive. Guiding coalitions.* Please."

Helen crawled into bed.

"And the same old arguments among the faculty. Tenured versus non-tenured. Who will teach freshman comp? The value of Tolstoy and Dostoevsky in the twenty-first century. I wanted to scream."

Helen pulled the blanket over her head.

"And you. You and your trademark Pinot Grigio grin. The wine wasn't that good. I couldn't believe the menu. When will college kitchens learn to prepare something other than chicken?"

Helen turned onto her stomach and buried her head under a pillow.

"Your suave Dr. Marcotte. How he fawned over you. If I treated you that way, you'd shoot me."

"Try it," she said under the covers.

"I wouldn't mind him if he didn't resemble George Clooney. You know he's on the prowl, don't you?"

Helen sprang up. "Stop it. Dr. Marcotte is a gentleman. He is not a hustler." She sat, crossing her arms. "You and I have a few hours together, and you act like a child."

Harold threw the towel on a chair. "Oh, do I?"

"I'd be upset if the whole conversation wasn't so absurd," Helen said. "And you. Did you know your voice raises an octave when you're angry?" She chuckled. "You sound like your Irish mother."

"I am angry," Harold shouted.

"Wait," Helen shouted back. "You found the chicken marsala predictable. The wine wasn't reserve vintage. What about the canned music? Too many violins? You're being over-critical." She wrapped the sheet around her body. "Let's talk about professional jargon. Have you listened to your old speeches, read your old memos? *Actionable. Core competency. Skill set. Traction.* Those words and phrases made me shudder. They still do."

Hal tapped on the door and opened it. "Pardon me for intruding. Missy forgot Marshmallow and can't sleep without her." He looked at Helen, sitting in bed. At Harold, standing on the opposite side of the room in pajama bottoms. "Did I hear shouting?"

Helen glanced at Harold and said, "We're having a discussion."

"If that was a discussion, I'd hate to have a fight with you." Harold looked at Hal. "Did you see your mother today? How she allowed Mr. Smooth to paw her?"

"Harold, you're tired and upset. Let it go," Helen said.

"You're the one who told me to deal with my feelings, not stuff them." Harold turned to Hal. "Tell me what you saw."

Hal wrung his hands, looked at Helen, and sighed. "I saw Mother having a good time, a meaningful conversation. It was good to see her smile. Good to hear her being appreciated. I didn't see any untoward conduct."

"You'd defend her if she held a knife to my throat."

"You asked for my observation, and I gave it to you," Hal said as he glared at Harold. "Am I not allowed an opinion?"

"You are allowed an *informed* opinion."

"Good ol' Dad, master of the left-handed compliment," Hal said.

"That wasn't a compliment. That was an insult."

"Mother, unless you ask me to stay, I'm leaving. If you find his childish conduct unbearable, call. We have space at the motel. Now, where's Marshmallow?"

"I'm fine, Hal," Helen said. "We're fine. Say goodnight to the family for me."

When Hal left, Helen rose from the bed and walked to Harold. "You heard what I said. We're fine." She reached to kiss his cheek. "We're fine. Now come to bed."

"I won't sleep." Harold reached for his pants and shirt. "Not until I cool down. You have anything harder than Pinot Grigio in the cupboard?"

"There's brandy, but should you drink it, what with your medications?"

"What about the park? Is it safe to walk at night?"

"At this time of night, every second walker is law enforcement."

How would she know?

Harold downed a shot of brandy and wandered to the walking path in the park. A runner and her dog raced by. He found a bench below a street light and threw his arms along the backrest. Oak leaves filtered a harvest moon that dipped between slotted clouds. A breeze ruffled the tree, freeing acorns that bounced off the asphalt path.

The brandy warmed him, relaxed him. A man and woman approached his bench, walking hand in hand. "Good evening." The man nodded to Harold.

"Good evening to you."

"Wonderful night for a walk," the woman added.

"Yes," Harold agreed. "A beautiful night." He leaned back. A lone man approached his bench, stooped, shuffling, his fists clenched. "Good evening," Harold said.

The man continued walking, head lowered, grumbling incoherently to himself.

The alarm at six startled Harold. He sprang and slapped the snooze button. "What a shocking way to waken. I haven't heard one of those for years."

Helen lifted herself and rested on an elbow. "Life is full of shocking surprises." She brushed fingers through her hair. "Rough night?"

Harold sat in bed, exercising his fingers, his hands, his arms.

"Feel up for the long drive home?" Helen asked. "The kids will be here at seven. We have time for coffee and a short walk to the lake."

They carried mugs across the park to the walking path and sat on a bench. Morning runners wearing sweatbands and tortured expressions hustled past. A blue-haired matron in a melon jumpsuit and matching shoes walked her corgi. A young mother pushed a twin-stroller while conversing on a cell phone.

The lake wore a civilized calm. No nature-laden breeze. No primordial boulders stacked in haphazard abandon. Fog wrapped the shoreline. Off to the right, gauzy sailboats listed like toys.

Picnic tables and signage replaced white birch and blazing columbine. NO LIFEGUARD ON DUTY. PLEASE CLEAN UP AFTER YOUR PET. PARK CLOSES AT 10 PM.

"This is not *our* lake," Harold said.

"Is this where you spent your late afternoon yesterday?" Helen asked. "Walking along the lake?"

"I had to cram four days of walking into one session. Two hours. I thought it would calm me. It didn't." He leaned back on the bench, legs spread wide, an arm wrapped around Helen's shoulder. "Since my medical *event*, I've thought about the days I have remaining, the days *we* have remaining. I thought I could allow you to explore your prospects." He tightened his grip on her arm.

Helen snugged her sweater and snuggled close. A squirrel scampered down the tree and sat on his haunches in front of them. A passing dog barked and tugged at his leash.

"While I walked, I saw a species of skipper butterflies we don't have further north, one I don't have in my collection. I followed it, plant to plant, flower to flower. When it landed, I felt an old urge to capture it, add it to my collection. I stopped. It was beautiful as long as it was free. Captured, it would fade and die. I chastised myself for wanting it."

He relaxed his hold on her and placed his hands in his lap. "Thus, in my best business jargon, in a zero-sum game, as much as

I want you, I set you free."

She stood, walked in front of him, and held his face in her hands. "I'm not going anywhere." She kissed him. "And neither are you."

Far on the lake, a freighter headed north, sounding its basso fog horn, appearing and disappearing in the morning mist.

LAMB

It started some forty years ago as an annual fishing trip, four school buds breaking away to Mille Lacs Lake after Labor Day. By then, vacationers from the twin cities with school-age children had fled. By then, bars and restaurants lowered their prices to appeal to the locals. By then, Iowans had emptied their cans of Iowa gas and their boxes of Iowa groceries, filled their coolers with Minnesota sunfish, and fled the low-fee county camp sites in their Iowa campers.

After a few consecutive years, the fishing trip appeared religiously on the four friends' calendars and earned the lofty title of tradition. One guy included it in his wedding vows.

Not only was the trip a tradition, so were assignments. Rocky kept outboards running. Tad built a legendary three-course Bloody Mary and sautéed a mean pan of walleyes. Bear scoured camp areas for wood and kept bonfires burning. Doc, fastidious Doctor Mike, maintained the campsite, sweeping the tent back when they camped in tents, washed dishes, strung a clothesline to dry rain-soaked gear.

No one claimed the assignment of catching fish. That's not what the weekend was about.

This year it rained on arrival Friday night. Rained hard like a collapsed celestial dam complete with a strobe lightning show and thunderous applause. They sat under the rollup canopy outside Rocky's travel trailer nursing beer and catching up on the year's history.

"We've come a long way since we started this tradition." Rocky pointed to the trailer. "Most of us have." He leaned back in his king-size lawn chair, belly cascading over his belt. Rocky had quit truck driving a couple years earlier when he failed the CDL for health reasons and now operated a beef cattle operation. Twenty-some years of truck-stop cuisine had taken its toll. "Tad."

Rocky pointed his beer can at him. "You were in charge of food and beer. If we drink all the beer you brought, we'll die of alcohol poisoning."

Tad sat in the semi-circle in camo fatigues and OD T-shirt and an expression of perpetual apprehension. He puffed a cigar. "Happy to be of service." Tad worked road construction in spring, summer, and fall living in a trailer half the size of Rocky's. Winters, he returned to his parents' farm close to the grandkids.

"Bear," Rocky continued, "you were in charge of firewood and watercraft and you brought this beautiful pontoon with upholstered deck chairs and beer coolers. Barbecue grill and a stereo sound system." He pointed to the boat still attached to the travel trailer. "It must have cost a bundle."

"An early retirement gift to myself," Bear said. "Maggie gets credit for the accessories. She's an interior designer when she's not curling hair."

"I was in charge of lodging." Rocky pointed to the trailer. "And you each have your own bed, if not your own bedroom."

"Bravo." Tad sat without expression. "Have a cigar."

"And you, Doctor Mike." Rocky bit off the tip. "You were in charge of weather. You let us down, brother." He reached his hand out from under the canopy, snapped it back, and dried it on his pants leg.

Doc leaned back in his chair, hands folded behind his head. "I bundled all the clouds and let them dump on us tonight. Blue skies and sunshine the rest of the weekend." Doc had a short drive to the lake, leaving from his clinic in Cambridge. He scanned the group and rubbed his chin. "Am I the only one who shaves?"

A flash of lightning struck, followed milliseconds later by earthshaking thunder. Tad launched his beer can in the air. "Holy shit." He grabbed another from the cooler and guzzled.

Doc retrieved the beer can and dropped it in a basket. "Rocky, you were in charge of the topic for this year's personal seminar series. I remember our inaugural topic—the first time I got laid. One year it was why I did or didn't serve in the military. Another was five things I want to do before I die. What's this year's topic?"

"I've thought about that a lot." Rocky blew a cloud of smoke over his head. "We're all getting grayer. Time for a little gravitas." He scanned his friends. "This year's topic—how does it feel to kill someone, either accidentally or on purpose. And how do you deal with it."

Silence, except for the clatter of rain on the canopy.

"You have a day to think about it." Rocky eyed the group. "Recitation is tomorrow night."

Another flash of lightning, less brilliant. Thunder, less immediate.

Rocky pointed his bottle at Tad. "You ought to ace this one, what with your two tours in Vietnam."

"I try not to think about it."

"And you, Bear. Deputy sheriff. I expect you racked up a few casualties."

"I winged a few. None of them fatal."

"How about you, Doc? Any assisted suicides? Mercy killings? Bungled surgeries?"

Doc knocked on the wooden armrest of his camp chair. "So far, I've been lucky." He hesitated. "Well, maybe one."

Rocky tipped his beer can and crushed it. "I smashed into a young woman driver who lost it on a patch of ice when I drove semi. Took me a long time before I could look in the mirror."

More silence. The rain eased. Lightning became remote, thunder indistinct.

Rocky stood. "I'm going to hit the sack. Hard day's driving, towing this Taj Mahal and Bear's showboat."

Tad stood too. "I'm going before you. Hope to fall asleep before you break into your snore mode."

Bear stood and moved his chair closer to Doc's. "Wish I could build a fire. So much easier to tell lies in front of a fire." He walked from under the canopy and glanced around the campsite, surveying firewood.

"So, retirement's in the offing?" Doc said. "Hope you've got a bucket full of challenges waiting. I've lost way too many patients who retired from work and retired from life."

"Not to worry. If I can't keep myself busy, Maggie will. How about you? Any retirement plans?"

"It's never occurred to me."

Rain stopped, except when wind shook it from leaves. A moth buzzed the lantern hanging from the canopy.

"Strange coincidence." Doc stared at the beer can in his hands. "Rocky mentioning killing someone. This afternoon, I drove by the academy I attended in my freshman high school year.

Remember? I didn't join you guys until our sophomore year."

"Don't recall. Want another beer?"

"I haven't seen the academy since my mother and I made the trip way back then. She wanted to talk to the Abbot. It was after Easter." Doc looked at the sky. Wind had scattered the clouds, and an occasional star peeked through. "I had done something stupid, very stupid, in response to what I perceived to be a threat."

Doc set his beer can down and rubbed his face. "In retrospect, it wasn't a threat. It was retaliation. I remember the grieved tone of the Abbot's voice when my mother asked for an explanation.

"'Father Ambrose took his own life,' the Abbot said. 'Shot himself. May God forgive him. Pray for his family.'"

Easter break at Agnus Dei Academy, and the boarding school student body had left for a long weekend. The dormitory was empty, save for three students—a foreign exchange student from Ireland, a displaced foster-home resident, and Mike Becker, with a home to return to, but no bus fare.

On Good Friday night, the usually cramped and rowdy dormitory was cavernous, quiet, ominous. Warm spring temperatures expanded the building's beams and struts; dissonant cracks echoed from hallway to hallway. The breeze through open windows scoured the stale air of winter.

Easter fell late that year, the twenty-fifth of April. Students had mowed Academy grounds, and the smell of fresh-cut grass rose to Mike's second story window, reminding him that his dad Leo would be prowling the fields now, assessing winterkill and measuring the height of first-crop alfalfa. His mother Ellie would be planting peas and potatoes in her garden and starting tomato plants in a hotbed on the south wall of the granary.

Leo Becker had knocked around in life, moving the family from farm to farm, scratching out a living, searching for a geographic *sweet spot*. Success was beyond his ken. He knew that, and concentrated on survival.

Ellie Becker was the daughter of a town family whose father enjoyed a prosperous career, allowing the children to finish high school and consider college. Books lined a wall in their parlor, and a Victrola spun recordings of Mozart and Handel and Chopin.

Ellie yielded her first three sons to Leo for the farm. Her

fourth and middle child Mike she retained, and into him she poured her love for music, her fondness for nature, her passion for books and education. She defended Mike, hid his misdeeds from Leo. When Mike torched his brothers' fort in revenge for their teasing, Ellie protected him. "Likely the boys were smoking in there."

"The boys weren't playing in the fort," Leo said.

"They were yesterday. Probably smoldered all night." She talked to Mike about the folly of revenge, how two wrongs don't make a right.

His conduct troubled her. During the spring school year, Mike tried out for baseball, the smallest kid on the junior varsity team. "You can't throw, you can't catch," the coach said, "and your strike zone could be measured in inches. I'll make you equipment manager."

Mike had issues with first baseman Blake who tossed his glove and bat at the end of practice. When Mike stooped to retrieve it, he'd get a baseball in the leg, the butt and a hearty chorus of laughter.

Mike's job was to inventory equipment after practice and account for all bats, gloves, and balls. He slipped the bat and glove Blake used into Blake's locker and reported it missing. "Probably stolen," he said.

When the rouse was exposed, the principal summoned Mrs. Becker and Mike into his office.

"You get all excited if my boy pulls a prank." She crossed her arms. "But you do nothing to stop the bullying. Nothing."

Her protection worked for Mike.

Neighbor Reilly badgered him about his size, called him Shorty or Peanut or Shrimp. Ridiculed him because he couldn't drive a tractor. Belly-laughed and called him Lightning when Mike pounded a nail. *You never strike the same place twice.*

Mike retaliated. Sunday morning, he lay in bed upstairs.

"Time to get ready for church," his mother called.

"I don't feel good," he moaned.

She climbed the stairs. "What's the problem?"

"Pain down here." He pressed his stomach. "What does appendicitis feel like?"

Mrs. Becker placed a hand under her left rib, then under her right. "You get this pain in your side. Don't remember which side." She pulled a blanket under his chin. "Sleep this one out. I'll check on you when I get home. You won't die within an hour."

Mike watched the Reilly driveway from his upstairs window. Their family car left for church within minutes of Mike's family. Mike dressed, hustled to the neighbor's farm, and opened the barnyard gates. The Holsteins stared at Mike, stared at the open gate, then filed out, heading for the alfalfa field, Mrs. Reilly's garden, a huge stand of field corn.

Back home, he watched the cows graze in the Reilly front yard, saw the Reilly car stop at the mailbox and kids chase the cows back, saw his family stop and herd stragglers from the cornfield to the barn.

Mrs. Becker climbed the stairs when she returned. "Somebody opened the gates at Reilly's." She took Mike's temperature. "Mr. Reilly says he knows who did it."

Mike held the thermometer under his tongue and gaped a surprised look.

"Those cows could have bloated and died. I know you don't like him, but the world is full of Mr. Reillys. You'll have to learn to deal with them. And not through revenge."

"But . . ." Mike mouthed over the thermometer. He didn't buy it.

The parish priest stopped Leo and Ellie after mass on Vocations Sunday. "God has blessed you with seven children." He placed an arm on their shoulders. "You owe one back to the Lord."

"Let 'em take Mike," Leo said later. "He'll never make a farmer."

Now Mike lay on his bed in the silent dormitory, exhaustion from mowing grass and trimming shrubbery tempered by a steaming shower. The Irish exchange student slept on the far side of the dorm, the foster-home student on the first floor. Outside, a paschal moon cast a shaft of light across the foot of the bed. Mike slept.

The bed moved, the footboard creaked. Mike lay with eyes closed. His heart knocked against his chest. Beads of sweat broke out on his upper lip.

Weight shifted. Mike opened his eyes. A tall, square-shouldered figure sat silhouetted in the moonlight. The man rose and moved away from the bed. Mike craned for an identity. The shadowed features were indistinct, the form unfamiliar. When it passed a moonlit window, he saw a plaid shirt, red plaid.

Mike waited, listened, and lowered his feet to the cool tile floor and stood, tentative and trembling. At the window, he stared down at dark forms of lilac bushes and mock orange in the courtyard. Silence.

Easter Monday, classes resumed. The dormitory buzzed with students in new shirts and trousers, stashing packages of cookies and bars, jellybeans and chocolate eggs. Mike left the dormitory to meet Rob in the courtyard.

Rob was a senior, committed to the seminary and, in time, to the priesthood. His stocky build, his cropped blond hair, his generous smile suggested a life of well-being. Mike hadn't understood why Rob selected him to mentor, to befriend. Why? "You remind me of my little brother."

Rob talked about his Easter holiday, played down the family dinner, the weighty conversations with his father, the doting excesses of his mother. "And what did you do for three days?" he asked Mike.

Mike hesitated. He flushed. "You're not going to believe this." He described how he awakened to the movement and sound of weight shifting at the foot of his bed, how the figure rose and silently departed when Mike stirred. "Not one night, but all three nights."

"The guy sounds too big to have been either of the other students." Rob looked puzzled. "And you couldn't recognize him?"

"He wore the same shirt every night. A red plaid shirt. That's all I could see."

"You've got to report this. Ask to see the Prefect."

In the courtyard the following night, Rob asked if Mike had reported the incidents.

"Yeah. The Prefect wrote something on a notebook, asked if I recognized the visitor, asked the same questions you did." Mike trembled and glanced over his shoulder. "I think he shrugged it off as an overactive imagination."

As a senior, Rob knew the faculty and administration well, both their professional and personal lives. Father Ambrose, the Prefect, kept a 12-gauge shotgun in his room and hunted small game. He remembered his hunting shirt. "I don't think you'll get cooperation from him. Let me mull this."

Days later, they entered the Abbot's office located in the monastery wing. Mike told his story again. The visitor, the shirt, the conversation with the Prefect.

The Abbot patted Mike on the back. "I'll take care of it."

In the courtyard after evening study hall, Mike told Rob. "I think Father Ambrose heard from the Abbot. When I glance up, he's staring at me. He doesn't call on me to recite in Latin class. He watches me when I come and go. He probably knows where I am right now." He glanced over his shoulder.

"He's doing the same thing to me. Don't worry. We did the right thing."

They continued to meet in the courtyard comparing notes. Tulips bloomed around them in strict rectangles. Forsythias glowed in a moonlit out-of-context exuberance. A center fountain gurgled behind their bench.

"Any word from Father Ambrose?" Rob asked.

"None. And I'm getting scared." Mike's voice broke with fear.

Rob reached to put his arm around Mike. To comfort him.

A blinding light flashed. "Well, isn't this a cozy love scene?" Father Ambrose stepped from behind a lilac bush, his fingers twiddling and laced across his stomach. A camera dangled from a strap around his neck. "We have rules about this kind of conduct." His eyebrows quivered, his Dick Tracy jaw squared.

The next day, Rob was gone. The Abbot's office cited personal reasons. Mike roamed the halls and classrooms and dormitory. He had no opportunity to talk to his friend, to say goodbye. Though Rob had done nothing dishonorable, a hint of scandal would be ruinous to his family. He left, Mike surmised, with an understanding. And a threat.

Days and nights melded in eerie confusion and torment for Mike. Voices were white noise. Food was bland, indigestible. Sleep impossible. Surveillance was constant. Everywhere he turned, Father Ambrose was watching. He wrote to his mother. She wrote back, promising to pray for him.

Paddy, the Irish exchange student, sat next to Mike at supper. A senior seminarian intoned the New Testament from the Abbot's table as students ate in silence.

Blessed are you when men reproach you, and persecute you and, speaking falsely, say all manner of evil against you, for my sake. Rejoice and exalt, because your reward is great in heaven.

Mike sat locked in the tortured spinning of his own thoughts. He poked at his peas, divided his mashed potatoes into squares. Paddy noted his withdrawal and nudged him. "What's the matter, boyo?" he whispered. "Having a bad time without Rob?"

Mike wanted to tell Paddy his story. "Just having trouble with the Prefect." The words slid out of the corner of his mouth.

"Get in line," Paddy whispered. "He has a reputation for manhandling the smallest kids in class."

Afternoons at five, priests gathered in the monastery chapel to read the Breviary and recite the Litany of the Saints. Mike knew Father Ambrose's room among those circled around the altar and prayer area, knew the priest was regularly late for prayer because of his duties as Prefect.

Mike's throat was dry, his heart pounded as he stole to the priests' chapel and opened Father Ambrose's door, slipping into the small, windowless room with its musky odor. Furnishings were sparse: a narrow cot, a kneeling bench before a crucifix, books stacked on a small desk beside a reading lamp and clock—*Confessions of Saint Augustine*, Thomas A. Kempis's *Imitation of Christ*, *Lives of the Saints*. A closet door stood ajar. Mike swung it open. On plain wooden hangers hung a cassock, black suit, hunting clothes, red plaid shirt.

He waited in the center of the room, the silence intensified by the incessant ticking clock. His belly knotted, his palms grew greasy with sweat. From here, he heard priests return to their rooms and enter the chapel area to pray in a monotonic hum.

Five-thirty. Mike removed his shirt.

The door opened. "What?" Father Ambrose stood in the doorway. He stepped inside and closed the door, cutting off view of the boy sitting on his bed. "What are you doing here?" His voice hissed with shock and sudden fear.

"I think I have poison ivy, Father. Would you rub calamine lotion on my back?"

"Are you crazy? Go to the infirmary."

"I was there and they gave me lotion, Father. But I can't reach my back."

Father Ambrose stammered. He turned to stare at the door separating him from his fellow priests and the prayerful Abbot kneeling at the altar. Muted prayer, the low, repetitive chants of *pray for us*, hummed like a beehive.

Father Ambrose grabbed the lotion, pounded a few drops in his hand, and flung the tube on the bed. His motions were cold, robotic. Mike lifted his undershirt to expose unblemished skin. Father Ambrose slapped the lotion on his back and rubbed it with quick, rough strokes. Again, Mike handed him the tube, and the priest repeated the motion, this time slower, gentler, wider, lower.

Mike jumped for the door, grabbed his shirt, and ran into the prayer area.

"Leave me alone," he screamed. "Leave me alone."

Toward midnight, after the rain subsided and the wind relaxed, Mike sat on a camp chair, his head buried in his hands. Bear crushed his beer can and tossed it in the basket. Silence, except for Rocky's lusty snore inside the trailer. A sliver of moon broke through clouds and cast timid shadows on the campsite.

Bear rose and reached for the lantern. "You want some time alone?"

Mike lifted his head. "There's more."

Bear lowered the lantern flame and sat.

"Today, when I drove past Agnus Dei Academy, I turned around and drove back to the church connected to it. In the parking lot, the carillon bells sounded, ringing the hour. The same bells that rang years ago. I slowed and stopped in the drive, trance-like. A driver tapped his horn and startled me."

Mike sat erect, staring at Bear. An owl called. Another answered.

"I walked up the steps to the church, just as I had done a hundred times years ago and dipped my fingers in the holy water font. Several old women prayed near the confessional in the dim nave.

"After high school, after I left home, I shunned the confessional. Partly because I didn't believe in it. Partly because, whether I believe or not, it holds bad juju. And what I had to confess was no small matter.

"The church still felt dank and chilly. Votive lights flickered in the rack and smelled of hot wax, just as they had done years ago. I slid in a pew next to the old women and assessed the situation. For years, I couldn't enter a church without thinking about Father Ambrose. Here, he was front and center and, when I closed my eyes to shut him out, he was sitting on my bed in the dormitory. I stumbled out of the pew and raced for the door."

Mike stopped and lowered his head in his hands again. Raindrops tapped on the canopy.

Bear stood. "Have you asked God's forgiveness, Mike?"

"Yes, and I felt it."

"Have your friends and family forgiven you?"

"Those I've told, yes."

"Have you forgiven yourself?"

Silence.

"Maybe," Mike mumbled.

"Maybe?"

Silence again, then Rocky's dissonant snoring.

"Yes, I forgive myself."

"And I forgive you too, for what it's worth." Bear parked a hand on Mike's shoulder. "Let's call it a day."

Gopher

Gopher Graham leaned low over the pool table, his belly pressed against the rail. He squinted down table, pointed at the thirteen ball, and tapped the corner pocket. His tourney opponent rested his chin on an upright cue and smirked at his pals. No one could make that nine-thirteen combo. Gopher steadied himself, braced a stubby finger against the felt tabletop, and cocked his arm. The cue stick glided like a piston rod, kissing the cue ball, brushing the nine, grazing the thirteen. It rolled, rolled, rolled against the rail into the corner pocket. Plunk. Gopher straightened, grinned at the crowd, and reached for his root beer.

Damn, it was good to be back with the gang.

Gopher's world upended when he won the million-dollar Power Ball jackpot. He wouldn't have splurged on a Power Ball ticket, but when the Broken Hart celebrated its grand opening with new owners, Gopher won a door prize of five tickets. He tucked them in the kitchen calendar pocket and forgot them. When news broke that the winning ticket was purchased in Minnesota and not claimed, the Broken Hart manager asked Gopher if he checked his tickets. "You could be a rich man, my friend."

Rich man was not in Gopher's lexicon. When his dad died and his mother moved to Good Shepherd Assisted Living, he sold the dairy cows and split the proceeds with sister Diane. For spending money, he trapped pocket gophers, rampant out in sand country. Neighbors hired him, paid him a dollar apiece. The townships matched that in bounty. On a good day, he'd trap forty gophers; on a great day, fifty. A hundred dollars a day. Not rich, but with the farm paid for and rent from cornfields and hay land, he satisfied his needs. And one *want*—a four-wheeler to run his trap line.

His pool pals razzed him, asked what thrill he got matching

GOPHER

wits with a rodent. He'd grin and swig a root beer. "Easier than milking cows morning and night." Razzing was old hat for Gopher. Years earlier in high school, when Gopher weighed in at two-hundred and thirty pounds, the football coach drafted him as defensive end. After a dozen sacked quarterbacks, half of them carried out on stretchers, the school's athletic director opted to save the district insurance money and retired him.

Monday morning after realizing he held the winning numbers, Gopher drove to town for a meeting with a representative of the Lottery Association and the bank president. He donned a fresh pair of bib overalls that strained at the waist, a faded T-shirt, eight-inch lace-up boots. When he removed his red Funk's Seed Corn hat in the bank, pinkish-white skin on his forehead contrasted with his leather-tanned cheeks.

After fifteen minutes, a sweating Gopher walked out the bank door, took a deep breath, and drove to the Broken Hart, labored breathing, white knuckles gripping the wheel. Outside, an early morning calm prevailed. In the bar, Gopher walked by the pool table and tapped the cue ball.

"Mornin', Mr. Greenbacks." The manager pressed hamburger patties on the grill table. "Can I get you the usual? It's on the house."

Gopher smiled an oafish grin and nodded. "Yep."

The manager wiped his hands on an apron and snapped a can of A&W. He rested his hand on Gopher's shoulder. "A million bucks is a lot of money." He smiled. "A whole lot of money."

Gopher stared through grimy glasses. He chugged his root beer and mugged a half-smile.

"You know it's customary for winners to show their appreciation. Share their good fortune with the establishment that sold the ticket."

Gopher swirled the can between his chubby fingers.

"Ten percent is common, you know. Let's see. Ten percent of a million is a hundred thousand. Damn near pay off our mortgage."

"It ain't a million. After taxes, it's about $675,000. And I'm not taking a lump sum. I'm taking a yearly payoff."

"Well, I'm sure we'd be willing to take our share on some kind of extended pay schedule."

Gopher took another swig and grinned at the manager. "I'm

hungry. Make me a double cheeseburger." He reached for an unfamiliar wad of bills. "And make it to go."

"A million dollars is a great gift from the Lord." Pastor Louise stood outside the screen door at Gopher's farm, talking above a snarling Bruno inside. "A generous gift from a beneficent Lord."

Gopher chewed his cheeseburger and held a finger on the screen door hook. He pushed Bruno away with his boot.

Pastor Louise kept one eye on the dog and tapped the New Testament in her hand. "You know, the Lord giveth and the Lord taketh away."

Gopher grinned and snugged his finger on the hook.

Pastor Louise licked the tip of her finger and opened the New Testament to a red-ribbon bookmarked page. "Mark 10: 25. *'For it is easier for a camel to pass through the eye of a needle than for a rich man to enter the kingdom of heaven.'*"

Gopher grinned. "I'm familiar with what the Bible says, ma'am."

Pastor Louise lifted a single braid and placed it on the shoulder of her gray cardigan. "Then you know what the Old Testament says about tithing. Ten percent back to the Lord. The Lord looks kindly on a generous heart."

The phone rang and Gopher glanced at his watch. "Sorry, Pastor, but I have to take this. I called my sister to help me manage my good fortune. I'll let you know what she says."

Pastor Louise clamped the Bible closed and stared through the screen.

Gopher turned away and picked up the kitchen phone. "Hi, sis."

"This isn't your sis, Gopher. This is Rick Mason down at Mason Motors. How ya doin'?"

Gopher held the phone away from his ear. "I'm expecting a call from my sister."

"Well, sir, this won't take long. I just want to congratulate you on your stroke of good luck. And I want to remind you that a man in your new income bracket deserves to ride around in appropriate style."

Gopher kept the phone away from his ear and thought about his sister Diane. Smart girl, inherited her mother's low-key sensibility, her slight stature, her intellect. Diane had a knack for

GOPHER

numbers, coasted through algebra, geometry, trig, and calculus in high school. Cruised through four years at Moorhead State on a full scholarship, graduating with a double-major in finance and accounting. Hired by a big Charitable Foundation in St. Paul first as analyst, then as account exec, and finally CFO.

"Now, Gopher, you've been real happy with that 2000 Silverado we sold you, right?" Rick Mason was on a roll. "And you've been real happy with the service we give you, right, Gopher? Well, sir, I have right here on my lot a new High Country Silverado with your name printed all over it. Four-door double cab, V-8 engine, monster tires, heated leather upholstered seats, GPS. All that, Gopher, in a knockout siren red package."

"What's GPS?"

"I was hopin' you'd ask. C'mon in and I'll show you. With GPS, you'll never get lost again."

"I never was lost."

"Of course not, Gopher. Not a smart man like you." He paused. "What d'ya say, Gopher? You want to come to town and I'll buy you dinner, or shall I drive out to the farm?"

Gopher stared at the phone, then glanced out the window. Murphy was negotiating the rutted driveway on his bicycle. "I got company. I have to hang up."

"Not a problem, Gopher. No sir, not a problem at all. I'll call back a little later. Now you have yourself a good day, hear?"

Gopher nudged Bruno off his boot and opened the screen door. "C'mon in, Murphy. Your Old Milwaukee's in the fridge."

"Damn woman driver." Murphy slid bicycle clips off his lanky pant legs onto his boots. His oversized jeans were belted at the waist with clothesline; his flannel shirt, worn summer and winter, sported a snoose box ring on the pocket. "Damn near run me over down the road. Looked madder than a wet hen. Wonder what turned her crank." He opened his beer and took a long swig. The bicycle ride to Gopher's farm exhausted him. But without a driver's license, without a car, options were limited. Maybe if he had passed the driver's license written exam and gotten a permit . . . Maybe if he learned to drive in reverse and parallel park . . .

"If it was a black Buick sedan, that was Pastor Louise. She believes that part of the Bible that says 'Ask and you shall receive.'" Gopher opened a root beer. "Sit down, Murphy, and help me with a plan. You know I won the Power Ball jackpot, right?"

"The what?"

"I won a lot of money in the lottery, and people won't leave me alone. I've got to get out of Dodge. Soon."

"You want me to stay here at the farm and keep an eye on Bruno while you're gone?"

"No, I want you and Bruno to come with me. We'll drive to the Black Hills of South Dakota. See Mount Rushmore. Let some of the dust settle around here."

"What day is today?" Murphy looked at the calendar. "Monday the fourteenth. I can't go until the seventeenth. My county check comes on the seventeenth."

"How much is your check?"

"$374.40."

"Hell, I'll give you $500, and your check'll be waiting for you when you get back."

Murphy took a swallow of beer and licked his lips. "I don't have any Sunday clothes."

"We'll pass a dozen Walmarts between here and there." Gopher looked at Murphy's bowl of unruly hair. "We also might want to stop at a barber shop, get you a store-bought haircut and shave."

Murphy rubbed his gray stubbled chin. "How 'bout your truck? Ready to make the trip?"

"I got the rest of the day to change oil, air up the spare, check the lights—head lights, taillights, brake lights. Interior light never did work. I'll run my gopher line and pick up the traps." Gopher grinned and swigged his root beer. "Be ready at eight-thirty tomorrow morning. I have to get outta here early. The WCCO television crew left a message on my answering machine. They'll be here at ten."

Murphy was glassy-eyed. "What if the truck breaks down? What if we get lost? What if . . . ?"

"Just be ready at 8:30. I'll stop and talk to Deputy Sheriff Bear before I pick you up."

Gopher pressed the call button at the county Justice Building the next morning and waited to be buzzed in.

"Mornin', Gopher." Deputy Sheriff Bear offered his hand. "Congratulations."

"You heard already?"

"A dozen times. Two of your neighbors called to complain about the traffic on your road. Gawkers wanting to see the site of

GOPHER

the new Gopher Manor."

"That's what I want to talk to you about. I'm getting too much attention. Gotta get away for a while. Murphy and me are going out to the Black Hills. Will you drive in my yard now and then? Leave fresh tire tracks in the driveway?"

"We can do that, Gopher. You got the place secured?"

"There's nothing to secure. The back door is locked, but it'll give if you lean into it. Front door never has been unlocked that I know of."

"Consider it done. You might be in a position to do me a favor down the road. Young Stub Norton will be eligible for work release in a month or so. Problem is, no work. No legitimate skills either. Wondering if you'd be willing to take him on out at the farm a couple days a week. Help with projects. Teach him to trap."

"His mom Rhonda and my sister Diane were best friends in high school. I'll see what I can do."

"You know where you're going?" Murphy sat in the passenger seat, arm resting on the open window. Bruno slept beside him, head on his lap. Along the highway, cornfields tasseled and soybeans covered the ground in a blanket of sage green. A milk truck honked and passed. Off in the distance, a water tower poked through the tree line.

"We'll stay on Highway 71 south all the way to 14, then head west through the whole state of South Dakota. I don't like freeways." He pointed to a patch of dense green oaks surrounding a silver-blue lake. "I like to see the countryside."

"We gonna break for dinner before we get there?"

"We're gonna break for dinner and supper. Maybe spend a night in a motel. Then break for breakfast and dinner again before we get to the Black Hills."

"You trust this old girl to make it that far?"

Gopher patted the dashboard. "I know every breath she takes. And I have the tool box in back if I need it."

Murphy read aloud each traffic sign and billboard they passed. REDUCED SPEED AHEAD, CAUTION LOOSE GRAVEL, CLOVERLEAF MOTEL. He paused. "I've never slept in a motel."

"Neither have I. But that's what they're there for. I'll stop for gas in Redwood Falls. My trucker friend crows about a good café there. We'll try them for dinner."

"I can tell we're heading south." Murphy slipped out of his

shirt. "It's getting warmer. How long before we stop?"

Highway 71 rolled south through small town after small town where pickups nosed into the curb in front of restaurants for morning coffee. And between, verdant fields of corn and beans, alfalfa and sunflowers. An occasional silver mailbox marked a homestead—large white house, barns, machine sheds, Harvestore silos, a half-dozen John Deere tractors. More often, a rusty mailbox, a gate blocking the weeded driveway. Deserted buildings, a screen door flapping in the breeze, a windmill in lazy rotation.

Gopher slowed at the Redwood Falls city limits, stopped for gas, and parked at the station. He patted his wallet. "Better put your shirt back on." He glanced down Second Street toward the Calf Fiend Café. "There's our dinner."

"Sounds like a coffee house and I don't drink coffee."

Inside, they sat at a booth and stared at the menu printed on a chalkboard. "Dinner's on me." Gopher clapped his hands. "Order what you want."

"Good afternoon, gentlemen." A waitress held two glasses of water. "Need more time, or do you know what you want?"

"Double cheeseburger for me." Gopher clamped his hands together and tapped the table. "And a root beer."

"Sorry, we don't serve cheeseburgers. How about a Philly steak sandwich? Same thing. Beef and cheese."

Gopher grinned. "Works for me. And a hamburger off the kids' menu to go."

Murphy shot him a glance. "What's that for?"

"Bruno."

"I'll have the same thing he's having, only I'll have a beer. You got Old Milwaukee?"

"Sorry again. But I have great coffee. Mocha. Latte. Espresso."

"Don't touch the stuff. Water's okay."

Gopher watched her wiggle to the kitchen. "This is your last meal in Minnesota. Enjoy."

They divided the last of a monster Babe Ruth brownie from the café when they crossed into South Dakota. "I'll be damned," Murphy yelled. "Looks just like Minnesota."

After Brookings and Huron, small towns grew smaller. One-stoplight towns gave way to no-stoplight towns, then NO SPEED

GOPHER

LIMIT towns. Beyond the last deserted bungalow, banks of combines marauded grain fields, chaff glistening in their wake like gold dust. Loaded trucks inched off the fields onto the highway spitting clods of dirt and obstructing the view. Gopher leaned back and braced his hands against the steering wheel. "Guess I'll have to slow down and take my place in line."

More small towns. Miller. Ree Heights. Highmore with a boarded Texaco station, its bullet-ridden sign advertising gas for ninety-nine nine, weeds growing through cracks in the concrete. Three towns with a combined population of a couple hundred.

Miles of grain fields gave way to miles of grazing land. Rolling hills gave way to flat prairie. No billboards. No mailboxes. No grazing cattle. No utility poles. And then, no fences. Ten, fifteen, twenty miles before they met another vehicle. Ahead, the highway stretched arrow-straight. Further ahead, you could see the curvature of the earth.

Gopher shook his head. "Man, that's a whole lot of nothing."

A few more small towns. Holabird and Harrold, with Co-op grocery, senior center, and three churches.

"Pierre Twenty Miles." Gopher read a sign outside Blunt. "The sun'll be in my eyes soon. We'll stop for supper in Pierre and stay in a motel. My trucker friend recommended a Super 8 a couple blocks off the highway." He looked at Murphy who didn't respond. Murphy slept, head tilted back, cap over his eyes, mouth open. Bruno slept too, his head resting on Murphy's lap.

"Welcome, gents. How can I help you today?" The tanned motel clerk wore a SAVE A HORSE, RIDE A COWBOY T-shirt. The turquoise and silver clip that circled her ponytail matched her turquoise and silver pendant.

"You gotta room for two?" Gopher rested his arms on the counter and grinned.

"Sure, hon. How many nights?"

"Just one. Just tonight. What's your rate for first-time Minnesotans?"

"For you, $63, plus tax. How many beds?"

"Well, there's me and my friend Murphy."

The clerk stared over the rims of her glasses. "How many beds?"

"Two."

Murphy walked around the lobby—the pamphlet racks, the candy machine, the soda dispenser, the split-rock fireplace with leather chairs, the *Sports Afield* magazines on the coffee table. He joined Gopher at the counter and spied a bowl of Life Savers. The clerk pointed with a turquoise-ringed finger. "Help yourself."

"Any problem if I bring my pup Bruno in?"

"If your pup is under fifteen pounds, no problem. Otherwise, $20 additional."

"Bruno weighed more than fifteen pounds when he was born."

"I love dogs," the clerk said. "What breed is he?"

"Breeds. Part mastiff, part good neighborhood." He reached for his billfold and pulled out a hundred-dollar bill.

"You can pay with cash, but I'll need to see a credit card."

"Don't have a credit card. Don't need a credit card. You got a problem with cash?"

"The credit card is more for identification. We miss a few towels, we know how to find you." She handed him the registration form. "Initial here and here and sign here. How about your friend? Does he have a credit card?"

"Look." Gopher opened his wallet—twenties, fifties, a wad of hundred-dollar bills.

The clerk jolted. "Do yourself a favor, my friend. Don't ever do that again. You're lucky you're in an honest respectable establishment." She pointed her pen at Gopher's wallet. "Put that in a safe place. You probably don't have access to your bank, so keep it in your socks, your shorts, any place out of sight."

Gopher gave her a quizzical stare.

"I'll give you room 118, down the hall and to the right. Complimentary breakfast begins at six."

Back on U.S. 14 the next morning, Murphy rubbed his belly. "You know you snore like a steam engine."

Gopher grinned. "How many waffles did you eat this morning?"

"What was I to do? She kept making them for me. By the way, you forgot your change at the table." He handed Gopher a five-dollar bill.

"Lotsa things I want to see out here." Murphy shuffled through a handful of brochures. "Reptile Gardens, Dinosaur Park, Big Thunder Goldmine, Crazy Horse Monument."

GOPHER

"Don't forget Mount Rushmore. I suppose we'll have the same problem getting a motel out there."

"No problem for me." Murphy petted Bruno's head. "Bruno and me'll sleep in the cargo box."

The motels in Rapid City declined credit card-less travelers. "Try Rockerville down the highway." Same thing there. "Try Hill City down the highway. There's a few mom and pop motels there that might take you in."

On the highway to Hill City, signs announced Cosmos Mystery Cave, souvenir shops in Keystone, the cut-off to Mount Rushmore. "Hey, when are we going to stop?" Murphy asked.

"Not until we find a motel."

The motels in Hill City repeated the same *no credit card, no room message*. "Try the Old Bones Woman Cabins up on Old Hill City Road. She might set you up."

The highway twisted out of Hill City, through forests of black spruce, canyons of exposed granite, vistas of mountain meadows. High on a darkened slope, a lone aspen shone gold in the late afternoon sun.

A sign constructed of weathered cattle bones marked the entrance of Old Bones Woman Cabins. A woman tended a fire beneath a hanging pot beside the house marked OFFICE. WELCOME.

Gopher shouted from the truck. "You got a cabin for a couple weary travelers, ma'am? And we don't have a credit card." Bruno pushed his head out the window.

"I have a cabin, and I don't take credit cards." She put her arm on her hip and brushed silver wisps of hair from her face. "And that dog of yours is welcome if he stays out of my bones." She motioned them toward a rustic cabin 4, sided with pine slabs. Inside, one room with two double beds. "There's a shared bath with cabin 3, but no one to share it with."

Gopher punched the mattress. "We'll take it. Can you recommend a restaurant in town for supper?"

"Sorry. I don't eat in town. All I know is what other people tell me. Let me know if you want to join me for supper tomorrow night. I like the company."

"What are you cooking in the pot?" Murphy asked.

"I'm boiling the hide off elk bones. I get them from an elk game farm manager out of Silver City. I read bones to tell the future, and elk bones have spiritual significance."

"You're a gypsy fortune teller?"

"No. I read bones. The bones tell me the future."

"Man, we hit the jackpot." Gopher raised his arms like a ref signaling a touchdown. "I want you to read my bones before we leave. How about tomorrow when we get back from Mount Rushmore?"

"I'll be ready for you."

"Are you a native out here?" Gopher asked.

"No. I'm a transplant, like everybody else. From Denver. Taught history there until I got interested in the paranormal."

"Whatever that is," Gopher said.

Murphy chimed in. "Denver's in Colorado. My dad went there once to a livestock show."

"Your dad was a beef rancher?"

"No, he drove a truck."

"C'mon, Murphy. Let's find us some supper."

"The Country Inn is less than five minutes from here. I can't recommend it, but from what I hear, if you like fried food, you're in luck. I'll get you a map."

Inside the Country Inn, air smelled of fried onions, fried hamburger, fried bacon. A few patrons, tourists in pastel and primary cottons, locals in denim and chambray, chatted at tables or leaned on the bar. Gopher looked down at his bib overalls, not local Levi's and not tourist gaudy. He shrugged his shoulders and took a seat at an empty table. Murphy cased the joint. "Look, Gopher. Slot machines."

A smiling waitress carried water glasses and menus. "Welcome, gents. Don't recall seeing you here before. My name is Julie, and I'm your waitress tonight."

"Well, Julie, I'll have a double bacon cheeseburger, if you have such a thing. And a root beer. Corner my friend over there and ask him what he wants."

Murphy walked to the table after giving Julie his order, his head bobbing from one gang of slots to another. "I'm gonna try my luck tonight. See if some of your good luck rubs off on me."

"You're wasting your money."

"And you're hogging all the good luck."

After supper, Murphy ordered another Old Milwaukee and headed for the slots. Other patrons were leaving. Julie washed glasses behind the bar. Murphy glanced at her. "Hey, how do you work these things?"

"I'll show you but I gotta tell you this. We close in ten minutes. Don't start a lucky streak and have to break it."

"Not likely," Gopher called from the table.

Julie coached Murphy in the art of slots. Within a minute, he won $100. In another few minutes, another $100. "Don't forget what I told you." Julie walked back to the bar.

Murphy continued, but not winning. "Time to close," Julie called. "You all come back soon."

"Oh, I'll be back for sure." Murphy smiled, exposing yellowed ill-fitting dentures, like something bought in a mail-order catalog.

Wednesday morning, and Gopher waved to the Old Bones Woman from his pickup. "On our way to Mount Rushmore. Murphy wants to buy some T-shirts. Back after dinner for my bones reading."

"I'll be ready," the woman answered. "And I have stew in the pot for supper."

Heading back toward Hill City, they passed the mountain meadow vistas, the granite walls, the black spruce forests they had seen yesterday in afternoon light. This morning, the light was clearer, the colors cleaner. The lone aspen on the darkened slope shown a lemon yellow. "I heard mountain light was different," Gopher said. "Now I know what they mean."

"Mount Rushmore Parking," Murphy shouted, pointing at a sign. "That's us. Think we'll have any problem bringing Bruno in?"

"I'll put him on a leash and pretend I'm blind."

Murphy pointed at another sign. "Wow. Ten dollars to park. That's a lotta money for a small space for a short time."

"What else ya gonna do?"

They walked up the stairs from the parking ramp, Gopher leading Bruno. Early morning, and already crowds of tourists blocked the promenade leading to the monument, grinning for selfies or posing for group pictures. Above them, across a valley and framed by flags from fifty states, the gigantic monument loomed.

"George Washington." Murphy pointed. "And Abraham Lincoln."

"Thomas Jefferson and Theodore Roosevelt." Gopher completed the roster.

"Wow." Murphy stood stunned. "That's a lotta rock. I saw a gift shop back there. Let's get some souvenirs."

They took an alternate route back to the cabin, through Keystone where, at Murphy's insistence, they parked. A hundred gift stores, T-shirt shops, and curiosities. Caramel corn stands and ice cream parlors. Guided tour buses. Everybody hawking wares from the sidewalk. "Let's get outta here." Gopher grabbed Murphy by the arm. "I can't breathe. We'll have dinner when we're out of this traffic."

"Give me just a minute." Murphy grabbed his sleeve. "I want to buy this baseball cap."

Back at the Old Bones Woman's cabins, Gopher leaned out of the cab. "You ready for my bones reading?"

"Yes, sir. I have the embers hot and ready to go."

They sat around the fire pit where three rocks supported a grill. "Give me a couple minutes to get into my spiritual state." She placed her face in her hands and bowed her head. A breeze carried a hint of sage and tousled her hair. Down in the valley, crows called. Trails of heady pine smoke twirled in the breeze. The woman lifted her head and placed a bone on the grill. Bruno cocked his head. "This is an elk shoulder blade. I'll set it above the embers until it starts to crack. The cracks are what I read."

Gopher leaned forward, elbows on knees. Murphy petted Bruno.

In a short time, the bleached white bone turned to tan. Old Bones Woman watched for cracks to form. "There," she said. "Beautiful cracks and lots of them. Lots to tell us."

She lifted the bone from the grill and placed it on a flat rock. "My, what's this? See this large triangle? That's a sign of good luck. Have you had such an event recently?"

Gopher nodded his head.

"Then dark spots. Random bad luck. Short lived, but significant enough to require attention."

Gopher nodded again. "I could tell you stories."

"Then this line points to a feminine characteristic. A woman. Small. A good woman. Honest. Caring. Intelligent."

"That could be my sister Diane."

"See the connection between the triangle and the feminine characteristic? That woman will guide you through your good luck."

GOPHER

"How about my bad luck?"

"The line goes nowhere. You're stuck with that. Does any of this make sense?"

"Sure. My sister's a financial officer for a big foundation in St. Paul."

"CPA," Murphy added.

Gopher cocked his head. "What I didn't tell you is I won a million-dollar Power Ball jackpot."

"Before taxes," Murphy added again.

Gopher sat erect. "I don't need any more money, and I don't need a hundred people telling me how to spend it. Maybe I unload my good luck problem on my sister Diane."

Old Bones Woman continued. "You see this prominent crack? It's a decision line. On the top of the bone, the crack goes all the way to the end. On the other side, it may not. The decision is often associated with love. More often money." She traced the line with her finger. "If you make the right decision, it's easy going." She flipped the bone. "Oh, oh. Not the case here. The line ends in rubble. Bad decision, big trouble."

Gopher stared at the bone, then at the woman. "There's no love in my life, so it must be money. What do I do now?"

"Think about it. Then proceed with confidence."

"How much do I owe you? And could we have supper as soon as that stew is done? We skipped dinner because I couldn't deal with the crowds. I've seen more people today than I see in a year at home."

"No charge for the bones reading. I'll consider it practice for the group of women coming next week. Supper's on in a half-hour."

"Good." Murphy clapped his hands. "After that, we're off to the Country Inn to start working on *my* fortune."

"Not until I have my nap." Gopher stood. "I'm still shot from driving yesterday."

When they pulled into the Country Inn at six, the lot was filled with pickups, motorcycles, a couple tourist buses. Murphy scanned for a parking spot. "What's this all about?"

Gopher pointed to a sign at the entrance. WEDNESDAY NIGHT SPECIAL. TWO FOR ONE DRINKS. TWO FOR ONE BURGERS. "We seem to attract people wherever we go."

Gopher pulled into a space on the far side of the building.

Murphy sprang out of the seat. "You gonna lock it up?"

"I got the best security system in the world right here." Gopher patted Bruno's neck. "Take good care of this, big guy, and I'll bring you a hamburger."

Inside, the tables were full. The jukebox played a Ronnie Milsap song. Lights from the slot machines flashed brilliant pinks and blues and greens in strobe precision. A constant synthesized din jingle-jangled from the slots. Julie met them carrying a tray of burgers. "Welcome back, gentlemen. There might be a couple seats at the bar. Seat yourself."

Gopher ordered a root beer and a hamburger to go. Murphy headed for the slot where he won yesterday. He patted it with loving fingers. "Speak to me, girl."

Within minutes, he won a $100 jackpot. "Guess I still have my touch," he whispered to Gopher.

"If you still have a brain, you'd quit while you're ahead."

Murphy placed one-dollar bets, five-dollar bets, ten-dollar bets, all at break-neck speed.

Gopher grinned. "I've never seen you work so fast."

Then, a red light over Murphy's machine flashed and rotated. A siren sounded. All the lights on the machine flashed. *K-ching, k-ching, k-ching.* Murphy held the machine with both hands. "Holy shit, Gopher."

The manager of the Country Inn walked over. "Congratulations. You won our weekly $2,500 jackpot. You want your winnings in fifties, hundred-dollar bills, what?"

"I've never touched a hundred-dollar bill."

"Well, you will tonight. By the way, we have a $2,500 maximum daily payout per customer. You'll have to drop by tomorrow if you win any more tonight."

"You mean I can't play anymore tonight?"

"You can play, but you won't get paid. House rules. We can't keep a million dollars in cash in this place."

"Damn. Just when I was getting hot. That's more money in fifteen minutes than I make in six months."

Julie counted out the bills and handed them to Murphy. "Congratulations, big guy. Sign here for the IRS. And here's a spot for your tip." She waited for him to sign.

"What shall I do?" Murphy asked Gopher.

"Do whatever you want. And don't tell me what you did."

Murphy wrote a number and handed the slip to Julie. She

scowled. "Well, I'll be damned. Stiffed again."

"What do you think, Murphy? Enough excitement for one day? Let's head for the cabin."

Gopher picked up the hamburger and walked to the truck, along a porch decorated with blinking Christmas lights. Two men leaned on the porch rail chatting, smoking. "Congratulations." One man held his hand out to shake. "Fun to outsmart the smart guys, right?"

Murphy grabbed his hand on the run. "Thanks."

"Not so much fun for them to cut you off when you're hot though," the other said. Both wore Stetsons with sunglasses parked on the brim, western shirts and jeans, cowboy boots.

"Right." Murphy walked behind Gopher.

"If you want to cash in on your hot streak, there's another small casino a few miles from here."

"On our way home," the first stranger added. "If you follow us, we'll show you where it is."

Murphy stopped.

"Real friendly folks," the second stranger yelled. "And their machines aren't strung as tight as these." He flipped his cigarette in the parking lot. "Follow us if you're interested." The two men moseyed to a new GMC pickup.

"What do you think, Gopher? Can I try it one more time? I've never been this lucky in my life. I don't want to stop now. Let's follow them."

"I think it's a stupid idea, but they seem like decent folks. We'll go for one hour max. Okay?"

A few miles down the highway at an intersection, the GMC signal lights blinked. The truck stopped. Gopher stopped behind it. The GMC driver leaned out his window. "Come here, and I'll give you directions. We go right here, you go left."

Gopher hesitated, then opened the door.

"And tell your friend we have some tokens good for drinks and snacks at the casino. He can get them from my buddy Mac here."

"Stay close to me, Murphy," Gopher whispered. "This may not turn out so good."

When Gopher and Murphy were outside their truck, the two GMC men opened their doors and stepped out. The driver held a gun. "Thought you guys might want to share your good luck with a good Samaritan." He pointed the gun at Murphy. We know how much you have. Drop it on the ground."

Murphy looked at Gopher.

"Drop it."

"And you," the driver pointed at Gopher, "drop your billfold. And empty your pockets."

Gopher tossed his billfold and money on the ground.

"Now stand back and no one'll get hurt." He pointed to Mac. "Pick up the loot. See, you guys? I told you no one would get hurt. You guys won't need your truck for a while." He pointed to Mac again. "Grab the keys out of the ignition and toss them in the woods. They can find them in the morning."

Mac opened the door of the darkened cab to reach for the keys. Bruno snarled and bit his arm. Mac jumped. "Holy shit." He pulled away. Bruno leapt from the cab, snarling, snapping, biting.

Mac yelled. "Get that son-of-a-bitch off me." He ran toward his truck with Bruno clamped on a large chunk of his thigh. "Shoot the son-of-a-bitch," he screamed to his partner. He fell behind the truck, Bruno shaking, tearing the man's shirt and jeans.

"I can't shoot him. I'll shoot you." He turned to Gopher. "Call that dog off."

Gopher stood, saying nothing. Murphy put his hands over his eyes.

Mac screamed. "Kill that dog before I bleed to death."

The driver walked to the downed man as he tried to pull himself under the truck. He lifted his leg to kick Bruno. Gopher lowered his chest and rushed the driver, hitting him in the back with a force that propelled him over the dog into the ditch, Gopher on top of him. Gopher stood. "Stay, Bruno," he yelled. He lifted the prostrate driver by the collar and shook him. "Not surprised your gun landed somewhere in the ditch."

Bruno snarled.

"And you, Mac or whatever your name is, drop our money.

"Now get in your truck, and I'll call Bruno off," Gopher said. "Better get your friend Mac to a hospital quick. Bruno is not current on his rabies shots."

Thursday morning, and Gopher and Murphy tossed their duffel bags in the truck box. Bruno jumped in the cab. "I'm coming over to settle up," Gopher called to Old Bones Woman. "And can I use your phone? I want to call my sister."

GOPHER

"That was a close one last night." Murphy sat in the cab as they left Hill City. "I thought we were goners."

"I never thought they'd shoot us. And they would have got only got a small chunk of my money. The rest was in my shorts. Let's stop at McDonald's for breakfast."

Now, the road back home. Rapid City, then I-90 to Wall where Murphy pleaded to stop. Then north off the freeway through Quinn, Cottonwood, Philip—the little towns that break the monotony of the wide and handsome prairie. Through Pierre and Huron. Gopher held the wheel with both hands. "I'm driving straight through. Not stopping 'til we get home. Can't wait to play some pool and get back on my trap line." He glanced at Murphy, asleep with Bruno snoring on his lap.

Before driving to the farm, Gopher stopped at the sheriff's office. "Anything I should know?" he asked Bear.

"Everything under control." Bear rose to shake his hand. "We put a tow cable across your driveway to keep the visitors out. Here's the key to the padlock. How was the trip?"

"Good to get away, great to get back. We saw a lot of scenery and met a spooky lady who helped me decide what to do with my good fortune."

"Sounds suspicious."

"Nope. My sister Diane is handling everything for me. A huge chunk goes to the community college to establish an ag campus. I may donate the farm someday. Another huge chunk goes to a scholarship for farm students."

"Anything for Gopher?"

"A tad. I don't need much. But there's a new bike for Murphy."

"I suggest you call Tim at the *Review Messenger* and give him the scoop. If people know the money's spoken for, they'll leave you alone."

Back at the Broken Hart, Gopher leaned low over the pool table, his belly pressed against the rail. He squinted down table, pointed at the thirteen ball, and tapped the corner pocket. His tourney opponent rested his chin on an upright cue and grinned at his pals. No one could make that nine-thirteen combo. Gopher steadied himself, braced a stubby finger against the felt tabletop, and cocked his arm.

Damn, it was good to be back with the gang.

CHAMELEON

By evening at Lois's farm, a November afternoon breeze from the Dakotas had wheeled around to a brisk nor'wester. White oaks and popple trees shivered, filling the air with twirling leaves, blanketing the yard like confetti. Wilhelm Wagner walked from the barn, pushed his cap back, and wiped his brow.

He checked his watch—six-thirty. Lois would have supper ready at seven. Not enough daylight to re-nail the jury-rigged corral fence. Not enough time to drive to his home place and check livestock. Too much time to walk into the kitchen and listen to new wife Lois's assault on Asian beetles climbing the screens or bull thistles from the pasture scattering seed on her lawn. Or about Will's tread-sole boots tracking dirt on her clean kitchen linoleum.

Will walked to the barn, rubbing his face, hoping to wipe away this afternoon's harangue, hoping to discredit his housekeeper Darla's story. *Stupid woman. What the hell does she know?*

Wind in this country blew itself out around sundown. Will had time before supper to drag the tarps of leaves Lois had vacuumed to the burn barrel. *I'll cut Darla off. Make her suffer.* As he dragged, he created a path through the carpet of new fallen leaves. The tarps, bulky and awkward, were heavy to pull. He walked backwards, tugging side to side.

At the burn barrel, Will spit on his finger and lifted it. He scooped armloads of leaves in the barrel, made a final wind check, and lit a match. The leaves ignited, filling the air with gray smoke and the sweet smell of autumn. Will walked to the barn for a pitchfork. When he looked back, blazing flames from the barrel lit the early darkness. A gust of wind scattered burning leaves across the lawn, toward the garage, the barn, the machine shed.

Lois yelled from the porch. "Holy shit. I'll call 911."

Will stomped on the flaming leaves, tried to rake them with

his fork, was blinded by smoke.

Lois ran to the barn. "Grab some gunny sacks. And turn the hydrant on."

Will followed her into the barn. Found sacks. Grabbed the hose and wet the sacks. Lois ran toward the house, dampening burning leaves that crept toward the porch. Will stretched the hose to reach the utility pole that flamed at the base.

"Aim it at the garage," Lois yelled. She uncoiled the hose at the house spigot. Sprayed the porch, the siding, the roof.

Wind blew flaming leaves to the barn. Century-old siding ignited like kindling. Will sprayed the walls and swung his gunny sack. An explosion behind him spun him around. The garage was aflame. Lois's Buick inside. He ran to the garage, pressed the door opener, hopped in the car. He spun out, squealing in reverse through flames until he reached a burned-out area. He ran back for the hose. Couldn't see Lois or the house for smoke. Called her name. "Lois. Lois."

Felt a huge pain, a huge crippling pain. He grabbed his chest and collapsed in a writhing, tumbling frenzy.

"Dar . . ."

Lois ran to him and dragged him to a water-soaked patch. "Will," she screamed. "Will. Will."

Two cars with sirens wailing and lights flashing broke through the smoke. One, a fire department vehicle with EMTs. The other, the county sheriff. Deputy Bear rushed from the squad and directed the EMTs to Will. "They'll take care of him, Lois. Are you okay?"

"The house," she screamed. "The house."

Bear grabbed a hose and saturated the siding, the porch rails that smoldered, the flaming trellis that held a charred skeleton of clematis.

A firetruck screamed to a halt in the driveway, lights flashing, firefighters scrambling like ants. Burning fragments of straw from the barn floated in the air. Lois motioned for Bear to wet her gunny sack.

"We're saving the house," Bear yelled. "Lucky we haven't lost power. The electric wires in the garage, in the barn . . ."

An EMT in yellow Bunker gear ran to Lois. "We're taking him in."

"Is he okay?"

The EMT placed a hand on her shoulder, held it there a

moment too long, then ran toward the flashing lights.

"I feel like I'll get in trouble talking about a dead man." Ex-wife Gena lowered her head, stirred and stirred her coffee. "Get in trouble complaining about him, criticizing him."

Lois shook her spoon. "You'll get in more trouble talking about a live man. Dead men don't argue."

Darla sat between them nursing a glass of water. "From what I hear, you two aren't talking about the same man. At least not the Will I knew."

They sat in the church basement waiting for the last of friends and neighbors to leave. On one side of the room, cheerless yellow concrete walls displayed art by vacation bible school students; on the other in large script, the Ten Commandments, the Beatitudes. A floor fan by the kitchen blended the aroma of coffee and the dank odor of moist basement.

In the kitchen, Daughters of Martha washed dishes in silence. A few in ruffled aprons circulated in the dining area, retrieving coffee mugs and wiping tables. As well-wishers left, they patted Lois on the shoulder. *I'm sorry. He was a good man,* they said. Lois stared ahead, nodded, and mouthed a thank you. *He'll get his just rewards in heaven.*

A few recognized Gena and jerked their heads in surprise. One of the town wags snapped, "I didn't expect to see you here. It must be fifteen years since you walked out on him."

"Sixteen." Gena stared ahead. "Bye now."

"The grave diggers." Lois shook her head. "I saw them sitting on a tombstone, leaning on their shovels, waiting like a pair of vultures. I told them to scram, don't come back until later." A shaft of late afternoon sunshine from a basement window highlighted her tight-curled gray hair. "They said today was the last day of goose season, so they'd hunt until sundown and then come back. Don't need to be reminded that *dust thou art.*"

Pastor Lundgren walked down the stairs and headed for Lois. "Ma'am, this was Will's." He held a Bible.

Lois looked at the book. "What would I want with a Lutheran Study Bible? Keep it at the church." She pursed her lips and stared ahead.

"This is the Bible Will read from in confirmation class years ago." He opened the book. "See? It has his signature. It's a beautiful memento of him."

"Thanks, but I have enough mementoes. Gena, do you want it?"

Gena chuckled and pushed faded blond hair behind her ear. "The Will I knew didn't read Bibles."

"Find a home for it." Lois glanced at the pastor, flipping her hand, dismissing him.

Darla reached to the pastor. "I'll take it."

"Will's dad left a tidy sum to this church in his will." Lois twirled her cup. "Lundgren's probably hoping for something in Will's. Good luck to him."

"Will and a Bible? What's that all about?" Gena asked. "He was a wild and crazy guy when we were married. What's that commandment about coveting thy neighbor's wife? I was his neighbor's wife, and he coveted me."

Darla elbowed her. "Not that you played hard to get."

Gena grinned. "Remember my first ex? Jim? He was a loser from day one. Had a few bad habits, like unemployment and drugs and motorcycles and parties. No visible means of support. He kick-started my caretaker instinct. Gave me someone to take care of—him. And our kid eventually."

Gena filled her coffee cup. "Will was young—forties when we got married. Said he was too bashful to be with a woman before that." She laughed as if remembering a dirty joke. "When he changed his mind, I was ready for picking. The lowest of low hanging fruit. He was a rank amateur, practically a virgin. I had to teach him everything he knew."

Darla grinned again. "Seems like you did a good job."

"How would you know?"

Darla twirled her finger in mousy gray-brown hair. "Just saying . . ."

"Will was sweet," Gena continued. "When I told him I wanted a horse, that's what I got for an engagement present. Got jewelry eventually." Gena glanced sideways at Darla. "What are those red marks on your wrists? Looks painful."

Darla pulled the sleeves of her cardigan sweater down. "Nothing. I have a bad habit of saving rubber bands on my wrists at work. Forgot to take them off."

"Sounds kinky." Gena chuckled. "Reminds me of Will. He was hooked on porn, had a ton of tapes." She stopped and sipped her coffee. "I shouldn't be talking bad about him. Not today."

Lois shook her finger at Gena. "When Will and I got married, I told him if he was looking for a woman to bounce around on all night, to keep on looking." She snapped her head.

"Did you love him, Lois?" Darla asked.

"Hell, no. It was a marriage of convenience." She swung at a fly. "Some marriages are made in heaven. Ours was made in an accountant's office."

Gena gave her a quizzical look. "Doesn't sound like the answer I'd expect from a strict Catholic."

"We planned to have the marriage blessed by a priest at Christmas. Never got around to it."

Darla turned to Gena. "How about you? Did you love him?"

"He was my road out of Dodge. Love him? No, I guess not. I knew from day one I'd leave him."

"Why did you have his kid?"

"I felt I owed him that. Speaking of kids, where are my boys?"

"They're at the Broken Hart, spending time with old friends. They wanted something stronger than lemonade." Darla rose. "I better get back there. I think that's where everyone is headed."

Gena waved. "Say *hi* to my sons."

"Before you go," Lois pointed at Darla, "keep cleaning Will's house until his estate is settled. Until we find out who owns it."

"I won't be alone out there with that creep of a hired man."

"What day do you clean?"

"Usually Saturday afternoons."

"I can't be there then." Lois shook her head. "Mass at five-thirty. Who went with you before?"

"Well . . . Will would usually show up." She held the Bible and twirled the car keys on her finger. "I'd better be going." She walked up the stairs.

Gena stood on the back porch of the once-pretentious house, peered through the screen door, then turned back to look at the yard, the barn.

"It's not much, but it's home." Will opened the screen door. "Dad built the house seventy-five years ago. I lived here all my life. Plenty of rooms, and plenty of room for remodeling."

Gena held a sleeping child and peeked into the kitchen, then

CHAMELEON

back toward the barn beyond the yard littered with renegade machine parts, a stalled lawn mower, a tipped wooden rocker swing. And weeds. Thistles.

Will pointed her toward the kitchen and walked in. "Don't expect to see it in the Parade of Homes." He turned on a burner under the coffee pot.

Gena glanced at the kitchen, the tall white cupboards, the yellow canister set with red lids and fruit decals, the sun-bleached curtains with red rickrack. They proceeded to the dining room where newspapers and magazines cluttered a massive table surrounded by six high-back chairs and a littered buffet. The living room with two overstuffed chairs and matching maroon frieze couch which sported a lace doily on the back cushion. On the walls, mounted deer heads, an oval framed sepia portrait of man, woman, and child, and a black velvet rendition of the Last Supper.

Will opened a door off the living room. "This was Dad's study." Inside, two leather wing chairs bracketed a walnut executive desk with green-shaded desk lamp and marble pen stand. Certificates, diplomas, and framed photographs of blue ribbon cattle standing beside a man, Will's father, dotted the paneled walls.

Gena patted the sleeping baby. "Where is our bedroom, and where is Baby Jim's?"

Will pointed to an open staircase carpeted with a threadbare maroon runner. Upstairs, he opened the door to his bedroom. "Pardon the mess. That's forty-some years of my junk." He turned off a VCR monitor that blinked red and hummed on a vanity. "His bedroom is across the hall."

Gena opened the door to Baby Jim's bedroom. "Take that stuff off the bed so I can lay him down."

Will piled boxes on the floor, draped coats over the footboard, and stacked magazines in the corner.

"Better shake the spread out the window." Gena rubbed her finger on a window sill. "Must be an inch of dust."

She laid the sleeping child on the bed and boxed him in with piles of clothes and pillows. "I'm thirsty. Let's have coffee."

Gena led Will downstairs. "I have a surprise for you." Will cleared breakfast dishes. "After coffee, I'll show you."

"You spoil me rotten. I hope I know what it is." She threw her arms around his neck and kissed him. "All this pasture, and all these barns, and all this space to ride."

"I didn't stop with one horse." Will poured her coffee. "I bought you two-hundred and fifty of them."

"You're teasing me. Did you know I was barrel racing champ in high school? I've wanted my own gaming horse ever since."

"I think you'll like what you see."

The baby cried from his bedroom. Gena sat, holding her coffee, surveying the kitchen, the refrigerator door decorated with magnets, the teapot electric clock on the wall, unplugged. She pointed to a cabinet door. "That's last year's calendar."

"Don't you think he'll be confused?" Will nodded toward the staircase. "Not in his own crib?"

"He'll be all right, but he'll be hungry. Got a can of soup? I'll get him."

After coffee, they walked outside into a bright Indian summer afternoon. The windmill creaked from a south breeze. Leaves raced across the gravel drive. Will carried the boy, switching arm to arm, and nudged Gena toward the garage.

"What's that doing here?" Gena asked, pointing to a house trailer overgrown with vines and tucked in a grove of box elders.

"That's where the housekeeper lived. And the hired men. I don't think Dad ever set foot in the barn. Unless he led a tour."

"I want to see the barn." Gena grabbed his arm. "Does it have horse stalls?" They walked into the milking parlor. "What a perfect space for a tack room. Just get rid of that bulk tank. And running water and a floor drain. I could shower a horse right here."

Will stood holding the boy who reached for an ancient bug strip. "Dad raised registered Holsteins. Show cattle. The barn hasn't been used since he died. I suppose it could convert to a stable."

"And the corral outside. A perfect riding ring. And the haymow. What a spot for our wedding dance."

"Slow down, girl." Will laughed. "Don't you think we should concentrate on the house before we remodel the barn?"

"Hell, no. Who would spend time in a house with this set-up?" She walked to Will and slipped her arm around his waist. "I don't know what my special surprise is, but could I trade it for a horse?"

"I'll show you." They walked to a three-stall garage where

CHAMELEON

he handed her a garage door opener. The door creaked up. Inside sat a bright red GMC Jimmy Blazer. "What do you think, Gena? Still want to trade it for a horse?"

Gena walked around the vehicle.

Will walked with the boy to the tail gate and pointed. "Look, Jimmy. It has your name on it."

"I see right now it needs a trailer hitch, and a trailer." Gena grabbed his arm. "And a couple horses to transport."

Bill patted his wallet. "I think we can manage that."

"I know the horse I want." Gena broke into a dance and waved her arms. "We can find one for you. The Huntersville Fall Trail Ride is next weekend. Let's go for it."

Will shrugged. Horseback riding? Not his strong suit. But Gena's excitement was contagious. What the hell.

Friday afternoon arrived in a blaze of fall color. Gena led her Appaloosa Nickels out of the trailer and tied him to a side bar. Rigs were parked in tight spaces in the campground, some with campfires, some with music blaring, horses munching out of feedbags, dogs wandering and sniffing tires.

"Bring your horse out." Gena brushed Nickels. "Great weekend for a ride. What's his name again?"

"Don't remember. I call him *Horse*." Will struggled with a hesitant palomino. "Who are all these people and where do they come from?"

Nickels nickered at horses scrounging in a neighbor's makeshift rope corral.

"I don't know, but by Sunday, I'll know everybody here. There's a short get-acquainted ride at six tonight, and the big ride starts tomorrow at ten. What a weekend."

"Hey, Gena. Is that you? Is that your horse?"

"Hey, Cody, That's me. That's my horse. That's my rig. And that's my husband-to-be Will."

"Wow. Looks like you struck it rich." He tipped his hat to Will. "Congratulations. Save a dance for me tonight, Gena."

Gena waved him on and tethered Nickels to the trailer. "You getting that horse of yours to pay attention?"

"I think he hates me. I think the feeling is mutual."

"Let me help." She grabbed the lead rope. "Piece of cake."

Will followed her out of the trailer. "Who's the cowboy?"

"Cody. We served on the sheriff's posse. I expect the whole

posse gang will be here. Let's saddle up and try these ponies out."

"I'm beginning to think I made a bad decision."

"You just gotta let him know who's boss. How long since you've been on a horse?"

"First grade. Merry-go-round at the county fair. Seemed silly then. Seems silly now."

Gena put her hands on her hips. "Cowboy up. Let's get these saddles on."

Will wrestled with the saddle. "What's the dance Cody mentioned?"

"Standard operating procedure. Dances Friday and Saturday nights. Great country western bands. After a few drinks, every guy looks like Tim McGraw. Every gal looks like Faith Hill. I wouldn't miss it."

A cowboy sauntered up to the trailer. "Gena, I heard you were here. Too early to kiss the bride?"

"About a month too early, Jackson."

"You the prospective groom?" Jackson reached a hand to Will. "Great catch for you, this woman. Drop over to our campsite tonight. I'll buy you the refreshment of your choice."

Gena tugged at the cinch. "Where are you?"

"At the end of the campground. Way back where no one can complain about our rowdy behavior."

"We'll find you." Gena grabbed a bridle. "Be on your way, my friend. We have to test-drive these ponies before the ride." She finished saddling Nickels and straightened the saddle on Horse. "Get on, Will. I'll adjust your stirrups."

"What are your friends going to do when they run out of Wyoming city names?" Will climbed into the saddle, his legs stiff, his hands fiddling with the reins.

"Loosen up, Cowboy. You look like a scarecrow."

"I can identify with the *scare* part."

A lone rider stopped at their trailer. "Well, the rumors are true," a cowgirl twanged. "Good to see you, Gena."

"Let me guess." Will put a finger to his lips. "Your name is . . . Cheyenne."

"Close. Name is Helena."

"Good to meet you, Helena. I'm your neighbor. Name's Billings."

Gena tied a red bandanna around her neck. "Word sure gets around fast. How are you, Helena?" She pointed to Will. "This is my betrothed. How about we catch up with you later for the early ride?"

"Love to have you. Welcome aboard, Billings." She smacked her horse on the rump.

"We'll ride to the river, Will. See if these ponies need a drink of water." Gena swung into the saddle. "Follow me."

Pickups and horse trailers inched down makeshift roads to campsites. Cowboys waved. "Howdy, Gena." A cowgirl dragged a rope full of firewood behind her horse and yelled, "Beautiful day for a ride." They rode through heady smoke of jack pine campfires, past the well where kids pumped buckets of water, past faded canvas tents and spendy live-in trailers.

Gena lifted her hat and raised her arms. "This is what I live for."

"Bet I'm the only guy in a ten-mile radius without a cowboy hat."

"You're the only guy in a ten-mile radius wearing loafers."

At the river landing, Nickels walked into the water, splashed it with a hoof, and drank. Horse stood at the shore, hesitating, dancing. Will jerked the reins. "Come on, Horse. The water's fine."

"Slap him on the ass," Gena yelled.

Will hit him with his baseball cap. Horse jumped in, twirled, twirled again, and reared. Will flew into the river.

"And me without a camera." Gena laughed when Will rose to his knees.

He stooped, raking sand with his fingers. "Lost my glasses." He stood when he found them and led Horse out of the river, his soaked shirt and jeans clinging like skin. "This is not going to work." Will scanned the landing, happy to see no other riders in the vicinity. "How about I go home, change clothes, and pick up Baby Jimmy from the sitter. We'll join you for breakfast in the morning."

"Your choice. You're going to miss a lot of fun."

"I'm not sure I'd live to tell about it."

Morning sun enflamed the timid aspens and maples and red oak, rendering them painted ladies. Will parked by the trailer and lifted Baby Jim out of the car seat. Dew, a couple degrees short of frost, glittered from grass blades. Geese honked from the river. The air tasted Canadian, the fresh, edgy bite of impending winter that contradicted the warm and heady aroma of ripe foliage.

The campsite was quiet. Campfires smoldered, gasping for life and breathing ghostly wisps of wood smoke. A horse nickered. Another answered. No one moved.

Will walked to the trailer, Baby Jim on his shoulders. The horses lifted their heads from the feedbag and stared.

"Want to see Mommy?" Will asked.

He rapped on the door of the sleeping compartment, then opened it. No one there. The bed was made. No clothes on the floor, no glasses or bottles on the nightstand. A tinge of concern mutated into a wave of worry. "Where's Mommy?"

They walked through the campground, Will glancing left and right, waiting, wondering. An acrid bile taste built in his throat.

"Mommy, Mommy," Baby Jim yelled.

Walking up the path, smoothing her shirt and jeans, running fingers through her hair, Gena sauntered forward with a confident stride. "Just out for a walk," she said. "Couldn't sleep in those tight quarters." She kissed them. "Ready for breakfast?"

A din of animated conversation floated from a group of men at the far end of the church basement.

"I wish those freeloaders would leave." Lois turned her head toward the last of the funeral well-wishers. "Who are they?"

Gena turned. "I recognize the fat one, the auctioneer at the livestock sale barn. The rest must be buyers and sellers. Will's customers."

Lois signaled to the Daughters of Martha. "Put the sandwiches and bars away. Those guys won't leave until the food's gone."

"Where is Darla getting all her information?" Gena asked. "She seems to know everything about everybody."

"When you're a barmaid in this town, you gotta know everything." Lois drummed her fingers. "What she don't know, she invents."

"Did you notice how she hemmed and hawed when you asked her who was around when she cleaned Will's house?"

"Will was goofy, but not Darla goofy," Lois replied.

"Don't be too sure. He was a straight arrow when I married

him. Sure, he tried some of my bad habits—drugs, rock concerts, the fetish stuff. But he never bought into it."

"Fetish stuff?"

"Never mind. Point being, when he saw that side of me, he got worried. Not so much about me. About Baby Jim. Afraid to adopt him. Afraid he might end up with a hydrocephalic."

"This shit I don't need to know." Lois stood and grabbed her purse while the last well-wishers talked their way to the staircase. "Anyway, it looks like the kid turned out fine. One head, two arms, ten fingers."

Gena stood. "Hell, Will was more of a parent than I was. He took Jimmy in when I left years ago."

Lois waved a thank you to the kitchen crew. "Who filed for divorce? You or him?"

"Don't recall. I was under the influence 24/7. A lawyer friend of mine knew Will was loaded, knew he was a softie. Cost Will a bundle, but he was glad to be rid of me. Of course, he had a bundle." She fingered imaginary bills. "Daddy's money. No skin off his ass. Off his pride, maybe, but not off his ass."

Lois grabbed a handrail at the stairs. "What screwball thing did you do to tip the scale?"

"Remember when I won that trip to Jamaica on the radio call-in show? Of course you don't. I told Will a break from farming would be good for him. Not during haying season, he said. I told him I'd take my sister. Problem was, I didn't have a sister. But I did know this sweet young cowboy with a cute ass."

Lois sneered. "And by this time, you were pregnant with his kid?"

"I don't know. It was all so crazy then."

Lois and Gena stood in the parking lot, Gena twiddling keys to her pickup. "When did you and Will tie the knot? And why? Talk about an unlikely couple."

Lois looked at Gena over the top of her glasses. "Nothing unlikely about it at all. Roy and Will were partners. Owned hundreds of head of livestock together. Cattle prices were in the toilet when Roy died. Not the best time to sell and split the proceeds. The accountant suggested we rewrite the partnership agreement. Or just get married."

A pickup drove past them and tapped the horn. Lois waved without looking. "I didn't need Will, but I didn't need to be single and alone either. Married would work. We sealed it within a week at the courthouse. Didn't tell anyone for months. Not even the kids."

Lois swayed in loose-fit jeans from the accountant's office to her car leading Will, a black bling purse swinging from her shoulder.

"Well, what now, partner?" Will asked.

She turned when Will reached for her arm. "We may as well get it over with. We can stop at Court Administration and see what the procedure is."

When Will drove to town for tractor parts the following week, Lois stopped mowing mid-lawn and rode with him to the courthouse.

Inside, Will plunked a check on the counter. "The budget wedding package, please."

"You have an appointment with a judge?"

"Yep."

"You have a witness?"

"I was thinking about you."

They waited on a wood bench outside the courtroom, Will hoping to not see neighbors, Lois picking at her fingernails. The courtroom doors opened and the judge walked toward them holding a portfolio and Bible. "Congratulations." She smiled. "Follow me."

The judge wore a black pants suit, white satin blouse, permed hair, makeup, jewelry, heels—the whole shebang. She trailed a heady aroma of spicy perfume.

"I hate her," Lois murmured.

Fifteen minutes later, descending the courthouse steps, Will asked, "You have time for coffee? I'm buying."

They sat in McDonald's overlooking the highway where a wrecker and tow truck were disentangling an SUV from an aggressive rear-ending pickup. Red, white, and blue lights flashed from a dozen squads. Highway traffic paraded through the parking lot to avoid the chaos.

Lois twirled her wedding ring. "This thing itches." She slid it off her finger. "Whose was it?"

Will turned from the commotion outside, surprised, maybe

hurt. "I bought it."

Lois stirred her coffee with the plastic swizzle stick. "Will you be moving your stuff to my house? We'll have to establish ground rules."

"Like what?"

"Like I'm not giving up my bedroom." Lois's voice squeaked with conviction. "Not even sharing it."

Will glanced at the other tables and spoke in low monotone. "Isn't there something in the Bible that says a marriage isn't valid until it's consummated?"

"I don't know what you're talking about, but if it's what I think it is, you and I read different Bibles." She continued to stir her coffee. "And don't make any plans for me late Saturday afternoons. I go to mass at 5:30."

"Fine. I go to the Broken Hart every morning at seven for coffee."

"You go to church anymore?" Lois asked.

"Twice a year. Easter and Christmas. But I give them a hefty hunk of change then. In memory of Mom and Dad."

Lois shook her finger at him. "Make sure it comes out of your checking account. And speaking of finances, have you read the prenups the accountant prepared?"

Will shook his head.

Lois pulled an envelope from her purse. "My farm and land are mine. So are my savings and my checking accounts, my IRAs and my cattle. Your farm and land and current assets are yours, as are your cattle. We split the large equipment fifty-fifty. The small equipment stays on the farms where it presently resides." She folded the paper. "I hope nobody's stupid enough to dispute that."

Will would learn Lois was like that—determined, dispassionate, non-negotiable, even for a good night kiss. He moved a few work clothes that afternoon and slept in the spare bedroom. As he drifted toward sleep, he sensed the presence of his good friend and partner Roy and felt relieved, happy to sleep alone, to not violate their friendship.

The arrangement worked for a time for Will. He would have felt embarrassed, emasculated if someone questioned him, but no one did. No one seemed to know. Or care. He drove to coffee each morning from Lois's house. His fellow coffee drinkers knew he had cattle at Roy's farm, Roy had tractors and haybines and balers at his farm. They didn't question him.

Will had met Roy when he was loan officer at the bank where his dad chaired the Board of Directors. When his dad died, Will was free to quit banking and live the life he fantasized—a beef cattle operation at his dad's farm a mile as the crow flies from Roy. Roy squired him to cattle auctions, coached him on cattle breeds and equipment brands. Within a month, Will listed his occupation as *rancher*.

With Roy dead and Will sleeping in his house, he felt a new frustration, one maybe caused by the living arrangement, or one caused by the prospect of the impending harvest without Roy's decision-making. Will would have to hire help. Mechanics was not his strong suit.

Neither was celibacy.

Although townspeople thought Will was single, he couldn't risk a liaison with a local woman. Lois would cut his nuts off. And there wasn't time to shop for relief in a distant small town.

The morning he lost the shake for coffee at the Broken Hart, he stood at the counter waiting to pay. Darla gathered mugs and spoons and waved goodbye to the men. Will gawked at her breasts looming over the table. When she placed the mugs in the dishwasher, she stood alone with Will.

"Eight bucks." She wiped her hands on her apron.

Will handed her a ten. "Keep it."

"Thanks a lot. I need that. Been a tough week."

"Tough?"

She sighed "Hubby needs dental work and his insurance doesn't cover it. The nursing home is trying a workaround, but it looks like I'll be stuck with a thousand bucks' worth of extractions and fillings. It doesn't make sense, what with his life expectancy."

Will sucked a toothpick and studied her.

"What are you looking at?" Darla asked.

"I was thinking." Will measured his words. "I'm looking for a housecleaner. You have Saturdays off, right?"

Darla nodded.

"Would you be willing to come out Saturday afternoon? I'd pay you twice what you make here."

Darla tied a napkin around her finger. "That's generous of you, Will." She remembered the long driveway lined with oak trees, the huge white house on the knoll with tall pillars. She wondered about the eerie feeling of a house without a woman. "Would I be alone?"

Will smiled and felt a tingle of excitement in his groin. "I'll make it a point to be there."

Will sat at the supper table, silent, scarfing down a plate of roast beef and mashed potatoes.

Lois fingered through the mail as she ate, separating junk mail from bills. Her eyes squinted as they read, her upper lip puckered like corduroy.

"You know what day today is?" Will asked with a hint of cheeriness.

Lois looked at him. "Thursday."

"And our anniversary. Three months to the day."

Lois opened bills and stacked empty envelopes in the pile of ads.

"I have a gift for you." Will reached in his pocket for a small black velvet box and handed it to Lois. "Happy anniversary."

Lois shot him an accusing glance and opened the box. She said nothing.

"Like it?" Will asked.

Lois lifted a necklace. "Whose was it?"

"I bought it."

She placed it back in the box. "I can't imagine where I'd wear it. Or why."

"I thought all women liked jewelry."

"You'll find I'm not like all women."

"It was fun buying it for you." Will leaned back in his chair. "Better to give than receive."

"Don't do that." Lois pointed to the chair legs. "You'll make dents in the linoleum." She opened the gift box and closed it. "Sorry if I'm not appreciative, but I have reasons. When Roy bought me a gift, it was always after he had done something stupid. With another woman usually. Poor guy, he was transparent as glass. And he couldn't live with guilt." She stared at Will. "Of course you're not Catholic. You don't know what guilt is."

Will choked a nervous laugh, leaned back and immediately leaned forward. The television droned in the living room, an ad for auto insurance, a reminder to watch Macy's Thanksgiving Day parade.

Lois continued to open and close the box. "We'll have to let the kids in on our arrangement someday. I was thinking about cooking Thanksgiving dinner."

Will contained a sigh and relaxed, like a drowning man thrown a life raft.

"How many in your family?" she asked.

"Two sons, two girlfriends."

"Ten in mine. With you and me, that's sixteen. Eight at this table, four at the kitchen counter, and four at TV tables in the living room."

"I'm surprised your kids haven't dropped in," Will said. "They don't live that far away."

"I told them I'm not a baby sitter, and this house isn't a day care center. That goes for your grandkids, too, when you have them."

"Well, I'm going to miss the crazy man." Gena stood with Lois in the church parking lot. "I don't expect he remembered me in his will."

"He remembered your kids. Told me that when we signed the prenups. They'll be some rich dudes."

"How about the home place? The house and eighty acres? Wonder who gets that."

"Hope he willed that to Darla." Lois turned toward her car. "Seems she spent most of her time there."

Darla stood at the kitchen sink in Will's house washing coffee cups and wiping the counter. The room smelled of Pine-Sol. Tammy Wynette wailed from the living room radio. Will leaned on the kitchen archway. "Great job. The house hasn't been this clean since Mom died."

Darla rolled down her sleeves and dried her hands. "Anything else, boss?"

Will glanced at the teapot wall clock. Five-fifteen. Lois would be en route to church. "You asked me to remind you to clean the washroom sink that's soaking in Old Dutch cleanser."

Darla clicked her tongue and brushed past Will at the archway. She walked to the washroom, Will behind her. At the sink, he pressed against her back and cupped her breasts in his hands. In the mirror, she saw his questioning smile. She reached behind her, searching, fondling.

"It's a shame to mess up the bed." Will led her to the living room floor.

Will checked his watch—6:30. "Gotta leave. Chores to do at Roy's." He grabbed his clothes from the floor.

"You mean you have chores to do at Lois's, don't you?" Darla laughed. "Everybody knows you live there."

"Suppose I could have guessed it." He reached in his pocket and handed her two hundred-dollar bills. "Well worth it. Can I count on you next week?"

Darla sat on the floor untangling her bra straps. "I suppose I should feel guilty, but I don't."

Will checked his watch again. "I suppose I shouldn't feel guilty, but I do." He handed her a house key. "Come anytime next Saturday. I'll see you at coffee Monday morning."

"Mind if I have a cigarette before we leave?" Darla knelt, smoothing her hair. "Sit with me a while."

"I'd rather you didn't smoke." Will held his throat. "Allergies."

Will visited the home place daily, checking cattle, maintaining machines, monitoring the hired man's progress. He fixed lunch at noon in his kitchen, napped in his own bedroom, his own bed. *This is home.*

Tomorrow, Saturday, was Darla's cleaning day. Would she wait until noon? Arrive early? Not come at all? She had acted noncommittal at coffee klatch in the morning, the same snappy rejoinders to him that she snapped at other men, the same racy innuendos. He had tried to catch her eye on the way out of the Broken Hart, but she turned and walked into the cooler.

Will stood in the entry, smiling at the living room carpet. How adventurous was she? How imaginative? How far was she willing to go? Before he left his house, he tossed Bondage and Leather magazines on the coffee table, a fetish supply catalog on the kitchen table, a cock ring on his bed stand. Conversation starters.

Late Saturday morning, he drove by her house. The garage

door was open, the car gone. He told Lois before dinner he had to rush back to his farm.

"You're spending a lot of time there." She slapped a cover on a boiling pot.

"Gotta tighten belts on the corn chopper, grease it up." He lathered his hands and wiped his face.

Lois dropped her head and peered over her glasses. "Since when did you turn mechanic?"

Will hid behind the towel, felt his pulse quicken, his temperature spike.

"You still have that goofy hired man?" Lois asked. "Or did you trade him in for a goofy hired woman?" She placed a plate of baloney on the table. "I'll have supper ready before I go to church. Eat if you're hungry. Don't wait for me."

After dinner, Will did a few chores around Lois's farm. Darla would have had time to wash dishes, dry mop the downstairs wood floors, bag recyclables, would have had time to notice the magazines and the hardware.

When he walked in his house, Darla vacuumed the upstairs bedroom, her back to him. Will walked to her and grabbed her hips.

She screamed, jumped, lost her balance and landed on the bed. She rolled over to face him, her arms extended, her hands flat. "Oh, my god. You startled me."

He fell on the bed, half-covering her. "Sorry about that. I was checking your reflexes." He glanced at the hardware on the bed stand. "Looks like I forgot to put away my toys. I did put away my magazines and catalogs though, right?"

"Wrong."

He stretched her hands to the corner bedposts and smiled, nose to nose. "You ever been handcuffed?" He rose from the bed, opened a drawer of the vanity and fingered through tapes, selecting one and slipping it into the VCR. "Watch this."

Days tumbled forward for Will, bliss to misery, contentment to frustration. Today he leaned on the corral fence at his farm, content, smiling at columns of plastic-wrapped silage and rows of baled hay. Angus beef cows, already bloated with pregnancy, munched at bale feeders. A six-month supply of feed, tractors

CHAMELEON

winterized and waterers insulated, calves separated and weaned—all that redeemed him, validated him. *I'm a rancher. Roy would be proud of me.* He felt a strange sense of well-being, a feeling maybe undeserved.

He walked from the corral to his house. Today was Friday, and Darla would come tomorrow. *Is that why I feel giddy? The cuffs were fun. What shall we try next?*

At supper with Lois Friday night, she asked about preparations for winter at *her* farm after Will related the status at his.

"You're good. Cattle are all home from summer pasture. You've got a year's supply of haylage. There's open water in the creek."

Lois spooned beef stew on her plate. "I hear Darla's driving to your farm. What's that all about?"

Will reached for a napkin, chewed for a few seconds and swallowed. "She still cleans the house. Hired man lives there now." He hesitated until he created a story. "The guy's a slob. I want to clean the house up and rent it someday."

Next day, a mild November afternoon, Will opened the windows in his bedroom. The bed was made, throw pillows fluffed, furniture dusted and smelling of polish. Darla walked in drying herself with a towel. He held her in a body hug.

"Want to switch roles?"

"What are you talking about?"

"You take charge."

She laughed. "You're crazy."

"I'm serious. Here, blindfold me. Slap these cuffs on me."

"No way."

Will squeezed her arms. "I'm ordering you. Do it."

She tied a blindfold over his eyes, cuffed his wrists, and pushed him on the bed. She cuffed his ankles, then the bedposts.

"Now, reach in the satchel for the little leather switch. Tickle me. Punish me. I've been a very bad boy."

She rubbed the switch across his chest, his belly.

"Harder, harder. I've been a very bad boy."

She switched him harder.

"Harder. Harder."

After the house cleaning, after the cuffs and switches and paddles, after the lovemaking, Darla brewed a pot of coffee. She smiled a sardonic smile of superiority. "I think I figured you out." She reached in her purse for a cigarette. "Yes, I figured you out." She nodded her head and flicked the lighter.

Will brought two mugs from the cupboard. "Figured what out?"

"Did you know my mother and your mother were high school classmates? Best friends?"

"Never heard her mention it."

"What do you remember about her?"

"Not much. I was young when she died." Will sat at the table and rubbed his red arms.

"Do you know how she died?"

"Dad wouldn't talk about it. No one else told me."

Darla inhaled and leaned against the fridge, her arms crossed. "He punished her to death."

"What?"

"He punished her to death. Cut her off from her family. Wouldn't let her drive. Wouldn't let her have company. Worse than that, he beat her. Mother drove her to the grocery store on Fridays. She told Mother everything. Showed her the welts."

Will stared at Darla. "I'm supposed to believe that?"

"Do you remember her funeral? Remember the closed casket? Do you know why it was closed? Mother knew."

"It was my first and only funeral. I thought all caskets were closed."

"Your mother's body was battered. Her eyes were blackened. Your dad had enough money and clout to silence the undertaker."

Will slammed his fist on the table. "Stop it. First off, I don't believe you. Second, why are you telling me this shit?"

"I watched you and Gena when you were married. You, buying her attention, not buying her love. Not Gena. You, not trusting her. You, stomping out of the Broken Hart when she wanted one more drink, then threatening her. Idle threats, for sure. But there was meanness in your eyes."

"You're crazy, woman." Will stared out the kitchen window. A barn cat stalked a flock of pigeons feeding beside the silo.

"Do you remember when your mother's sister, your aunt Margaret, moved in to care for you? Mother does. They were friends from school too. Any idea why she left within a couple weeks?"

"She found another job." The coffee pot stopped gurgling and Will tapped his cup on the table.

"Uh-uh." Darla poured the coffee. "She found out what was going on. Tried to spirit you away, but your dad quashed it. Ever wonder why you're into whips and paddles? Maybe you're wired for it."

Will glanced at his dad's family portrait in the living room.

"And now you're married to Lois," Darla continued. "How's it going? You love her? Trust her?"

"Enough of this shit." Will spilled his coffee. "Where the hell are you going with this?"

"You think a barmaid doesn't see what's going on?" Darla blurted. "Doesn't hear what people say? This much I know." Darla shook a spoon at him. Shook it like Lois did. "A man like you won't find a woman he can live happily ever after with. You don't trust women. And why should you? They walk out on you. Desert you. Cheat on you. Die on you. Your mother. Your aunt. Lord knows how many housekeepers. And Gena."

Will rose. His pulse quickened, his face reddened, his fists clenched. "You lyin' bitch."

"Relax, Will." Darla sat at the table and sipped her coffee. "Why should I lie to you? We're not married." She stared at him like a cat toying with a cornered mouse. "I just want to let you know you're not likely to find happiness with any woman. A few minutes of happiness, maybe, but not long term. You can give money and you can give presents, and I appreciate that. But you can't give love. Love requires trust, and you don't trust women. You never will."

"I'm doing fine."

"No, you're not." Darla sat and held his gaze. "That's okay with me, because I'm married. A few minutes of happiness is all I need. But," she stood, smiling, and grabbed Will by the shoulders and pressed against him, "let's make love one more time before I leave."

Will backed against the doorway. His chin quivered, his eyes teared. "Can I trust *you*?"

Darla inhaled, then dropped her cigarette in the coffee cup. She rose and exhaled in his direction. "Can you?"

Darla climbed the stairs from the church basement and walked to her car, the Bible under her arm. Main Street was empty and gray. A north wind scattered leaves along the pavement. Inside her car, she checked the satchel behind the seat. Still there. She heard Will's words. *If anything happens to me, get rid of this stuff.* Instead of turning right to the Broken Hart, she turned left to the cemetery.

The sun hovered on the tree line, casting shadows that stretched across the highway. *The gravediggers are still goose hunting. Time to dispose of the goods.*

At the gravesite, she stood holding the satchel and Bible. The bare casket lay below in a concrete crypt, its mahogany cover sparkling with coins of golden popple. She choked, closed her eyes, and held the satchel over the grave. Shaking. Sobbing. Her knees trembled, her legs weakened. She tottered back, afraid she'd fall.

She scanned the area. Alone, except for popples and maples trembling like mourners and Norway pines along the cemetery fence moaning in the wind. A tiny eddy of leaves danced along the ground beside the open grave, then disappeared.

She opened the satchel. Bright chrome inside reflected a final sliver of daylight. She grabbed the handcuffs and stuffed them in her coat pocket, then placed the Bible in the duffel and dropped it in the grave.

"Goodbye, Will." She wiped her eyes with her sleeve. "Goodbye. I love you."

Epilogue

Today's the day. Sheriff Troy, my boss, left the office after a hearty handshake and said thanks. Said he'd see me at the party. The dispatcher gave me a hug and a cute teddy bear. The office gals baked a pan of brownies and served coffee all afternoon.

Now, I have a few personal items to pack—the photographs of Maggie and son Brian, my favorite coffee mug, and framed citations and certificates which I'll toss in the dumpster on the way out.

Bittersweet, sitting in this old leather chair for the last time. I open the file drawer and flip through case folders and thumb through my log book. Memories pop out of cases I've investigated or people I've booked. Interesting, isn't it, how certain small-town folks are immune to consequences, folks who achieve status that places them above reproach.

Joy, for example, thrice-married widow on the prowl for victim number four. Joy, paragon of virtue in her youth, only child of esteemed Reverend Martin Luther Johnston. Accustomed to having it her way. Who would risk damnation by the esteemed reverend by criticizing his daughter?

Wilhelm Wagner Sr., Will's dad, another example. Bought his way into the community. Approved bank loans to those who kowtowed to him. Meager merchants on Main Street and marginal farmers wouldn't lock horns with him. They turned the other way when his domestic violence was broached.

Doc Brust, my veterinarian. He's safely above the fray. Could circulate a ton of rumors about his bevy of nightly visitors at the mansion. Nobody says a word.

How do I know this? I listen, and my sweet wife Maggie hears it, or doesn't hear it, at the salon. It's the little people who bear the brunt of small town chatter. The Gopher Grahams, the

Rooster Dunnes, the bottom-of-the-ladder barmaids like Darla. Create a rumor about them and it spreads like wildfire.

Tomorrow at this time, I'll be a free man. Tomorrow and the rest of my life. Time in the morning for a second cup of coffee with Maggie waiting for the kids and grandkids to rise and shine. Maybe ask Brian to join me at the men's coffee klatch to give him a peek at how locals view his old man. Maybe state my case for retiring and cut off all speculation, me being in the social stratum not immune to gossip. Maybe harness Misty and take the grandkids for a sleigh ride on the cutter if snow continues. Maybe contact the sheriff's posse and volunteer my services.

Cases closed, at least for me. Maggie will be getting dressed now. Brian and family are home for the occasion. I have a retirement party to attend. No speeches.

Removing this badge is like removing an arm. Or a heart.

Made in the USA
Columbia, SC
21 June 2018